MARK ROBSON

IMPERIAL TRAITOR

For Cameron and Ella
may you never lose your love of stories.

SIMON AND SCHUSTER
First published in Great Britain in 2007 by Simon & Schuster UK Ltd
A CBS COMPANY

1 3 5 7 9 10 8 6 4 2

Simon & Schuster UK Ltd
Africa House
64–78 Kingsway
London WC2B 6AH

A CIP catalogue record for this book is available from the British Library

ISBN-13: 978-1-8473-8035-7

www.markrobsonauthor.com

www.simonsays.co.uk

Typeset by Rowland Phototypesetting Ltd,
Bury St Edmunds, Suffolk
Printed and bound in Great Britain by
Cox & Wyman Ltd, Reading Berks

DRAMATIS PERSONAE

REYNIK – Legionnaire of the General's Elite Legion. Trained by Femke to infiltrate the Guild of Assassins. Bearer of the Wolf Spider icon.

FEMKE – Talented young spy for the Emperor of Shandar. Mistress of disguise.

SHALIDAR – Member of the Guild of Assassins (bearer of the Dragon icon) and long time adversary of Femke.

SURABAR – Ex-military General of the Shandese Legions. Now Emperor of Shandar.

LORD TREMARLE – Powerful 'old school' Lord of Shandar.

KALHEEN – Palace servant who accompanied Femke on her mission to Thrandor. Son of Rikala the seamstress.

LORD KEMPTEN – 'Old school' Lord of Shandar. Regent of the Shandese Empire in Emperor Surabar's absence.

LADY KEMPTEN – Gracious Lady wife of Lord Kempten. Affectionately known as Izzie by her husband.

DANNI – House maid to Lord and Lady Kempten.

TOOMAS – An unscrupulous tattle tout.

LORD FERDAND – Master Spy. Mentor of Femke. Missing, presumed dead for two years. Now the Guildmaster of the Guild of Assassins.

SHANTELLA – Member of the Guild of Assassins – Brother Fox. The sole female member of the Guild.

OTHER ASSASSINS – Brothers: Firedrake, Scorpion, Bear, Viper and Cougar.

LORD BORCHMAN – Shrewd 'old school' Lord of Shandar. Contender for the Mantle of Emperor.

LORD REAVIS – Lord of Shandar. Contender for the Mantle of Emperor.

LORD MARNILLUS – Powerful Lord of Shandar. Leading contender for the Mantle of Emperor.

JABAL – Grand Magician. Member of the Council of Magicians and tutor at the Academy of Magicians in Terilla.

CALVYN – An acolyte magician. Also known as Lord Shanier, scourge of the Legions, due to a recent incident that resulted in the loss of five Imperial Legions.

ALTMAN – Butler to Lord Kempten.

DERRIGAN DARKWEAVER – Long dead magician. Creator of the magical icons utilised by the Guild.

COMMANDER LUTALO – Commander of the Elite First Legion. Father of Reynik.

DEVARUSSO – Flamboyant leader of a troupe of travelling actors.

SERRIUS – Widely regarded as the deadliest gladiator ever to tread the sands of the arena in Shandrim. Retired after sustaining a serious injury.

NADREK – A top gladiator.

DERRYN AND BARTOK – Street entertainers. Talented knife throwers.

CHAPTER ONE

The shadow glided silently across the wall like a giant spider, limbs spread and finding purchase with apparent ease. Given the assassin's height above the ground, any watcher would have marvelled at the confidence with which the dark shape moved, but none saw him.

Shalidar was ever aware of the deadly drop, but totally unafraid. He breathed easily, his mind focused and calm as he reached for his next hold. He had always been an exceptional climber. His lean, athletic frame and strong fingers made the impossible appear natural. Edging confidently across a narrow ledge, he paused at the window high above the ground. It was bolted shut. Momentary irritation niggled, but did not distract him from his goal. He no longer had current passwords to access the Imperial Palace by conventional entrances, but such a minor problem would not prevent him from reaching his target.

He moved on. A gust of wind tugged at his cloak and he paused a moment, clinging to the wall like a limpet as he waited for the destabilising force to subside. The wind died to a gentle sigh and he made another series of moves. The next window was not far. A glance around the frame revealed the drapes to be open. The room inside was dark. Another glance and a warm feeling of success heated his gut. The window bolt was open.

Lifting the window whilst precariously perched on the narrowest of ledges took extraordinary balance, but there had never been anything ordinary about Shalidar. Without making a sound, he opened the window and slipped inside, silently closing it behind him.

'Is this a step too far?' he wondered as he crossed the room to the door. 'Will the Guildmaster accept yet another circumstantial excuse?'

Shalidar listened at the door for a moment. All was quiet in the corridor outside. He slipped out and flitted along the passageway on silent feet. His clear mental map of the Palace allowed him to move without hesitation, but a sudden wave of doubt made him pause in the shadow of a doorway.

The Palace appeared silent and deserted. It was dangerous to stay in any one place for too long, but he needed a few moments to settle his indecision. If he killed Emperor Surabar, the ex-General would become the second bearer of the Imperial Mantle he had assassinated inside a year. For the first hit he had enjoyed the benefit of the perfect cover, but he had no such protection this time. If he killed Surabar, concealing his involvement from the Guild would be impossible. The Guild would use truth serum to force information from him if they felt it necessary. The thought made him shudder.

The Assassins' Creed forbade a member of the Guild to kill the Emperor. The penalty for doing so was death. Shalidar had twisted the creed on many occasions to suit his need, but he had stretched his luck to the limit during recent months. The Guildmaster's patience with him was wearing thin, but the reward was tantalising: legal inheritance to a powerful noble House. If he were to play his hand well, such a position might ultimately see the Emperor's Mantle placed on his own shoulders. It hardly seemed possible, but Lord Tremarle was serious. Shalidar was sure of it. The death of the Lord's last remaining son, Danar, followed by that of his best friend, Lord Lacedian, had provided a powerful if misguided motive for seeing the Emperor dead. However, to capitalise on the old man's misconceived notion of revenge, Shalidar would have to gamble with his own life. Did he dare?

His turbulent thoughts began to calm and his dark eyes glittered with calculating malice. He slid out from the doorway and moved noiselessly forwards into the depths of the Palace. It was late. The passageways were quiet. Getting close to the Emperor's study without being seen would not be difficult.

He had come to the Palace to look for Wolf Spider. His reason for being here was legitimate. The Guildmaster had tasked him to kill the young man who had infiltrated the Guild. Wolf Spider's links to the Emperor were beyond doubt. The legitimacy of his presence in the depths of the Imperial Palace gave Shalidar further reason to consider making the hit tonight. But how could he make the hit look accidental? If his target had been anyone other than the Emperor, he would have used Wolf Spider as a smokescreen without hesitation. But the Guildmaster was no fool. It would not take him long to work out what Shalidar was about.

The assassin moved like a phantom through the Palace, gliding smoothly from one dark recess to the next. There were some sounds of movement from within rooms on either side of the passageways, but no one disturbed him as he threaded his way into the heart of the Emperor's domain.

The smell of polish and cleaning wax hung heavy in the air, as it always did in the Palace corridors. Despite the high ceilings and the inevitable smoky odour from the burning torches that lit the inner walkways, every door, every wooden panel, every surface gleamed with the effort of generations of Palace staff.

As he expected, two guards held post outside the Emperor's study. They were dressed in full ceremonial armour and were armed with swords, knives, and what looked like miniature crossbows. Crossbows! That was a development he had not considered. It was most unusual to arm indoor guards with mid-range weapons.

Shalidar held his position. He was hidden in deep shadow some distance along the corridor from where the two men were standing silent and alert. Torches were alight in the Emperor's study. He could see the light shining through the narrow windows that opened high in the wall of the passageway. Surabar was there, but the assassin had no way of getting any closer without revealing himself to the guards. As things stood, he would have to kill them to get to Surabar. He was not prepared to test the guards' marksmanship in order to get close enough to guarantee clean kills. The risk was too great. He needed a diversion: something to draw the guards away from the door, or distract them.

Fire was always good, but he did not want to risk burning down the Imperial Palace. No. He needed something spectacular, but not life threatening – an occurrence that would catch everyone's attention and draw the Emperor from his study.

The question remained: what? Unusually he found himself bereft of ideas to begin with. Then the seed of an idea germinated within his mind. Within seconds it flourished and grew. It was genius, he decided – a plan worthy of the Dragon. Everything he needed was here in the Palace. A surge of excitement filled his belly with fire. Hugging the shadows, he slipped away and made for one of the Palace's many drawing rooms.

It did not take long for Shalidar to find what he needed. There was a writing desk with all the necessary implements in a nearby room. Writing was not something he made a habit of, as it left a trail that could be traced. However, in this case it was necessary. He lit a candle at the writing desk and began. Once he had drafted his letter, he rewrote it neatly in a bold, flowing script. With the final copy finished to his satisfaction, he set fire to the draft. This he threw into the fireplace and watched to make sure it was totally consumed before returning to his polished version.

He blew gently on the ink for a moment to help it finish drying, then folded the letter neatly and melted wax over the join to seal it. There was a generic Imperial household seal on the desk, so Shalidar pressed it into the drying wax. It was a nice touch, he decided with a twisted grin.

Next he needed someone to deliver it. Speaking to somebody would generate another piece of traceable evidence that he could do without, but it did not cause him great concern. By the time he was finished, any lasting evidence would be blurred.

He snuffed out the candle and left the drawing room. Nobody was abroad in the Palace at this time of night. The only people still at work were the cooks, who were preparing the food for the morning. Shalidar made for the servants' exit, but not with the intention of leaving. Instead he went to the cloakroom near the external door. It took but a few moments to find what he was looking for.

Wrapping an Imperial guard's long night cloak around his shoulders, he gathered his hair at the back of his head and put on a helmet. He turned up the collar of the cloak to hide any telltale tufts of his unmilitarylike locks trailing from the back of the helmet. Once dressed in his crude disguise, he surveyed the effect in a large wall mirror. His dark eyes scanned up and down the reflection, noting every detail. His boots were not regulation style, but he did not intend to let anyone see his feet. He would pass at first glance as an Imperial guard, and that was all that mattered. As a final matter of more important detail, he rubbed at his cheeks to make them flush as if he had just walked in from the cold. Perfect, he decided.

Without pause he turned and crossed the hallway to the entrance to the kitchens. He opened the door a little and leaned through the narrow gap such that just his head and shoulders were inside.

'Anyone here know someone called Kalheen?' he asked, looking around and making eye contact with each of the handful of cooks on the late-evening shift.

'Yeah, I know Kalheen. He's floor staff. He doesn't work here in the kitchens,' one of them answered, suspicion in his eyes.

'Do you know where his quarters are?' Shalidar asked. 'I have a letter for him. The girl said it was very urgent – something to do with life and death. Might be a family member or something.'

The kitchen hand looked across with an enquiring expression at one of the older men. The response was a terse nod. 'No problem,' he said, 'I'll take the letter. If he's in his room, I'll have it in his hands in a few minutes.'

'Thanks for that. It'll save me getting into trouble for being away from my post too long. You know what security's like at the moment. Everyone's paranoid.'

There was a general grumbling agreement to that statement. Without fully entering the kitchen, Shalidar handed the letter to the man and then withdrew, closing the door behind him. It was a few steps to the external door. He exited swiftly, pleased with the success of his ploy.

Once outside, he moved instantly into the nearest deep shadow. He needed to give the cook a good head start, so he counted slowly to one hundred. As he counted he removed the cloak and helmet and stowed them under a nearby shrub. With the count complete, he re-entered through the door. If Brother Falcon's description of Kalheen were accurate, then the man's gullibility would lead him to act swiftly. Shalidar knew he had very little time to get into position. Every second counted.

He set off through the maze of corridors at a brisk walk. His eyes and ears strained ahead for any sign of movement. Intimate knowledge of the Palace served him well, as his indirect route through the less frequently used passageways gave him a clear path to his observation point in the shadows near the Emperor's study. Nothing had changed. The guards were still in position. The Emperor's study was still lit. As long as Kalheen took the bait, the Emperor would be hard pressed not to come to the door when it began.

Kalheen awoke with a start from his sleep. Someone was knocking insistently at his door.

'Wha . . . what? It can't be morning already? Shand! Have I overslept again?' he muttered as he rubbed at his eyes and tried to focus on something. 'Who is it? What do you want?' he called more loudly.

'Letter for you. Urgent I'm told. Do you want me to slide it under the door?' replied a voice.

It was not a voice that was instantly familiar, though something in Kalheen's mind told him he should know the person to whom the voice belonged.

'A letter?' he asked. 'Who's it from?'

'I don't know. A girl sent it apparently. Said it was a matter of life or death . . .'

'Mother!' Kalheen exclaimed, instantly fearing the worst. He leaped from his bed and stumbled across to the door. Flinging it open, he grabbed the letter from the messenger's hand with a worried mumble of thanks.

The kitchen hand was a little put out by Kalheen's abruptness, but the pale look of shock and concern on the servant's round face was enough to make forgiving his rudeness easy.

'I'd better get back to the kitchen. I hope the news is not all bad,' the messenger said, backing away.

'Thanks,' Kalheen mumbled, his attention totally fixed on the folded, sealed note held between his fat, trembling fingers. There was no question of his lighting the torch in his room. His hands were shaking too much to contemplate trying to kindle a flame. Heedless of anyone else seeing him in his rumpled old nightshirt, he walked the few paces along the corridor to where the nearest lit torch was bracketed and took a closer look at the letter. The handwriting was not his mother's. Was that good or bad? He did not like to think. It was sealed with an Imperial seal, so someone here in the Palace had written it. 'Who in the Palace would write to me on a matter of life and death,' he thought. Was this some sort of practical joke? If so, then it was not funny.

He broke the seal and opened up the letter. His eyes widened as he began to read.

Dear Kalheen,

I'm sorry to contact you like this, but I need your help. There are traitors at work in the Palace. The Emperor's life is in danger. If I cannot flush them out into the open, then I fear he will not live to see the dawn.

There are not many in the Palace I can trust. After our recent trip to Thrandor together, I know I can count on you. What I need you to do is simple, but of the utmost importance. If you do it right, then it could make the difference between the Emperor living, or dying tonight.

Go immediately to the Imperial Bell Tower. Don't delay. When you get there, go inside and barricade the door from within. Then ring the Imperial Bell. Don't stop ringing it until the guards break in. The bell will panic the traitors into action. I will do the rest.

Burn this letter as soon as you have read it. Don't wait, Kalheen. Go now. I'm counting on you.

Yours in haste,
Femke

Femke! He had hardly seen so much as a glimpse of the Imperial spy since they had returned from Thrandor, and now this. He was to be an agent: an agent for an Imperial spy. Just the thought of it sent pictures and potential stories spinning through his mind in a kaleidoscope of images. It was all he could do to bring himself to his senses. He had no time to waste in idle dreaming. Femke needed his help now, and he, Kalheen, would not let her down.

'Burn the letter first,' he muttered, lifting it to the flame of the torch and setting light to the corner. The parchment caught and the flame spread rapidly across the sheet. He held it as long as he could before dropping it onto the stone floor. The flame consumed the letter, leaving only a few wafer-thin pieces of curled black ash.

Kalheen raced back into his room. There was no time to dress, but he could not run around the Palace with nothing on but his nightshirt. He slipped his boots onto his bare feet and grabbed his cloak from the peg on the back of the door. Wrapping it around his body, he set off through the Palace as fast as he could walk.

The bell tower was located in the main west wing of the central Palace structure. Kalheen did not encounter anyone during his brisk transit. The door to the ground floor of the tower was not locked, but neither was there any light inside. It took a moment of fumbling around in the darkness before he located a torch and pulled it from the wall bracket. He lit it from one of the torches in the corridor outside and re-entered the tower.

Once inside, he lit two further torches. There was plenty of material with which to barricade the door. The tower was not in regular use. Its function by design was that of announcing the passing of an Emperor. As this was such an irregular and infrequent occurrence, the Palace staff had utilised much of the ground floor space for many years as a storage area for excess furniture. Dressers, tables, chairs, a chaise longue, bookcases and a host of smaller items lined the walls of the lower tower lobby. Aside from the access to the central staircase, there was little floor space that was clear.

The staircase climbed a single floor to a square chamber

with no doors. The chamber was undecorated save for a large, circular rug. The deep pile of finest wool was woven with the Imperial Seal of Shandar in rich gold and silver against a background of deepest royal purple.

A single rope with an intricate end knot hung through a small round hole in the ceiling. Many spans above, in the lofty heights of the belfry, the rope was attached to the swinging mechanism of the great Imperial Bell. Access to the belfry was through a trap door via a ladder fixed to the north wall of the tower, but Kalheen had no need to climb further.

After his initial swift scout around to make sure that he was alone, Kalheen placed his lit torch back in the wall bracket on the ground floor and set to work building the barricade. He was determined to help Femke to the best of his ability, but he was also aware of the time constraints. Using every ounce of his bulk, he heaved a large, heavy bookcase across to block the doorway first. Then, working swiftly and systematically, he piled more and more furniture behind it. After a few minutes he was sweating profusely. It was the most physically demanding exercise he had done in months.

'That'll have to do,' he panted softly, surveying his handiwork with a self-satisfied eye. Taking the nearby torch from its bracket again, he headed up the stairs to where the bell pull beckoned. There was a bracket on the south wall for his torch. He jammed it into the bracket and he grabbed hold of the rope with both hands. 'OK, Femke – here it comes.'

*

At the first toll of the bell, the two guards at the door to the Emperor's study looked at one another in confusion and alarm. At the second resounding DONG, they began talking urgently in fierce whispers.

Shalidar drew a knife from his boot. His heart pounded as he crouched in the shadows. He was poised, ready to leap at the first sign of the Emperor. Would he come out? Would the bell prove sufficiently appealing bait? Or would the canny old General see through the trap and go to ground?

DONG, DONG, DONG . . .

The bell tolled loud and insistent. All over the Palace people began to move. Groups congregated in the hallways and corridors asking if it could be true. Was the Emperor dead? How had he died? Why was the bell tolling now? Would it not have been better to wait until morning?

Off-duty guards scrambled to dress. On-duty guards milled in confusion, asking directions of their superiors where they could. Senior guards and guard commanders did their utmost to display a calm front as they were bombarded with questions from all quarters.

'Come on! Come on!' Shalidar urged through gritted teeth. 'You can't resist this, you old meddler.'

If the Emperor did not show within the next few seconds, Shalidar knew he would have to abandon the hit and move into a better position in order to escape the Palace unnoticed. The guard commanders would not take long to collect their thoughts and come running.

. . . DONG, DONG, DONG . . .

'Damn you, Surabar!' he swore under his breath. Time had run out.

Keeping to the shadows, Shalidar began edging away from the study. He moved slowly to avoid drawing the attention of the guards. As he did so, he could hear the sound of running footsteps approaching along an intersecting passageway. They were still some distance away, but they were closing fast. Just then, the door to the Emperor's study opened. The two guards turned to face the Emperor.

It had worked, but the window of opportunity was very small if he was to strike and still make a clean getaway. Shalidar had never been one to play safe. He leaped into motion the moment the door began to move. His target was in sight. The focus of the guards was away from the corridor. He was committed.

The sound of the bell brought Emperor Surabar to his feet as if he were propelled from his seat. His chair tipped backwards, but he spun and caught it before it fell.

'What in Shand's name . . .' he began, his voice trailing off as the bell tolled a second time.

The bell tolled again and again, the sorrowful tones reverberating through the Palace. Instinct carried him around the desk and towards the door, but he paused before his hand touched the handle. Was this a trap? Did someone want him to move from his study? On the other hand someone could be trying to draw the guards away in order to trap him inside. 'Damned if I move and damned if I don't,' he thought grimly. 'Whatever I do is likely to be wrong.' Maybe someone was playing a prank.

It seemed unlikely. This had the feel of an assassination attempt.

He raised his hand towards the door handle again. Once more he stopped. Should he open the door or barricade it? His desk was heavy. It would slow down any potential assailant. There were weapons on the wall that he could wield if it came to it. 'If I open the door, I would be a fool to do so unprepared,' he thought. He went to the nearest wall and drew a sword from its ornamental scabbard. He hefted it to test the weight and balance of the blade. It was a little heavier than he preferred, but it was a good weapon. 'It will do,' he decided.

The guards turned inwards towards him as he opened the door. They looked confused and worried. A movement to his left caught his eye. He recognised Shalidar instantly. The assassin was almost upon the left-hand guard. Surabar opened his mouth to give warning, but the assassin struck before he had a chance to speak. A crossbow bolt flashed past him from left to right, missing his chest by no more than a hand span. Before he had a chance to raise his sword more than halfway to the horizontal, pain erupted in his right side. His breath froze in his throat and he lost his grip on the sword. The passageway tilted alarmingly as his legs collapsed from under him. His mind could not fathom what had happened. His perspective of the corridor was wrong. It made no sense. Shalidar had been attacking from his left. What had hit him from the right?

Then Shalidar was standing over him. The assassin's cold smile was more than he could bear. Fury burned within him, a white-hot hatred that spewed a string of curses to his lips. The strange thing was he could not articulate them. His body was not responding. Nothing made sense. The world was spinning out of control. He was choking, drowning in a sea of fiery red anger.

Shalidar speared down the corridor with barely a whisper of sound to mark his passing. The Emperor saw him before either of the guards, but by then it was too late. The assassin rammed his knife at the thin metal backplate of the nearest guard with his left hand. The ceremonial armour was not designed to withstand a strike of such force. The knife sliced right through the metal. The man stiffened with shock and pain. At the same time Shalidar grabbed the guard's right hand, which was holding the mini crossbow. In the blink of an eye, he had angled the weapon up at the second guard and triggered the firing mechanism. There was a *thunk*, *thud*, followed by a short pause and then another *thunk*, *thud*.

Shalidar shoved the dying guard forward and drew another knife, but his work was done. The first *thunk*, *thud*, sounds had marked the release of the crossbow bolt and the projectile striking the second guard high in the chest. This second guard, thrown back by the force of the bolt, had then inadvertently squeezed the trigger on his own crossbow resulting in the second rapid sequence of sounds. To the assassin's delight, the stray bolt fired by the dying guard had struck the Emperor in the side of his ribcage. Fired at point-blank range, the arrow had penetrated deep into his chest.

Both guards and the Emperor fell almost simultaneously,

the Emperor's sword clattering on the floor. The two guards were as good as dead before they fell. The Emperor's wound was also mortal. Blood flowed freely from the wound in his side, and frothed at his mouth and nose. The bolt had clearly punctured his right lung. Without a miracle, the Emperor would be dead inside the next few minutes, most likely by drowning in his own blood. It was tempting to finish him, but Shalidar thought better of it. Chance had played in his favour. He would no longer have to worry about the Guild subjecting him to truth serum. He had not directly killed the Emperor and he could say so in all truth.

Under the influence of truth serum no man could lie. There was a way to beat the power of the potion. He had done it once before. The method was not pleasant, but the stakes were so high, he would have been willing to endure the discomfort, the feelings of violation and the risk of betrayal involved in allowing a sorcerer to meddle with his memories. Old Memison had already delved through Shalidar's memories once. He knew enough of the assassin's past to see him executed a hundred times over. Whatever else the sorcerer might be, he had proved himself to be no tattler.

Emperor Surabar was slumped in the doorway, neither sitting nor lying. He opened his mouth to speak, but no sound made it past his lips. He coughed. More blood bubbled and dribbled from his mouth. His eyes burned with hatred more intense than any Shalidar had ever seen. For the slightest moment he felt a cold shiver run down his spine, then a shout sounded behind him. A group of guards were rounding the corner from a side corridor. The guard who had shouted was loading a crossbow. Shalidar did not hesitate. He hurdled the bodies of the guards and sprinted off down the corridor.

The assassin darted into the first side passage to his left. As he did so a crossbow bolt ricocheted off the wall behind him, missing him by no more than a finger's width. High on adrenalin he raced down the passageway and turned again, this time through an unmarked door that led to a service stairwell. It was well that he knew the Palace intimately, for without such knowledge, escape would be unlikely.

The bell would have put the guards on full alert at all the outer gates. They did not normally check people exiting the Palace, but under the circumstances it was unlikely that he would get past them without being stopped. That left two options. He could hide within the Palace, or he could exit the Palace by a route that the guards would not be watching. The latter option was preferable. Once the guards got organised, they would search the Palace thoroughly. Shalidar was sure that some of the hiding places he knew would fool the guards, but there was always the chance that one of them might get lucky.

Foregoing the obvious exits, he turned left and climbed up the stairs. With feather-light footsteps he raced up a floor, taking the steps two at a time. The stairwell was square with the steps turning at each corner. He reached the landing area and opened the door into the top-floor corridor system. A smile touched his lips briefly as he paused in the doorway, for he could hear his pursuers clattering downwards and away from him. 'So far, so good,' he thought.

There were folk gathering in the corridor and there was a buzz of speculation. The bell was still tolling its mournful message. Kalheen must have done a good job of barricading the door, Shalidar realised. The guards would certainly be trying to get into the tower by now.

Twice people tried to question the assassin as he passed, but he brushed them aside by frowning and claiming important Imperial business. His purposeful stride and officious manner were enough to prevent bystanders impeding his progress.

When he reached the end of the corridor, he turned right and then immediately left into the drawing room there. Nobody was inside. Shalidar closed the door behind him. There was enough light from the windows that he did not need to light a torch. He crossed the room to the window nearest the left corner. It opened easily. He looked out across the Palace grounds and over the outer wall to the cluttered hotchpotch of buildings that crowded around the Imperial stronghold. It looked almost as if the city buildings were bustling around the Palace, pushing and shoving one another to try to get as close as possible.

Shalidar's eyes swept downwards to the area below the window. It was a long way to the ground, but he had made the climb safely before on several occasions. The descent was not difficult for a talented climber, but there was always a risk of falling, no matter how slight.

Shalidar switched his focus back inside for a moment. He reached up and twisted the right-hand end stop from the curtain pole. The curtain was easy to remove. The heavy material had hung from as high as he could reach to the floor – a useful length. He rolled it into a bundle and leaned out of the window to see if he could see anyone moving about in the Palace grounds below. There did not appear to be anyone around. This was not a surprise. The guards were most likely concentrated around the gates. He dropped the bundle and watched as it descended to the ground. The thud as it landed was clearly audible despite the tolling of the bell. He waited for a moment to see if the noise aroused any interest. No one came running.

With one last look around, he climbed out of the window and eased along the ledge to the nearest corner of the building. The fancy stonework that decorated the corners of the Palace buildings offered plenty of handholds. The only disadvantage was that descending a corner made him more visible against the night sky. His silhouette would stand out far more readily than if he descended a flat wall.

He descended quickly, making the fancy cornerstones and gargoyles appear much like a ladder as his hands and feet found purchase with ease. No more than two minutes later he was back on solid ground. There was plenty of deep shadow in the Palace gardens. His black cloak, leggings and boots made him feel all but invisible. He scouted the ground under the window and retrieved the curtain bundle.

'Hey, you! Stop where you are!'

Instinctive reaction made Shalidar glance up. It was a mistake. His face reflected the moonlight, giving a clearer target for the guards to aim at.

'How in Shand's name did he get down there?' a voice

exclaimed from a second window. The assassin's face split into a wide grin at the comment. 'Let them wonder,' he thought. It was unlikely that the guards would follow his path down the side of the building. He exploded into a sprint across the gardens.

His muscles automatically tensed at the *thunk*, *thunk* sound of two crossbow bolts being released, but the shots were wild. He did not even hear the bolts land. The crossbows used by the guards were not renowned for their accuracy. There was always the chance of a lucky shot, but they were more for short range and deterrence than for use as a precision long-range weapon. As soon as he had run a reasonable distance from the main building, he knew he was in little danger from those in the upper-floor windows.

He reached the outer wall of the Palace gardens. The wall was high, more than twice as tall as he was, and topped with iron spikes. The creamy-coloured stone had been rendered smooth. There was no way of climbing it without a rope . . . or a curtain, Shalidar thought with a grin. He unrolled the material with a flick and then whipped it up towards the spikes on the top of the wall. His first attempt failed to snag anything, but his second tangled on two of the iron spikes. Working quickly he twisted the material until it became like a thick rope and then, with one final tug to ensure it was secure enough to take his weight, he began to climb.

A crossbow bolt clattered against the wall about three paces to his right. To get an arrow that close was a good shot considering the range, but close was not good enough. He walked up the wall, pulling hand over hand as he climbed the makeshift rope. The cloth began to rip as he reached the crown of the wall, but the hem acted as a stop point for the tear. The ascent took seconds. Pausing a moment to fasten the curtain material more securely, he stepped carefully over the spikes and flipped the trailing end over to the other side of the wall.

With a last glance back at the Palace, he took a double handful of cloth in preparation to begin his descent. As he did so there was a sickening thud combined with an explosion of pain in his right thigh. The shock and pain took him by surprise. In what seemed like slow motion, Shalidar lost his balance and toppled off the wall.

CHAPTER TWO

'Is this it?' Reynik asked, keeping his voice low.

'Yes, this is the place,' Femke replied. 'He's many things, but pretentious is not one of them.'

Reynik nodded. If Femke said this plain-looking country house was where they were going, he would follow her with the utmost confidence. The young woman spy was not much older than he was, but she had a wealth of experience.

'Should we go straight up to the house?' he asked.

Femke paused for a moment before answering. Her head tipped back just a fraction as she gave the surrounding countryside a sweep with her piercing, grey-blue eyes. The sun was sinking fast into the west. It would soon be dusk. 'We should take a few precautions first. I'm sure we've not been followed, but there's always the chance that someone has employed a watcher to monitor the estate. Let's split up and circle the house. Stay at a good distance, and try to keep out of direct line of sight where you can. We don't want to alarm those inside.'

Standing in her stirrups, Femke looked over the high hedge between the lane and the outer gardens of the country house. The house looked large, but simple in design with little outward evidence that it belonged to a Lord of substance. The only clue was in the quality of the build. The walls were thick and strong. They were made from large, regular blocks of the local grey stone. This did little to enhance the beauty of the building. There were no fancy gables or elegant balconies. The house was a straightforward, oblong-shaped structure – solid and practical.

The gardens were extensive, but laid out with a simple elegance that required minimal maintenance. Much of the land surrounding the house was set to grass. The exceptions were an orchard to the west that looked to be a mixture of apple and plum trees, and a few borders filled with ornamental shrubs and trees.

Here and there were signs of a woman's touch. Window boxes filled with early-blooming flowers softened the looming greyness of the house, and carefully-tended hanging baskets hung from large iron brackets to either side of the main doorway. A cast-iron table surrounded by four chairs rested next to a small pond in the outer gardens. The table and chairs had been placed such that two large trees growing nearby would offer them shade in the heat of a summer afternoon. A small willow tree, recently planted, overhung the water. If Femke had to judge, she would say it was the Lady of the house who organised the maintenance of the grounds, most likely taking an active hand with some of the finer details.

'You circle to the west. I'll go east. I'll meet you by that cedar tree over there,' she said softly, pointing to a huge, spreading tree just visible beyond and to the left of the house. 'Keep your eyes and ears open. If anyone is watching, they'll not be obvious. Remember what I taught you about how agents camouflage their positions. A watcher will not be easy to see, but only the very best leave no signs of their presence.'

'And if I do find a watcher?'

'Leave him alone,' Femke ordered. 'Note his position, but don't give any indication you've seen him. Rendezvous with me by the cedar. We'll tackle any trouble together. Let's not take unnecessary risks.'

Reynik nodded and, with a gentle tug, turned his horse to the left. Initially he backtracked down the lane along which they had approached. He kept his mount at a slow, steady walk. Making noise on horseback was inevitable, but at a walking pace the noise was not great. He had few worries about encountering danger that he could not handle out here in the countryside. After the events of the previous evening, it was hard to imagine he would ever face such danger again.

'Complacency will get you killed, son,' his father had told him. The words echoed in his mind, ringing with sad irony given his father's fate. Killed by the assassin, Shalidar, in the heart of his Legion's campsite, it was difficult not to question if complacency had played a part in his death.

Thoughts of his father brought with them a welter of emotions. The sharp pain of grief brought fresh tears to his tired eyes. Fierce anger and the burning desire for vengeance see-sawed with the feeling that losing his father's strength had somehow made him weak and helpless. The conflicting feelings were confusing and overwhelming, and his ability to cope with them was not helped by his extreme fatigue.

He dashed the tears from his cheeks. No matter how his father had died, Reynik was not ready to abandon his words of wisdom. Lutalo's advice had served him well during the last two years. Not many young soldiers enjoyed the privilege of having an experienced Legion Commander for a father; even fewer could boast one who was willing to act as a personal tutor. The military insights he had gained had given him a huge advantage during his training as a Legionnaire. However, none of his lessons had prepared him for the situations he had faced during the past few days.

As he rode, he did his best to stay alert. Vivid flashbacks to his running battle with a string of top assassins the night before, combined with a lack of sleep, did not help. He could feel his concentration waning, but he felt helpless. He tried splashing his face with cold water from his canteen as he rode, but his focus continued to slip in and out.

'Come on!' he urged himself in a muttered growl. 'Get a grip, Reynik. Don't let yourself down now.'

A short while later, Reynik reached the cedar tree. He had noted nothing unusual, but as he rubbed at his cheeks and eyes in an effort to stimulate life back into his face, he wondered if he would have noticed even the most obvious of watchers in his current state. He had to admit it was unlikely.

He did not have to wait long for Femke. She looked shattered too. But despite the dark rings under her eyes, she had an air of alertness about her that he knew he did not share.

'Anything?' she asked.

He shook his head. 'Not that I saw, but I'm not in much of a state to be positive about my sweep.'

'I didn't see anything either. We'll have to risk it. We both need rest, and if someone is out there, he knows we're here now anyway. We might as well go in.'

Rather than circle all the way back to the main entrance, they decided to use a path in towards the house that Femke had noted not far from their current position. The stables were on this side of the house, so the path was likely one used for recreational riding, rather than a thoroughfare. More to the point, it saved unnecessary riding, which was welcome on many counts.

Femke had never been comfortable riding a horse. She had spent a lot of time in a saddle during her recent mission to Thrandor, but she was a realist when it came to her abilities. As a horsewoman, she knew she was more adequate than accomplished. They had been riding less than a day from Shandrim, but Femke's thighs were stiff from the journey.

Reynik had fared better, but was more than a little pleased that they had reached their destination. He had ridden extensively as a boy, but he was suffering the intense weariness that follows a sustained rush of adrenalin combined with the emotional weight of losing his father. His night of danger had passed. He had not rested in nearly two days. All he wanted to do now was to bathe and sleep – not necessarily in that order.

As they neared the stables, it became apparent that their approach had not gone unnoticed. A stable boy stepped out to meet them, walking forward with confidence, but not so quickly as to frighten the horses. He took the reins of Femke's horse while she dismounted, patting her horse's neck and talking to it in a low, warm voice as she stepped clear. Reynik dismounted without assistance, but the boy was quick to take his reins as well.

'My Lord and Lady Kempten have been informed of your arrival. Danni, one of our maids, will show you the way. If you could meet her at the door over there, please?' he said politely.

'Our bags—' Reynik began.

'Can wait,' Femke interrupted. 'We should attend the Lord and Lady, Reynik. That's what we're here for. We'll be staying tonight. Could you see that our bags are taken to our rooms, please?' she asked the stable boy.

'Of course, ma'am. Leave it to me.'

They walked to the door that the stable boy had pointed to and went inside. A young girl in a grey dress with a white apron was waiting for them. She curtsied as they entered.

'May I take your cloaks?' she asked in a timid voice.

'Thank you, Danni. That would be most kind,' Femke responded, smiling warmly at her. She removed her cloak and draped it over the girl's proffered arm. Reynik added his and nodded his thanks. 'We were told you would take us to see the Lord and Lady. Do you know if they're ready to receive us? Our business with them is urgent, but we don't want to offend them by appearing in our travelling gear and smelling of horses.'

'That's all right, my Lady. Lord Kempten said that I was to show you to his study right away.'

'Very good. Lead on then.'

The passageway along which Danni initially led them was narrow and dark. It was clearly a part of the house used solely by the servants. Once through the end door, however, the change was startling. The grey exterior of the house had not visually prepared them for what awaited inside. The central hallway of the house was stunning.

Everything was clean, bright and tasteful. Exposed beams contrasted with the fresh whiteness of the ceiling. Rich panelling of shining teak was offset by subtle shades of green, and everywhere they looked the furnishings were made with materials of the highest quality. There were none of the usual trappings commonly found in the houses of Lords and Ladies of the Imperial Court. Where one would expect to find suits of armour guarding various areas of the entrance hall, instead there were huge potted plants and ornamental trees. Where one would expect to find crossed swords, or ceremonial weapons hanging on the walls, instead there were a series of exquisitely painted landscapes. A wide, wooden staircase climbed from the centre of the room up and away from the main entrance door. The feeling of life and vibrancy was amazing.

Handmade rugs, coloured to fit the theme of the hall, were carefully arranged to soften the expanse of polished wood. Tastefully-placed dahl tables boasted occasional ornaments of great workmanship and detail. The person who had arranged the décor in the hallway had great skill. The effect was one of simple elegance. There was nothing pretentious or overbearing, yet there was no mistaking that someone of class and distinction lived here.

Danni led them around the hall and up the central staircase to the first floor. Here they turned left and along the upper landing to a door on the left. She stopped and knocked twice before entering.

'Your guests, my Lord,' she said, her voice still sounding timid despite her attempt to speak up as she announced them.

'Ah, Femke, Reynik, do come in. This is a nice surprise. I was not expecting visitors from Shandrim for some time yet. Thank you, Danni. Would you be so kind as to bring our guests some refreshments? I'm sure they would appreciate a bite to eat and something to drink after their journey.'

Lord Kempten was dressed in country-styled green trousers and a cream-coloured tunic, with a brown leather jerkin over the top. His grey hair was slicked back and his face appeared freshly shaven. He looked every inch the country gentleman.

'Thank you, Lord Kempten, that would be most welcome,' Femke said, giving a slight bow. Reynik also bowed, feeling stiff and awkward next to Femke. She had a way of appearing at home in every situation.

Lady Kempten rose from her chair near the window and walked to her husband's side. She, too, looked very different from the way she dressed for Court. A dress of subtle shades of green, brown and cream, with lacework at the neck and cuffs gave a more rustic look to her inherent elegance, and her hair was clipped into a ponytail for practicality. 'Welcome. Come and sit down with us. You must be tired.'

'Thank you, my Lady,' Femke replied, 'but we're not really in a fit state to sit. We're both caked in grime from our travels, and are somewhat fragrant with the smell of our horses.'

'Not to worry, Femke. A little dirt can be cleaned away,' Lord Kempten said quickly. 'I assume you bear important tidings, or you would not be here. Come. Take a seat. We crave your news.'

'Thank you again then, my Lord,' she said gratefully. 'A comfortable seat would be nice after a day of bouncing in my saddle. I never was much of a rider.'

Femke and Reynik sat in the chairs that the Lord and Lady directed them to. Reynik was happy to let Femke do the talking. He was not comfortable trying to talk politics and high-level strategy. He understood it well enough, but he preferred action to words. Lord and Lady Kempten sat down. For a moment there was an uncomfortable silence.

'It might be better if we allow the servants to bring the food and wine before we speak of the pressing matters that brought you here,' Lord Kempten observed. 'I suspect we will not want other ears listening to what you have to say.'

'Begging my Lord's pardon, but do you think Lady Kempten should be party to this conversation? Some of the knowledge I'll be imparting is highly dangerous; it may place her in grave danger of becoming a target for the Guild of Assassins.'

'No offence is taken, Femke, but Izzie and I have decided that whatever the future holds for us, we shall face it together. I have put her through enough traumas recently. After she discovered that my assassination was a fake, we discussed the situation. I trust Izzie implicitly. Even if you were to order her to leave now by the will of the Emperor, I would share any information with her later. We're in this together, for better or worse.'

'As you will, my Lord.'

For the next few minutes there followed an awkward exchange of small talk. The light was dimming fast. Lady Kempten lit a taper from the fire. There were several candles around the room. She lit them all in turn. After their sleepless night and the long ride out from Shandrim, the flickering light and warm room made for a soporific atmosphere. When the servants brought the light refreshments, Lord Kempten thanked them politely and then made it clear he did not want to be disturbed again before dinner. The main meal was not due to be served for at least two hours, so this would give them plenty of time for private discussion.

Once the servants had left, Femke began to talk. Reynik listened and tucked into the food. There was a plate of sliced bread, butter, cheese, sliced meat, and a pot of steaming hot dahl from which he poured himself a generous mug. The hot stimulant drink helped prolong his ability to focus. With Femke cast in the role of narrator, Reynik poured her a cup of dahl and sliced her some bread and cheese. She nodded her thanks and continued her report, taking occasional sips of the dahl and nibbles at the food during natural breaks in the flow.

Lady Kempten was quick to point out to Reynik that this food was just a snack to keep the hunger pangs at bay. They would dine more formally an hour after sunset.

The story took a considerable time to tell. When she reached its conclusion, both Lord and Lady Kempten had wide eyes. In contrast, Reynik was fighting hard to keep his eyes open. The comfortable seat, the warmth from the fireplace and the food in his stomach were making it increasingly difficult to stay awake. The stimulant properties of the hot dahl had helped initially, but he was fighting a losing battle.

'Shand, no! Surabar dead! This is disastrous!' Kempten said, his shock and instant grief draining the colour from his face. 'He will be sadly missed, Femke. The man was a genius at organisation. Given time he could have been the best Emperor Shandar has ever seen.'

Lady Kempten's face was also pale and grave as she took in the news. 'How sure are you of your deductions, Femke? Are you certain it's the old spymaster, Lord Ferdand, who is leading the Guild? He's been missing and assumed dead for some years, hasn't he? I always took him for a loyal subject of the Emperor. Did you see him clearly?' she asked.

'Positive, my Lady – one hundred percent. I'd know my old mentor anywhere. It was strange to see him after so long. I feel I should be happy that he's alive. Instead all I feel is anger. He has betrayed the principles he claimed were precious to him. I admit the location of the Guild's head-quarters is supposition, but it's based on a lot of strong circumstantial evidence. If I were a gambler, I would bet heavily on my theory. As for the Emperor's death, well all we can tell you is that the Imperial Bell was tolling for a long time. I think we have to accept the fact that Emperor Surabar has breathed his last.' Femke turned her head towards Lord Kempten and looked at him until he met her gaze. 'This does, of course, make you the rightful Emperor Designate.'

'Emperor Designate . . . hmm, yes,' Kempten muttered thoughtfully, returning her strong stare for a moment before looking away.

'Isn't there something of a problem there?' Lady Kempten said pointedly. 'As far as everyone at Court is concerned, my husband is dead and buried. Why should they now announce him the rightful Emperor Designate?'

Femke grinned, mischief lighting up her eyes. 'As your husband will be quick to affirm, Emperor Surabar was a clever man, my Lady. The senior Lords are certain to take control of the Palace now. When they find Surabar's Last Will and Testament in his study they will be glad to find your husband declared as his rightful heir. It would be logical for them to think Surabar did not get around to changing it after Lord Kempten's death. They will read out his will in the Imperial Court, as is the requirement. No doubt they will openly display great sorrow that Lord Kempten is not able to take up the Mantle. Inside, how-ever, they will rejoice, for this will open the way for one of their own to assume the Mantle in his stead. It should be noted that even if they crown one of their own as Emperor, under Shandese law your husband would still be entitled to take up the Mantle at any time.'

'It was a part of the plan that Surabar disclosed to me before he arranged my "death", darling. I'm sorry. I didn't think it would be appropriate to mention it.' Lord Kempten looked sheepish.

Lady Kempten raised one eyebrow quizzically and the set of her jaw made her look uncharacteristically dangerous as she turned to her husband. 'Well, dear, why would you? Becoming the next Emperor of Shandar is hardly something that will affect our family, now, is it? Not appropriate to mention it!'

'Would you like us to leave?' Femke offered. She turned to find Reynik's head had slumped forward on his chest. He was fast asleep.

'No, dear, you're fine where you are,' Lady Kempten said firmly. 'Besides, your friend there looks very comfortable. I'd hate to disturb him. A little embarrassment might do my husband the world of good. I love him dearly, but he's so single-minded. He can be very thoughtless at times. I'm first to applaud his dedication to the Empire and to his job, but you would think he might mention something like being officially next in line for the Mantle.'

'Now, Izzie, dear—'

'Don't even think about "Izzie, dearing" me! I'm not going to interfere with your plans. You know me better than that. But I am disappointed that you didn't see fit to tell me something so important to our future. Our future: that's you, me, and our children, dear. You do remember us, don't you? Were you planning to write us a letter about it?'

'Please, Izzie, don't be like that. You know I don't conceal things from you unless I have to. To be honest, I didn't expect to ever find myself in this position. Emperor Surabar named me as his heir as a stopgap measure. He was watching the nobility for suitable candidates to replace him. He didn't want the Mantle. He intended to renounce it as soon as he found a Lord whom he felt would make a sound replacement. The man was a very talented leader and not one to be easily fooled. He knew what he was looking for, but that bunch of self-centred idiots at Court were so set on deposing him, they blinded themselves to his abilities and intentions.'

Femke coughed pointedly at this, and both the Lord and Lady turned to look at her.

'Begging your pardons, my Lord, my Lady, but I think you should know that Emperor Surabar found the person to whom he intended to transfer power.'

'Really? Who?' they asked in unison.

'You, my Lord. Emperor Surabar told me last week that his admiration for you had grown considerably since your short period of Regency. The only reason he had not already abdicated in your favour was his mission to destroy the Guild of Assassins. He knew that having stirred the hornets' nest, he needed to follow his plan through to its conclusion. He had no intention of leaving you with a huge unholy mess to sort out when you came to power. It was a matter of personal pride for him to leave you with a state of stability in Shandrim from which you could build. When he began the conflict with the Guild, I don't think he realised how difficult a campaign it would prove to be, but he was doing everything in his power to resolve the situation quickly. He intended to give you some warning, my Lord. However, it seems he has not been given the chance.'

'He chose me? But he knew ... I mean you must have told him about . . . I don't understand.'

Lady Kempten laughed. 'Secrets within secrets! What a life you spies and politicians have! Well, my dear, I will forgive you your oversight this time. Don't let it happen again. If I am to be an Empress, then I should be kept far better informed.'

Femke smiled and nodded her head. Lady Kempten had become a lot more assertive since her husband's fake assassination.

'What are your thoughts on the Guild, my Lord? Assuming you take power, do you intend to adopt Emperor Surabar's goal of destroying it, or are you going to let them resume business as usual?'

Lord Kempten clasped his hands together in front of his body and leaned forward. Then he stood up and began pacing around the room. Femke and Lady Kempten followed him with their eyes. 'I don't know,' he said after a short pause. 'I've not got used to the idea that I might be the next Emperor yet. *If* I were to take the Mantle, then deciding my policies would not be something I would leap into without a good deal of consideration. If the Guild has assassinated the Emperor, as looks likely, then the Assassins' Creed is no longer operating. In that case I'll have little choice but to continue working towards their destruction. If they did not kill him – if he died through a misfortune, or because of something unrelated to the Guild – then, well ... I'll have to think long and hard about it. In that circumstance I would be protected by the creed, but Izzie and the children would not. The Legions were Surabar's family. That's where the Guild struck to hurt him. I'm not willing to place my family in that sort of danger.'

Lord Kempten's final statement hung in the air. An awkward silence followed. It was the slightest of sounds that drew Femke's attention, but she knew instantly what it was. Waving to the Kemptens to attract their attention, she indicated that someone was listening at the door and for them to keep talking. She got to her feet, placed a hand over Reynik's mouth and shook him awake with the other. He awoke with a start. His eyes met hers. It took no more than a second for understanding to spark in his gaze. Trouble!

Femke removed her hand from his mouth, and with simple hand gestures she outlined her plan. The Kemptens stumbled over their words as they initiated a nonsensical argument over how their children would react to being moved into the Imperial Palace, but they kept talking whilst Femke and Reynik moved silently to the door. Lady Kempten's expression was one of astonishment and horror as a concealed blade appeared in the spy's hand. Reynik grabbed the door handle and wrenched the door open, allowing Femke to leap through.

No one was there, but out of the corner of her eye, she

noticed a shadowy figure slipping away down the stairs. In an instant, she was in pursuit. Reynik was no more than a pace or two behind. They reached the stairs. The figure was near the bottom.

'Stop where you are! Move and you'll die.' Reynik's bellowed order was so unexpected it made Femke jump. To her surprise, the figure froze. They reached her in seconds. It was Danni, the maid. She was already weeping and shaking with terror.

'Come with me, Danni,' Femke said, her voice calm and soothing. 'Don't do anything foolish. We don't want to hurt you. We just need to ask you a few questions.' The girl did not look like a professional agent, but the spy knew all too well that appearances could be deceptive. 'Now, let's go slowly back up the stairs, Danni. I have a knife here. The blade is poisoned. I'm going to keep it well away from your body to avoid any accidents, but you must do as you're told. Do you understand?'

Danni nodded. Tears streamed down her face. Her weeping was so intense that she could not control her breathing. She juddered and convulsed with every attempted inhalation. Femke was not sure whether to feel sorry for the girl, or impressed by her dissembling.

Doors in the hallway twitched as curious servants peeped out to see what was happening. Reynik's thunderous shout must have been heard through most of the house. Femke led Danni back up the stairway at knifepoint. Reynik took a good look around the hallway to make sure they had not missed anything obvious. Content that they had captured their quarry, he followed them up.

Before entering the drawing room where the Lord and Lady awaited them, Femke gave Reynik her knife while she searched Danni for weapons. She found nothing. As an extra precaution, she had the maid remove her shoes before leading her in to see the Kemptens.

'What's this about, Femke? What has Danni done?' Lady Kempten asked, clearly upset to see her maid in such distress.

'I'm not sure yet, my Lady. I hope we're about to find out,' Femke replied, turning her tone cold for the benefit of her prisoner. 'Danni – if that is your real name – who are you working for?'

'L . . . L . . . Lord and Lady Kempten,' she spluttered.

'Come along, Danni, you know what I'm talking about. Who *else* are you working for? Who is paying you to spy on the Kempten family? There's no point denying it. You were listening at the door. Who is your employer, Danni?'

'I don't know what you m . . . mean. I'm just a m . . . m . . . maid.'

'All right, Danni, have it your way. I'm going to search your room now. Lady Kempten, would you expect your maids to be able to read or write? Also, how much money do you pay your house staff, please? I shall be interested to see what turns up in Danni's room.'

Lady Kempten did not get a chance to answer. Danni's eyes had gone wide at the mention of writing. 'Toomas,' she gasped. 'I work for Toomas.'

'The tattle tout?'

'That's him,' Danni said, nodding. 'He pays me for information. When Lord Kempten became Regent, Toomas

40

contacted me and offered me money for any interesting snippets of information about the family. I didn't see any great harm in it. When the news came that Lord Kempten was dead, I thought it would stop. I was quite disappointed, because I had managed to save a goodly sum in a short time.'

'But it didn't stop, did it?' prompted Femke with a sigh.

'No, Miss. Lady Kempten brought me here with her, and I learned that my Lord was not dead. I realised that Toomas would pay a lot of money for that knowledge. I'm sorry. It was wrong of me, but my dream has always been to save enough money for a little place of my own. I realised that this could be my chance to realise that dream. For something this big, Toomas would likely give me enough to complete my deposit. When you arrived earlier I saw another chance to increase my income from Toomas and I took it.'

'Does this Toomas already know that I'm alive?' Lord Kempten asked, his voice gruff with anger.

'Yes, my Lord. I sent word to him some time ago. I've not received any payment yet, but I know he will have the information by now. I had hoped to gain information today to use as a lever to speed up his payment.'

'Shand alive! If a tattle tout knows I'm alive, then half of Shandrim will know it too!'

Femke shook her head. 'Not necessarily, my Lord. Toomas is an old hand at the trading of information. The trick with it is to know when the information is at its most valuable. When it's announced in the Imperial Court that you are the rightful successor to the Mantle, the information will suddenly gain great value to those who wish power for themselves. If we're quick, we might be able to prevent Toomas from damaging our cause.'

'What are you suggesting, Femke?' Lord Kempten asked, watching her response intently.

'I would have thought that clear, my Lord. Someone must pay Toomas a visit.' She turned to Danni again. 'Are there any more like you here, Danni? Should we be looking for others in the employ of tattle touts?'

Danni looked genuinely surprised. 'I don't think so, Miss Femke. I'm not aware of any – honest, I'm not.'

Femke believed her. She was not a good liar and her vehemence seemed genuine. 'Very well. Do you have anywhere you can effectively confine her for the time being, my Lord? I don't think she's dangerous, but she cannot be allowed to communicate with the world outside this house for a while.'

'I'll see to it,' Lady Kempten offered. 'If Reynik would escort us, I'll lead the way.'

'Of course, my Lady.'

Femke waited until the three of them were out of earshot and then turned back to Lord Kempten. He still looked angry, but there was also an air of thoughtfulness about him.

'How much do you think she heard, Femke?'

'I'm not entirely sure, my Lord. I suggest you keep her isolated until any information she could have gleaned is no longer relevant. It will be onerous, but I believe it's for the best.'

Lord Kempten wore a dark frown as he considered and

dismissed possible alternatives. 'I agree,' he said after a moment. 'I'll see to it.'

'My Lord, there are other issues we need to discuss,' Femke added. 'You might want to consider moving your family. If I don't get to Toomas in time, there is no telling what the Guild might do.'

Lord Kempten's face paled. 'Where would I move them to?' he asked. 'I can't send them back to the city and I don't have anywhere else.'

'It's just something to consider, my Lord. Think on it. If you feel it necessary, then you'll think of somewhere. Information is going to be key to this whole situation. He who controls the information flow will control the situation. I'll get to Toomas as soon as I can. Experience tells me he's highly unlikely to have sold news of you yet. He will know the potential value of that information and will seek to gain the maximum yield possible from it.'

'Very well, I'll give it some thought,' he said. 'Is there anything else?'

'Yes, my Lord. We need confirmation that the Guild Headquarters is under the Imperial Palace. Even if you decided not to pursue their destruction, this knowledge would give you an edge in dealing with them in future. I would also suggest we research a way of disrupting their transportation system. That will require specialist knowledge. We need the help of a magician – preferably a powerful one who knows what he's about. Do you know of any we might approach?'

Lord Kempten nodded. 'I do know such a man. He is a member of the Council of Magicians. I could send for him, but Terilla is a long ride. Assuming he left as soon as he received my message, it would be nigh on a week before he could get here.'

Femke sighed and shrugged. 'A lot can happen in a week, my Lord, but we'll need his input if we're to learn how we can interrupt the Guild's use of magic. Also, he might know if it's possible to break the bond between Reynik and the spider icon safely. I'm worried that the icons might have more powers than we've seen to date. I'd hate to think of the Guild having some sort of control over him that we don't understand. We need more information, but we're unlikely to find answers from within Shandrim. Please send for this magician and stress the urgency of the situation without giving away too many specifics.'

Lord Kempten nodded thoughtfully. 'Time flows quickly during times of turbulence,' he observed. 'Decisive action will rule the day, I feel. Damn it! Surabar was far better at this sort of thing than I. It feels as if I'm walking on the top of a high wall; one bad step and I could fall.'

'In that case, my Lord, I have one final piece of advice.'

'Yes?'

'Keep moving forwards and, whatever you do, don't look down!'

CHAPTER THREE

Shalidar fell, but he did not let go of the curtain material. The top half of his body tipped outwards from the wall until it reached about sixty degrees. The material pulled tight with a jolt. His arms took the initial strain, but he could not prevent his body spinning sideways until his right shoulder impacted the wall. Before he knew it, he was hanging from the wall with the cloth slipping through his fingers.

He swung, his body scraping against the stone. The pain from the arrow in his leg fogged his senses with a mist of red. He clung on desperately, trying with all his might to restore a stable grip on the material, but in vain. He accelerated towards the ground, the cloth burning his palms until he was forced to let go entirely. The last few feet he fell unchecked, but he had done enough to ensure his fall would not be fatal.

He hit the ground hard, his legs folding underneath him until his knees hit his chest. The feathered tail of the crossbow bolt jammed hard against his ribcage, driving the point of the arrow even further into the taut thigh muscle. He cried out. He could not help it. The pain was excruciating. He rolled on the ground for a moment, clutching at the area around the arrow wound and groaning in agony.

Despite the pain, Shalidar had too much to lose by getting caught. He knew that if he could just get back to his transfer stone, he would have the chance to inherit Tremarle's House. It was a powerful incentive.

With gritted teeth, he forced his body upright and hobbled away from the wall. There were a few families in the street, following the road around the Palace wall towards the gathering area at the main gates. He snarled in their direction. It was enough. They hurried on their way, adults pointedly looking away and desperately urging their fascinated children to do likewise.

Fear would keep them from bothering him while he was close by, but he knew the city patrols would soon hear of his presence. He had to get out of sight as quickly as he could. There was a dark alleyway on the far side of the street. Shalidar limped across to the entrance and embraced the darkness as he moved away from the Palace with all speed.

He could put little weight on his right leg, which made stealthy movement difficult. However, even with his injury, Shalidar moved more quietly than most. A limping ghost, he navigated his way through the maze of back streets. Despite the blinding pain, he did not stop until he reached his transfer stone nearly a half hour later.

The familiar sensation of transfer was bliss. For an

instant the pain in his leg dissolved into a million tiny fragments. The coalescence in his private chamber was not so pleasant, but it did bring with it the knowledge that he was safe for the time being: providing the Guildmaster would accept his innocence in the matter of the death of Emperor Surabar, of course.

'Don't invite more trouble,' he muttered as he staggered over to a chair. 'One thing at a time.'

The bell to attract the attention of one of the serving staff was on the dahl table nearby. With a groan, Shalidar stretched across, grabbed it, and rang it several times before placing it where he could reach it more easily. He sat back and waited. The servants were efficient. He knew he would not have to wait long.

One of the brown-robed men appeared within a minute. Shalidar did not need to see the servant's expression under his deep hood to sense his surprise.

'Sir?' he asked, giving his customary bow.

'Fetch alcohol, hot boiled water and plenty of cloths,' Shalidar ordered.

'Of course, sir,' the servant replied. 'Anything else?'

'Well, I'd appreciate the help of someone who has drawn arrows before, if we have anyone. I'd do this myself, but I might not retain consciousness long enough to clean up afterwards.'

'Very good, sir. I'll see to it at once.'

The servant turned and left at a run. When he returned a few minutes later, Shalidar was surprised to see the figure accompanying him. It was the Guildmaster. Shalidar struggled to sit upright.

'I would stand, Guildmaster,' he said with a grimace, 'but I'm somewhat hampered right now.'

'So I see.' The Guildmaster's soft voice gave away nothing. He moved forward to inspect the wound. 'Might I ask who bestowed this little gift on you? It doesn't seem like Brother Wolf Spider's style somehow.'

'One of the Imperial guards, I imagine,' Shalidar replied with a shrug. 'I didn't actually see it coming.'

'So you've been at the Palace. And did you apprehend our young infiltrator?'

'No, Guildmaster.'

'Hardly a great surprise given that he came back here,' Ferdand observed, remaining still as he watched for Shalidar's reaction.

Shalidar's eyes narrowed as he tried to see past the rim of the Guildmaster's dark hood. It was no use. He could just about make out the tip of the old man's nose. He would have given a lot to see Ferdand's expression. He had never learned to read the inflections in the old Lord's voice. Was he being serious, or was he conducting some subtle test?

'It seems that when he left in a hurry earlier today,' the Guildmaster continued, 'he left something behind . . . well, when I say "something", it would actually be more accurate to say "someone".'

'Femke?'

'Precisely. Hmm, this is going to hurt. Would you like something to bite on?'

'Thanks, but no. Did you catch her?' Shalidar asked, unable to totally conceal a note of hope in his tone.

The Guildmaster did not say anything for a moment. He dipped a small towel in the hot water and wrung it out. He placed it around the entry point of the bolt and braced Shalidar's leg with his left hand as he grasped the protruding feathered shaft with his right.

'No,' he said slowly, 'she got away. As did young Wolf Spider.'

With a sharp pull, he wrenched the arrow from Shalidar's leg. The assassin gasped at the pain, but did not cry out. 'You were lucky,' the Guildmaster noted as he clamped the cloth over the hole and held the bloodied bolt up to inspect it. 'There's been a recent trend of cutting barbs on the shafts of these. They tear the flesh when they are removed. This is a straight shaft with a normal point. The wound is deep, but it didn't hit the bone and it doesn't look as if it severed any major blood vessels. You will have to avoid running or any strenuous exercise for a while, but a normal padded dressing and bandage should see it heal well. I'm sure I don't need to lecture you on changing the dressings regularly.'

Shalidar shook his head. With iron control, he calmed his breathing until he felt he could speak normally. When he did so, his voice was strained, but he spoke with a normal tempo.

'Who have you sent after them?' he asked.

'Cougar, Viper and Bear are all out in the city with orders to find and kill Wolf Spider. Brothers Firedrake and Griffin are watching his transfer stones. As Wolf Spider managed to get in and out again via the stone that Firedrake was supposed to be watching, I assume that Wolf Spider

49

has neutralised him. The alarm has not rung, so he cannot be dead, but I've sent Brother Fox to see if she can find out where he is.'

'And Femke? Have you sent anyone after her?'

Shalidar could feel the intensity of the gaze emanating from under the Guildmaster's deep hood. He had pushed the old man before about disposing of Femke. His previous attempts to secure permission to kill her had failed. After the incident at Mantor, Shalidar had felt sure the Guildmaster would authorise her termination, but instead it had felt as if he had been shielding her. The feeling had to be nonsense, of course. The Guildmaster was renowned amongst the Brothers for his neutrality.

To Shalidar's amazement, the old man began to laugh.

'There's no need to go after Femke,' he chuckled. 'She will find a way to come back and visit us soon enough.'

'She will?' Shalidar could not imagine why.

'Yes,' the Guildmaster said confidently. 'She discovered something here that will draw her back like a moth to the light. When she comes, we'll be waiting for her. In the meantime we'll have our scouts in the city watch for both Femke and Wolf Spider. They'll not run far and there are some people in the city with whom I know Femke deals regularly. I'll have them watched. The infiltrators will surface, just you wait and see.' The Guildmaster turned to the servant who had been standing in silence at the far side of the room. 'Help Brother Dragon bind his wound, would you? I have to get back to the central chamber. I'm expecting reports at any time.'

'Guildmaster, there is something I need to report before you go,' Shalidar said quickly.

The cloaked figure halted in his tracks and turned slowly to face Shalidar once more. 'Yes? What's that, Brother Dragon?'

'It's the Emperor, Guildmaster. He's dead.'

The Guildmaster froze for a second as he assimilated Shalidar's statement.

'And how, exactly, did he die, Brother Dragon?'

For the first time in a very long time, Shalidar could sense something of the emotions riding under the surface of the Guildmaster's calm voice. Anger, disbelief and in-credulity were discernible in his tone, though his speech did not rise one decibel above his normal mellow volume.

'It seems a trap was laid for me,' Shalidar began. 'It was a subtle one and I walked straight into it. I should have realised they would expect me to go to the Palace after Wolf Spider. It was one of the more obvious places to look, after all. I was forced to fight my way free. I killed two of the Emperor's guards, but not Surabar. He was shot by one of his own men in the crossfire. When I passed him, he had a bolt buried in his chest. I left in a hurry, so I did not see him breathe his last, but the arrow had clearly punctured his lung. He had minutes to live at best.'

The Guildmaster was silent for a moment. Shalidar concentrated on breathing calmly as he imagined what was going through the old man's mind.

'I can't let this go, Brother Dragon. You know that. Your actions with relation to the creed are in question here. Even if you're telling the truth, the Palace will be sure to circulate a different version of events, most likely calling it an assassination by the Guild. There will have to be an investigation. In the meantime, you're to remain here in your quarters. If you leave at any time without permission, then I'll take that as an admission of guilt and you can be sure I'll not rest until you perish. I'll send the entire Brotherhood after you if I have to. You will answer for this. Shand's teeth, Shalidar! Why, when things go wrong, do I always find you at the centre of them?'

Shalidar shrugged, but his expression offered no apology.

'If it helps, Guildmaster, I will take a truth test.'

'You would submit voluntarily to truth serum?' Ferdand was genuinely surprised by the offer.

'I would – providing *you* administer it,' Shalidar answered. 'I presume the normal protocols will be applied and the questions will be limited to my involvement in the death of Surabar. I, like everyone else here, have secrets I would not wish to be exposed.'

The Guildmaster nodded. It was no small gesture to submit to truth serum. The side effects of the potion could be dangerous, even fatal for a few. It also left one wide open to abuse.

'It would be suitable proof to the Guild of your innocence,' he said thoughtfully. 'Under the circumstances, I believe it necessary that you provide such proof. I'll not say that I'm sorry to see the back of Surabar. He hasn't made my life easy during the last couple of months. However, if his demise is to be at the expense of the reputation of our Guild, the price outweighs the convenience of his death. Very well, I shall see it arranged. I'll also ensure we have as many Brothers as possible present to bear witness. I don't want any conspiracy theories growing within the Guild. We must remain united now more than ever before. If we can ride this out, then a new Emperor will most likely rescind the order declaring us *anaethus drax*. Assuming all goes well over the next few weeks, we could be back to business as usual.'

'The sooner the truth test can be arranged, the better,' Shalidar replied. 'I know how fast rumours grow. If resolved quickly, there will be far less speculation.' *Besides, I have business to do,* he added silently. *Tremarle will need guidance if he's to take power. He will need his son.*

Dong. The first doleful ring of the Imperial Bell rang out across the city. Cougar saw his chance and took it. A moment's inattention by one of the soldiers was all he needed. In a flash, he had relieved the distracted Legionnaire of his weapon and begun dealing out blows in rapid succession.

Viper reacted so fast that it appeared to the Legionnaires as if the two assassins had planned the escape in detail together. The two men, who had been all but carrying him along the street, did not stand a chance. They were both unconscious before they realised what was happening.

The patrol group of six Legionnaires had been leading them through the city towards the military campsite on the outskirts. By chance, their route took the patrol close to Cougar's second transfer point. He knew that if they timed their strike right, he and Viper could get away from the soldiers and transfer back to the Guild headquarters before anyone else had a chance to intervene.

Viper had been feigning semi-consciousness since the men had hauled him upright off the street. Cougar had picked up on the subtle signs his fellow assassin had been giving. He knew he could count on support when he initiated the break.

The pair downed four of the six soldiers before they had a chance to react. The last two drew weapons and met Cougar's stolen blade in a rapid exchange of clashing blows. Viper turned and ran up the nearest side street. Cougar leaped away from the two soldiers and sprinted after him. To his relief the soldiers did not follow. A glance over his shoulder saw them attending to their fallen colleagues.

'Viper! Take the next left,' Cougar called softly. Viper complied. 'Stop there a moment. They're not following.'

In the distance, the Imperial Bell was still ringing. Cougar caught up with Viper and they exchanged knowing looks. If the bell was to be believed, then the Emperor was dead.

'What do you reckon?' Viper asked. 'Is it for real?'

'I don't know,' Cougar replied. 'I wouldn't put it past Wolf Spider to have arranged it as a diversion. He's the Emperor's man. The Emperor is desperate to see the Guild destroyed. If it served his purpose, then I imagine he would allow the bell to be rung. People will surely gather at the Palace gates to hear the news. He could be planning to use the crowd as a smokescreen, but to what purpose?'

Viper scratched an eyebrow thoughtfully. 'I can't think of one. Why would he need a crowd at the Palace gates? It doesn't make any sense to me. Do you think we should go and take a look, or is that what Wolf Spider is hoping? Perhaps he is trying to lure as many of us into the crowd as possible.'

'To be honest, I don't care,' Cougar said bluntly. 'I need to go and clean up my face. I want to know how badly he cut me with that blasted stave. My cheek feels swollen and I want to remove any splinters from it as fast as possible.'

'It looks ugly,' Viper confirmed, 'but I don't think it's deep. I can't see any splinters in this light, but that doesn't mean there aren't any.'

Cougar looked at the unfamiliar face of his fellow Guild member. He had never seen the man's features before tonight, as he had been accepted into membership more recently than Viper. 'Your face isn't exactly a bunch of flowers either, Brother. Your left eye looks as if it's blackening and I can almost feel the lump on your right temple. He must have caught you with a good crack there.'

Viper probed the lump gently with a finger. He winced. 'I'll treat him with a bit more respect next time. It seems the Emperor's man is more talented than I gave him credit for. He'll live to regret today, though. Mark my words, Cougar, I don't take kindly to being made to look the fool.'

'You speak for both of us there. I'm going back to the Guild to get cleaned up. I suppose we had better make a report to the Guildmaster as well.'

'Let's not rush to communicate our failure, Brother,' Viper suggested. 'How about we get cleaned up and meet again in an hour? If we're lucky, we might even catch young Wolf Spider tonight.'

'A sound plan,' Cougar replied. 'Where shall we meet?'

'The front door of the Old Crossbow?'

'I'll see you there in an hour.'

Shantella watched the Guildmaster pacing the central chamber and a sly smile crossed her face. He was losing control. She could sense it. He was vulnerable, but she had no intention of revealing her hand too early. For now she would continue to play the loyal Guild member and wait for the perfect moment to strike. 'I found Firedrake, Guildmaster,' she called, drawing his instant attention.

The Guildmaster walked across the meeting hall to Fox's booth. He had not heard her arrive, but that was not surprising. Most of the Brothers were very stealthy in their movements.

'Well done, Brother Fox. Where was he?'

'He wasn't where he was supposed to be, so it took me a while to find him. He was lying at the roadside a couple of streets away, completely unconscious. Do you want my report here, or shall we retire to my quarters where it is more comfortable? I have an excellent bottle of wine that is crying out to be opened.'

'Another time, maybe,' the Guildmaster replied, his voice remaining neutral. 'I'd prefer your report here. I'm still waiting to hear from Cougar, Viper and Bear.'

Shantella sat down and stretched out her long legs like a cat. 'Very well,' she said, a hint of disappointment audible in her sultry tones. 'I couldn't wake him, and he was too heavy for me to carry, so I had a couple of men from a nearby inn carry him to one of the guest rooms there. I paid the innkeeper well to see that he was left in peace. Judging by the lumps on his left temple and the top of his head, I doubt that he'll be waking up any time soon. It would be unfortunate if someone sought to take advantage of his condition and tried to steal his icon.'

'Indeed. To lose any more Brothers now would be a disaster. We have already lost Brother Scorpion tonight.'

'Really? Do you know how he died, Guildmaster? Where did it happen?'

'He was killed here in the complex, guarding Wolf Spider's room. He was taken by surprise. It seems Brother Wolf Spider left a guest hidden in his quarters during his last visit. With Wolf Spider already gone, Scorpion had no reason to expect an attack from within the complex. He stood little chance.'

'A shame,' she observed. 'I take it the intruder has been dealt with?'

'No. She escaped.'

'She?' Shantella said, clearly savouring the word. 'Ah, let me guess – the Emperor's pet spy. I've heard tell of her, but I have no idea what she looks like. How did she escape without an icon? Surely that's impossible.'

'Wolf Spider came back for her,' the Guildmaster replied.

'That makes sense. Is she pretty?'

The Guildmaster paused for a second before answering. 'She can be attractive if she so chooses. Is that relevant?'

'It is if you're a woman, Guildmaster. Beauty can be a powerful weapon in itself if used properly. But I digress. If the bell rings true, then Scorpion was not the only one to die tonight.'

'You refer to the Emperor, I trust?'

'Ah! You have heard then.' Shantella was disappointed that she was not the first to bring the news.

'Brother Dragon told me.'

'And did Brother Dragon know any more than the fact the Imperial bell is ringing?' she asked shrewdly.

Under his deep hood, Ferdand grimaced. Shantella really was a fox, he decided. She was far too perceptive for her own good sometimes.

'That is between Brother Dragon and me for the time being,' he replied slowly, knowing that she would read his response as easily as she would a book.

'Of course, Guildmaster,' she purred. 'And what of Wolf Spider? Has anyone located him yet?'

'Now just wait a minute! Who is reporting to whom, here, Brother Fox?' he asked and then chuckled to take the sting from his words. 'I had hoped you would have news of him. I've not heard anything yet. Do you have anything else to report tonight?'

'Only that half of the population of the city is gathered in front of the Palace seeking news. The streets are full of people teeming towards the city centre. It's chaos out there.'

'It's to be expected, I suppose. Another inevitability is the call on our services by about half of the nobility over the next few days. I think we're going to need a Guild meeting at the first opportunity to discuss the situation. I don't want Brothers accepting hits until I can get a clear picture of the power structure in Shandrim. There's no doubt we stand to benefit from this turn of events –

particularly if the right person takes up the Mantle.'

'Surely everyone is fair game until the coronation,' the Fox observed. The anticipation in her voice was clear. 'The trick will be to ensure that a candidate who is sympathetic to our cause is left standing.'

'Sometimes, Brother Fox, I wonder if the wrong person was chosen to be Guildmaster. Thank you for your report. Please go back and check on Brother Firedrake first thing in the morning. If he is able to move, bring him back. It would be safer for him to recover here. In the meantime get some sleep while you can. I suspect that it may be a rare commodity in the next few days.'

Femke looked across at Reynik and shook her head. 'You know, that moustache and goatee beard do make you look totally different. You've made me jump a couple of times when looking across at you. The combination of the facial hair and the clothing is very effective. It's like riding with a total stranger.'

'That's the idea, isn't it?' Reynik replied. 'I'd be worried if you looked at me and saw Reynik, the Legionnaire, or Reynik, the assassin.'

'True, but I kind of like both of those Reyniks. Reynik the merchant is a bit . . . hairy and foppish for my taste.'

'Ah! That's a shame, because this particular merchant is rather partial to redheads.'

Femke did look striking with a cascade of deep ginger curls. She had dyed her eyebrows to match and wore make-up that accentuated her cheeks and lips. A Lady's riding dress in heavy blue material, topped with a matching cape and hood, gave her a wealthy appearance without being extravagant. This was very much a new disguise, made up from things borrowed from Lady Kempten, but it was very effective. It was hard to imagine her infiltrating the Guild of Assassins when she was dressed up in such ladylike clothing, yet she seemed as at home as she did when dressed in black and armed to the teeth.

'Femke, about the other night . . .'

'The kiss was a mistake,' Femke interjected quickly.

'Kisses.'

'Kisses?'

'There were two,' Reynik pointed out. 'The first before we went into the Guild headquarters and the second after we escaped.'

'Ah, yes! I'd forgotten about the second one. Well, that was a mistake as well. I'm sorry, Reynik. I shouldn't have kissed you at all. You saw in Thrandor that mixing relationships and missions is not a good idea. I've been burned once. I don't want to go through that again.'

Reynik's heart sank. He had been expecting something like this, but had been hoping it would not happen. The optimist in him had been convinced that Femke had opened the door for him to pursue a relationship with her. With all the bad things that had happened over the last few days, he had been hoping to keep one positive thing to focus on. He was not sure he was emotionally prepared for her to slam the door in his face.

They had been riding for several hours now. For the most part they had ridden in silence. When they had spoken, it had been to discuss how they would tackle their individual tasks when they reached Shandrim. Reynik had wanted so much to tell Femke how he felt about her ever since he had rescued her from the Guild headquarters. Somehow the moment had never felt right. Now, he thought bitterly, it looked as if he had left it too late.

'Is there any point in my trying to change your mind?' he asked.

'Don't, Reynik – please don't.'

He sighed. 'I guess not then. Femke, I know I'm young – I can't change my age. I . . . I suppose I just want to say that I like you a lot. I'm no playboy like Danar. I just know that I like you. I care about what happens to you. More than anything else I would like to know that you were safe and that you care about me in the same way.'

'It's not an age thing, Reynik. I just can't do it. I can't. I'm sorry. It won't work. It's just . . . no. Leave it be. Maybe, when all this is finished . . .'

There it was – the rejection he had feared, followed by the carrot. His stomach churned and a bitter taste settled on the back of his tongue, but as her sentence petered out he was left with the feeling that not all was lost. She had made it sound as if she might consider him as a partner if they successfully completed their mission to destroy the Guild. Was this an attempt to let him down gently? He hoped not. He had a glimmer of hope. It was enough for now. He would press forward and do his best to keep them both alive.

Femke was a survivor. If any woman could find a way through the deadly maze that faced them, she could. He knew he would do better to look after his own skin than to worry about hers, yet she was not infallible. He had seen that in her too.

'Nothing is ever easy, is it?' he said with an edge of bitterness in his voice that, despite his best efforts, he could not conceal.

'No. I don't remember the last time I felt something was easy. But then, the best things in life are worth fighting for,' she said with a sad smile.

'I'll bear that in mind.'

For much of the rest of the day an awkward cloud of silence hung over them. The wind picked up, carrying showers of cold, driving rain. With cloaks drawn close and hoods pulled down over their faces in an effort to keep out the wet, it was easy for each of them to feel some sense of solitude.

The miles slipped past as Femke dictated a punishing pace. She was determined to get to the city before nightfall. There was a chance that she could complete the most pressing part of her mission today. If Toomas was at home, she felt she should be able to silence him without the need for violence.

They reached the outskirts in the late afternoon. A heavy shower had just blown through, leaving everything dripping. Puddles filled every hole in the street, and rivulets of filthy water ran along the gutters. The afternoon sunshine reflected light off the buildings in all directions, making the city look bright and freshly washed, though the smell in the streets told a different story.

Returning to the city after spending time in the country-side was always an assault on the olfactory system. City dwellers were used to the all-pervading smell generated by the mass of humanity. The inadequate sewerage system meant that raw sewage would often run through open gutters. Attempts to mask the resulting stench mingled with the smells of open-air market stalls trading in foodstuffs, exotic spices and perfumes. The combination of odours made for a heady brew, bordering on overpowering for those not used to it.

Reynik wrinkled his nose in disgust.

'It's hard to use the words "home, sweet home" when it smells like this,' he observed as their horses plodded through the muck of the street.

'It's part of the price one pays for the sophistication of city life,' Femke replied with a wry smile. 'There are times when I wonder if it's all worth it. Are you all set?'

'I think so.'

'Good. All being well, I'll meet you at The Horseman inn in the southeast quarter in two days. We'll meet at the fourth call after midday. If I'm not there by the sixth call, then go back to the country estate without me. I shall do the same if you're not there. Getting what information we have to Lord Kempten is to be the priority. Take care of yourself.'

'You too.'

Femke turned her horse to the right and directed it up one of the more open side streets. The house of Toomas was some distance from here, but she was content that she would now reach it before sunset. The district in which Toomas lived was a rough place after nightfall. Thieves and muggers were commonplace there. This did not particularly concern her, as she was used to operating in all areas of the city. Common sense, however, dictated that she should not take unnecessary risks. Dressed as she was, she would make a tempting target for a thief. Even the least skilled of footpads could get lucky, and Femke had no intention of making careless mistakes.

CHAPTER FOUR

'I've found it!' Lord Reavis exclaimed, his pitch rising with excitement as he announced his discovery. 'Look, it's Surabar's Last Will and Testament. The scroll is sealed with the Imperial Seal and clearly marked. Should we open it?'

Lord Borchman looked up from the stack of parchments he had been leafing through. Lord Reavis always seemed to look jolly, regardless of his emotions. His curly grey hair, rounded face and dimpled cheeks gave him the appearance of a gentle old grandfather. His blue eyes were bright under his bushy white eyebrows and laughter lines served to further his jovial image. Borchman kept his thin face serious as he considered the implications of his fellow Lord's question.

'It might be better to wait until we have a quorum, Reavis,' he said thoughtfully. 'It wouldn't look good if we were to break the seal without the other candidates present. If Surabar has named a successor in that document, then it would be far better for us all to be present at its opening. That way, if the contents are at all contentious, as I suspect they will be, then we'll be able to make a considered response. Put it on the desk here with these other parchments. There are more things here of which the Court should be made aware. It seems Emperor Surabar was a busy man.'

Lord Reavis reluctantly placed the scroll on the desk. 'Why are we looking through his things if we're not going to take advantage of what we find?' he asked.

'The others will likely be here within the hour. That we have stolen the march on them gives the two of us a momentary advantage. We can control what information is released and in what fashion, but Marnillus still has the better of us when it comes to supporters in Court. You can bet he will be manipulating the Court before Surabar's body is put to rest.'

'Marnillus is a fool. He'd be a disastrous Emperor,' Reavis spat.

'On that we're agreed, but his voice holds a lot of sway in Court,' Borchman replied. 'He'll be difficult to defeat.'

'Not if he were to have a fatal accident. With Surabar dead, the Guild of Assassins will be looking to re-establish their role in Shandese politics. What if you and I were to demonstrate our willingness to see the *anaethus drax* declaration lifted by placing a contract jointly? We would win the support of the Guildmaster, dispose of our most influential opponent and save money into the bargain. What do you think?'

'I think you're getting ahead of yourself, Lord Reavis –

that's what I think,' Borchman replied carefully. It was hard to visualise Reavis ordering assassinations. He did not look the sort of person to even consider it, but appearances were deceptive, as Borchman well knew. 'Let's wait until the contents of Surabar's will have been examined, shall we?' he suggested. 'When I know what the crafty old fox put in there, I might consider your proposal. If I were to gain the Mantle, I'd prefer to do it without too much bloodshed, if possible.'

Borchman returned to his scrutiny of the stack of parchments on the Emperor's desk, but his mind was not on the task. If Reavis were already thinking about assassinating other candidates, how long would it take for others to have similar thoughts? Not long. He would need to take steps to protect himself from the bloodbath that looked poised to begin.

Marnillus would have a heavy guard as a matter of course. He had done so for some years. Would it help him, if a contract were placed? Borchman doubted it. One only had to look at what happened here. The Emperor was in his study with two guards at the door and who knows how many more around the Palace, but an assassin had still penetrated the defences. Someone had killed Surabar and tried to cover his tracks by making it look as if one of the guards had pulled the trigger.

If the assassin had not been seen escaping, it would have been hard to deny the evidence. The fact that the killer had also escaped the Palace despite the entire Imperial guard force being alerted to his presence lent more weight to the argument that the Emperor's death had been orchestrated by the Guild. If they had abandoned their creed, then the Guild had become more dangerous than ever before. It was a chilling thought.

Reavis was a fool in many ways. If it came down to the two of them in the Imperial race, then Borchman did not believe he would have a problem winning the support of the Court. However, by using the Guild, Reavis became a fool indiscriminately wielding a deadly weapon. As far as he knew, the Guild did not place a filter on their customers other than their ability to pay enough gold. As long as the contract did not contravene their creed, then the Guild usually accepted contracts without question. The coming days would be fraught with danger for the Imperial candidates.

'Who allowed you access to the Emperor's study?'

It was Lord Marnillus. The bluster and outrage clearly identified him. Lord Borchman could picture the man's broad frame, richly ornamented apparel and self-important posturing without needing to look up.

'Good evening, Lord Marnillus,' Borchman replied, keeping his tone level and his eyes on the parchments he was leafing through. 'One might ask the same question of you. With the Emperor gone there is no one to grant or deny access to the senior Lords now. We were looking to see if he left any instructions against this eventuality. It appears he did.'

'Surabar left a will? Where is it? What does it say?'

'Not so fast, Marnillus,' Borchman warned, keeping his tone civil, but firm. 'The Emperor did leave a will, but it is sealed. We did not open it, as not all the candidates were here. Besides, I think it more appropriate that it should be read in open Court, don't you? That way there can be no dispute as to the contents.'

'You think!' Marnillus sneered. 'Pah! You *don't* think – either of you. There's a mob growing at the gates of the Palace. They need a leader – one who will unite them and inspire them, one who will keep them calm in this time of uncertainty.'

'And there's no question as to who that leader should be, I suppose.' Lord Borchman did not bother hiding his sarcasm.

'None,' Marnillus replied without pause. 'I have the support of the Court. You cannot deny it. I should take the Mantle now and speak to the people.'

'Over my dead body!' exploded Reavis. 'You have a slim majority, Marnillus. You know the rules as well as any of us. Surabar may have seized power from under our noses, but the Court will not sit by and let that happen again. Against Surabar we were powerless because he had total control of the Legions. He could have crushed all or any one of us like flies if he'd wanted. He took the Mantle in a bloodless coup, but if you were to try such a thing – well, let's just say you wouldn't want to try it.'

'Is that a threat, Reavis? It sounds rather hollow to me.'

'Don't push it, Marnillus,' Borchman warned. 'It would not do for more blood to be spilled here today. The will shall be read in open Court. I'll see that it gets there without being tampered with. Do you wish to call my integrity into question, or will you trust me to bring the scroll without tampering with the seal?'

Calling the integrity of another Lord into question was as good as issuing a challenge to a duel. Marnillus was no fool. Although Borchman was no longer young, he had been a master swordsman as a youth and he was still remarkably fit and trim for his age. He was tall and slim, with a long reach. Marnillus, for all his bluster and posing, was not as fit as he made out. He knew he would be unlikely to prevail over the wiry, silver-haired Borchman.

'No, Lord Borchman, I do not question your integrity. I shall see to it that the Court is convened as soon as possible. This situation needs to be resolved quickly. We cannot allow Shandrim to degenerate into chaos.'

'I quite agree,' Borchman replied, looking up to meet the eyes of his opponent. 'As long as that damned bell keeps ringing there is little chance of anyone not realising that an imminent session of Court is likely.' It will likely be the most interesting Court session we've seen in many a year, he added silently. He ran a finger down the side of the stack of parchments on the desk. You were so darned well organised, Surabar, I would not be surprised to see you reach from beyond the grave and put everyone in line with your blasted Legion logic.

The Guildmaster looked around at the booths from his podium. Fourteen were occupied. Fourteen out of twenty – a third of the Guild dead, unaccounted for, or incapacitated. It was not a pretty state of affairs.

As they recited the creed, he fingered his own silver icon under his robe, feeling the sleek lines of the panther. In his youth he had felt he resembled his emblem: powerful, silent and deadly. Now he felt none of those things. More than anything he felt his age pressing down on him, an ever-present weight of years that was slowly curving his spine and sapping his strength. It was interesting how some of the Brothers served to increase that weight, whilst the presence of others served to help him feel young again. His eyes came to rest on the dragon emblem. Shalidar fell squarely in the former of the two categories.

Ferdand had never liked Shalidar. Since he had risen to the post of Guildmaster, Ferdand had come to know all the assassins. There was a streak of arrogance in most of them, but every meeting with Shalidar had left a bitter taste in his mouth. If the Guild were not in a state of weakness, he would be all too glad to find Shalidar guilty today. In his heart he still secretly wished for that outcome. There was very little that would give him more pleasure than to plunge his dagger into Shalidar's heart and watch the light fade from his eyes. Somehow, he doubted that would happen.

The bearer of the dragon icon had volunteered for this truth test. He would never have done so if he had not been confident he would pass. With his ability to wriggle his way out of the most impossible situations, if there had been an eel icon, then Shalidar would have been ideally suited to it. The Guildmaster could only assume on this occasion that Shalidar really was free from guilt, as the line of questions he had agreed to answer under the influence of truth serum would be damning if answered with responses other than those expected of him.

The final echoes of the creed faded. The dim hall fell

silent. The Guildmaster raised his right hand towards the dragon emblem.

'Brother Dragon, come forward,' he intoned with solemn formality.

None of the other assassins knew what was about to happen. The silence thickened with an air of mystery and expectation. Hooded and cloaked as always in the presence of the other assassins, Shalidar limped forwards until he was standing in front of the podium.

'Brothers, you're all aware of the death of the Emperor last night. What most of you do not know is that Brother Dragon was at the scene when the Emperor was killed. He claims innocence in the matter. I am going to test that claim. It's good that you're all here to witness this, as it concerns the very core of the creed that we have just recited.'

Two servants emerged from the stairwell that led down into the Guildmaster's private quarters. They walked forwards and positioned themselves either side of Shalidar, one taking each arm. The Guildmaster descended from his podium and walked around to stand in front of Shalidar. From under his cloak, the Guildmaster drew a small glass vial containing a dark purple fluid. He held it up high above his head.

'For those of you who have never seen this before, it is truth serum. Any person under the influence of this substance cannot tell a lie. It is very powerful. No one has ever been known to withhold a truthful response to questions posed whilst in its power. Truth serum is also dangerous. Some suffer violent reactions to ingesting it, the most extreme of which can result in death. I should state for the record that Brother Dragon volunteered to take this truth test as he felt it necessary to prove his innocence in the death of the Emperor. There will no doubt be speculation amongst the population of Shandrim as to our involvement. It is therefore important for all of us to know what really happened.'

The Guildmaster's mellow tones had an unusually hard edge to them.

'Brother Dragon, are you still willing to undergo this test?' he asked.

'I am.'

Shalidar made the simple statement with a firm voice. Ferdand could see his dark eyes glinting beneath his hood. They held a challenge that set the Guildmaster's teeth on edge.

'Then drink.'

To make sure the slippery assassin did not palm the vial and replace it with one of his own, Ferdand removed the stopper and poured the thick, sticky liquid into Shalidar's mouth. He watched as Shalidar made a swallowing motion.

'May I see the inside of your mouth, please?'

Shalidar opened his mouth. His tongue was stained purple, right to the back. He had definitely drunk it down.

'He has drunk the serum,' Ferdand announced. 'It will be fully effective inside a minute and last for about half an hour. I should make it clear that in order to protect Brother Dragon from revealing unrelated secrets, I shall adhere to Guild protocol and only ask questions relating to the death of the Emperor. Providing he is innocent of breaching the creed in the matter of the Emperor's death, then he will be taken straight to his quarters. He shall then be left alone until the effects of the serum have worn off.'

The Guildmaster fell silent and focused on what he could see of Shalidar's face. The assassin's eyes began to lose focus. His pupils enlarged until they were totally dilated. Suddenly Shalidar staggered. The two servants were quick to take his weight and hold him steady. The Guildmaster waited, prolonging the silence. He wanted to be absolutely sure that there was no chance of Shalidar shamming. The dim light of the chamber tingled with a thickening air of breathless anticipation. All eyes stared unblinking at the four figures by the Guildmaster's podium.

With slow, deliberate movements, the Guildmaster drew a dagger from beneath his cloak. The steel blade glinted in the flickering torchlight as he brought it up in front of his face in a salute before stepping forwards to place the point lightly against Shalidar's chest. Standing this close he could see the slackness in Shalidar's features. It was clear the truth serum had him in its grip.

'Brother Dragon,' he began, 'where were you at the time the Emperor received his fatal wound?'

Shalidar stared vacantly at the Guildmaster.

'In the Imperial Palace, not five paces from where the Emperor was standing,' he answered, his voice sounding flat and hollow.

'What were you doing in the Palace?'

'I was looking for Brother Wolf Spider . . .'

The Guildmaster was about to ask his next question, but he paused as he noted something unfinished in the way Shalidar had intoned his sentence. A strange look of mingled shock and horror crept over Shalidar's face as he fought an internal battle to conceal information.

'. . . and . . .'

The connective had come out unbidden. Beads of sweat formed on Shalidar's brow as he fought with all his strength against the effect of the drug. It was a battle he could never hope to win.

'And?' the Guildmaster prompted.

'. . . and for Femke, the Imperial spy,' Shalidar said, his voice managing to convey his anger at this revelation despite being as flat and hollow as before.

Ferdand's hand clenched the dagger and inadvertently pressed it a little harder against Shalidar's chest. The revelation did not constitute a breech of the creed, though it did show intent to do so. Ferdand could not kill him for intent. He would need more than that to justify plunging his blade into Shalidar's heart.

'Did you kill Emperor Surabar?' he asked.

'No!' Shalidar replied immediately.

Was that relief in his tone? Ferdand wondered. It was hard to tell, though the anger in his previous statement had been clear.

'Did you arrange for anyone else to kill the Emperor?' he asked.

'No.' Again, Shalidar answered without hesitation.

'How did the Emperor die?'

'He was accidentally shot by one of his own guards.'

Clear, precise answers, with no sign of internal struggle: Shalidar was telling the truth. The Guildmaster slowly, almost reluctantly, raised his dagger in front of his face again and replaced it inside his cloak.

'Do any question the validity of Brother Dragon's answers?' he asked. Nothing would please him more than to have a reason to continue questioning Shalidar.

None of the Brothers responded.

Reluctantly he nodded to the servants for them to take Shalidar to his quarters. As they moved to comply, Ferdand caught a last glimpse of Shalidar's face. There was a curious smugness about his features that made Ferdand's blood boil. Somehow Shalidar had done it again. He had concealed something. Ferdand did not know how he had done it, but his instincts told him that Shalidar had somehow engineered the death of the Emperor. However, they had agreed the scope of the questions beforehand. Ferdand was a man of his word. Shalidar had answered the critical questions in a way that could not be denied. He had clearly not killed the Emperor by his own hand. Nor had he paid another to make the hit. So what had he done?

The Guildmaster was very thoughtful as he climbed back up into his pulpit-like podium. The Shalidar mystery was one for another time. Brother Dragon would not be involved in any of the upcoming hits, due to his injury. The next few weeks looked to offer an opportunity for the Guild to recover some of its recent losses due to the *anaethus drax* declaration. The trick would be managing this time of opportunity in a way that would secure the Guild's future.

'Brothers, we have seen Brother Dragon prove his innocence in the matter of the Emperor's death.' The words tasted sour as he pronounced them, but he kept his tone positive. 'Now that we have ascertained this, we can return to business in the knowledge that the creed has not been compromised. The inevitable race for the Mantle has already begun. There are five Lords currently looking to claim power. I have already received word from three of those five stating that they wish to make use of our services in the near future. Each of them has also promised the reinstatement of our Guild status and the repeal of the *anaethus drax* order.'

'But can we trust any of these Lords, Guildmaster?' The voice came from the alcove bearing the insignia of a viper. 'We don't want to find ourselves faced with another Surabar. Are there any of them who stand above the rest?'

'Good questions, Brother Viper. This is what we must determine before we take on any contracts over the coming weeks. Although there are five Lords who have currently declared their intention to claim the Mantle, they will not necessarily be the only ones to do so. There may well be late entrants into this contest. We will need to be cautious and alert to changes if we are to ensure our position in society is fully restored.'

'So if we are offered contracts?' The sultry tones of the Fox were unmistakeable in any meeting.

'You're to bring them to me before accepting them, Brother Fox. I will control which are accepted. It looks likely there will be plenty of work to go around. If we get this right, the Guild will be secure for many years, so I don't want to see anyone getting greedy. Once we have the right person in power, you'll all be free to go back to working as normal. In the meantime, please bear with the restrictions. They should not be in place for long.'

The Guildmaster paused for a moment. He had thought long and hard about his next point of order, but was still not totally convinced he had chosen the right people.

'Brothers Cougar and Bear, I want you to continue the search for Brother Wolf Spider. This is to take priority over any other work. You will be recompensed for your time. Brothers Viper and Fox, you are to look for the spy, Femke, and will also be paid for this task. It's possible that you will find them together, but I want to cover the option that they may choose to work independently. Wolf Spider, you may kill on sight, but I would like you to take Femke alive if at all possible. I have unfinished business with that young lady. Any questions?'

'Just one, Guildmaster,' the Fox said quickly. 'Do you have any idea where we should start looking?'

'As it happens, I do, Brother Fox. I'll brief the four of you on possibilities at the end of this meeting. Now if there is nothing else on that subject, I shall move on to more mundane matters . . .'

'Yes?' Toomas asked, cautiously cracking the door open. 'What can I do for you?'

He eased the door open a little further as he took in the wealthy-looking young woman in her riding dress and cape. The horse tied to the rail looked tired. Logic dictated it was unlikely she had been sent by any of his rivals here in the city to make trouble for him.

'I'd like to come in for a chat, if I may,' Femke answered,

giving him a weary smile to accentuate her appearance of harmlessness.

'Are you buying or selling?'

'That depends,' she temporised. 'To start with, I just want to come in for a chat. I've come a long way to talk to you, Toomas. I promise you'll learn something to your benefit, but no money need change hands.'

Suspicion played on his face.

'If you're not here to buy or sell, then I'm not interested,' he said, convinced that she was wasting his time. 'Good day to you, lady.'

Toomas made to close the door, but had moved it no more than a couple of finger widths before Femke stopped it with her foot. He hardly saw her move, but as if by magic a knife had appeared in her right hand and she had it at his throat before he could so much as flinch.

'In that case, I'm afraid I'm going to have to insist,' she replied.

The expression on his face turned from suspicion to fear. He let go of the door and allowed her to open it.

'Who sent you?' he asked, his voice cracking on the last syllable. 'If it's Tullis, then he's got it all wrong. It wasn't me who leaked information of his affair to his wife.'

Femke stepped forwards, forcing him back into the hallway with the point of her blade. Without taking her eyes off him, she closed the door behind her.

'Where can we sit in comfort, Toomas? I don't want any interruptions for a while. Is there anyone else in the house?'

'No,' he said nervously. 'There's no one else. I live alone – always have.'

'Very well. Where you do you suggest we go to be comfortable? I'll not trouble you for food or drink. A chair and a quick chat will be fine.'

'Over there – the door to the left of the hat stand – it's the living room. We can sit in comfort in there.' Toomas was shaking by now and Femke could see it.

'Good,' she said. 'Now, turn around and lead the way. Don't try anything silly. All I want to do is talk. If, however, you get ideas that involve pain on my part, then I will stick you like a pig. Remember Commander Chorain?'

The tattle tout's eyes went wide. 'Was he the commander who died in the street not far from the arena last year?'

'Indeed. I didn't want to kill him, but I was under orders. Don't make me do something I will regret later.'

'I thought he died of heart failure.'

'He did,' Femke confirmed, her voice cold and heartless. 'Heart failure induced by a particularly rare and nasty poison being introduced into his bloodstream. This blade is tipped with the same poison, so I wouldn't recommend any sudden moves.'

The blade was not poisoned, but Toomas was sure to be more cautious if he thought it was. First impressions were that he was not taking any chances. He turned very carefully and led the way into the living room.

Despite the tattle tout's assertion that there was no one else in the house, she entered the room with a certain amount of caution. She pushed the door until the handle met the wall before crossing the threshold. As she moved through the doorway, she scanned the room. There was nowhere for anyone to hide. The chairs and the chaise longue all had long wooden legs, denying cover for a man to hide behind, or underneath. The curtains did not reach the floor and there were no obvious places large enough to conceal a person. It was possible Toomas had the room this way for the exact purpose of preventing people from hiding here.

The room was furnished with items of quality. Toomas was clearly doing well from his trade. There were rugs of the finest wool on the floor and the walls were adorned with paintings and hangings created by artists and weavers of the highest calibre. The curtains looked to be made from velvet, which had never been cheap. Femke was quietly impressed. She had used Toomas on several occasions both for buying and selling information, but it was clear that he had managed to build an extensive customer base in what could clearly be a lucrative trade.

He indicated to a seat for Femke, but she declined, making him sit there instead. Then she pulled a second chair across until it was facing him. A faint smell of incense lingered in the air. Femke breathed it in, enjoying the hints of wood and lavender, but the scent looked to be doing little to calm the tattle tout's nerves. He was pale and sweating as she sat down.

'What is it you want to know?' he asked. 'I'm not a violent man. I never have been. I wouldn't deliberately hurt anyone . . .'

'Save it, Toomas! You would sell your grandmother if you thought she would bring a good price. I know your reputation as a tattle tout. I also happen to know that you managed to place one of your people inside Lord

Kempten's household. She has passed you information that could make you a lot of money if sold to the right people. I'm not here to take away your profit – merely to delay it a little. This will work to your advantage in the long run. Trust me in this.'

The tattle tout's eyes narrowed when she mentioned 'a lot of money'. His mind was clearly working fast to see how he could twist this situation to his advantage.

'Lord Kempten did not die in the assassination attempt, so what? Unless . . . unless he was to be Surabar's successor! Oh, ho, ho! That's it, isn't it? Kempten's assassination was a scam to get him out of harm's way in case the Guild decided to take him out. Does that mean that Lord Lacedian's assassination was also a farce?'

'I'm not here to give you additional information, Toomas,' Femke said firmly. 'I'm here to suppress information that should not be released until the time is right. If you're good, then I will allow you to sell the information in due course, but only when *I'm* ready for it to be sold. If word that Lord Kempten is alive becomes known before I'm ready, then I'll hold you responsible regardless of where the information comes from. Do you understand me?'

Toomas showed no sign of having heard a word that she had said. His eyes looked distant as his mind processed this new piece of information and fitted it together with other snippets he had gathered. Suddenly his eyes went wide.

'You worked for Surabar,' he said, his tone suggesting his certainty. 'Surabar organised for Kempten to disappear, which means he most likely organised the death of

Lacedian. Surabar detested assassinations. It's why he declared the Guild of Assassins *anaethus drax*. Why then would he go against his most basic of principles?'

Femke did not answer. Toomas's finger tapped against his forehead for a moment like a woodpecker tapping at a tree.

'Unless . . . yes! The only reason he would do that would be to get someone into the Guild. That's what was going on! The Guild must have discovered the infiltrator and gone after him. Running battles on the streets, assassins fighting assassins, it all makes sense now. But who killed the Emperor? The Guild would not have done that. It doesn't fit with the rest of the pattern.'

Toomas was very good at piecing things together, Femke conceded silently. Possibly too good for his own well-being. She had kept her features unmoving as he speculated on the Emperor's activities, but she knew all too well that Toomas would be a master of reading emotions and responses. Ferdand had taught her to conceal her emotions, but it would not surprise her to find that Toomas could read her reactions in spite of that training.

Femke raised her knife threateningly. 'Toomas, I repeat, you are not to sell news of Lord Kempten until I say you can. Are you listening to me? If you do not answer, I'll kill you now and have done with it.'

That got his attention.

'Yes, yes, I understand,' he assured her quickly. 'Please don't do anything rash. I don't like restrictions, but I'm no fool. I'll hold on to the information for now. Five Lords were angling for the Mantle before the Emperor's death. I've no doubt more will enter the running before the end.

A delay will enable me to determine who is likely to pay the most.'

'Good. I'm glad we understand each other. I shall get in touch again in due course. Make sure my next visit is not an unpleasant one, Toomas. Keep your word and you will live to enjoy your fortune. Get greedy and you will not see another season.'

Rising to her feet, she kept her knife in front of her as she moved carefully around Toomas towards the door. He leaned forwards to get up as well.

'No. Stay where you are. I'll see myself out. When you hear the front door close, you may move. Goodbye, Toomas. Until we meet again.'

He did not answer. His eyes were already distant as he set to sifting through the information he had gleaned to see if anything else would fall into place. Femke was tempted to open and close the front door so silently that he would not hear her leave. However, she was not looking to antagonise him – just to control him. She slipped out of the lounge and across the hall to the front door. When she opened the door, her horse looked up and gave a resigned snort. Femke smiled. She closed the door firmly behind her and walked across to the animal, patting its neck and untying the reins from the fence post.

'It's OK, girl. We're not going far.'

The horse snorted again and nodded her head. Femke swung up into the saddle and turned her mount back up the street along which they had approached. She had an inn in mind for the night. It was not particularly salubrious, but it was not one of her usual haunts. The last thing she wanted to do was to be second-guessed by Ferdand. She knew she would have to be very careful if she were to avoid tangling with the Guild again over the next couple of days.

Several turnings later, the slightest of noises behind her raised the hairs on the back of Femke's neck. Trying to appear casual, she looked around. She could see nothing. The long shadows of evening were deepening. Whatever had made the noise was well hidden, but it served to warn her of the possibility she might have picked up a follower.

CHAPTER FIVE

Reynik looked around the vast hall of the city library and his heart sank. There was an army of books, thousands upon thousands of them, marching in rows along the bookshelves. Within each of those volumes were hundreds of pages, and on each page were hundreds of words. Large high windows admitted shafts of light: great diagonal vessels filled with a swirling miasma of dust. Despite its size, the hall felt musty and close. The smell of leather and beeswax hung in the air as thickly as the dust. Reynik pinched his nose, twitching and rubbing it to try to relieve the itching sensation that had begun the moment he had stepped through the door.

When he and Femke had decided this was the most likely avenue for finding proof of the location of the assassins' lair, he had pictured skimming through a few books and the answers leaping out at him. The reality of the magnitude of his task was overwhelming. One look at the huge walls of books made scouting around the Imperial

Palace and counting vents, as Femke had first thought, seem a lot more appealing.

Proving that the Guild of Assassins' headquarters was below the Imperial Palace was never likely to be an easy task. Femke's initial idea of seeing how many vents actually emerged within the Palace and comparing the number with those found outside was sound in principle, but getting access to every underground room and cellar in the Palace would be all but impossible. What he needed was written evidence – if there were any.

What were the chances that the Guild allowed anything to be written down? Little to none, most likely, he thought with a silent sigh of resignation. The search here could prove futile, but he felt he had more chance of finding something here than he did of penetrating the Palace at the moment. The Palace guard had at least doubled over the last few days. No doubt the Lords looking to gain the Mantle would verge on paranoid over the coming weeks – with good reason.

The library appeared empty. Reynik began walking from one bookcase to the next, scanning the spines for anything that might lead him to the section he required. The only sound was the distant noise of people outside the building and that of his footsteps, which seemed almost to echo around the great space. The near silence added to the feeling of reverential awe that the room inspired. Reynik began to place his feet with more care, hardly daring to breathe for fear of polluting the stillness.

'Can I help you?' The voice was female and soft.

Reynik turned in surprise. Despite the silence, he had

not sensed her moving up behind him. Femke would not have been impressed to see him caught off guard so easily. The young woman he faced was taller than average, and slim, with willowy limbs and a friendly smile that looked almost apologetic.

'Are you the librarian? It's just that I thought . . .'

'That the librarian would be a man?' she asked, her expression hardening to a reproving stare. 'You're not the first, and you won't be the last. Now, what can I do for you? Are you looking for something specific?'

'Yes, I suppose I am,' Reynik replied, giving her his most winning smile in an effort to make up for his unfortunate opening comment. 'I'm something of an architect. I design buildings for the nobility: mansions, large houses, you know the sort of thing. I was wondering, do you have anything by the architects or builders of the Imperial Palace. The buildings that make up the complex are fascinating, and I would love to get some sort of insight into what the designers were thinking when they built certain elements of it.'

His obvious enthusiasm for his subject made a positive impression. The librarian's face softened again as she replied.

'The Imperial Palace? Yes, well we don't have floorplans, or the like, of course. Such information is not open to the general public. However, we're bound to have something that will interest you. Come with me. I think I know where we should begin looking, but it would be as well to check in the index first. That is what it's for, after all. All the books and documents here have been stored in order of the date of printing and cross-referenced by subject matter. I don't know how much we will have in the way of material, but if you give me a moment, then we should be able to find something for you to read.'

The librarian led Reynik across to a large table on which was the biggest index system he had ever seen. Flicking through the boxes of filed parchment, the librarian quickly found what she was looking for. Nodding to herself, she murmured pleased-sounding noises as she made mental notes of her findings.

'As I thought,' she said. 'We need to look over here.'

Once again she led him across the library, this time to the end furthest from the main doors. She did not hesitate, but led him straight to a particular shelf where she proceeded to run her index finger along the spines until she found what she was looking for.

'Here's one . . . and here's another,' she said, tipping each out in turn and passing them to Reynik. 'There should also be some more over here. Yes, here we are. There are several more here. Hmm, that's odd!'

'What?' Reynik asked, his ears pricking immediately. 'What's odd?'

'Two of these have been tagged, but I've never seen tags this colour before.'

'Tagged? What does that mean?' he asked, sensing potential trouble.

'It's part of our library administration system. Normally a tagged book has particular handling restrictions. For example if this were a blue tag, then the book could only be handled in the presence of a librarian. If it were a gold tag, then the book is regarded as so rare as to be priceless. Those books may only be viewed in a locked side room. Books with gold tags are obviously not kept out on the general shelves, but you get the idea. I've been working here a couple of years now, but I've not noticed any books with a black tag before. I'd better go and check what the handling restriction on these books are before I let you look through them, if that's all right.'

Reynik regarded her for a moment, looking for any hint that there might be more to the tags than she was letting on. Either she was telling the truth, or she was an extraordinarily accomplished liar, he thought.

'That's fine,' he said, putting his discomfort down to unwarranted paranoia. 'Go ahead. I've plenty here to be getting along with.'

Reynik took his stack of books across to a nearby table and shuffled through the volumes before choosing which one to begin. The tome he picked was thick and looked to contain a lot of detail. He had barely skimmed the preface before the librarian returned.

'Sorry about that,' she said, her face a little flushed. 'The tags were old; left over from a previous indexing system, I believe. I've removed them now. Here you are.'

He thanked her as she handed over the books and she gave him a weak smile before beating a hasty retreat. There was something strange going on here, he realised. The librarian had seemed perfectly organised and confident before finding them. It was true that no one liked to look the fool. Maybe she felt her lack of knowledge about the tags made her look unprofessional in some way. Regardless of the reason for her fluster, he determined to keep an eye on her as best he could whilst reading the books. He knew he could not be too careful whilst in the heart of Shandrim.

Reynik placed the two books on the top of the stack and returned to his first choice of text. He was not a fast reader. This was going to take some time. Opening the front cover with a sigh, he began reading. Within a few minutes the text drew him in such that he forgot his intention of monitoring the librarian.

At the other end of the library the young woman sat down at her desk, pulled out a piece of parchment and, with shaking hands, swiftly scratched out a short note. She signed it, folded it and sealed it with the city library seal. She glanced nervously across the hall at where the young man sat reading. He looked oblivious to her, lost in the pages of the book in front of him. She rose silently from her table, crossed the short distance to the main door and slipped outside. The grand entrance steps between the twin columns led down to a small square.

It took less than a minute for her to find a boy willing to run an errand for a few copper sennuts. As she watched him race off down the street clutching the letter, the librarian wondered what would happen next. The instructions in her desk on what to do if someone asked for those two books had been strange. The administrative notes had led her to a sealed letter placed on a high shelf in an obscure corner of one of the side rooms. The letter had clearly been there, unopened, for some years. The instructions it contained were most specific, and a little worrying. She had the distinct feeling that by following them she had made trouble for the man in the library, but what was she to do? The letter was clear: if it were found she had not complied with the instructions, she would lose her job. She loved working in the library. It was the most rewarding job she had ever done. She did not know what sort of trouble she had made for the young man, but she feared the worst.

Femke knew that it would be impossible to lose a competent tail on horseback in the city without setting off at a gallop through the streets. A galloping horse would create so much noise it would leave a trail of witnesses that even the least skilled of trackers could follow.

It was irritating, but she knew she had to change her plan. Thoughts of a bath and a hot meal would have to wait a little longer. If she were to lose a shadow, particularly one with any skill, then she would have to dispense with her horse. She thought hard for a moment. Deception and caution would be the key. If there were someone following her – someone sent by the Guild – then whatever she did would have to be slick if she were to shake him.

It took a few seconds, but she formulated a new plan. There was an inn not two streets away that would serve her initial purpose. The prickling sensation on the back of her neck had not gone away. She felt sure now that someone was creeping along behind her. It was not that she heard or saw anything to confirm it, but more like a sixth sense – a certainty that someone was watching. It was not a comfortable feeling. If the watcher had a distance weapon like a crossbow, or even a throwing knife, she would make an easy target. The temptation to kick her weary horse into a gallop was strong, but she suppressed it. Keeping her horse at a steady, plodding pace, Femke forced herself to stay calm and show no outward sign of her unease.

Every step seemed to take forever. In reality it was a mere handful of minutes later when she guided her mount around the final corner and up to the inn. The stable boy was quick to take the reins and help her out of the saddle. She thanked him for his swift attention and gave him a few coppers.

'Do you know if there are any spare rooms tonight?' she asked as she handed him his tip.

'Yes, my Lady. Plenty.'

'That's good. Thank you.' She set off towards the main door, but turned just before she reached it. 'Would you mind bringing my saddlebags inside, please?' she called.

'No problem, my Lady. I'll just settle her into a stable and I'll be right with you.'

Femke took the opportunity to surreptitiously scan the street as she turned back to the front door. She saw nothing, but then she did not expect to. A skilled operative would never be seen so easily.

She went inside. The taproom was all but empty. Those who were there looked to be the sort of regulars who wore grooves in the furniture. They all appeared so at home, they could have been a part of the decor. The proprietor took one look at her clothing and a broad smile crossed his face. In an unconscious gesture, he swept his few remaining hairs across the top of his head as if trying to conceal his almost complete baldness.

'Come in, my Lady. Take a seat. What can I get you? You look as if you have travelled some distance today,' he said, bustling up to her and making a great fuss of taking her hand and leading her to a nearby table.

'Actually I was wondering if it would be possible to take a room for the night,' she replied, sitting down gracefully into a chair. 'It has been a long day.'

'Of course, my Lady! No problem at all. Just you wait there a moment and I'll go and see which rooms we have available. I'll be right with you. Did you want me to bring you something while you wait?'

The innkeeper brushed instinctively at the grubby apron spread across his ample torso. Femke glanced at his hands. At least he had clean nails, she thought. That was a good sign. His face looked flushed, though the room was not overly warm. She could only presume that this was his normal complexion.

'Would it be too presumptuous to ask for food and drink to be taken to my room?' she asked. 'I'd appreciate some privacy and quiet this evening, as I'm tired and not in the mood for company.'

He nodded, his expression one of understanding.

'I'll take your order shortly,' he replied. 'Just bear with me whilst I arrange a room for you. I'll be back in a moment.'

Femke looked around. The taproom was typical of the locality: dimly lit, a low ceiling with exposed beams, and tables of various shapes and sizes, many of them showing the signs of repairs. The room smelled of smoke from the open fire mixed with odours of cooking food and a hint of stale beer, most likely from spillages that had not been properly cleaned up. The smell was not unpleasant, but neither did it cause her to inhale deeply to soak it up.

The door of the inn opened again and a figure, hooded and cloaked in black, stepped in across the threshold. Femke instinctively reached for her most accessible blade. The stranger took a couple of steps inside, threw back his hood and unbuttoned his cloak. Several of the regulars instantly called out greetings. He was clearly well known here. She let out the breath she had instinctively held. Blood pounded in her ears as she felt the burn of adrenalin deep in her gut. She began to relax a little again, though she remained edgy. She watched the newcomer carefully until one of the serving girls had brought him a drink and he had settled himself at a table with two of the other regulars.

After a couple of minutes the innkeeper bustled back into the room. 'I have a room that should meet your needs, my Lady,' he said in a low voice. 'Come this way, please.'

Femke got to her feet and allowed the innkeeper to lead her through a doorway into the heart of the inn. The corridor was narrow, and a rickety wooden staircase at the end of it climbed steeply around two right-angled corners to the first floor. There was another narrow passageway at the top of the stairs. Doors were situated at regular intervals along both walls. The innkeeper led her forwards until they reached the penultimate door on the right. Here he stopped and produced a large iron key from his apron pocket.

'This will be your room, my Lady. It's one of our better ones.'

Femke stepped through the door and into the bedroom. It looked comfortable, if a bit spartan. There was a bed, a single chair, a small chest of drawers, a boot rack, a cloak stand and a tiny dahl table. The walls were decorated with hangings that had seen better days. Bare wooden floorboards were covered in two places by small rugs – one next to the bed and one in front of the chest of drawers. There was also a small, wall-mounted mirror at an average lady's face height above the dahl table.

'This will do fine, thank you,' she assured him.

'Very good, my Lady. Young Thommis will be up with your saddlebags shortly. Now, what would you like to eat? We have roast beef and vegetables, or rabbit pie, on the menu tonight.'

'Some of the beef and vegetables will be fine, thank you. And a small glass of ale, please.'

'Beef and vegetables with a small glass of ale – no problem. I'll be back with your food just as soon as I can. Will there be anything else, my Lady?'

Femke was tempted to ask for a tub of water in which to bathe, but she did not anticipate staying long enough to enjoy a bath. 'No,' she said, giving him a tired smile. 'The food and drink will be all, thanks.'

The innkeeper withdrew. As soon as she was sure he was not going to re-enter, she went straight to the window and partially opened it. A glance outside revealed that her room was at the back of the inn – ideal for her purposes. She opened it further and leaned out. There were no obvious climbing routes down to the rear courtyard, but that was not a major problem. She had a small length of rope in her saddlebags. All she had to do was to wait for the stable boy.

It would be as well for her to eat here. Working on the assumption that she had been followed, her tail would most likely watch the inn for some time to confirm she was planning to stay, before going either to report or to fetch some back-up. It would be a fine line between waiting long enough that the watcher would be fooled and so long that he could leave and return with help. She hoped the innkeeper's 'just as soon as I can' would not be too long.

Femke had barely sat down in the solitary chair when there was a tap at the door.

'Come in,' she called. It was Thommis with her saddle-bags. 'Just put them on the bed for now, thank you.'

'Will that be all, my Lady?'

'Yes, thank you, Thommis ... actually, no. There is something else you can do for me. If you have time, I'd really appreciate it if you could give my horse a rub down and a good brushing. She worked hard today. Would a senna cover it?'

The stable boy's eyes lit up. 'Yes, my Lady, a senna would be fine.'

Femke dug in her purse and flipped the silver coin to him. He plucked it from the air and gave a rough imitation of a bow.

'I'll see to it that she gets a good feed of mash as well, my Lady. She'll have her hay, of course, but I've always found that horses recover faster if they're fed an oat mash after a particularly hard day.'

Thommis left with a bounce in his step. Femke smiled at his enthusiasm. No sooner had he gone than her food arrived. It was still early evening, and the inn was not yet busy. The innkeeper was clearly looking to stay ahead of his customers for as long as he could.

The tray of food was steaming, and the aroma of it set her stomach rumbling the moment the innkeeper brought it in through the door. Femke waited until he left and then tucked in with some enthusiasm of her own. The beef had been cooked for longer than she preferred, but the vegetables were as she liked them and the thick, meaty gravy masked any dryness of the meat. The ale was strong. As soon as she took her first sip she was glad that she had only ordered a small glass. Overall, the meal was just what she needed.

Replete, she put the tray on the small dahl table and opened her saddlebags. Within a few moments she had spread the contents over the bedcovers. It was time to move again, time to utilise her unique talents for disguise and deception.

Off came the red curls and the dark blue riding dress and boots. On went a wig of dark brown, shoulder-length hair, a tunic and trousers of cream and brown respectively, topped with a hooded cape of darkest black. Brown leather ankle boots finished the outfit. A pot of flesh-coloured cream changed the complexion of her face and hands to a darker shade. Having done so, Femke then took her make-up pencils and, using the small wall mirror, changed both the colour and shape of her eyebrows. A vial of sticky black liquid and a tiny round brush served to darken her eyelashes, and a further vial and brush decorated her eyelids.

The overall effect was remarkable. The person looking back at her from the mirror looked nothing like the one who had been there but a few moments earlier. Femke admired her handiwork for a few seconds, then gathered her weaponry and concealed it about her person.

It was a shame to have to leave the dress, but she could not carry it. The saddlebags were bulky and did not lend themselves to being carried far, but she did not want to advertise the fact that she had been in disguise by leaving everything behind. The dress was one thing, but her other changes of appearance were something else.

Femke took the length of rope from the bed, and looked around for somewhere to secure it. There was not much choice. Her best anchor point was a bed leg. The bed was up against the wall nearest to the window already. All she needed to do was to drag the bottom of the bed across until it was under the window. The bed was heavy and solidly built. Once in position it would be unlikely to go anywhere.

Moving the bed was a slow job, as she did not want to transmit the noise of moving it through the floor. The last thing she wanted was the innkeeper knocking on the door to find out what she was up to. Once it was right underneath the window, Femke tied the rope securely to one of the foot-end legs.

The innkeeper had appeared a decent-enough fellow, so she put an appropriate amount of money on the chest of drawers to pay for her accommodation and food. It was unlikely that she would be able to return to the inn to take her horse, so the innkeeper was set to do rather well at her expense.

She slung the saddlebags over her shoulder, wrapped the rope around her back and, holding on to the rope tightly, she climbed out through the window. Step by step she shuffled down the wall. Balance was not easy to maintain with the saddlebags weighing her down on one side, but she was careful and made the descent without incident. Once on the ground, she ran silently across the courtyard to see which street the back gate opened into.

Dusk had given way to full dark. It was hard to make anything out in the back street, but Femke was confident of her bearings. She could not take her saddlebags with her to the next inn – without a horse they would raise too many questions. Slipping out into the darkness, she drew her hood over her head and crept along the streets looking for a likely alleyway in which to conceal them. She did not have to go far, which was a blessing as the bags were heavy.

The alley she chose was littered with discarded rubbish. Femke took a few moments to bury her saddlebags under a pile of old cloth and other discarded junk. Having done so, she sniffed gingerly at her hands. They stank. If she could, she would have to clean them before seeking out another inn.

She returned to the mouth of the alleyway with her thoughts focused on looking for a water butt. If the street she entered had not been so silent, she would never have heard the whisper of the descending cosh. As it was, she had no time to avoid it. Instinct helped her to fall with the blow, lessening the impact, but it was not enough. The hollow-sounding thud as it hit the back of her head, together with an explosion of yellow stars in her eyes, were the last things she experienced before the vacuum of unconsciousness sucked her into its void.

Shalidar paused for a moment in the shadows. He was directly opposite Lord Tremarle's town house. The immediate effects of the truth serum had worn off. Shalidar had regained full control of his mental functions again, but had been left with an intense headache. He felt as if someone had pierced the back of his head with a metal spike and was tweaking it at random intervals to deliver extra-sharp lances of pain. It was excruciating, but things could have been worse. If the Guildmaster had paused just a little longer between his second and third questions, Shalidar's life would have been forfeit. He shuddered at the memory.

As soon as he had been asked what he had been doing in the Palace at the time of the Emperor's death, Shalidar had realised his error. If left to answer for long enough, he would have revealed his intention to kill the Emperor. He had thought his truthful answer that he had been looking for Wolf Spider would allow him to control his reaction to the serum. He had been wrong. The serum had allowed him no control at all. He had felt compelled to tell everything, rather than just the part he wanted. He had been fortunate the Guildmaster had interpreted his reluctant admission that he had also been looking for Femke as his only secret from that question. A pause of a few more seconds and Shalidar knew he would have told more – much more.

Once again he had gambled. Once again he had emerged triumphant. There were times when he felt invincible, but this was not one of them. He had pushed his luck to the limit this time. He was no fool. He knew this sort of luck could not last forever. A certain amount of prudence would now be required if he were to see his ultimate plan through.

He checked the street. It was clear. A glimmer of light leaked out between the drapes in Tremarle's drawing-room window. Despite the late hour it looked as though the old Lord was not yet in bed. Shalidar was pleased. It meant he would not have to make much noise to attract his attention.

With a second quick glance up and down the street, Shalidar limped out into the open and across to Tremarle's front door. He gave the door three quick raps with his knuckles. He paused for a second and did it again. Lord Tremarle did not keep him waiting long.

'I wondered if that might be you. Come inside. Quickly.'

Shalidar did not answer, but limped in through the door and across the hallway to the drawing-room. Tremarle closed the door and followed him, also closing the drawing room door as he entered.

The fire had burned low, but the room was comfortably warm. Shalidar gingerly lowered himself into one of the armchairs near the fireplace. It felt good to take the weight off his injured leg. Tremarle crossed the room to the drinks cabinet and held up two glasses.

'Drink?' he asked.

Shalidar thought for a moment. 'I wouldn't usually, but I believe I will, thank you.'

As he moved to pour two generous glasses of red wine, Tremarle could not help but take several glances at the man he was to adopt as his son. Both of his true sons were dead. Both had died in unfortunate circumstances – the eldest, Danar, as a direct result of Surabar's blackmailing him into going to Thrandor.

Would he have been as proud of Danar if *he* had just assassinated the Emperor? It was a ridiculous question. If Danar had lived, Tremarle would have had no reason to see the Emperor dead. As it was, Shalidar had brought Tremarle's vengeance to fruition. He had avenged the death of his eldest son and earned his place at Tremarle's side. He was of perfect age and maturity to take Danar's place as heir to the House of Tremarle. It was still the House of Tremarle while he lived. Why should he not choose a strong successor, rather than allow the noble name of Tremarle to die, his House subsumed into another as if it had never existed?

As he walked across and handed Shalidar one of the glasses, he looked into the calm eyes of the assassin. The eye contact gave Tremarle further feelings of assurance that he had made a good choice. Shalidar might be cold, but in time he would make a formidable leader for the House.

'So what happened?' Tremarle asked as he sat down in a chair positioned to the other side of the fireplace. 'I heard the Imperial Bell. I therefore conclude that you succeeded, but I see you have suffered an injury. Is it bad? Do you need any medical aid? Are the two incidents related?'

'It's bad, but I've suffered worse. I took a crossbow bolt in the leg during my exit from the Palace. It was unfortunate, but injuries are a risk that one in my profession learns to live with.'

'I hope you feel your reward on this occasion will be worth the pain you have suffered . . . son.'

'You have signed the legal adoption?' Shalidar asked.

'Yes. It's on my desk. I'll show you before you leave. The only reason it's not been lodged with the Court is that I was waiting to show it to you first.'

'That was most thoughtful of you, Lord Tremarle. As it happens, it might be better if you wait until my leg has healed before submitting it. Several people saw me with the bolt in my leg during my escape. The authorities will no doubt have the militia look for a man with a wound in his right leg. I would not want to bring them to your door. It would be most unfortunate if someone were to tie the person running from the Palace with your newly-adopted son. There are plenty of Noble Houses who will fall under suspicion for the Emperor's death. Let's not invite trouble by giving them a reason to investigate our activities.'

'Quite right!' Tremarle said emphatically. 'However, I might be able to help speed your recovery a little. I have an expensive ointment in my possession for just such a flesh wound. I bought it from a magician in anticipation of one of my sons coming home with a duelling injury. They were both rather impetuous. Danar in particular was renowned for his dalliances with the young Ladies of the Court. He was ever in danger of being challenged. The magician

104

assured me that the ointment would speed up the healing of flesh wounds several fold.'

'The use of such an ointment would be much appreciated,' Shalidar admitted. 'Is it somewhere to hand?'

'Indeed. Wait there, I'll just be a moment.'

Tremarle put down his glass, got up and left the room. Shalidar sipped at his wine. It was a good vintage, but the combination of his headache and the constant throbbing pain in his leg seemed to sap something from the flavour. He wanted to get up and look at the papers that declared him heir to the House of Tremarle, but to do so would be to invite more pain. He thought better of it.

The old Lord was not long. He returned with a plain earthenware pot, which he handed to Shalidar.

'Use it sparingly. I'm told it is very potent.'

'Thank you. I shall.'

'Now, Shalidar, as you are now my adopted son and heir, I wondered if we might discuss how to best present you to the Court. How many of the nobility would know you by face as a member of the Guild?'

Shalidar thought for a moment. 'I think I can safely say that no more than one or two from the Court would know that for sure, though some others might suspect. Those who do know are sensible enough to keep their mouths shut. I was seen openly in the Palace for over two years, so many know my face and name. However, to my knowledge, the only people aside from select clients who knew I was a Guild member were the Emperor and a few of his spies. Most thought I was one of His Imperial Majesty's advisors, which, in a manner of speaking, I was. Advisors go in and out of fashion, so no one has questioned why I'm no longer in Imperial favour. In truth, I have managed a successful business as a merchant in my spare time for years now. Recent events in Thrandor have damaged the business, but it has not been destroyed. I intend to rebuild it in due course.'

'A merchant,' Tremarle repeated thoughtfully. 'Yes, that would be respectable enough, assuming the goods you're trading in are of sufficient standing.'

'I've traded in expensive cloths, quality silverwork and jewellery. I'd say my business was respectable enough for most.'

'Yes, yes! No offence was meant. That will be fine – more than acceptable as an occupation for the heir to the House of Tremarle.'

'Indeed,' Shalidar agreed, 'but will it be good enough for the heir to the Imperial Mantle?'

'I beg your pardon! What are you talking about, Shalidar?'

'It's quite simple really, *father*. I'm asking you to propose yourself as a candidate in the succession.'

CHAPTER SIX

Reynik's attention was dragged from his book by the sound of the librarian suffering a loud coughing fit. As he looked up he became aware of the stiffness in his back and shoulders. He had not realised how long he had been sat motionless, reading. The librarian had risen from her table, but was doubled over and coughing as if something were choking her. Was she gesturing? His eyes swept across to the main doors. Two men in dark cloaks had just entered. As soon as he saw them his blood ran cold. He ducked down to hide behind his book, but it was too late. Cougar had seen him.

Reynik did not know the other man, but it was likely he would be another Guild member. His heart raced. He had to get out of the library – and fast! The only weapons he had about his person were his knives. Cougar was wearing a sword. At first glance the other man appeared to be unarmed, though this was unlikely to be the case. Reynik's options were limited. All the windows in the library were far too high to reach. There were some side doors, but for all he knew, they could lead to dead ends. His only sure way out was through the main door at the front. To get there he would have to get past the two men.

Closing the book, Reynik got to his feet. Thinking fast, his mind spun with possible options, but as fast as ideas came he dismissed them.

Cougar brushed past the librarian. He touched the other man's arm and silently indicated Reynik's position. They split without exchanging a word and walked forward with deadly purpose. Cougar closed in from Reynik's left, while the other man approached from his right. Reynik held his position. If he moved, the two assassins would alter track and corner him. At present they were between him and the one known exit. They had all the angles covered. His thought was to draw them in close and then somehow create an opening through which to make his escape. Unfortunately it was the 'somehow' that was causing him the problems.

'Hey! What do you think you're doing? If you two gentlemen are thinking of making trouble, then you can leave right now.' The librarian bristled with anger, her coughing fit miraculously forgotten.

Reynik grabbed the largest of the books from the table. 'Get out of here. They won't leave witnesses,' he advised her urgently, his head moving from side to side as he tried to watch both men approach. 'Run! Don't get involved.'

As if to confirm Reynik's summation of the situation, Cougar drew his sword. The librarian's eyes went wide as realisation dawned. She gave a squeak of terror, turned and fled across the library, stumbling over her feet as she went. She disappeared out through one of the side doors. Reynik noted which one she had gone through, as it was likely to lead to an exit. Cougar noted it too.

'There's nowhere to go, Wolf Spider. You're mine this time. Your spy friend was captured last night, but your fate is not to be so kind. The Guildmaster wants nothing from you other than your head.'

Reynik's heart sank. They had Femke! He had to get away. If she had been taken to the Guild headquarters, there would be no way out for her unless he could stay alive.

The assassins were getting close. Their cold eyes held no mercy. Reynik met their stares with what he hoped was a cool front. Inside he was on the verge of panic. It was his final flitting scan around the library for anything he might have missed that sparked inspiration. Hope flared.

In a single spinning motion Reynik flung his large book at Cougar, turned, picked up his chair and hurled it at the other man. The solid-looking assassin brushed it aside with an arm as if flicking away an imaginary fly, but the projectiles had given Reynik the vital second or two he needed.

Without pause, Reynik vaulted up onto the table. To the two assassins' amazement, however, he did not cross it and run for the door as they anticipated. Instead he turned and exploded into a froglike leap back towards the huge bookcase behind the table. He grabbed the top, finding a good handhold as the bookcase tipped with the impact of his weight. For a moment, he thought the bookcase was going to fall, but it faltered and then rocked back towards the upright. Clinging to the top, Reynik waited until the critical moment and then threw all his weight backwards to accelerate the movement of the bookcase back towards his attackers.

For a moment it appeared his weight was not enough, the bookcase teetered once again at the point of no return. This time, however, Reynik's weight on the down-going side made the vital difference. The two assassins, Cougar with sword raised and ready to strike, suddenly found themselves bombarded by a deluge of falling books, followed by the crushing weight of the huge wooden bookcase.

Reynik tried to throw himself clear, but realised too late that this was impossible. The only thing that saved all three men from being crushed by the massive weight of the bookcase was the strength and solidity of the table at which Reynik had been working. The bookcase impacted the table and stopped with an almighty crash. Reynik landed awkwardly, colliding first with the far side of the table before falling to the floor. The remaining books from the top three bookshelves fell on top of him. The two assassins were trapped in the narrow wedge between the bookcase and the table, having been first buried under the majority of the falling books.

Reynik groaned as he rolled over, gaining first his hands and knees, then staggering to his feet. He felt bruised and battered, both front and back. There was a noise of movement under the table. At least one of the two assassins was trying to get out. The warm rush of adrenalin burned in his belly once more. Forcing his pain-filled body into a lurching run, he crossed the library towards the front door.

As he ran, he saw the shocked face of the librarian peering round the side door through which he had seen her run a few moments earlier.

'Come with me,' he called to her. 'If you want to live, come with me now.' He held out his hand towards her. 'Quickly!' he added, urgency making his tone harsh.

The young woman tentatively emerged from her hiding place and took his outstretched hand. A glance back revealed Cougar's companion emerging from under the table. His face was twisted with anger. Reynik began running towards the door. The librarian needed no further encouragement. She ran alongside him with light-footed steps. Together they burst out through the door of the library and into the midday sunshine.

The small square outside was bustling with people going about their daily business. After a long morning spent in the quiet of the library, Reynik suffered a momentary shock as he emerged into such a hive of activity. He paused for a split second as he took in the noise and motion around the busy junction, then he raced down the steps between the grand circular columns. At street level he turned to his right and ran along the pavement, turning immediately right again along the first street he reached. The librarian ran with him, silent and unquestioning; most likely still in shock, Reynik realised.

'Listen,' he said, keeping his voice low and urgent. 'I'm sorry you got involved in this, but if I'd left you in the library those men would most likely have killed you. I'm afraid you won't be able to return there for some time.'

'Why not? Who were those men? What did they want?'

Reynik steered them left along a back alley and stopped for a moment, pulling her close in to the wall out of sight. He peered around the corner, looking back down the street. There was no immediate sign of pursuit, but he knew the two assassins would not give up easily. He turned towards her only to find her face uncomfortably close. Her proximity and the fact that she was still clutching his hand tightly suddenly filtered through his thoughts of the assassins and the dangers they posed.

She was not quite as tall as he was. Her head tilted back just a fraction as she regarded him with her intelligent, brown eyes. For a moment he considered how much he should say. The more she knew, the more reason the Guild would have to seek her out. There was a faint scent about her; sweet, like rose petals mixed with a hint of lavender. It wafted and curled around him with invisible fingers that tickled his nose and ignited his blood.

'Shand blast all women!' he thought. 'Why did the creator make them so damned intoxicating?' With alarm, he noted what looked like hero worship in her expression. There was something about her vulnerability that made him feel most uncomfortable.

'Assassins,' he said, trying desperately to snap out of his daze. 'Cold-blooded killers who don't hesitate to dispose of any who cross them. I don't know how they found me at the library, but you saw too much. They would not leave any alive who could identify them.'

The woman blushed and looked down at her feet. 'I think I'm to blame for them finding you at the library,' she said sheepishly.

Reynik put a finger under her chin and gently lifted it until she was forced to meet his gaze. To his surprise there were the beginnings of tears welling in her eyes.

'What did you do?' he asked.

'It was the tags in the books you were looking at. There were strange instructions relating to them. Any librarian noting people reading books tagged with that colour are instructed to send word to the bakery on the Western Avenue. The message was simply to say "library" to the senior baker. It did seem strange. I had not noted this instruction before, but then I'd never noted any books with that colour tag before. I cannot imagine there are many.'

'I think if you were to look carefully through the entire library, you would find the only books with that colour tag were the ones I was looking at,' Reynik replied thoughtfully. He removed his finger from under her chin. 'Which means I was on the right track, even if I didn't find what I was looking for. It wasn't your fault. You were only following your instructions. Don't worry about it.'

'That's easy for you to say. What am I supposed to do now? You say I can't go back to the library. Should I go home? If they wanted to find me it would not be hard for them to find out where I live. I have made no secret of my address. Will they seek me out there?'

'To be honest, I don't know,' Reynik admitted. 'It would be safer for you to avoid going home for a while. I would take you with me, but that would place you in more danger. I'll see you to safety, but then you'll have to take your chances alone. My advice is to get out of Shandrim. Go away somewhere – anywhere. If you stay quiet and out of sight the Guild will forget you in time.'

Reynik snuck another look around the corner and pulled back immediately. Cougar's associate was coming along the road towards their turning. The man was still some distance away but it was clear they had dallied too long. Reynik raised a finger to his lips and noted the fear return to her eyes. Silently he gestured his intentions and they set off along the back alley at a fast, but noiseless, walk. To run now would draw attention. He needed a weapon if he was to face the man on equal terms. If given the choice, however, he would rather not face the man at all.

They rounded a corner, taking them out of sight of the main road. Reynik thought about pausing again to see if the man entered the alley. He decided better of it, electing instead to continue to the end and onto another major street.

When they emerged from the alley, a street market lined both sides of the road. The cries of competing stall-holders imparted a sense of energy to the atmosphere. The air was thick with a rich mixture of smells. The scent of exotic foreign spices mixed with aromas of fresh vegetables and cooking meat. One only had to take a few paces to experience the fragrance of freshly-cured leather competing with those of burning incense oils and the smell of freshly-baked bread.

The librarian gripped Reynik's hand even more tightly as he led her into the thick of the thrumming market. Together they threaded through the milling shoppers and between the stalls until the crowds began to thin out. They were almost at the end of the market area when he spotted the stall.

'Over here,' he said softly, drawing her across the road. The stall sold weapons, both new and old. On the table were knives, daggers, crossbows, hatchets and short swords. Shields of all shapes and sizes were hanging from the awning frame, both on the horizontal bar across the front of the stall and on all four of the uprights. In stands behind the table were long swords, bows, pikes and pole arms of several varieties, double-handed battleaxes and a bundle of staves. It was the last item that had caught Reynik's eye.

'Can I have a look at one of your staves?' he asked.

The stallholder drew one at random from the bundle and passed it across the table. When placed upright on the ground it proved to be slightly longer than Reynik was tall. He ran his hands along the surface of the wood. It was smooth and polished to a deep, glossy shine. The weight was good too – heavy enough to be solid, but not so heavy that it would be awkward to manoeuvre.

'How much?' Reynik inquired indifferently.

'Five senna.'

'Five!' he exclaimed, his voice outraged. 'You have to be joking! It's a piece of wood, for Shand's sake! You can cut a branch from a tree and make one of these in five minutes. I'll give you two.'

'How many trees do you see around here?' The stall-holder replied with a shrug. 'A lot of work went into polishing that stave. Four senna.'

'Three and I'll take it, but not a sennut more.'

Reynik held out the stave for the stallholder to take back. The man looked him in the eye to see if he could squeeze a final offer. Reynik looked back, his expression unwavering. The stallholder sighed.

'Three senna then,' he said in a dejected voice.

Reynik counted out the silver coins from his purse and handed them to the stallholder, who pocketed them swiftly.

With a stave in his hand, Reynik felt a lot more comfortable. It was tempting to tell the librarian that she would be safe now and send her on her way. The problem was that he knew it would be a lie. Despite it having been her actions that had led the Guild to him, he felt an annoying, irrational sense of responsibility towards her.

Angry with himself for being so weak, he grabbed her hand again, leading her away from the stall and along the street until they left the market behind altogether. He looked back a few times, but there was no sign of the assassins. Although he did not relax completely, it was with growing confidence that he moved through the streets towards the inn where he had spent the previous night. His horse and bags were still there. He was keen to retrieve them. The big question mark in his mind was over what he should do next.

The further he got from the library, the more it sunk in that he was alone and vulnerable here in Shandrim. He glanced down at the librarian's hand in his and wondered who was gaining more comfort from the physical contact? She should be safe now. He could send her on her way.

There was a multiple street junction ahead. He would do it there, he decided.

His mind reeled with a confused jumble of events, facts and possibilities that were likely to leave him with a severe headache. The Guild had captured Femke. Cougar had said nothing about her being killed, which gave him hope that they would keep her alive for the time being.

He knew that Femke would not give up hope. He had seen that side of her while they were in Mantor. But what could he do to help her? It made no sense for him to try to penetrate the Guild headquarters on his own. The Wolf Spider quarters would no doubt be under heavy guard, particularly now that they had Femke. He had returned for her once. They would be sure to take precautions against him trying again.

If he could get some of those crystals that Femke had used in Mantor to incapacitate the Royal Guards, maybe it would give him the edge he needed to storm in and take her. No, it was a fool's chance, he decided. He needed more than parlour tricks. To rescue Femke from the Guild, he would need some serious backup.

When Cougar stepped out of the side street not ten paces in front of them, it was hard to say who was more surprised. Judging by the expression on Cougar's face, Reynik realised that the assassin had found them by chance. Both men were quick to react. Reynik let go of the young woman's hand and charged at Cougar, whose sword seemed almost to leap from its scabbard.

'Run!' Reynik shouted, not looking back to see if the young woman had complied. His focus was fixed on his enemy, who was ready for him as he closed the distance between them.

The first clash was fast and furious. Reynik landed a jabbing blow with his stave to Cougar's shoulder. The assassin opened a cut on Reynik's right forearm. The assassin backed off, but Reynik moved in concert to deny him the chance to recover his poise. He pressed forwards, raining blows on the assassin in an avalanche. Any lesser swordsman would have been overwhelmed by the fury and speed of that attack, but Cougar did not lose his poise. He backed away calmly, deflecting blow after blow with his blade. Reynik managed to get a few strikes past the assassin's guard, but none that were telling.

Reynik was mid-swing when something hard smashed into the back of his left shoulder. Pain burned like molten fire as his left hand lost its grip on the stave and fell, useless to his side. He followed the swing through by gripping more tightly with his right hand. Cougar deflected it easily. Reynik ducked and twisted to try to fix a position on his new adversary whilst leaping momentarily clear of Cougar's reach. Something dark and round whistled past him. There was a hollow sounding *thunk* and a groan. Reynik twisted again in time to see Cougar, eyes rolled back, collapsing as if someone had just melted every bone in his body.

Pain and confusion warred within Reynik. He whirled, his senses scrabbling to find a logical explanation for what was happening. It took a moment for the cobblestone in the librarian's hand to register in his mind. Her face held a look of iron determination that he would not have expected in one with such a delicate appearance.

'You can put the stone down now,' he said gently. 'I don't think you'll be needing it.'

'Is he . . . is he . . .' The young woman could not finish her sentence.

'Dead?' Reynik guessed. 'I'm not sure. Let's take a look, shall we?'

The assassin had dropped his sword as he fell. Reynik kicked the weapon out of the killer's reach and gestured for the librarian to pick it up. He did not want to risk Cougar coming around with a weapon close to hand. Life was gradually returning to his left arm, though it was incredibly painful to move. He flexed his fingers a few times and, putting his staff down for a moment, he rubbed his shoulder gently. It did not feel as if anything was broken, but he doubted he would get full strength back in his arm for at least a couple of hours.

'Sorry about your shoulder,' the young woman apologised. 'I thought I had a clear shot at him, but you moved just as I threw. To be honest the first throw was a bit of a sighter. I haven't had to throw for some time.'

'You're forgiven,' Reynik replied. 'To look at you, I'd never have guessed you would have the strength to throw something with that much force. I'm just glad that you hit your target with the second shot. He would have finished me within a few seconds otherwise.'

'My brothers and I used to compete as youngsters at who could throw stones the furthest. Being the eldest, I had a slight advantage for a while, but it became harder to win as my brothers got older and stronger. In the end I realised I could no longer hope to beat them, so I changed the rules.

That's the benefit of being the eldest. Instead of competing for distance, we made targets to knock down. I practised a lot and became very accurate. It seems I haven't totally lost my skill.'

Reynik picked up his stave again. Keeping his distance, he prodded the motionless body of Cougar in several places. The assassin did not flinch. It looked very much as though he was dead, or at least deeply unconscious. If he was bluffing, he was doing a very good job of it, Reynik decided.

The street was still empty, but someone could come along at any moment. Reynik did not want to be caught standing over an unconscious man with a weapon in his hand.

With a heave, Reynik rolled Cougar over. A quick scan over the man's body revealed what he was looking for. The decorative, clip-on, silver belt buckle in the shape of a cougar's head told him instantly that the assassin was still alive. If he had been dead, the icon would have returned automatically to the Guild. For an instant, Reynik hesitated. He had spared Cougar's life at their last encounter. The assassin had tried to kill him again. It was clear that the man would not give up, but was that justification enough to kill him in cold blood?

Reynik gritted his teeth. If their positions had been reversed, Cougar would not have hesitated, but that did not make it any more right. He was out of time. Taking a deep breath, he unclipped the silver buckle from Cougar's belt.

'What are you doing?' the librarian asked anxiously. 'Are you going to rob him?'

'Not exactly,' Reynik replied. He got to his feet, fingering the icon as his conscience played havoc with his emotions. 'You had better go. You should be safe enough now. Just keep heading along that alley there. If you do have to visit your home to gather possessions, then do it quickly. Get out of the city as fast as you can. Go. You need to get away from here before we're seen.'

'But what about you?'

'I'll be fine now,' Reynik assured her. 'Thanks again for your help. I won't forget it.'

She nodded, a haunted look of rejection in her eyes. 'I won't forget you either. Good luck.'

'You too.' He watched for a moment as she set off up the street. A part of him wanted to keep her close and look after her. In his heart, however, he knew he had done the right thing. She would not have survived long in the cutthroat world of espionage and political intrigue.

He turned and threw the silver buckle as hard as he could back along the street. Cougar's body convulsed once and then lay still again. Reynik did not look down at the body. Nor did he watch to see the sparkle of energy as the silver icon vanished before striking the cobblestones. Instead he walked purposefully away from the scene, deliberately taking a different road from that of the young woman. He had sent a message to the Guild that they could not ignore. The Guildmaster would not know how Cougar had died, though he would guess who had caused his demise.

To kill in self-defence was honourable. What he had just done made him feel as bad as he had after he had assassinated Lord Lacedian in order to infiltrate the Guild.

For good or bad, it was done. He knew he had to move on. Femke's life could depend on what he did next. A horrible thought struck him. What if the Guildmaster took her life in direct response to the death of Cougar? That was a consequence he had not considered.

'Oh, Shand!' he muttered softly. 'What have I done?'

As the world swam slowly back into a hazy sense of reality, Femke became aware that all was not well. At first she felt overwhelmed by confusion and pain. Her head was pounding and her hands and feet throbbed with a counterpoint rhythm that was most disconcerting.

She tried to move, only to find her limbs would not respond. Where was she? Her blurred vision slowly cleared until, with effort, she found she could focus for a few seconds. The concentration required to control her sight made the pain in her head sharper, but she was determined to place her surroundings.

The room she was in had no windows. What light there was danced and flickered. It made maintaining her concentration all the more difficult. She closed her eyes to shut out the disturbing blurry images. Her mind turned to the question of how she had got here. Slowly, piece by piece, her memory returned. She remembered visiting Toomas. What information had she sought? Or had she been selling? She did remember climbing out of an inn window, though. Why had she done that?

It took some time, but she gradually filled in the gaps in her memory. Eventually Femke organised her thoughts into a chronological chain of events that led up to the last moment she remembered before waking here. Then the realisation dawned on her – someone had clubbed her out cold.

She tried to move again. Her limbs would not respond. Panic gripped her gut with icy fingers. Was she paralysed? Had she lost the use of her arms and legs? With grim determination she forced her eyes back into focus and discovered one of the sources of her discomfort. Her wrists were tied to the arms of the chair in which she was sitting. It was fair to assume that her ankles were similarly tied. Whoever had tied the bonds had not shown much concern for her circulation. Her hands and feet felt swollen with trapped blood. It was no wonder they were throbbing with pain.

Dizziness and a wave of nausea swept over her. The room began to spin and tumble. Femke knew she was sitting motionless in a chair, but reality and perception had become detached. It took every ounce of her will to re-establish her sense of balance and avoid ejecting the contents of her stomach. The effort left her breathless, but she succeeded.

'She's coming around. Go and tell the Guildmaster,' she heard a voice say.

Quiet footsteps set off at a quick pace out of view. The voice was that of a woman, low and sultry. Her reference to the Guildmaster confirmed Femke's worst fear – she was back in the Guild headquarters. The woman was behind her and to her right. Had she been there all along? It seemed likely. But who was she? The voice had a lilt to it that sounded vaguely familiar. Maybe hearing a little more of the woman's speech would spark her memory.

'Hello? Who are you?' Femke asked. 'Why have you brought me here?'

'Come now, Femke. You know perfectly well why you've been brought here. You cannot meddle in the affairs of the Guild without consequence. As for who I am – that is something I'm forbidden to reveal even to a condemned prisoner.'

The voice was tantalising. It was both familiar, and yet not so. When the woman had first spoken, Femke had felt positive that the speaker was someone she had met before. Now she was not so sure. Maybe the voice reminded her of someone – but whom? As she tried to sift through memories her head pounded all the more. It was no use. The pain was too intense for her to retain any sort of coherence in her thinking. A name would come to her in time – if she had time enough. Formulating a plan of escape was far more important right now.

'What's the matter, Femke? Feeling fragile, are we?'

The woman's voice almost purred with pleasure, her taunting barbed with poisonous sarcasm. Femke had heard enough to brand the voice into her mind so she felt no need to respond to provocation. 'With luck,' she thought, 'I'll get the last laugh here.' The thought fired her with a feeling of positive energy that spread through her body. Gradually the pounding in her head reduced, and by wriggling her fingers and toes, she found that the pressure in her hands and feet eased.

The sound of approaching footsteps sharpened her focus further.

'Thank you, Brother Fox, you may leave us.'

It was Ferdand, but which role would he play this time? Ferdand the mentor? Ferdand the master spy? Ferdand the Guildmaster? Or would he accept himself for what he was: Ferdand the traitor.

'Very well, Guildmaster,' the woman purred. 'Call me if you have need. I'll not go far.'

Femke's mouth felt suddenly dry as a mixture of fear and fury caused her tongue to stick to the roof of her mouth. Anger gave her limbs renewed strength. She strained silently against her bonds with every ounce of force she could muster. Her efforts did not go without notice.

'Don't be foolish, Femke. I taught you better than that. In situations like these you need to apply your brain rather than brawn.'

'Is that what you did when you sold your soul to the Guild?' she spat in reply.

Lord Ferdand walked around until he was standing in front of her. Drawing his hood back he regarded her face to face. His expression held a degree of resignation and hurt at Femke's accusation.

'My reasons for joining the Guild are not important today,' he said, keeping his voice flat and emotionless. Then he lowered his voice to barely more than a whisper. 'Right now I have a bigger problem than explaining my history to you. Answer me this – how on earth am I to extricate you from this mess without having to order your execution?'

CHAPTER SEVEN

Reynik passed the reins of his horse to the stable boy and stomped across the courtyard. His face mirrored the shade of the clouds that raced across the sky above. Rain sheeted down around him in torrents, but his anger had carried him beyond caring. That his path, arrow straight, took him through deep puddles of water went without notice.

'Where's Femke?' Lord Kempten asked anxiously. 'I thought you were planning to come back together.' He was waiting in the doorway, his silver-grey eyebrows drawn together with concern and his eyes betraying his confusion.

'Captured,' Reynik spat, his eyes flashing with barely-contained fury. 'The whole trip was a disaster from start to finish.'

From the moment he had been forced to accept that Femke was not going to meet him at their pre-determined rendezvous point, his temper had deteriorated into the foulest mood he could remember. It seemed everything had conspired against him. His placid, accepting nature had finally reached a limit and something inside him had snapped. His temper was now beyond the point of reason. He was almost enjoying being angry. It felt good to have a focus for his outburst.

Lord Kempten was not impressed. The look he gave Reynik left him in no doubt that he would not tolerate such behaviour.

'Failure is no excuse for an ill manner, young man. Now, let's have that again in a civil fashion, with a few more details, please.'

Reynik sighed heavily and tipped his face up skyward for a moment, closing his eyes. The rain pounded his face, washing across his cheeks and down his neck. Lord Kempten's rebuke struck deep. The discipline of his childhood began to reassert reason and control. Suddenly the rain felt good again. It hid his tears and saved him the embarrassment of exposing his weakness. His anger drained away with the raindrops.

'Apologies, my Lord, but I bring bad news,' he said, his tone heavy with weariness. 'It appears the enemy has captured Femke. Please, my Lord, forgive my temper. It has not been a good few days. Before I elaborate, though, I would prefer it if we could retire to your study.'

'Apology accepted, Reynik. Please, don't stand on the doorstep any longer. Come in. You'll need to dry out and warm up after your long ride. It would be remiss of me to have you fall ill through my lack of hospitality.' He led the way into the back hall and took Reynik's dripping cloak from him.

'Thank you, my Lord. The journey from Shandrim was

miserable. Dry clothes and some food will doubtless improve my temper.'

'Do you have any dry clothes in your pack?' Kempten asked. 'If not I'm sure we'll be able to find you something warm and dry to wear.'

'I'm not sure, my Lord. It would not surprise me to find my pack full of water. The rain has not stopped since I left the city.'

'Then we'll make that the first priority.'

Lord Kempten called for a servant and issued him with a list of instructions. Reynik was shown to the room in which he had stayed during his previous short stay. On opening his pack he found everything to be wet, or at best, damp. The servant attending him was quick to bring suitable replacement garments.

As soon as he had changed, Reynik went to the drawing room where he and Femke had last met with the Kemptens. Lord and Lady Kempten were already there. On entering, Reynik felt a strange sense that he had lived through this scene before. Perhaps it was because the Kemptens were sitting in exactly the same places as they had done on his previous visit. It was hard to say. Lady Kempten was busy stirring a large pot of freshly-brewed dahl. She looked up and smiled as Reynik entered. Lord Kempten got up and closed the door behind Reynik, locking it in an effort to prevent interruptions.

It was Lady Kempten who spoke first.

'Welcome, Reynik. Hot food should arrive shortly. The cook is busy preparing something quick as we're between meals. My husband told me the essence of your bad news.

Please do tell us more. I understand the situation is bleak.'

'A good summation, my Lady,' he replied, taking a seat. 'Femke's capture by the Guild has severely weakened our position.' He felt the black mood threatening again, but he clamped down on his emotions. Now that he was dry and had calmed down, he felt thoroughly rotten about his earlier behaviour. He silently vowed not to add Lady Kempten to his list of social blunders.

'Reynik, please fill us in on the details of your trip,' Lord Kempten urged. 'With Femke taken, is all lost?'

'No, my Lord, I don't believe it is.'

Reynik gave a brief run down of his experiences in Shandrim. In particular he recounted Cougar's words as close to verbatim as he could remember. His throat felt tight as he told how he had gone to the rendezvous point in the hope that Cougar had been lying, but how his hopes had been dashed when Femke had not appeared. He had not wanted to return without her, but her last instructions were very specific. He spoke of his temptation to try a rescue mission, and his anticipation that the Guild would be expecting him. He found it hard to justify why he had not followed through with his plan to retrieve her.

'It was not the danger, you understand,' he explained. 'If I'd failed, you would have been left with nothing, my Lord: no information and no operatives. I could not in all conscience risk that outcome. However, I don't think we should give up on her yet.' His voice was passionate as he set out his reasoning. 'The Guildmaster clearly wanted to question her. Ferdand wouldn't kill her if he felt she had valuable information to give. Femke was his protégé.

I'm hoping that this history with her will make him reluctant to kill her out of hand. It should buy us extra time. Also, Femke would not release information quickly. It stands to reason that she could remain alive for some time.'

Lord Kempten shook his head. 'Don't get your hopes up too high, Reynik,' he said. 'If the Guild of Assassins wants information from Femke, then she'll have little choice but to give it. They will break her quickly, or kill her. I doubt they'll linger over her interrogation.'

Reynik looked to Lady Kempten for support, but her face was grave. He would get no help from her, he realised. Reynik was not ready to back down yet, though. Femke was too special to be cast aside so easily. 'Then we should aim to rescue her sooner, rather than later, my Lord,' he insisted.

'I don't think a rescue attempt would be a good idea, Reynik,' Lord Kempten replied. 'If Femke is to escape the Guild, then she'll have to do it on her own.'

'But that's impossible! As far as we know, there's no way out unless you have an icon.' Without thinking, Reynik's hand reached into the top of his borrowed tunic and touched the silver wolf spider hidden there. As soon as he realised what he was doing, he pulled his hand away as if burned. 'Please my Lord, I beg you – don't abandon her. Femke has demonstrated unswerving loyalty to the Empire in the face of numerous dangers. She has always put duty first. Will you now just abandon her because the situation looks dire?'

'Do you think I have no feelings, Reynik?' Kempten

replied fiercely. 'Femke saved my life once. I'll never forget what she did for me that day. I owe her a great debt, but my duty is to the Empire first. Femke more than anyone would understand this. If I gamble everything she's worked for in a high-risk effort to save her, do you think she'll thank me? Of course she won't! Don't make the mistake of thinking me heartless, Reynik. When it comes to protecting those I care about, I take my obligations very seriously. However, I must also temper my personal decisions with my position as Emperor Designate.'

With the suddenness of a volcanic explosion, white-hot fury erupted inside Reynik. The rage made his earlier temper feel insignificant by comparison. He shot to his feet as if catapulted.

'Does that mean you're going to step forward and take the Mantle, my Lord?' he growled, his eyes flashing with the heat of his anger. 'Femke told me you had doubts – something to do with putting the safety of your family before your duty as Emperor. Is this how it's going to be? A rule for one and a different rule for the other? If I'm out of order here, then fine – throw me out. But if you're going to spend your time as Emperor displaying such hypocrisy, then I can promise you now that you won't enjoy much support from your subjects.'

The look on Lord Kempten's face at the outburst lent justification to his vehemence. His words had struck a nerve.

Reynik knew he would feel remorse later, but right now he did not care. What was there left to lose? All he had ever wanted was to become a Legionnaire and climb the ranks

131

like his father. He had worked hard and achieved the first part of his dream, but for what? At the Emperor's bidding he had stained his soul with blood and made an enemy of the Guild of Assassins. He could no longer return to his Legion for fear of the Guild tracking him down. Assassins had also taken the lives of his uncle and his father. Femke was his one remaining love. He was not about to stand by and let the enemy take her without a fight.

'Now listen here, Reynik! Don't you—' Lord Kempten began.

A knock at the door coincided with a plea from Lady Kempten. 'Gentlemen, please!' Her voice was firm, cutting off her husband's angry retort. 'That's quite enough. We all need time to calm down and think things over. Nothing productive is likely to come of a discussion where passions are so fiercely defended. Let's save judgement on what should be done until we've slept on it. Reynik's food is here. He needs to eat. The poor man looks famished. Let's not forget that we're all on the same side here.'

'But—' Lord Kempten began.

'Not another word on the subject. Think on it, gentlemen.' She opened the door and a servant entered with a tray of steaming food. 'Thinking time will benefit us all. The dawn will bring a fresh perspective and new ideas.'

Lord Borchman looked out at the gathered noblemen of the Imperial Court and considered his chances of success. Under his cool, collected exterior, his nerves jangled. For the gamblers, he suspected he would attract pretty good odds. He was not the front-runner – Marnillus had enjoyed a small margin for some time, but he knew he would pull more of the vote than several of the other candidates. The test would come when the less likely candidates fell away. To whom would the free voters then migrate? Would they see through the bluster of Marnillus?

He and the other six candidates for the Mantle were standing in a line at the front of the courtroom for all to see. Each had spoken in turn, giving a simple statement of their intent to become the next Emperor. Two late entrants into the running had complicated the dynamics of the race.

The surprise entrant, and the one giving him most cause for worry, was Lord Tremarle. Aside from Marnillus, Tremarle was likely to become his main opponent. Those in the Court looking for a traditionalist Emperor would likely be split between them, as their views were broadly similar. Given that Marnillus was the front-runner, Borchman would not be surprised if the braggart met with an unfortunate accident in the imminent future. He had no intention of employing assassins, but had little doubt that others would be doing so. If Marnillus were to fall, then it was not hard to see who would emerge from the chasing pack.

Had Tremarle not entered the race, Borchman would have expected the gruff old Lord to vote for him. Why had he entered? He had never shown any open interest in becoming the next Emperor before Surabar's death. There was something different about him since the Emperor's assassination. He seemed more alive than he had for some time. By chance, Borchman had noticed the look in the old man's eyes as Surabar's body was laid to rest. It had bordered on triumph – hardly a fitting emotion in the midst of the public mourning and the pomp and ceremony of such a solemn occasion. It had almost seemed as if, until that moment, Tremarle had expected Surabar to be faking the whole scene, and at any instant he might appear at the head of a column of troops to complete some incredibly clever military ruse. Well, Borchman knew without doubt that this could not happen. As was traditional, the body had been arranged for all to see and carried with all due respect to its place of rest. He had seen it up close. It was definitely Surabar, and he was most certainly dead. However, a hunch told him there was more to Tremarle's entry into the race for the Mantle than met the eye.

If Borchman had been surprised to see triumph in Tremarle's eyes at Surabar's funeral, the opposite was true of seeing it in the eyes of Marnillus when they had read the contents of Surabar's will to the Court. That a legal successor was named had been a bit of a surprise; that Surabar had not got around to changing his will after Kempten's recent demise was not. With the way open to take the Mantle, Marnillus looked to push his advantage by asking for an immediate commencement to the selection process. There had been protests, but Marnillus had managed to quash them. Each candidate in turn would now have the chance to speak to the Court in an effort to win votes to their cause.

Selecting an Emperor had never been a quick process in Shandar. History had shown time and again that it had taken days, and sometimes weeks, for a clear winner to emerge. Now began the dangerous time. It would not be long before the killing began. The question was not whether there would be assassinations, but who would be the first to die?

'You expect me to believe you?' Femke asked, bitterness flowing from every syllable. 'After all the lies you fed me! Do you really expect me to believe anything you say, ever again?'

Femke was not touched by the hurt in Ferdand's eyes. He had always been a good actor. For all she knew, this was just one more little scene in his grand play.

'Femke, you do me a cruel injustice,' he replied. 'I have loved you like a daughter since the day I took you into my home. Yes, I lied to you. It was for your protection. I didn't want to risk the Guild drawing you into their web. Even when I was chosen as Guildmaster here and forced to disappear from public life, I tried to keep people watching out for you. It's to your credit that they have not always been skilled enough to keep up – you learned your lessons well. I never stopped following your career with the interest of a loving parent who has allowed his child the independence of adulthood.'

Femke allowed a wry smile to cross her face. 'You always have an answer for everything, don't you? I suppose that Shalidar was a part of your little watching party as well. If so, then your loving father act is thinner than you might imagine.'

Ferdand's face darkened at the mention of Shalidar.

'Absolutely not!' he snarled with quiet vehemence. 'I wouldn't trust Shalidar as far as I could pick him up and throw him. He's been a thorn in my side from the day he first set foot in this place. My enmity for him was never feigned. I'd like nothing more than to see him fall from his self-built pedestal. You might not want to believe me, but I'll swear any oath you name that this is the truth, Femke.'

It was hard to imagine anyone faking such intensity of feeling, but even so she could not bring herself to believe her old mentor. If she were to rely on him telling the truth in one area, then it would be easy to start off down the slippery slope of accepting what he said in many others. That was a path down which she had no desire to go again. However, one truth she could not deny in what Ferdand had said so far was that using her brains was the only way out of this situation. She needed to control her anger at her old mentor's duplicity if she were to have a chance of getting away.

An idea flashed into her mind. She relaxed into the chair still further as she contemplated her response. Two could play the deception game.

'Very well, I can accept that,' she said reluctantly. 'But if you have these fatherly feelings for me, will you not demonstrate them now? Release my bonds. I already know that there's no way out of this place unless one wears the icon of an assassin, so I couldn't run far.'

Ferdand regarded her closely for a moment and then turned his head aside. He began pacing slowly back and forth in front of her, his face a picture of contemplation. After a moment or two he spoke.

'I'm inclined to let you have your little victory,' he said carefully. 'However, if I release your bonds you'll have to behave. Any thoughts of using me as a hostage to get out of the complex should be discarded right now. It's a rule of this place that there's no such thing as a hostage situation. If you try to use me as a shield, they'll kill me without a second thought. There are several assassins who would be only too pleased to see me die, as they feel they're in the running to be the next Guildmaster.'

Femke pursed her lips as she thought this through. Once again Ferdand had appeared to read her thoughts. It was an uncanny knack he had that had always been irritating, but now was verging on intolerable.

'Also,' he continued, 'if you kill me, then what will you have achieved? There are Guild servants everywhere, and many assassins who would think no more of killing you than they would of discarding a broken arrow. If you were lucky, you might get past one, but they would get you in the end. Just as they will get young Reynik.'

So Reynik was still at large. That was good to know. Femke tried again.

'Accepted,' she said. 'I'll not try to hold you hostage. You know I'm not the sort for suicide, so I'm not ready to kill you just yet either.' It was true. Much as it would be tempting to kill him and take her chances, logic dictated she should bide her time for a better opportunity. 'That's not to say I won't come after you eventually. I doubt I'll ever forgive you your web of deceit.'

'Think, Femke – think back to when you first began to learn the skills of espionage. What did I tell you about killing?'

It was not hard. The words were etched on her memory.

Ferdand's words had made a big impression on her, as until that time she had not even considered the possibility she might be required to spill blood in her role as a spy.

'You told me there might be times when I was forced to kill in self-defence; that I might also be required to kill for the good of the Empire, but that the only person whom I should allow to assign me such a task was the Emperor.'

'You always were good at listening,' he said with a pleased, fatherly smile. 'Femke, you have succeeded where I failed. I shaped you through your training to be the perfect spy. Sadly I must now admit that I did not mould you in my own image, but in the image of that which I had always intended to be. My career was poisoned many years ago.'

He sighed and knelt down in front of her chair. With his right hand he drew a knife from under his cloak and carefully sliced through her bonds one by one. For a moment his eyes met hers, but he looked away quickly, not able to take the accusation in her gaze.

'One could say I was a victim of my own success,' he continued, 'just as Reynik has now become a victim of his. There's no way out of the Guild for him, Femke, other than through death. If he does not return to renew his bond with the master stone every six months, his icon will return of its own accord. When it does so, he will die. He showed his hand too early. The Guild now knows him for an infiltrator. He'll be eliminated one way or another.'

Reynik had not had his icon long. There was still a considerable amount of time in which to find a way of breaking his bond with the icon. What if there was no way of breaking the link? That did not bear thinking about. Femke began gently rubbing her wrists and ankles to encourage the blood flow. Her mind raced, but she knew she must concentrate on listening. Ferdand was giving away Guild secrets. She could not afford to miss a word. There would be time later to think on how she could use the information to her advantage. Ferdand stood up, stepped back, and began to pace up and down, taking care to maintain a wary watch on her as he continued to speak.

'Once Surabar declared us *anaethus drax* I was living in dread of him sending you to find us. It occurred to me that if anyone could find a way to get to us here, it would be you. I knew in the case of this eventuality, I would be faced with a terrible choice. I must admit that I did not foresee you training another to do it. Was that your idea?'

'No. It was the Emperor's plan.'

'Then Surabar was more clever than I imagined. Reynik was a good choice, although several of the Guild members suspected him from the moment he arrived. Shalidar was one of them. In some ways it was because he was so suspicious that I really wanted to believe in Reynik. Nothing would have pleased me more than to prove Shalidar wrong.'

The prickling pain of returning blood circulation to her hands made it difficult to interpret the sensations from her fingertips. With ginger care she explored the area on the back of her head where she had been clubbed. It all felt swollen, but she was not too sure how badly. One good thing was that there appeared to be no broken skin. Satisfied that the damage to her skull was not too bad, she rubbed again at her wrists and ankles, gently massaging blood back into the extremities of her limbs.

Ferdand paused in his pacing and looked at her intently. His hawkish features looked drawn and lined with age.

'I could not ignore your interference, Femke. Like it or not, I am Guildmaster here. I will only live as long as the Guild considers me to be doing a good job. When I fail in my duty as Guildmaster, then I'll be cast aside to make way for someone more able. By getting caught, you committed me to a path with few options. The choice I dreaded is nearly upon me. I can delay it a short while, but not forever. Whilst Reynik is at large I can keep you here as bait to try to draw him back. He came for you once. Who is to say he will not do so again?'

Femke prayed silently that Reynik would not be so foolish as to attempt a rescue, but he was young and rash. It would not surprise her to see him caught in such a fashion.

'What's the choice, Ferdand?' she asked. 'Maybe I can save you the trouble of choosing.'

His expression changed slightly to include annoyance.

'Don't get flippant, young lady. None of the options are pleasant.'

'Try me,' she replied, her blue-grey eyes steely as she invited the challenge.

'Very well! As I see it, I have three options. Firstly, I could have you killed – unpleasant, but simple. Secondly, I could make you one of the serving staff here at the Guild, where you'd remain for the rest of your life. The length of that lifespan would, of course, depend on how you adapted to life as a servant.' He paused.

'And the third option?'

His eyes suddenly bored into hers as if he were looking into her soul.

'The final option would be the worst, for if I took it I would have admitted failure in every area of my life. As a third option, I could induct you into the Guild as an assassin.'

CHAPTER EIGHT

'It's him,' Kempten confirmed, 'but I don't know his travelling companion.'

'At last!' Reynik breathed. He took another look out of the window at the two riders approaching the front of the house. It was strange, he thought. He had not been expecting the magician to look so ordinary. When he questioned his instinctive response, he realised that he was not sure what he had been expecting. The only magicians he had seen were those on the streets of the cities, employing their tricks to earn coin from passers-by. It was common for such folk to wear outlandish costumes to attract attention. He had never really considered what a true master magician would look like.

Lord Kempten left the room to go and welcome the new arrivals. Reynik followed him out of the study and down the main staircase. The butler was already at the front door. Reynik was impressed. The servants in this house did not miss much.

'The stable boy is on his way, my Lord,' the butler advised. 'He should be here in just a moment.'

'Good work, Altman. Could you have the kitchen staff prepare something for our guests? They must have ridden hard from Terilla to get here this quickly. I'd like to offer them our best hospitality.'

'Right away, my Lord.'

The butler strode across the hall, somehow managing to move at speed without appearing in a hurry. Kempten opened the front door and stepped out onto the threshold. Reynik followed him outside and stood to his right. The two riders drew to a halt in front of them. The younger of the two, a fair-haired young man who looked in his late teens or early twenties, vaulted down from his horse.

'Would you like a hand, Master?' he asked the older man.

'No, thank you, Calvyn. I'll manage.'

The old magician swung out of his saddle and lowered himself gently to the ground with the ease of one long accustomed to riding. As he turned and closed the distance between them, Reynik surveyed the man with interest. Heavy streaks of grey punctuated his long, dark hair, which he had tied back into a thick ponytail. His eyes were deep-set under heavy brows that again showed signs of once being a fierce black, but were now the colour of steel. He was shorter than average, and slim, yet there was an indefinable aura about him, a sense of presence that made him seem bigger than his physical dimensions. His face was deeply lined with the passage of many years, yet his dark blue eyes were alight with bright intelligence that lent his

143

features a more youthful edge. A man of fascinating contrasts, Reynik mused as Lord Kempten gripped the magician's hand in greeting.

'Welcome, Jabal, it has been far too long.'

'Indeed it has, Kempten, my old friend. Your message spoke of a matter of great urgency, so I came as fast as I could. I brought an acolyte with me – I hope you don't mind. I've been tutoring him recently and thought this would be a good opportunity to get him away from the stuffy confines of the Academy – broaden his horizons and all that. Not that this young fellow needs his horizons broadening that much. He's not your average acolyte.' He turned and beckoned to his travelling companion. 'Calvyn, come and meet Lord Kempten.'

The stable boy had arrived and taken control of the horses. The young man identified as Calvyn walked across to join his master. As he reached Jabal's side he stopped and gave a smart bow. Reynik's first impression of him was not that of a magician-in-training. His upright stance, short-cropped fair hair, precise movements and the sword at his side spoke more of a young man enrolled in military service. For a moment he wondered just what it meant to train as a magician.

'Welcome to my household, Calvyn. I hope you enjoy your stay with us. Please let me introduce you both to Reynik, another guest of my household, and a loyal servant of the Empire.'

'Loyal servant of the Empire – an interesting description,' thought Reynik as he shook hands with the two men. Legionnaire, spy and sometime assassin might be more accurate. 'A pleasure to meet you,' he said aloud.

'Come,' Kempten continued. 'Let's go inside and get you gentlemen some refreshments. I'm sure you could both do with something to eat and drink after your long journey.'

It was some time later when the four, together with Lady Kempten, were sitting in the study. The two magicians had changed out of their travelling clothes, eaten a meal and had listened intently as Lord Kempten outlined the current situation.

'Well, well! That's a bundle of news if ever I heard one,' Jabal muttered, as Kempten finished his tale. 'It's been many years since I read about the silver icons of the Guild of Assassins. I never thought to see one, never mind get involved in a plan to destroy them. And you wear one of these icons, Reynik? May I see it, please?'

'Of course, sir. Here . . .'

Reynik drew out the wolf spider from under his tunic, the silver glittering ominously on his chest as the master magician got out of his chair and approached him for a closer look. Jabal lifted it off Reynik's chest by one of the spider's legs and held it up, twisting and turning it in order to see it from all angles.

'Wonderful workmanship! Calvyn, take a look at this for a moment. You might recognise the handiwork.'

'I doubt it, master. I don't know very much about silverwork. Unless . . .'

Jabal looked at him and smiled. 'Yes. This was made by the same person who made the amulet that gave us all that trouble last year.'

Calvyn's eyes opened wide as he took a closer look at the silver spider pendant.

'Darkweaver!' he exclaimed softly. 'So is this made of blood silver as well?'

'No,' his master responded, shaking his head. 'He didn't discover the secret of blood silver until a little later in his career. If it had been made of blood silver, I would not have been handling it.'

'Blood silver, Jabal? You're talking in riddles. Why do you magicians always feel the need to be so mysterious?' asked Kempten, his tone curious.

Jabal gave a wry smile as he responded, but did not qualify the question with a direct response. 'Calvyn and I crossed paths with someone who carried a very special piece of this magician's work last year. Derrigan Darkweaver made these icons for the Guild in the early days after he gained his robes. He was looking to make a name for himself, so he took on several commissions of this sort. Silver was a substance he knew well. If the history books are correct, his father was a silversmith. He would no doubt have learned many secrets of the smithy trade at his father's knee.'

'So that's why he worked with silver!' Calvyn exclaimed. 'I thought it was just because silver was a substance that was receptive to magic.'

'I think the fact that silver and magic were a compatible mix was a happy coincidence for Derrigan. Most of his more impressive magic was wrought by combining his skills in both fields,' Jabal explained.

Lady Kempten coughed pointedly. 'This is an interesting

history lesson, gentlemen, but does knowing who made the icons help us in our bid to destroy them?'

'A most pertinent question, my Lady,' Jabal responded, giving a slight bow in her direction. 'As a magician it does at least give me some idea of what to expect. Darkweaver produced a surprisingly large number of powerful works of magic during his relatively short time as a magician. There is a reference in the Academy library about this particular group of icons. With your permission, Reynik, I'd like to try something that will tell me more.'

Reynik was intrigued. 'Go ahead,' he offered, secretly hoping he was about to see something magical happen.

Jabal reached inside his jacket and drew out a curiously-shaped piece of reddish-orange stone. It was rather like an oversized needle in shape, though shorter and much fatter. The elongated smooth shaft was about the thickness of a man's little finger. The pointed end was blunt and rounded whilst the other end sported a squat eye-shape. The magician held the eye over the spider icon and began to mutter something in a strange language. All eyes in the room focused on the two objects.

Whatever Reynik expected to happen, he had not thought it would involve pain. All of a sudden he felt an excruciating cramp in his chest and the room began to twist and distort before his eyes. He wanted to cry out, but he could not breathe. His body seemed to convulse, bend and stretch in ways that defied logic. Jabal was the only constant. His image did not distort one iota. He was solid, calm and unmoving in the midst of a maelstrom of surreal chaos. Then, as suddenly as the sensations began, normality was resumed. Reynik slumped back into his chair, his head spinning and his body totally drained of energy.

'What the hell did you do?' he gasped, clutching at his chest and attempting to rub away the phantom residue of the pain he had experienced.

'Hmm, that might be a little difficult to explain, Reynik. Sorry for any discomfort. The spider has more power than I anticipated. Calvyn, did you see the lines of force?' the magician asked as he placed the strange stone device back inside his cloak.

'Yes, Master. To break such a bond would surely cost Reynik his life.'

'I agree. The only way to deal safely with the magic in this icon is to destroy the master power source. Logic dictates that the bonding stone provides the main power for the network of force that links all the icons to their bearers. Break the bonds between the icons and the mother stone and all the subsidiary links between the icons and the assassins will fail as well. That's the theory anyway.'

'And if you're wrong?' Lord Kempten asked.

Jabal frowned. 'Well,' he said carefully, 'I do not normally err when it comes to such things. However, if the bonds were more complex than I believe them to be, then your objective would still be achieved. The Guild of Assassins would be destroyed. Unfortunately, the likely outcome in that case would be that anyone wearing an icon would die with the destruction of the stone.'

A cold silence enveloped the room as the magician's words sunk in. Reynik felt sick. It was hard to know how much of his nausea was a result of the magic Jabal had just performed and how much due to his ominous words. Nothing had gone right since Reynik had infiltrated the Guild. It was little short of miraculous that he was still alive, given all his encounters with the Guild assassins. The thought that, even if he were to take no further part in the conflict, by destroying the Guild his life may still be forfeit did not seem fair. Where was the justice in it?

He drew in a deep breath through his nose and exhaled slowly through pursed lips. He knew it was not his decision, but he was determined to have a say.

'We should do it,' he stated. Every eye in the room settled on him, but he ignored them all. He stared into space, reflecting on all the grievances he now held with the Guild. 'We should go ahead and do it,' he repeated firmly. 'We have come this far. We cannot back down now.'

'But the risk—' Lord Kempten began.

'Is no more than I have faced already. However, we need to be prepared for the more likely outcome. If the destruction of the stone merely breaks the link between the assassins and their icons, we will not destroy the Guild – merely break up its primary form of transport around the city and cause them to relocate their headquarters. We'll need to be prepared to round them all up and bring them to justice. It won't be easy.'

'There's another element to your situation, Reynik, of which you might not yet be aware,' Jabal said thoughtfully.

'More trouble, Jabal? Can it get much worse? What have we missed now?' Kempten asked, his voice heavy with dread.

To Kempten's surprise his friend did not reply to him, but instead looked Reynik squarely in the eyes. 'From what I read of the icons, I understand that Derrigan added a little safety device to ensure the assassins remained loyal to the Guild. How long have you had your icon, Reynik?'

'A week . . . ten days . . . I've not been counting.'

'Then I suggest you begin. If you do not return to the bonding stone within a certain time period, the icon will return on its own.'

'But that would mean . . .' Reynik did not finish his sentence.

'Yes, you'll die anyway,' Jabal confirmed.

'Very clever,' Lord Kempten said, nodding. 'I can see why the Guild had Derrigan instil the icons with that property. Do you know how long Reynik has, Jabal?'

'No. The text was not that specific. It could be anything from a matter of weeks to a period measured in years.'

Reynik was astonished by this development. 'Why didn't they tell me?' he asked. 'Do you think they knew who I was all along?'

'I doubt it,' Jabal replied. 'It's more likely that they don't tell new members about this until a probationary period has been completed.'

'So, the sand is trickling through the hourglass,' Lord Kempten observed thoughtfully. 'Does anyone have any suggestions?'

'Yes,' Reynik replied immediately. 'First, let me rescue Femke. I feel sure she's still alive. With Femke's resourcefulness, we would stand a much better chance of completing the rest of our objectives.'

'We've been through this, Reynik,' Kempten replied, a note of anger in his tone. 'It's too dangerous. Femke is lost to us. We must manage without her.'

'Femke?' asked Calvyn. 'That wouldn't be the same Femke who visited the King's Court in Mantor a few months ago, would it?'

Reynik looked at him with surprise. 'Yes. How did you know that?'

'I was there when she was introduced to the King. She did seem a sharp young woman. An ambassador, I believe.'

Lord Kempten gave an embarrassed cough and Lady Kempten smiled knowingly. Jabal raised an eyebrow at their response.

'I take it she's a little more than just an ambassador,' the magician observed with a straight face. 'As she's clearly not one of the Guild, then I assume she must be part of the Imperial spy network.'

'One of their best,' Kempten confirmed.

'I sensed something of her nature in the King's Court. She has a quick mind,' Calvyn said thoughtfully. 'As her mind harboured no hint of a threat to the King's immediate safety, I didn't interfere with her visit. The Guild is holding her prisoner, you say? Do you have a plan to get her out?'

'I have a rough plan,' Reynik replied. 'But it would be very risky.'

Calvyn turned to Jabal.

'Master, I should be able to reduce the risks involved. If I were to accompany Reynik into the Guild headquarters, I could shield us both long enough to see us safely in and out. If Femke is still alive, there are unlikely to be any in the Guild with the power to stop me from taking her.'

Jabal scratched at his right eyebrow as he considered Calvyn's proposal. He did not look happy about the idea, but he did not appear to be dismissing it out of hand.

'I'll think on it,' he said eventually. 'In the meantime, there are other details that will require attention. One in particular bothers me. I find it incomprehensible that the Guild would build their headquarters under the Imperial Palace without having some sort of conventional way in and out. If there were no conventional exit and I were to destroy the magical transportation system they use, they would be trapped in the Guild complex. This would be madness on the part of the Guild. I refuse to accept that any sane man would design such a place. There has to be another entrance, and we need to find it.'

'I was reading books on the construction of the Palace when the two assassins attacked me in the city library,' Reynik offered. 'There are two books there with tags that have clearly been put in place by the Guild. I suspect there may be information there that might lead us to a secret entrance. If so, it would likely be in the cellars of the Palace. It's a shame I can't ask the librarian. Unfortunately she had to leave Shandrim for her own safety. I'd be a fool to go back to the library now. The Guild will know that I haven't yet got what I was looking for. They'll more than likely have watchers looking for me to return. However, that doesn't preclude someone else from going.'

'I can do that,' Jabal volunteered. 'I can protect myself against any attack the Guild might try. I like libraries. They're places of calm and order.'

'If you'd seen Shandrim Library yesterday, you might have reservations about that statement,' Reynik laughed. 'It was anything but calm and orderly. As long as you're discreet about your research, I doubt you'll have problems. I can describe the books and the library tags you'll be looking for.'

Lord Kempten nodded and his lips tightened into a thin line. 'It sounds as if we have a plan,' he observed.

How Ferdand could ever believe Femke would join the Guild of Assassins in order to preserve her life was beyond her. He had listed it as an option, but he was making a big assumption: that she would consider joining those whom she had cast as her enemy. It had taken every ounce of self-control she possessed not to spit in his face at the mention of such an idea. She had been most grateful when he had been called away to a meeting shortly after telling her his perceived alternatives. His departure had given her a chance to re-establish a firmer control of her emotions.

She had searched the room thoroughly for anything that could be of use in an attempt to escape, but whoever had placed her here had done a good job of removing all potential weapons. There was little of use. The chair she had been tied to was sturdy enough. She could use it as a weapon if pushed, but it would not be manoeuvrable enough to be effective. It would be better used as a shield than a weapon in its current state. She could break it up and make something sharp from the pieces, but to do so would make noise. She could ill afford to draw attention to herself as potential trouble.

All major pieces of furniture had been removed. The only decoration she noted was a wooden plaque above the door with an elaborate sea snake carved into the face of it. There was a cloth mattress, poorly stuffed, on the floor. There was a flagon of water in one corner of the room, but aside from that, there was nothing that could be easily broken or robbed for potential materials. One thing she had noticed when Ferdand had left was that there was no bolt on the outside of the door. The only bolt was on the inside. It was clear that the Guild did not make a habit of holding prisoners.

This room was likely the bedroom of one of the assassins' suites. If the design of the suites were similar, then the door opened into the living area, which was consistent with the brief glimpse she had gained of the room beyond the door. Her cloak was on the mattress. The clasp had been removed, but the material had been left, presumably as a blanket. She picked it up and wrapped it around her left arm several times.

Placing her right hand on the door handle, she turned it as slowly as she could. Despite her best effort at silence, she was still turning it with infinite care when the handle was wrenched from her grasp and the point of a blade lunged towards her chest. It stopped just short of making contact, but was close enough to make her heart leap in fear. The bitter taste of bile rose to the back of her mouth.

'What d'you want?' the servant demanded. He was holding the sword as if he knew how to use it, which made what she had in mind far more dangerous. At least he was alone, she noted. If there had been more than one guarding the door, she would have given up there and then. The man's brown robe looked to be made of quite heavy material: another factor that did not help her cause.

'A d . . . drink, please, and some f . . . food if you have any,' she replied, her shaking voice only half feigned.

'There's water in the corner over there,' he said, pointing with his sword briefly before returning the tip to her chest. 'You'll have to wait for food like the rest of us. What's wrong with your arm?'

'Pins and needles: the pressure helps take away the discomfort and stops me scratching.'

Femke allowed her shoulders to slump and she began to turn to her right, back towards her prison. Out of the corner of her eye she noted the servant relaxing as she turned. He started to lower his guard with the sword just a fraction and reach for the door handle. Femke did not hesitate. She spun back to the left, brushing the sword blade aside with her wrapped left arm and driving the ball of her right foot up in a vicious kick at the man's groin. Her foot drove home with satisfying force. The man doubled over and lost his grip on the sword, which fell with a ringing clatter to the floor. Femke followed up her kick with a double-fisted strike to the back of the man's neck that sent him to the floor.

The pain she was left with in the sides of her hands bore testimony to how hard she had hit him. It was not surprising, therefore, that when he hit the floor the servant did not so much as groan. He was completely out cold.

Femke's breath hissed out through clenched teeth as she shook her hands in an effort to dispel the pain. She unwrapped her left arm and picked up the sword. Carrying such a weapon would be dangerous. She had no pretences of being a master swordswoman. If she were to face an assassin with a blade in her hand, it would guarantee her death.

She looked around for somewhere to put it out of the way. The best place she could think of was under her mattress. It had the advantage of being inside her prison, though it was a painfully obvious hiding place. All she could hope was that her captors would expect her to conceal acquired weapons with care. There was a slight chance that they would not check the obvious. She was under no illusions of her chances of escaping the Guild complex, but escape was not the only reason to break out from her single room. As every spy knew, information was often the key to controlling situations. Any intelligence she could gather by scouting the complex might prove crucial in the long run.

Having stowed the sword, Femke checked the servant for signs of consciousness. When she lifted his right eyelid, the iris did not contract at all. She pinched hard on one of his earlobes but he did not flinch. Given the lack of response she guessed he would remain unconscious for some time. His pulse was strong, so she had no worries about having inadvertently killed him.

She grabbed his arms and dragged him through into the room in which she had been held. As a finishing touch, she rolled him onto the mattress. Would they think to look under the mattress if he were found lying on it? Hopefully not.

Creeping out and across the living room, Femke paused by the outer door to listen. If there had been a further guard, surely he would have come running immediately at the sound of the falling sword, she thought. She opened the door. The corridor was empty: so far, so good.

Despite stretching, her muscles still felt stiff from her extended period of being tied in the chair, but Femke was so practised at moving silently that her body automatically compensated for any inflexibility. At first, she thought the noise she could hear was the faint guttering of the flames from the wall-mounted torches. She paused for a moment to listen. It was not the torches, she realised. The faint muttering was the distant sound of voices in discussion. Eagerly, but with even more caution, she moved forward to see if she could get close enough to hear what was being said.

As she approached the door at the end of the short corridor, it became clear that the voices were originating from the chamber beyond the door. It seemed likely that the door would open into a cubicle in the central chamber of the Guild. With painstaking care, Femke turned the handle and pushed the door open just a crack.

'So that leaves us with Marnillus, Borchman, Tremarle and Reavis.' It was Ferdand's voice. Femke leaned closer to the door. She smiled as she listened, silently thanking the designer of the central chamber. The acoustics in there made eavesdropping easy.

'Marnillus is an arrogant, self-centred fool who should have been drowned at birth,' offered an unknown voice.

'Self-centred and arrogant I would agree with,' the

Guildmaster replied. 'But a fool? I'm not so sure he's a fool. He currently holds the support of the majority of the Court. He would not hesitate to call on our services if he felt he needed them. Two of the other candidates have offered contracts on him. One has offered a significant sum.'

'Take the contract.'

'He would make a terrible Emperor.'

They did not know about Kempten. Excitement welled within Femke. The Guild sought to control the succession in their favour, but they had no idea that the race for the Mantle was an irrelevance.

'Very well,' she heard Ferdand say. 'Those who believe the Guild should accept the contract on Marnillus say "aye".'

A resounding chorus of 'aye' echoed in the chamber.

'Noted. What of Lord Reavis? It would be his contract that we would be fulfilling.'

'Reavis is a buffoon,' answered a different voice. 'Assassination would be his answer to every difficult question. He would bring plenty of trade for us, but would run the Empire to ruin in no time.'

'There's a contract on him, too. Should we take it?' asked Ferdand.

'No. By killing him as well, we would be too obviously controlling the outcome of the succession.' The voice was that of the woman who had been in Femke's chamber earlier. 'He's not likely to win enough votes from the Court. Leave him be.'

'I tend to agree.' Ferdand replied. 'Although the fees offered on some of these contracts are attractive, by showing restraint, we stand to gain in the longer term. What of the rest of you? Who thinks we should take the contract on Reavis?'

Femke judged that only two voices answered in the affirmative. It appeared that Lord Reavis had just won a reprieve.

'What of the last two? Brother Dragon, you have had dealings with Lord Tremarle. What do you make of him?'

'I have to confess a bias, Guildmaster.' Femke's blood ran cold as she identified the voice of Shalidar. 'As you well know, Lord Tremarle has used me as his assassin of choice for over a decade. My support for him as a candidate of choice should be taken with little weight, as his gaining the Mantle would place me in the enviable position of being the preferred assassin of the Emperor. Tremarle has not placed many contracts over the years, but those he has placed have been carefully considered. He is intelligent, conservative and he had no love for Surabar, which will win him much support amongst the "old school".'

'I'll bet you wouldn't remain his "assassin of choice" for long if he knew you killed his son,' Femke thought with a grimace. Mentally she noted it as an item for her agenda if she managed to get out of here.

'Thank you for your honesty, Brother Dragon. From what I've seen, much the same description could be said to apply to Lord Borchman.'

'Except that he never uses assassins,' another voice pointed out.

'What's that, Brother Viper?' Ferdand asked.

'It's true that Borchman had no love of Surabar,' Viper confirmed. 'But he also has no love of assassins. He has always dealt with his problems personally. To my knowledge he has killed three people in duels and severely scarred several others. I don't believe he would maintain the *anaethus drax* order, but I doubt you'd see many contracts coming from the Palace if Borchman wore the Mantle.'

'Interesting! That's something I'd not noticed about him. I'd assumed as he was "old school" that he would—'

With heart-stopping unexpectedness, something smashed into Femke from behind, catapulting her through the door and into the cubicle beyond. The door crashed against the wooden chair inside the cubicle and rebounded into the two sprawled bodies. The figure in his brown robes was up and raining punches down on Femke in a flash. He struck again and again in a barrage of blows. The assault was so sudden that she had no time to formulate a counterattack. All she could do was curl up in a ball and protect her face as best she could with her hands.

'STOP! Stand up and stand still. What's going on in there?' The Guildmaster's voice, normally gentle and kindly of tone, rang with anger and the full authority of his position.

The punches stopped, for which Femke was grateful, and the servant got to his feet. As he did so, he deliberately stood on the back of her left leg, causing her to cry out with the pain. She pulled her leg free from under his foot and squirmed on the floor. Gasping for breath and tears rolling down her cheeks, her mind worked frantically to find a way out.

'I'm sorry for the interruption, Guildmaster,' the servant apologised. 'I erred and the prisoner surprised me. I didn't want to repeat my mistake. The situation is under control now. I'll take her back to the cell. She'll not disturb you again.'

'How long ago did she escape her room?' There was no mistaking the anger in Ferdand's question.

'I'm sorry, Guildmaster, but it's hard to judge. Not long, but long enough to listen in on part of your meeting.'

'She's dangerous, Guildmaster. I've warned about her before. Holding her here is a mistake. We should kill her now,' Shalidar urged.

Femke groaned softly. 'Go to hell, Shalidar,' she muttered as she heard his plea. It was a comfort to know that Ferdand was unlikely to be persuaded by him. To her chagrin, a second voice added her support. It was the woman Ferdand had called the Fox.

'It's not often that Brother Dragon and I agree,' she said, 'but in this I have to concur, Guildmaster. She is a liability. The spy should die.'

CHAPTER NINE

'The glamour will hold until I dispel it.' Jabal's voice was at once confident and authoritative as he inspected the magical disguise he had woven around Lord Kempten. 'There are unlikely to be any in Shandrim with the power to penetrate the illusion. Now then, my friend, I suggest you stay at your town house while the rest of us are about our business in the city. We'll keep you informed of our progress and we'll fetch you when the time comes for you to claim the Mantle.'

'But my servants there won't recognise me,' Lord Kempten said, looking around in wonder at the group of strangers that he knew to be his travelling companions. They all looked totally unrecognisable. 'Why would they let me stay there?'

'Write a letter from Lord Kempten extending you an invitation,' Jabal suggested. 'Your handwriting and signature should be recognisable to them.'

'But my servants there think I'm dead.'

'So date the letter before you died,' the magician responded immediately. 'You're going to arrive travel-stained and weary. Who's to say you have not been on the road for weeks? It's up to you, my friend. You don't have to, but it will save you staying in an inn. I'm sure you would be more comfortable at home. Even staying in your own guest room should be better than waiting at some backstreet tavern.'

Jabal seemed to have all the answers. Kempten considered for a moment and nodded thoughtfully. He looked around again at his companions, still not quite able to bring his mind to accept what he was seeing.

Jabal's features and apparel had changed totally. His illusory face was broader and sterner than his real one. His hair appeared fully grey now, and thinning. It looked backcombed with grease to make it stay in place. His clothes were as sombre as his stare, grey and forbidding. Calvyn and Reynik could pass for brothers – very ugly brothers. The illusions that masked their features made them both look like tavern brawlers: big, broad-shouldered, square-jawed, with flattened noses, scruffy hair and a variety of scars. Their clothing looked as rough and battle-worn as they did. With their new personas there was little chance of any sober man picking a fight with them. They would appear in their element walking the backstreets of Shandrim.

Kempten's own appearance had changed to that of a slightly younger man. His clothing marked him as a scholar and his short, neatly-trimmed, black beard and waxed moustache added an edge of the eccentric to the image. Of course, none of it was real. He wondered what would happen if someone were to touch his face. Would they feel the beard? When he touched his face with his own fingers he could only feel his normal features. It was unlikely that he would find out. Who was likely to touch his face other than Izzie? And she was not with them.

It was an hour's ride to the edge of Shandrim – time for the party to split. The two young men would have made noticeably strange travelling companions for the others, so the plan was for Kempten to continue with Jabal to the edge of the city, whilst Reynik and Calvyn cut south to enter the city from a different quarter.

'Good luck, Reynik. Be careful,' Kempten said as they made ready to part ways.

'Thank you, my Lord. I'll do my best.' Reynik turned to Jabal. 'Good luck to you too, sir. Thank you for helping us. It feels good to have someone like you lending us your aid. Take care at the library.'

'I shall. We'll meet as agreed in two days.' The magician waved his acolyte to his side. Calvyn moved his horse alongside his master's. 'Don't do anything rash, Calvyn,' Jabal said in a low voice. 'Remember – magic is not the answer to everything. Minimise your use of it. If we keep the Guild in the dark as to our abilities, we maintain a powerful element of surprise for when we most need it.'

'I understand, Master.'

'Good. I'll see you at the rendezvous.'

'Whatever the spy has learned is of little import,' Ferdand said dismissively. 'She cannot escape the complex. I hear

164

your arguments, Brothers, but I disagree. Until Brother Wolf Spider has been dealt with, Femke is of more use to us alive.'

The Guildmaster kept his tone reasonable, but inside he was seething. What did Femke think she was doing? She was playing into Shalidar's hands. The dragon assassin was now gathering support amongst the other Guild members in calling for her death.

'I'm sorry, Guildmaster, but I don't see the logic in your argument,' objected Viper. 'What does it matter if the girl is alive or dead? Brother Wolf Spider knows we have her. He also knows that we would be unlikely to hold her anywhere but here, so we already have our lure. What does it matter if we kill her? He wouldn't know if she were still alive unless he came to find out.'

'There is logic, I can assure you, Brother Viper. One who wears an icon tied to his life force should realise that there are ways of discerning if a person is alive or not from a distance. There are those within Shandrim who can do this. Not many, I grant you, but they are there. Brother Wolf Spider has proved time and again that he's not without resources. We know that he cares for her. He has come back for her before. If we're to draw him into our trap, then we need to keep Femke alive a bit longer. Also, Wolf Spider has already demonstrated his ability to do the unexpected. If we were to be caught unawares, Femke may prove to be useful as leverage.'

'How long, Guildmaster?' asked Fox. 'We have Brothers maintaining a constant guard on Wolf Spider's quarters and now a guard on her. How long are we going to keep this up? It's a drain on our resources, aside from being interminably dull.'

'Patience, Brother Fox, patience. We shall continue for a week. If in that time we have still not seen any sign of Brother Wolf Spider, I shall reconsider. It may be that he has given up on her. If that is the case, then she has no further use as a lure, but we should allow some time to determine this. If he does not show, then we shall dispose of her.'

Femke squirmed on the floor of the cubicle as she listened to Ferdand's words. Somehow the Guildmaster's words stung every bit as much as the bruises from her beating. 'So much for the three options,' she thought. Even though logic dictated he would have to offer the Guild members some platitudes to justify their efforts, it still hurt to hear him speak of her so. Who was he lying to this time? Were the choices he had mentioned a fabrication, or was he really trying to help her? Ferdand was more of an enigma to her now than he had been as her mentor.

'Take her back to the cell.'

The servant standing over her bowed. 'Yes, Guildmaster,' he said with deference.

'And see that you do not fall for any of her tricks again. I don't want her interfering with any more Guild business.'

'Yes, Guildmaster. I promise she'll not give you any more cause for concern today.'

The man in the brown robes reached down and grabbed her by the hair. With brutal efficiency, she was yanked to her feet and guided back along the corridor to her cell. The guard hurled her across the threshold into the room that had been converted to serve as her cell. To her surprise, when she looked back towards the doorway he had followed her inside. The hood of his brown cloak was back up, but she could see the cruel twist of his lips. She did not need to see the rest of his features to know that he had violence in mind.

'You're going to pay for making me look the fool,' he hissed.

'Don't do it. You're making a big mistake,' she warned, her eyes flicking around the room as she considered her options.

'Oh, I won't kill you, but I am going to make you wish you'd never tricked your way past me.'

Femke shuffled backwards away from him, scrabbling across the floor on her hands and feet. He ran forward and kicked her hard on her right leg. She cried out at the pain, trying her best to drag her body clear. He came forward again, giving her another kick – this one so hard that it rolled her over. Her body came to rest next to the mattress.

A thought occurred to her. His scabbard was still empty. He had not found his sword. A third kick landed, his boot this time catching her in the kidney region of her lower back. The pain from the impact was excruciating. Any thought she had harboured about being the good prisoner and taking her beating disappeared in a flash of rage. Her body was hard up against the edge of the mattress, so it was easy for her to slide her hand underneath it. She found the blade with her fingers and worked her hand down until she reached the hilt.

'Stop!' she cried. 'Please, stop before you do something you regret.'

'Oh, I don't think you've quite had enough yet,' he replied, his voice cold with calculating cruelty.

A moment later his boot impacted her back once more, this time slightly higher. The kick brought another wave of pain. The senseless violence hardened her resolve. Her grip tightened on the sword hilt and she gritted her teeth as she released a snarl of determination. The guard was drawing his foot back as Femke rolled towards him. There was a scrape of metal against stone as she drew the sword out from beneath the mattress. The guard heard it, but did not have time to withdraw far enough to find safety. Femke's roll took her close. With all her remaining strength she thrust the blade up into the man's gut. His jaw dropped and his eyes bulged with the shock of the pain as he looked down at the blade protruding from his body. He staggered back a few steps, a horrible gurgle sounding in his throat. Then, with agonising slowness, he sunk to his knees, his hands clutching at the blade before falling with leaden finality onto his side.

Femke was breathing hard as she got to her knees. She could make out the pool of dark blood spreading from beneath his body. She was no stranger to blood and death, but the combination of her pain with the sight of the dead guard hit her hard. Nausea twisted her stomach and she retched, falling forwards onto all fours. The smell of her vomit triggered further spasms, each one hurting more than the last as her bruised muscles protested at the clenching strain.

It took some minutes before she regained control. As the spasms died away she felt momentarily drained – drained of strength, of hope and of spirit. At the same time she felt a sensation of deep uncleanliness, as if somehow, in her short time here, the dark filth of the assassins' killing mentality had stained her to the core. As she considered this, she realised that much of the sense of uncleanliness flowed from her history with Ferdand. It was he who had taught her how to kill. She had thought the lessons were to keep her safe during her life as a spy, but now she wondered if he had pursued a deeper motive all along.

The feelings of despair did not last long. As soon as she felt herself sinking into the rising well of negative thoughts, her spirit rallied. It was not her who was unclean, she realised. Her motives had never been dark. She could hold her head high in any company. Since entering the Imperial network her actions had never been driven by thoughts of self-interest, or personal gain. She would never follow in Ferdand's footsteps. She would die first.

The realisation that she was willing to sacrifice her life for her beliefs was timely. Only minutes ago there had been calls for her death. How much more would the Guild members call for her execution when they discovered the dead servant? She sighed. There was no escaping the fact that the situation was dire, but there had to be a way out. There always was. It was up to her to find it. For a moment she considered stealing the servant's robe and trying to get away from the body, but even assuming she could bluff her way out of the quarters, where would she go? Trying to run was unlikely to achieve anything. The Guild complex was big, but not big enough to remain hidden for long in the face of a determined search.

Femke got slowly to her feet and staggered over to the chair. It was facing the door. She had no energy to move it, so she sat down and rested her head in her hands.

As she sat, she thought. Memories of the Royal dungeon in Mantor flooded back. There she had faced the prospect of death at the end of a period of captivity. The situation had seemed dire, with little chance of salvation, but she had not lost hope. Reynik had been her lifeline to the outside world in Mantor. Once again he was her best hope of reprieve, but this time the odds were stacked against him like never before. The enemy expected him. The Guildmaster was laying traps for him. 'Webs with which to trap the Wolf Spider – how ironic,' she thought. 'A wolf spider doesn't weave webs! It has no need for them.'

For some reason this fact gave her hope. Did the Guild understand the nature of the beast they were trying to catch? Reynik was resourceful and a quick student. No matter what the odds, she would not give up hope.

'It's not over until the final curtain call and I'm not ready to take my last bow just yet.'

Shantella put the finishing touches to her make-up and took a moment to admire the results in the mirror. The meeting had not long since finished. To her delight, the best contract had fallen to her.

'Darling, you are to die for,' she purred, delighting in the *double entendre.* Turning her head from side to side she checked the symmetry of her artwork. It was perfect. The smile she gave herself before turning from the mirror accentuated her classic cheekbones. 'Time to go.'

Rising gracefully from her chair, she swept her dark cloak around her shoulders and pulled the hood carefully over her intricately-styled hair. The ring on the middle finger of her right hand glinted as she touched it to the transfer stone. A glow of power briefly illuminated the fox-head design on the ring as it made contact, and Shantella instinctively took a deep breath as she embraced the sensation of magic enveloping her.

Transfer always left her feeling flushed and alive. For her there was only one thrill greater: that of watching the life drain from the eyes of her victims. Shantella revelled in kills that allowed her to be close to her victim when he died. Tonight would be no exception.

Lord Marnillus should be at home. His was an impressive house – large and imposing. In some ways it was a reflection of the man. The down side to such a large building was that it offered many routes of entry for a person with the skills of the Fox. That she had visited the house on several other occasions over the years made it all the easier. Marnillus had always been one to show off his wealth and influence by holding extravagant parties. Shantella had attended several gatherings here in past years, employing various guises to locate previous targets. There was no detailed planning required for this hit. It was as straightforward as they came.

Assuming no complications, she would enter and exit

with the only person any the wiser being her target. Lord Marnillus, however, would not be telling anyone of his caller.

Shantella slipped silently out from the dark corner of the side street and set off on the short walk to find her intended victim. Her blood was fizzing through her veins as the aftereffects of the transfer mingled with the anticipation of a kill. Her sleek, lithe figure flowed through the dark with feline confidence. Thieves in the areas around her transfer points knew not to mess with her. Several had learned the hard way and word had not taken long to spread. She had little to fear until she reached areas of the city where she was not instantly recognised as predator, rather than prey.

The walk did not take much time, and entering the building even less. Locks and latches were rarely more than a brief inconvenience. The windows of the Marnillus residence had none that slowed her for more than a few seconds. Once inside she prowled up through the house until she found the Lord's bedroom. He slept alone, which simplified matters.

She cracked open the door and slipped inside, easing the door closed behind her.

'What the . . .?'

'Shh! Keep your voice down, my Lord,' she purred. 'We don't want to wake the rest of the household, do we?'

'No, but—' He pushed himself into a half-sitting position and the bedcovers slipped down to his stomach.

'I just *had* to come and see you. I do so love powerful men, and word has it in the city that you are destined to become the most powerful man in Shandar.'

The light was dim, but his eyes were well adjusted to the low light. As she spoke, Shantella slipped off her cloak. Marnillus was entranced. The strutting approach and the purring voice of the shadowy figure set his pulse racing.

'Yes, well . . . Wait a minute! I know you. You're—'

Shantella did not hesitate. The volume of his voice was increasing. If he were to wake others in the house, her escape would become complicated. Even as she pounced, the assassin whipped a cushion from a convenient chair. Her blade gleamed as it plunged down with unerring accuracy, slicing between his ribs and into his heart. The cushion, jammed firmly over the Lord's face, muffled his cries. He struggled, fighting with all his failing strength to break free, but he fought in vain. Shantella knew her trade. With the deathblow dealt, she concentrated on maintaining his silence, leaning on the cushion and restricting the thrashing of his arms.

A surge of triumph sent shivers thrilling up her spine as his struggles began to subside. Seeing his life ebb away made her feel more alive than ever.

'Goodbye, Marnillus,' she whispered.

Jabal looked at the Legionnaire with an expression of disbelief. 'Martial law? Since when has Shandrim been under martial law?'

'It's been implemented in the last few days, sir,' the soldier replied, looking pleased at an excuse to show off his knowledge to men of obvious status. 'Ever since Emperor Surabar was assassinated the city has been gradually descending into anarchy. Despite the new restrictions Lord

Marnillus was found dead in his bed a couple of days ago, sir. There have been several riots and a lot of unnecessary bloodshed. The official word on Marnillus is that he suffered heart failure in his sleep. Seems unlikely, if you ask me. The man was burly, it's true, but he wasn't particularly overweight. Most thought him to be in good physical health. If he died of natural causes, then it was a cruel twist of fate for him. After his death the remaining candidates for the Mantle suddenly decided that the streets were not safe after dark. That clinched it for me. He was assassinated. No doubt about it. The only question remaining is who commissioned the hit.'

The military blockade across the main road into Shandrim from the north was manned by no less than a dozen Legionnaires. Further along the street, Jabal could see evidence of more patrols moving through the city, all in full fighting gear. Whoever was organising the policing of the city was taking the situation very seriously.

'I see,' he said thoughtfully. 'Please, excuse our ignorance, for we have travelled quite some distance to get here. We're not up to date with current affairs in the capital. What restrictions are you placing on the citizens?'

'Adults are not to gather in groups larger than six,' the Legionnaire responded, his eyes automatically rising as he sought to recall the new rules. 'Any meeting larger than this must be authorised by the City Clerk's Office. No one is to be on the streets after dark. The eighth call currently marks the night call. You have just under an hour to get to where you're going, or you'll be taken off the streets by the patrols, questioned, and held overnight under guard.

I wouldn't recommend that. They have you sleep on the floor in a warehouse. It's very uncomfortable. I doubt there are many who actually get any sleep there.'

'In that case we had better be on our way. Thank you for your time.'

Jabal turned in his saddle towards Kempten, reached out and shook him by the hand. 'It was a pleasure to meet you, sir. Fate has rarely treated me to such an interesting travelling companion. Good luck with your research. I shall look out for a copy of your book when it's finished.'

Kempten gave a slight bow in his saddle. 'And I, yours, sir. Shand guide you and protect you. I hope we meet again some day.'

With the words of parting complete, the two crossed through the barrier and went their separate ways. Jabal continued straight down the main road towards the city centre, while Kempten turned right up the first main cross street. Neither of them looked back to see if the Legionnaires were taking note of where they had gone.

'The streets are crawling with soldiers. Is Shandrim always like this?' Calvyn asked, his voice sounding out of place emanating from the mouth of the illusory brutish figure.

Reynik shook his head, instinctively checking his own disguise to make sure the magic was still working. It was. 'Something major must have happened during the last few days,' he said. 'The streets were not being patrolled this heavily when I left, and the Legions had no blockades in place then.'

The sun had dropped below the horizon and dusk was

already beginning to concede the city to night. Their vantage point on the high ground to the west of the city suburbs gave them a good view over the western quarter. Patrols of soldiers were numerous, their torches bobbing through the city like dancing lines of tiny fireflies.

'Dodging patrols every other step of the way is not going to make it easy to move around the city,' Calvyn observed.

'We don't have much choice,' Reynik replied. 'I'd rather not try to penetrate the Guild during the day. They do most of their business by night, so there will likely be less of them in the complex after full dark. I doubt they'll be put off by the patrols. Come on. We'll just have to be careful to avoid being seen. We can't take the horses any closer to the city, but the nearest village is at least a league from here. Have you any ideas?'

'We could leave them here. They'll be as safe as anywhere else. We're a fair distance from the road. I'll place a compulsion on them not to stray far until we return. It's not a difficult spell. Just give me a minute.'

Calvyn began muttering in a strange tongue. A sensation of power tickled the back of Reynik's neck as the outlandish words rippled the air. The two horses pricked up their ears and turned to listen. With a final syllable of power, Calvyn completed his spell. A haunting echo hung in the air.

'It's done,' he said. 'They'll not stray of their own accord. Of course this will not prevent them from being taken by force, but if anyone does try, the horses will resist.'

Reynik nodded. The horses had already set to grazing,

seemingly content with their location. The two young men removed saddlebags, saddles and bridles from the animals, stowing the gear deep within a nearby thicket of hawthorn and brambles. Calvyn marked one of the trees with a series of small cuts. How he expected to find his mark, Reynik did not ask. Out of habit, he took a few moments to commit the patterns of trees and bushes to memory. Since training with Femke, his powers of observation had improved markedly. When he was content that he had a firm mental map of where their gear was, he led them down the side of the ridge towards the edge of the city.

The main roads were blockaded, but there were many ways into the city. Shandrim bore little resemblance to the Thrandorian capital, Mantor, with its great city wall and tightly controlled entry and exit points. Shandrim's walls had long since fallen into disrepair. Only a few small sections of the old walls were now maintained, more for their historic value than for any protective attributes. Once they had encircled what was now the central part of the city, but the population of Shandar's capital had outgrown the walls many centuries ago. There were now vastly more people living outside the original city wall than inside.

A string of successive Emperors had cared little for controlling the growth of the city boundaries, so the housing on the outskirts had been built with no sense of order. The chaotic tangle of streets and alleys between houses of all shapes and sizes gave the outer city a warren-like feel, dark and complex: a natural breeding ground for thievery and violence, to say nothing of vermin and disease. Public amenities were few, and there were great areas of housing that barely qualified as habitable. Most were wooden structures, cemented together with dried mud, whilst the more permanent stone-built dwellings were predominant in the richer areas towards the centre of the city. However, the darker aspects of life in the poorer districts did nothing to deter thousands from living there, each looking to claim their small slice of the wealth for which Shandrim was famed.

Defence of the city had not been a consideration for many generations. The might of the Legions had deterred even the most aggressive of nations from thoughts of conquest. Shandar had long been the aggressor, subsuming other societies and kingdoms into the Empire. It was inconceivable that any would be capable of sending armies here, to the seat of Shandar's power.

For Calvyn, entering one of the poorer districts came as a huge shock. The air was thick with the stench of human waste. The reek was so intense that he could taste it at the back of his tongue like a residue of foul treacle. Rats and smaller vermin were everywhere, scratching around in the mud of the alleyways and scuttling across the cobbled streets in numbers that made him shudder. It was clear from the animals' disinterest in the two men that they were seldom hunted. It was hard for him to imagine living in this fashion. His parents had not been wealthy by any stretch of the imagination, but no one in his poor country village had lived in such squalid conditions. He looked around with a mixture of distaste and horror. He dreaded to think what the insides of the buildings were like. It did not bear thinking about, he decided.

Steeling his nose and stomach, he did his best to ignore his surroundings and concentrate on following Reynik. He ranged ahead with his mind, seeking to locate the patrols before they ran into them. Whispered warnings to Reynik whenever he sensed people approaching saved them from inadvertent confrontations on more than one occasion. Progress was slow, but street by street and alley by alley they weaved a tortuous path through the city towards their goal.

It was getting late when they reached the entrance to the alley where the transfer stone unique to the wolf spider talisman was located. Dusk had long since given way to the full dark of night. Lurking in deep shadow and observing the alley in silence, the two young men held their position for a full half hour. Aside from the frequent scurry of rodents, nothing moved.

'Do you sense anyone nearby?' Reynik finally asked in a barely-audible whisper.

'No. The alley appears clear,' Calvyn replied softly.

'Is the transfer going to muddle your senses the way it did mine when I first used the icon?'

'I don't know until I try, but it shouldn't do. My mind has undergone a lot of specialist training to guard against magical interference. I'll try to protect my senses as we use the device.'

'The room we'll arrive in is certain to have a guard,' Reynik warned. 'For the first few seconds we'll be very vulnerable.'

'Understood,' Calvyn responded. 'I should be able to give us a certain amount of protection, but I don't want to alert the Guild to my abilities unless it becomes absolutely necessary.'

Reynik nodded. 'That makes sense. Are you ready? Then let's go.'

CHAPTER TEN

'You there! Stop where you are!'

No sooner had Reynik and Calvyn moved out from the shadows than the bellowed order froze them briefly in their tracks. They had been so focused on the alley and looking for possible watchers that they had not noticed a patrol of Legionnaires rounding the corner down the street to their left.

'Go! Go!' Reynik urged, his momentary surprise overcome. This was no time for explanations. He launched into a sprint, with Calvyn a step behind him. A few paces and the darkness of the alley swallowed them. The tromping sounds of running, booted feet closed quickly on their position. It took a moment for Reynik to find the right stone in the thick darkness.

'Here, hold this,' he ordered in a hoarse whisper, holding out the spider talisman. 'Here we go.'

He touched the icon to the transfer stone, belatedly remembering that he had meant to draw a weapon before entering the Guild complex. It was too late now. The magic was already swirling through him. Despite his previous exposure to the sensations, the feeling of exploding and coalescing left him unbalanced as he materialised in the wolf spider suite. Had he been alone, he would have died there and then. The assassin, Firedrake, who was on watch duty, was quick to react to their emergence. He had drawn and thrown a blade before their bodies had fully solidified, but Calvyn, too, was quick to react.

The blade in flight took a sudden swerve to the left, missing Reynik by the narrowest of margins. A second blade followed and that also flew in a curved path that defied the laws of nature. Firedrake gasped with surprise. He knew his throws had been good, but neither had found their mark. He was given no time to theorise on how he had missed. The man bearing the wolf spider icon had taken only an instant to recover, and was bearing down on him with a sword that had all but leaped into his hand.

Firedrake drew his own sword, his mind reeling in confusion. This was not the same young man who had been initiated into the Guild as Brother Wolf Spider. The person he had seen that day was boyish of face, and only of medium build. This man was broad-shouldered, muscular and ugly as chewed blackroot. It was impossible. Icons could not change hands without the death of the holder. There had been no initiation of another at the bonding stone. It made no sense.

He blocked the intruder's first swing, but he was unprepared for the speed and agility of the big man. Their blades rang no more than three times. Before Firedrake knew what had hit him, the bearer of the wolf spider icon had run him through. His fingers slackened on the hilt of his sword. The blade tumbled from his fingers, clattering to the floor with a loud jangle of metal on stone. His jaw slackened with shock and he looked down as his attacker pulled his blade free. The room jolted, then tilted, as he fell first to his knees and then onto his side. His hands sought the wound, but he could not feel anything. The light dimmed and the two men's whispered exchange echoed strangely in his ears, gradually fading as darkness overtook him.

Reynik shuddered as he pulled his blade clear of Firedrake's body. He had been given no choice. It was kill or be killed. That made the justification easier, but he doubted he would ever gain pleasure from taking a life, unless it was that of Shalidar.

'I'm pleased to see you didn't suffer any ill effects from the transfer,' he whispered to Calvyn. 'I don't know what you did to his knives, but thank you. I think that was Brother Firedrake. He and I have tangled before.'

'You were very fast. You're good with that sword.'

'Thanks. I had a good teacher.'

Reynik looked around at the familiar room, his eyes avoiding the body of the assassin. Much of the furniture had been moved back to where it had been positioned before Femke had barricaded herself in here after her successful spying escapade a couple of weeks ago. Some of the pieces showed signs of damage from that incident. The door to the corridor was the only real change. It was clearly new, the old one having been shattered.

'Is there any way you can use that sensing ability of yours to work out where Femke is being held?' Reynik asked softly. 'I don't want to test my skills further unless it becomes absolutely necessary.'

Calvyn's eyes went distant for a moment as he reached out with his mind. Reynik held his breath as he watched. It looked very strange to see a thuggish brute of a man in a trance. It seemed wrong. The glamour was a marvel, he decided. Even Femke could not have produced a disguise of this subtlety.

The moment passed and Calvyn gave a sigh.

'I can't tell,' he said. 'Whoever built this place was very clever. Someone has protected against the interference of magicians. There are magical echoes reverberating throughout the complex. I've touched Femke's mind once before in the Royal Palace at Mantor. I thought that I would be able to track her down easily, but all I can tell you is that she is still alive. I can feel her presence, but I wouldn't like to guess where she is. I might be able to narrow down her position as we move, but for the moment we'll have to search using conventional methods.'

A loud BONG suddenly reverberated through the complex. It sounded as if someone had just struck a massive gong with great force.

'What was that?' Calvyn whispered urgently. 'Have we set off an alarm?'

'I don't know,' Reynik replied, his brows drawn into a frown. 'I never heard that noise during my time here. I've no idea what it means. Come on, we'd better get near enough to the meeting chamber to see what happens. We might learn something to our advantage. We can retreat back here if need be. There's no other way into these apartments from within the complex.'

Calvyn nodded and signalled for Reynik to lead the way.

They moved swiftly but silently out of the chamber with swords held at the ready. There was no one in the corridor outside, so they sped along to the end. On reaching the door that led into the wolf spider alcove in the central chamber, Reynik opened the door just enough to peep through. Calvyn did not press to see, but reached out instead with his mind. He did not sustain the effort for more than a few seconds. Whatever was causing the magical interference was much stronger in the chamber ahead, and his attempt to sense the underground cavern left him feeling momentarily dizzy and confused. He leaned against the wall and rubbed his temples at the sudden flare of pain in his head.

At first, Reynik could see nothing. The light in the chamber was too dim. After a few moments his eyes began to adjust to the light. The shadowy figure of the Guildmaster was emerging from the stairwell close to the central podium.

'Who was it this time, Guildmaster?'

'I don't know yet, Brother Fox. I'm glad to see that it was not you. I'm going to the bonding stone now. Will you join me?'

'Of course, Guildmaster. Did we have anyone out on assignment tonight? I thought we were going to leave the rest of the Imperial candidates alone. The tattle on the

185

street is that the nobility are rallying behind our chosen man. I didn't expect more intervention on our part.'

'I've not ordered anything specific tonight,' Ferdand replied, 'but several of the Brothers are out in the city following up our ongoing commitments. You're right. The race for the Mantle is all but done. We'll see no further business this side of the final vote in the Imperial Court. It may be that the victor will wish to eliminate the other candidates afterwards in order to prevent any subsequent trouble. If that's the case, then we'll accept the commissions.'

Reynik watched as the slender figure of the woman assassin crossed the floor to join the Guildmaster. It was like watching seduction in motion. The Fox was a born tease, he decided. Even cloaked and hooded, she managed to make every movement play on a man's baser urges. 'That is one dangerous lady,' he thought with a grim smile of admiration.

He eased the door closed and turned back to Calvyn.

'I think I know what the sound was,' he whispered. 'They're going to the bonding stone. I think the sound must ring out when an icon returns from a dead assassin. I'm guessing that it must have taken Firedrake a few seconds to breathe his last. When they realise which icon it is that's returned, they'll be down here in a flash. We'll have to be quick if we're to get Femke out. They should be distracted for a few moments, but unless we can get in and out without delay this could get messy.'

The thought that his own icon could return to the bonding stone at any time made him grind his teeth in frustration. If he knew what deadline he was working to, he would feel a lot more comfortable about orchestrating this rescue. It seemed a waste to be this close and not take the opportunity of renewing the bond between his icon and the mother stone. That his life might prove forfeit as a result was a worrying possibility. However, to attempt to reach the bonding stone would increase the risk of death or capture by an unacceptable margin. Femke's rescue was the priority.

Calvyn nodded and pushed away from the wall. They cracked open the door again in time to see the Guildmaster and Fox disappearing into the passageway on the far side of the chamber. No sooner had Fox entered the mouth of it than the illusion of the wall reappeared, leaving no sign of the secret entrance.

'Now!' Reynik said softly. He whipped the door open and they both vaulted the waist-high wall, landing softly in the central area of the chamber. 'Which way?' he whispered.

Calvyn reached out once more with his mind and recoiled at the maelstrom of magical eddies and echoes. How could he make sense of anything in the midst of this? It took a moment, but his subconscious assimilated the sensations, converting them into images he could relate to.

Suddenly he was in another place: standing in the midst of an ornamental maze. It was night. A violent thunderstorm raged above him. There was a flash of lightning, followed instantly by a deafening crack of thunder. A vicious gust of wind buffeted him, upsetting his balance and making him stumble to one side. Invisible hands plucked debris from the ground, swirling it into the air and hurling it at him with formidable force. Rain battered him in torrents, jabbing his skin like a million ice-cold darts. The hedge tops swayed and danced, unearthly faces forming and disappearing in the clouds and leaves. They were laughing. Laughing at him?

For a moment it almost felt as if the whole earth were rocking. In his mind he called out, but his words were whipped away almost before they passed his lips. He laughed, lifting his face to the sky as the rain pummelled his skin. An edge of hysteria touched his voice as he realised the futility of his efforts. How could Femke possibly hear him in the midst of this? Yet, impossibly, somewhere in the midst of the noise and confusion, he could feel her presence. She was there. Waiting. Hoping to be rescued.

In the chamber he staggered forwards and Reynik caught his arm. Calvyn did not notice. He was lost. The real world had gone. All that remained was the maze and the storm. Reynik sensed his companion's mental struggle, but could do nothing other than offer him physical support.

In his mind, Calvyn ran forwards taking turns, left and right. At first he ran randomly, taking whichever turning presented itself next. A flying branch hit him across the face and he flinched, reeling from the pain of the impact. Then the thought struck him. If he worked methodically, he should eventually cover all parts of the maze. There must be a way of doing it. In simple mazes one could cover all parts of a maze by continually following the wall on one's left, allowing the wall to lead into all dead ends and back out again. The problem was, he had no way of knowing how complex this maze was. If he were to apply this principle in a large labyrinth, he was equally likely to walk around in circles forever.

Reynik started to panic. Seconds were ticking by. The Guildmaster was likely to return any moment. Calvyn had slipped into a trance and was showing no signs of surfacing. He shook the acolyte's arm, but got no response. They could not stay here. He tucked an arm around Calvyn's back and dragged him forwards.

A sudden gust of wind picked Calvyn from his feet and propelled him forwards. A dead end loomed. Flying through the air he smashed into it, the branches tearing at him like claws. He tumbled through to the other side. Nothing looked any different. He was still in the maze. He scrabbled to his feet. If anything the storm was getting stronger. Another flash of lightning split the sky and he flinched at the deafening clap of thunder that accompanied it. Another enormous gust of wind scooped his feet from under him and once again he was flung through the air. He had no more control than a branch ripped from a tree. Another hedge raced at him and he barely had time to shield his face as he ploughed into it with unstoppable momentum.

Half dragging, half carrying him, Reynik lurched around the perimeter of the chamber, taking Calvyn in front of one alcove after another.

Calvyn was beyond reason: battered, bruised and bleeding. The storm seemed almost sentient – toying with him, flinging him at will, first one way and then the other. He had to escape. Was there no way out? A presence suddenly reminded him of why he was there. She was close – very close. He could feel her. She was a haven of calm in the fury of the storm.

'The storm isn't real,' he told himself. 'You must withdraw – must break free. It's only a vision.' But no matter how he tried, he could not bring his mind back to reality. He tried forming focus pictures, but the storm kept breaking his concentration. He could feel the wind gathering its strength to hurl him forwards again. There was nothing for it. He reached for the handle of his sword and drew it, lifting it high above his head. Runes glowed brightly along the shining metal and the clouds seemed almost to growl, as if hawking up more energy. Then in a dazzling double fork, they spat an incandescent stream of lightning at the blade.

They had gone about a quarter of the way around when Calvyn suddenly took a sharp intake of breath. They stopped by the gate bearing the symbol of the sea serpent.

'In there,' Calvyn panted. 'She's in there.'

'Quick!' Reynik urged, his voice desperate. 'We've got to get out of sight.'

He dragged Calvyn forwards, staggering through the gate and into the alcove. They opened the door at the back and entered the corridor beyond. Calvyn paused, leaning against the wall and breathing heavily.

'Can you manage without me for a moment? I'll be right behind you,' he gasped.

'Are you sure you'll be all right?' Reynik whispered. 'What if someone comes this way?'

Calvyn nodded. 'I just need a few seconds. That chamber

has a . . . draining magical influence. Go. Get to Femke. I'll follow you.'

Reynik raced forwards, drawing a knife with each hand. It was foolhardy, but he knew that his only advantages now would be speed and the element of surprise. He had no idea how many guards the Guildmaster would have assigned to Femke, but there was no time to worry about it. He burst through the door at the end of the corridor and charged headlong into the living area of the assassin's chamber. On entry it became clear that the sea snake icon was still unassigned.

A servant, dressed in his brown robe but with the hood down, leaving his face exposed, was sitting on a chair by the far door reading a book. He leaped to his feet at Reynik's explosive entrance, but he was neither quick enough nor skilled enough to face such an opponent. Reynik's first throw was true, striking the servant in the chest with deadly force. He ran to the door where the servant had sat guard, scanning the room for hidden adversaries as he went. There were none. A lock and bolt looked to have been newly fitted. He drew the bolt, and tried the door. It was locked. 'No surprise there,' he muttered. A quick search of the servant for a key was not productive.

'Femke,' Reynik called in a hoarse whisper, rapping the door several times with his knuckles. 'Femke, it's me – Reynik.'

'Reynik! You fool! What are you doing here? It's a trap. The Guildmaster is expecting you.'

The sound of Femke's voice brought a smile to his face.

His blood was still racing and he felt a sudden dizziness at having located her.

'Never mind that,' he said. 'I've brought some help. Listen – do you know where the guard keeps the key to your room?'

'The guard doesn't have it. The key is normally held by the Guildmaster, or whichever assassin he assigns to bring me my meals. The servants are not trusted with the keys any more.'

'Shand's teeth!' Reynik swore, clenching his fists in frustration. 'How am I . . . Never mind. I have an idea.' He ran back to the door that led out into the corridor. Calvyn was just approaching it, still unsteady on his feet, but looking a little better. 'Can you open locks? The guard is dead, but he doesn't have a key.'

Calvyn nodded. 'Show me,' he said simply.

Reynik led him into the assassin's quarters and pointed at the door. Calvyn muttered something under his breath. There was an audible *snick* as the door unlocked and Femke opened it a split second later. She ran out and stopped dead in her tracks, her face totally shocked.

'You're not . . .'

It took a second for Reynik to realise what had caused her shock. The glamour had created a disguise beyond any that Femke could see through.

'Femke it *is* me, Reynik,' he whispered insistently, 'and this is Calvyn. He's an acolyte magician. He altered our appearances using magic. What you can see is just a glamour – a type of illusion. There's no time to explain details. We've got to get out of here . . .' He paused. Time had run out. There were voices in the corridor. Someone was coming.

'Looks like we have trouble already!' Femke muttered. She was wary. It sounded like Reynik and this was just the sort of madcap rescue he would try. The opportunity to leave her cell was not one to be missed, so she decided to run with it and ask questions later. 'Quick, get this off him. We need to buy some time. You'll have to bluff. Remember what Devarusso taught you.'

Together, the three raced to strip the servant of his brown robe. The loose-fitting nature of the garment worked in their favour and in just a few seconds, Reynik was throwing it over his head, whilst Calvyn and Femke lugged the dead body into the cell.

Femke was about to close the door behind her when she witnessed an unfortunate side effect of the glamour that Calvyn had cast. As Reynik was settling the garment around him, it was melting into the illusion, leaving him looking exactly as he had before, with no sign of the brown robe.

'Magician! Quick! The illusion,' she hissed, catching Calvyn by the arm and dragging him into a position to see Reynik.

Calvyn's brows drew together in a frown of concentration and he began muttering a spell. It seemed to go on and on, but there was no sign of any change in Reynik's appearance. Silently, Femke gestured at the door and without pausing in his strange muttering, Calvyn nodded for her to close it.

Reynik sat down slowly in the chair. He took a knife in

each hand and crossed his arms. By touch he inserted each hand and knife up the sleeve of the opposing arm. With his arms positioned over his chest in an effort to cover up the bloodstains he knew to be there, he waited. He could feel the hood over his head, but his clothes remained unchanged and the knives in his hands were all too visible.

The voices had stopped talking, but the sound of a single set of booted feet was approaching. Reynik knew he would have to be fast if it was one of the assassins. The invisible restriction of having his hands inside the sleeves of the servant's robe would not help. It was very tempting to pull them loose, but he resisted the urge, leaving it as late as he dared before committing to a fight. As the handle of the door turned, the air around Reynik shimmered. His proportions shrank back to normal size and the brown robe became visible. The glamour had been dispelled without a second to spare. He got to his feet and bowed low in the fashion of the servants as the Guildmaster entered.

'Is everything all right?' Ferdand asked him. 'Have you seen anything unusual here in the last few minutes?'

'Everything is fine, Guildmaster. Why? I heard the alarm. The loss of a Brother always makes for a bad day.' Reynik spoke deliberately, lowering the pitch of his voice slightly to add to his disguise.

'It appears Brother Wolf Spider has returned to the Guild complex. He managed to kill Brother Firedrake on his way in. I'll get more people down here to help you protect the prisoner as soon as I can. In the meantime, stay alert and keep a weapon to hand.'

'Yes, Guildmaster. I'll do my best.'

The figure in black turned to leave, but then paused and looked at Reynik again as if to say something else. Under the brown robes, Reynik could feel the pricking of the wolf spider talisman on his chest. He tensed further, preparing to leap into action, but to his relief the Guildmaster shook his head slightly and went out through the door.

Reynik listened to the retreating footsteps for a few moments to make sure the Guildmaster was really going. Satisfied, he got up and silently opened the door behind him. Femke came out as if catapulted. She gave him a brief hug.

'I heard,' she said simply. 'We don't have long. Your magician friend . . .'

'Calvyn.'

'Calvyn,' she repeated, nodding. 'Glamour or no glamour – he doesn't look well. Something here is affecting him. I think he's likely to be more of a hindrance than help in getting out of here.'

'We can't leave him,' Reynik said firmly. 'I'd never have found you without his aid.'

'I wasn't suggesting that we should. It'll just make a difficult situation worse, I meant. We'll have to help him along if we're to move at any speed, though what we'll do if we're attacked, I don't know.'

'You'll let me fend for myself,' Calvyn interrupted, appearing in the doorway with his sword already drawn. He leaned against the doorframe, his brutish face pale, but his eyes glittering with defiance. 'Let's go. Unless you know another way out of here, then we'd better get back to the transfer stone before they put a wall of assassins in our path. I won't use magic again except as a last resort. The magician who protected this place did a work of powerful magic that I don't understand. The effects are disorienting and draining. The longer I'm here, the worse it'll get. I must get out of here quickly.'

'You'll get no arguments on that score,' Femke said. She moved to Calvyn's left to offer her shoulder as a support, whilst Reynik moved to support Calvyn on his right. Reynik passed Femke one of his knives, replaced the second in his underarm holster and drew his sword. As quickly as they could, they crossed the room, exited the door and hobbled along the corridor. Intertwined as they were, they were neither speedy nor silent, but the distance to the central chamber was not great.

Femke took a moment to check the main chamber before opening the door fully. It appeared empty, but she knew it would not remain so for long. They stumbled in a tangled gaggle through the alcove, out of the gate and into the central area of the chamber. All thoughts of stealth had been abandoned now. Speed was the key. Once out in the unrestricted space of the main chamber, they picked up the pace.

'It's him! And he has the girl! STOP HIM!'

Digging into his deepest reserves, Calvyn somehow found more strength. He shook off the arms of the other two, gasping, 'Go! Go!' and ran headlong for the wolf spider alcove. All three reached it together, scrambling over the gate in a jumble of arms and legs. Femke fell, cursing as she went down. A knife glanced off the wall, showering sparks above where she had fallen. Reynik grabbed her wrist and hauled Femke to her feet even as Calvyn opened the door into the passageway beyond.

They slammed the door shut behind them and Calvyn stared at it for a moment, muttering something under his breath. He staggered as he stopped speaking. Sweat poured down his forehead.

Reynik gave him a quizzical look. 'I thought you said you weren't going to do any more magic.'

'It was only a simple spell,' Calvyn replied, pain lining his illusory features. 'It'll delay any pursuit for a few seconds.'

Something banged against the shut door, but it did not open. Reynik had no idea what Calvyn had done, for there was no lock on the door, but whatever spell he had cast appeared to be working. The new door at the other end of the corridor was shut. They gathered outside, breathing hard. On Reynik's signal they threw it open and charged.

Femke was first into the room. Shantella had a knife in the air almost before the door had swung fully open. As fast as Femke was, she was not fast enough to avoid the thrown blade. It slammed into her shoulder and she recoiled, crying out with pain and colliding with Reynik, who was right behind her.

Shantella threw a second blade, but Reynik anticipated her throw and avoided the blade with ease. Seeing she was outnumbered by three to one, Shantella darted through the back door into the bedroom area and slammed the door shut behind her. Reynik was content to let her hide. All he wanted was to get Femke and Calvyn out of the complex.

'Quickly!' he urged. He dragged Femke, still reeling with

shock at the knife buried in her shoulder, across to the transfer stone. He drew out the wolf spider icon. 'Come on, come on!' They transferred, all three touching the icon. It was only as he touched the icon to the transfer stone that Reynik thought to wonder if there was a limit to the number of people that the icon would transfer at any one time. As the universe stopped spinning and the sparkling stars receded, he was pleased to see that all three of them had made it.

'Holy Shand alive! Where did you lot spring from?'

Reynik groaned. The patrol that had followed him and Calvyn into the alley was still there. Of the three of them, he was the only one in any state to run. They were out of options. They would just have to surrender to the Legionnaires and live with the consequences.

'File leader! Over here – there's three of them.' The Legionnaire backed away slowly until more of the soldiers came running at his call. Reynik sheathed his sword, motioning for Calvyn to do the same. Femke had sunk to her knees with her right hand clasped to where the knife was sticking out of her left shoulder. Reynik knelt down beside her and turned her face gently to look at him. Tears were rolling down her cheeks. He did not know what to say. The knife had driven deep into her flesh. He did not dare to remove it without a medic on hand to clean and dress the wound properly.

'Everything's going to be all right, Femke,' he whispered softly. 'We'll be fine now. Trust me. I'll get us out of this.' He had no idea how he was going to fulfil his promise, but it seemed like the right thing to say.

'Drop your weapons and walk out of the alleyway – slowly,' the File Leader ordered. He was holding a torch in one hand and a short sword in the other. 'Don't make any sudden moves. I don't want any unnecessary nastiness.'

Reynik did as he was told, unclasping his sword belt and dropping it carefully in front of him. One by one he removed his remaining knives and dropped them next to the sword.

Calvyn dropped his belt knife, but instead of dropping his sword he placed the sheathed blade across his open palms in a non-threatening fashion and slowly took a pace forward. 'My sword is valuable,' he said calmly. 'I'd rather not drop it. Would one of your men look after it for me? I'm sure you'll return it to me when you feel it appropriate.'

'Valuable, is it?' the File Leader replied suspiciously. 'Very well. Tam, take his sword.'

One of the Legionnaires stepped forward, his stance cautious and his eyes darting back and forth between the three strangers. He took the sword from Calvyn, who remained totally still whilst he did so. A curious expression crossed the soldier's face as he lifted the sword from the magician's hands. Calvyn stepped back, saying nothing.

'And the girl?' the File Leader asked. 'Does she have any weapons?'

'Only the one stuck in her shoulder,' Reynik answered. 'You have nothing to fear from her. Listen, File Leader, I know I'm in no position to ask favours, but my friend here is badly in need of a medic. An assassin threw this blade. It may be poisoned. We need to get away from here fast. The Guild of Assassins is pursuing us. If we linger, they'll catch us. Neither you nor I want that.'

'The Guild?' The File Leader's face flickered between disbelief and fear. 'What would the Guild want with you?'

'A good question – but not one that I'm willing to answer here. Help us get away – preferably to somewhere that my friend can get medical attention – and I'll answer such questions.'

Reynik got back to his feet and gently helped Femke back upright. Calvyn helped support her on the other side. He was looking better by the second. Clearly being out of the influence of whatever magic had been worked in the Guild chambers was already having a restoring effect. Slowly stepping forwards, the three walked as directed out of the alleyway and onto the street. Inside, Reynik's heart was pumping fast. How long did they have before the place was swarming with assassins? Not long. If they were caught here, being surrounded by soldiers would not offer them much protection.

The File Leader did not look convinced, but he was wise enough not to take chances. Marshalling his men into a protective guard formation, he led them off at a fast pace towards the nearest command post.

CHAPTER ELEVEN

'The votes have been counted and the results confirmed. My Lords, I am pleased to announce that we have a new Emperor Designate. By a clear margin, the Imperial Court has decided that the next bearer of the Mantle of Shandar will be . . . Emperor Tremarle.'

Tremarle's knees nearly gave way as the full impact of the statement struck home. It seemed all but impossible that just a few short weeks ago he had thought the House of Tremarle to be dying. Now his name was to be elevated to the highest tier of all and he had his newly-adopted son to thank for that honour. He would never have believed his popularity amongst the other Lords was great enough for him to succeed in this race, yet the cheering, clapping throng before him should be enough to quash any final doubts.

Borchman was shaking his hand vigorously and the other remaining candidates were patting his back and shoulders in congratulation. The Imperial Court was alive with noise, but Tremarle could hear none of it. He was alone with his thoughts. Imperial politics had never been simple. He knew that he had not won through popularity alone. There had been a lot of dark undercurrents in this competition, not least of which had been the death of Marnillus. As he had not ordered the Lord's death, his victory felt wholesome and untainted by dark deeds. In his heart, however, he could not help but ponder what others had done in his name.

Shalidar, as his son and heir, had a place in the front row of the Court room today. For a moment, Tremarle met the man's dark eyes and his chest constricted with the cold breath of fear. Shalidar was smiling, but the expression did little to light up his face. For a moment it was as if someone had removed a veil from his sight and Tremarle glimpsed beyond the public façade. Beneath it a dark cloud of machination boiled and seethed, filled with dark motives, cunning and unscrupulous acts. The vision left a sour, oily taste in his mouth. All thoughts of a pure victory through fair competition vanished in that instant. The truth was there, glittering in Shalidar's eyes. The throne and the Mantle were his, but who had actually won the victory, and how, was a mystery that Tremarle did not think he would ever dare to unravel.

He was ushered forwards to give a speech. He had one prepared, of course, but for a moment the words escaped him and he just looked back and forth across the crowd of smiling, enthusiastic faces. He felt a fraud, but he knew he had come too far to back down. By fair means or foul, he had won this responsibility. It was what he did with it that people would remember him by.

Tremarle had never been an instinctive speaker. Despite his misgivings and inner desire to speak out about his sudden insight into the corruption within the election process, he began to recite the carefully-crafted words graciously accepting the role that the Court had placed upon him. All the excitement and applause died away to allow him his chance to speak. The speech was not long, but he had worked hard on it. After the initial thanks and acceptance he moved on to a more pointed theme.

'From the outset, I want it understood that my time as Emperor will be spent upholding the traditions and values that have been handed down to us by our forebears. Shandar has a rich history. It is this history that has shaped not just the Empire, but also the way in which all those who abide within it live their lives. All my life I have striven to honour the traditions and values of Shandar. If it is within my power, then the recent erosion of those traditions and values will stop. I shall be looking to you all for help during this time of restoration.'

He paused and there was much nodding and a mixture of gentle and enthusiastic clapping.

'As a first step towards restoration of order and tradition, I wish to state my intent to end the strife between the Imperial House and the Guild of Assassins. For centuries the Guild has been an accepted, if feared, part of the Shandese society. The recent feud instigated by my predecessor resulted in lamentable bloodshed. Many innocent people have lost their lives. It is time for the killing to stop. Although not within my powers as Emperor Designate, I want it known that my first action as Emperor will be to revoke the *anaethus drax* order on the Guild . . .'

Tremarle instinctively looked down at Shalidar. He did not let his eyes linger. The satisfaction he saw in the assassin's face was chilling. He wondered how long his adopted son would wait before he looked to take the Mantle for his own. It was an obvious step. He should have seen it from the beginning, but knowing that this was an inevitable end game gave Tremarle a slight edge. Conceding to Shalidar's wishes was likely to prolong the period before confrontation. This would give the old Lord a chance to marshal his resources. If Shalidar thought Tremarle was a puppet who would just step aside when he was ready to assume power, then it was the assassin who was poised for a shock.

Even as the old Lord finished off his speech to a thundering roll of applause, he felt himself harden inside. It felt as if he had made a deal with a prince of demons. The sourness of that act tainted his soul, but he knew the situation was not yet beyond redemption. This newfound power was his to wield, not Shalidar's. There was still a chance he could bring genuine honour to his family name.

Toomas rubbed his hands together and regarded the pile of gold on the table with greedy eyes. The figure in black stepped back and sneered at the tattle tout from beneath his hood. 'It's all yours if your information is as critical to the Guild's future as your message indicated.'

'Oh, it is! It is!' Toomas said enthusiastically. 'I've heard rumour that your Guildmaster has been controlling the outcome of the contest for the Mantle.'

'And if he has?'

'If he has, then he's been wasting the Guild's money,' Toomas replied with a sly chuckle. 'None of the candidates could hold the Mantle for long.'

'Really? And why, pray, is that?'

'Because Lord Kempten is not dead,' Toomas said, his eyes dancing as he savoured the words he had held back for so long.

'What! You're sure of this? Where is he?'

'I cannot vouch for where Lord Kempten is at any particular moment in time, but he has been in hiding with his family out in his country home. His assassination was a hoax designed to set you all looking for the killer. Surabar sought to infiltrate the Guild with his own man, though from what my eyes and ears tell me, you've already discovered the traitor. Tell me, have you caught him yet?'

The figure in black was silent for a moment as he considered the sly question.

'Do you have news of his whereabouts too?' the assassin asked gruffly.

Toomas grinned at the response. He had been right all along. What was more, his deductions had just gained him his next project. 'No,' he admitted, 'not yet, but you can be sure that you'll be quick to hear if I do.'

'The Guild would be most generous if you were to lead us to him.'

'I felt sure it would.'

The man in black left silently. Toomas did not rise to see

him out. The man was no threat at the moment. He wanted more information. Whilst that held true, Toomas knew he was safe.

The deal was done. He had waited and waited for the young woman to return, but she had not come back. The Lords vying for the Mantle had been jumping through the political hoops for a week or more. The final vote was today. If he had waited longer, he might have lost the market for his information. As it was, he had been forced to be creative with his sale, which had not been without considerable risk.

To Toomas's anguish, the richest Lord, Marnillus, had been removed early in the competition. Had he sold to Marnillus just before he was killed, the tattle tout knew he could have commanded an equally high price when he sold the information a second time. The loss of such a large potential income hurt him like a physical wound. Gold was his life. He cared about nothing else except his own skin.

It was the value he placed on his own life that had made him think twice about dealing with the Guild. However, his eyes and ears around Shandrim had brought him hints that the Guild was interfering with the race for the Mantle. That they had a vested interest in the outcome was not in question. What was debatable was how far they would go in order to get the Emperor of their choice on the throne.

The Guild had always been known for its neutrality in matters of state. They killed for all sides within the bounds of their creed. An Imperial succession with no clear qualification by blood had not occurred for many generations. The Guild would not be pleased to discover their attempts at controlling the outcome were in vain. As long as Lord Kempten was alive, he was the legal Emperor. Even in death it appeared Surabar was determined to have the last laugh at the Guild's expense.

'At the Guild's expense . . .' thought Toomas, carefully stacking the gold sen into piles on the table in front of him. 'I like that phrase. The Guild is dangerous, but it has deep pockets. With this sort of money up for grabs, the Imperial spy who infiltrated their number had better be good at running, because I'm going to put so many watchers out looking for him that he'll not be able to stick the tip of his nose above ground without my knowing it.'

Ferdand was furious. 'Firedrake dead, Wolf Spider escaped with the prisoner, and now this! How in Shand's name did the fact that Lord Kempten has surfaced alive and well at his country home escape the notice of our intelligence network?'

'I don't know, Guildmaster,' Viper replied. 'This tattle tout, Toomas, had a watcher within Kempten's staff. With Lord Kempten apparently dead, it appears that when Lady Kempten moved out to the country, the network no longer deemed it necessary to watch her household.'

'Let's be thankful that someone "deemed it necessary", shall we? It was expensive information, but timely, Brother Viper. Thank you.'

'I think you should also be aware that the tout knew about Wolf Spider being an infiltrator as well. He asked whether we'd caught him yet.'

'Good grief! Are the Guild's private affairs now open

knowledge?' the Guildmaster spluttered. 'I trust you have told him we'll buy any information that will lead to Wolf Spider's capture?'

Viper nodded.

'Good! Let's hope he proves more efficient than our network. In the meantime I have a task for you. Go to the Kempten country house. The creed says nothing about Emperor Designates. Kill him. If Kempten is not there, find his wife and bring her here – alive. She will be my lever on him if all else fails. I hardly need tell you there would be a big difference to the Guild between putting the Mantle on Tremarle's shoulders and having Kempten come back and take it.'

'Consider it done, Guildmaster,' Viper replied. 'But before I go there is another message that I've been asked to relay. One of our agents contacted me today. He said to tell you that Lord Tremarle has recently adopted a son in order to maintain his family line. His new heir is a man named Shalidar. He seemed to hold some significance to the information.'

The Guildmaster did not answer. He was too stunned. After a few moments he nodded and waved the assassin's dismissal, glad that Viper could not see his face. He waited until the assassin had exited his alcove before he began his muttered string of expletives. When he had finished swearing he fell silent for a moment as he reorganised his thoughts.

'Shalidar! I wish I'd killed him when I had the chance. He set this whole scenario up right under my nose!' he growled softly. 'I should have killed him. He's been a danger to the

Guild from the start, but this . . . this . . .' Ferdand could not finish the sentence.

He turned and crossed the chamber to the steps leading down to his quarters. His eyes were drawn to the dragon emblem as he walked. The dragon on the shield smirked at him, its golden eyes seemingly amused by his dilemma. Ferdand ground his teeth with anger. How he hated that icon.

It was tempting to go and confront Shalidar straight away, but he was wise enough to hold back. He would need to think carefully before taking that step. There had never been any taboos on one's position or trade outside of the Guild, but Shalidar was knowingly creating a set of circumstances never encountered before within the Guild's history. He was on the verge of setting up a paradox within the creed.

If Shalidar were to become the Emperor, or arguably even sole heir to the Mantle, then he would be protected by the creed. Once a dynasty was established, the accepted interpretation of the creed had always been that the Emperor's immediate descendents were also sacrosanct. The fact that he was not a blood son but an adopted son was unlikely to change that interpretation. This in turn meant he could break any one of the other tenets with impunity. The only punishment specified by the creed was death, but the Guild could not kill the Emperor or his immediate descendents. Shalidar had always been a maverick. How could the Guild ever hope to keep him in line once he enjoyed such immunity?

'As if I didn't have enough problems,' Ferdand muttered,

frowning at the dragon icon from under his hood. 'Trust *you* to bring me more.'

'I think the Guildmaster is losing control,' Shantella said softly.

Bear's eyes narrowed as he looked across his quarters at the hooded figure of the woman. He had a lot of respect for her as a killer. The Fox was a canny assassin, but there were times when he felt her to be too clever for her own good.

'And if he is?' he asked. 'What are you suggesting?'

'I'm not suggesting anything . . . yet,' Shantella replied, keeping a matter-of-fact tone and a casual stance. 'It's merely an observation. Listen. We've lost a quarter of our number during the last few months. The only new Brother we've recruited to fill those places was an infiltrator – the first successful one in many decades. We've resorted to holding a prisoner within the Guild headquarters, something else that has not been done in living memory. This was also a disaster, as she was rescued from the very heart of our complex despite the urging of some Brothers that she be terminated. I'd say the Guildmaster's grasp of our organisation is tenuous at best. I think we might have to start considering the possibility that his tenure as our leader could be drawing to a close, that's all.'

'Treachery, Fox? You sneak into my quarters to talk treachery! What if the Guildmaster were to come in now and find you here? Whatever else you may say about him, he's no fool. He would see straight through you.'

Shantella laughed. 'I doubt that. The Guildmaster would believe I had come here for a more base purpose. He perceives me as an insatiable seductress who enjoys taking risks. It's an appearance I've worked hard to cultivate in his presence. If I were found in the quarters of any of the other assassins, it's unlikely he would do more than give me a mild reprimand.'

'I'm not sure I want to listen to any more of this. You had better leave.'

Fox got to her feet and strutted across to the exit doorway. Bear could almost see her flaunting the splendid brush of her namesake as her hips swung beneath the black garb. She stopped for a moment, her slender fingers caressing the doorframe. Beneath her hood she smiled.

'Don't get me wrong, Brother. I don't want to take down the Guildmaster. I like him. Despite his failings, I'll not deny he's been a good leader. My problem is that I find myself asking if he is the *right* leader for what's ahead. Shandrim is changing, Brother. We will need to adapt if we're to survive. The Guildmaster is old. To give him his due, he is trying to develop new strategies to meet the new needs. In my view, however, I find it unlikely he will adapt fast enough. Ponder on it. I'll drop by again sometime.'

She was gone. Bear breathed out in a long sigh. The realisation that he had been unconsciously holding his breath made him realise anew what an effect the Fox had on men. What should he do now? Should he side with the Guildmaster and tell him the Fox was up to her tricks? He doubted he was the only Brother she had approached this way. Where would her scheming lead? Was she right? Was it time for a new leader? A lot of things had gone wrong for the Guild recently. Could things have been handled better?

'Damn you, Fox! Why couldn't you just let things lie?' he muttered.

Jabal squinted as he entered the library from the bright sunlight. Although the library was well served by large, high windows, there was a freshness and sparkle to the open air that was lacking in the great book-lined hall. The magician took an instinctive deep breath before stepping across the threshold.

As he entered through the double doors the library appeared a picture of serenity and order. The dust-filled, peaceful atmosphere of studiousness within its walls made it hard to picture the mess that Reynik had described resulting from his encounter with the two assassins just a few days earlier. There was no sign of it now. Equally, there was no sign of the young woman librarian he had described. A grim-faced old man sat at the librarian's desk, lost in a book. It seemed she had taken Reynik's advice.

The bookcase that Reynik had pulled over was back in place. Jabal meandered across to it as if looking around at random. When he reached it, the only hints of the recent action were the impact dents in the table-edge from the wooden uprights. All the books had been replaced. At least it looked that way at first glance.

'Can I help you?'

Jabal was momentarily startled. He had not heard the librarian move. This was unusual, as his hearing had always been keener than most. If the librarian could sneak up on him so easily, had he been overstating his confidence at being able to protect himself from assassins? He shook off the thought.

'No, I'm just browsing, thanks,' he replied casually.

'Very well. I'll be at my desk if you need me.' The old man's eyes narrowed for a moment, darting around Jabal's features as if constructing a detailed mental map of him.

'Am I being paranoid?' Jabal wondered, as the old librarian turned and re-crossed the library floor to his desk. The old man was wearing slippers, which would go some way to accounting for his silent movement, though the magician did note that the librarian's gait was not typical of an old man. Where most would shuffle, this man lifted and placed his feet with care.

It crossed Jabal's mind that he should probe the man with magic to ensure he was what he seemed, but he decided that to do so would be more likely to compromise his own disguise than to reveal anything useful. He turned his attention back to the bookcase. Taking care not to be too obvious, he scanned through the various categories until he found the area that dealt with the Imperial Palace. Sliding his eyes across the titles, he failed to pick out the two books Reynik had described.

Selecting a book from the shelf above, Jabal took it and walked around the nearest table to a spot where a shaft of light from one of the high windows would make reading his chosen text easy. It also had the advantage of placing him with his back to the librarian, and facing the shelf where the two books he was looking for should be situated. He sat down and opened his chosen book. For the next two minutes, he looked through the book with genuine interest.

Books had always fascinated him, and this one was no exception.

After what he deemed to be a suitable time, he looked up and scanned the shelf in a determined effort to locate the texts he was looking for. It did not take long for him to realise that they were no longer there.

Strange, he thought, scratching at one eyebrow as he considered the implications of this development. The Guild are clearly aware of the two books. From the description Reynik gave, the books had likely been in the library for centuries. The Guild had the books especially tagged such that they would know when people read them. Why would they choose to remove the books now, after all this time? Surely it had not taken this long for them to realise the danger of the information they contained? No. They must have known what was in the books, or they would not have tagged them in the first place.

To ask about the two books would be both obvious and dangerous. Whatever the reason for their removal, it appeared the library was now a dead end. Jabal remained a little while longer, browsing through his book before replacing it and leaving the library. He nodded at the librarian, giving him a friendly smile as he left. The sour old man's mouth did not so much as twitch in response.

'What happy circumstance it must be to enjoy such job satisfaction,' Jabal muttered under his breath as he re-emerged into the sunlight.

CHAPTER TWELVE

It took a moment for the words to take on meaning. Shalidar felt them settle in his belly like lead, heavy and poisonous. This was supposed to be his moment of triumph. If he had believed in such things, it would have been easy to feel that some higher power was toying with him – dangling sweetmeats under his nose and then whipping them away as soon as he made to bite.

'Where did this information come from, Guildmaster? Is the source reliable?' he asked, his voice like ice.

'It came from a tattle tout who knows better than to feed anything other than reliable information to the Guild.'

'I see. Does the Emperor Designate know?'

'I assume by that you mean *Lord* Tremarle,' Ferdand replied, enjoying the emphasis. 'I don't know, but I suspect the tattle tout will waste no time in selling him the information as well. From what I know of this tout, he is very adept at making the most out of such snippets.'

Shalidar began to feel sick. After all the risks he had taken it was hard to believe he had done it all for nothing. 'Kempten alive,' he thought. 'This is the doing of Femke and Wolf Spider. It has to be. Surabar was devious, but this feels more like Femke's work. If only you had listened to us and killed Femke when you had the chance, we could all have been spared from her meddling for good. Well, I'll not let her interfere any longer. Damn the consequences. The spy must die, and Wolf Spider with her.'

His chances for power were dissipating like the morning mist. Suddenly, warning bells began to ring in his head. 'Why are you telling me this now?' he asked, eyeing the Guildmaster suspiciously. 'It's important information – information that all Members of the Guild have a vested interest in. Surely this is worthy of calling a meeting, unless . . .'

He could feel the Guildmaster watching him from under his hood. The old man's eyes were watching his reactions with hawklike intensity. He knew. How much he knew remained to be seen. He met the Guildmaster's gaze with a look of defiance. There was no point in denying the basic facts.

'When were you going to tell me about your relationship with Tremarle, Brother Dragon?'

'I saw no reason to. I declared that I had an interest in seeing Lord Tremarle come to power. If I had announced to the Guild that I was his adopted son, then my anonymity would have been destroyed. That would have been against Guild policy.'

'I wasn't talking about announcing it to the Guild. You

216

know full well that I should have been informed of your adoption.'

'Why?' Shalidar challenged. 'At the time I was adopted, Lord Tremarle was just another nobleman. Are you telling me that none of the other members of our Guild are of noble blood? His bid for the Mantle came later.'

'At your bidding?'

'I'll not deny that I encouraged his ambition. In my position, who wouldn't?'

'Shand's teeth, Shalidar!' Ferdand exploded, his eyes alight with anger. 'You seem to delight in placing me in impossible situations! What exactly do you think I should do now? The true Emperor Designate is out there in hiding, no doubt planning to claim the Mantle when he is ready. He was Surabar's man through and through. You can bet your last copper sennut that when he returns, he will look to see the Guild destroyed. However, if I order him killed, I place you in direct line to the Mantle. Do that and I create a paradox.'

'A paradox, Guildmaster? How so?' he asked, his tone almost taunting.

'Don't toy with me, Shalidar. You know full well that as heir to the Mantle, you would be protected by the creed, yet as a Member of the Guild you should be bound by it. The two are mutually exclusive. It would place me in the impossible situation of having a Brother who could break the creed at will, with no fear of facing the consequences. I cannot allow that to happen.'

Shalidar shrugged, his eyes wary, waiting to see just how much more the Guildmaster knew. Had the old man seen through all his machinations? Had he discovered why Tremarle had adopted him? He paused for what seemed like an eternity, but the Guildmaster added nothing further. As the silence extended, his confidence began to return and he decided to take the initiative.

'So what are you going to do? Kill me now, while I have no status? What is my crime? Failing to tell you of a change in personal circumstance? I hardly think that warrants a death sentence. I have not broken the creed. I imagine you would experience considerable resistance from the Brothers to an execution of one of their number without good cause.'

The Guildmaster placed his hands together in front of his body and interlocked his fingers so tightly that they turned an ugly mixture of purple and white. Shalidar watched with wary fascination.

In truth, the application of the creed was not something he had fully considered during his manipulation of Tremarle. To his secret amusement he realised it was a measure of his disregard for the creed that he had neglected to think through the interplay of Guild rules with his change of status. The Lord was old. Shalidar had intended to wait for him to pass on naturally before taking the Mantle. The old man was as soft clay in Shalidar's hands. Tremarle would have ruled in name only.

Putting the complication of Lord Kempten aside for a moment, it had not occurred to him until now that once Tremarle had been crowned, Shalidar could have killed him and seized the Mantle for himself without fear of reprisal from the Guild. To think he had come so close to being untouchable!

'I've deferred the decision for now,' Ferdand said, his voice grim. 'But don't think I've dismissed the idea of having you killed. I want you to give thought to renouncing your adoption. Having a Brother in line to the Mantle, let alone wearing it, is inconceivable. I'll not allow it during my leadership.'

'Then you'd better start counting your days as Guild-master,' Shalidar thought, his cold anger warming swiftly to a fiery heat. 'With policies like that I'll use whatever means available to ensure you don't lead the Guild much longer.'

'Father?'

For a moment Reynik was stunned. Then a warm rush of joy flushed through him and he ran forward, wrapping his arms around Commander Lutalo in a tight embrace. It was hard to believe. The impossible dream had just come true. Tears of joy ran down his face in streams as he fought for control of his emotions. It did not seem a very manly reaction, but right now he had no cares for what anyone else thought of him. He was so ecstatic to find his father alive that he felt like dancing and singing at the top of his voice. Lutalo returned the hug, clearly thrilled to see him.

'It's good to see you, son. I've been worried about you,' Lutalo said with no sign of embarrassment.

'But how is this possible? I was convinced you were dead,' Reynik replied, dashing the tears from his cheeks. 'Shalidar told me he had killed you. Oh, father, I can't tell

you how wonderful it is to see you alive and well. But wait
. . . if you're alive, then who did Shalidar . . .'

'The assassin killed Sidis,' Lutalo said, his voice sad at
the reminder of the incident. 'I was just briefing him on
new security arrangements when the tip of a blade burst
through his chest. The assassin struck through the canvas
wall of the tent. I was livid, but grateful that he didn't
stop to confirm his kill. I'm a fair swordsman, but I'd not
have liked to face a Guild assassin without a few men to
back me up. It was a tragedy. Sidis may not have been the
best of File Leaders, but he did not deserve to die like that.'

For a moment, Reynik felt secretly pleased that Sidis
had died in place of his father. Sidis had been narrow-
minded, vindictive and petty, but his father was right –
none of those failings made him worthy of such a death.
Shalidar had murdered him without ever seeing his face
– an uncharacteristic mistake on Shalidar's part.

In his surprise and joy, he had momentarily forgotten
the urgency and danger of their situation. In a rush it
all came flooding back. Cold icicles of fear stabbed at
his heart, cutting through the warmth of his unexpected
reunion with the harsh revelation that all could yet be lost.
The realisation struck him like a physical blow.

'Father, we need your help,' he said in a rush. 'We're all
in terrible danger. We don't have long. The Guild could
attack at any moment. I doubt we were fast enough to get
here without picking up a tail somewhere along the way.
Femke needs medical attention, and Calvyn . . .'

'I'm fine,' Calvyn interrupted. 'It took a while to
shake off the effects of that chamber, but I'm almost fully

recovered now. Sir, if you can spare us some space in a quiet room, then I'll tend Femke. I have some skill with healing wounds. I should be able to throw the pursuers off our trail with a few illusions as well.'

'Illusions?' Lutalo asked.

'Calvyn is a magician, father. He's come with his master to help us defeat the Guild and restore order to Shandrim.'

Commander Lutalo regarded Calvyn closely, seeing only the rough, villainous features of his glamour image. Calvyn concentrated for a moment and dispersed the illusion. Lutalo's eyes widened with amazement. He rubbed at them and blinked several times as the thug transformed into fair-haired young man with something of a military air about him. The Commander did not know what to think. The young man's appearance still seemed at odds with his profession as a magician.

'Impressive,' he admitted. 'But which one is the real you?'

'This is,' Calvyn replied with a friendly grin. 'I was using the other persona as a deterrent. The illusion was designed to keep the criminal element of the city from messing with us. It worked, too.'

'I'm not surprised,' the Commander said, giving a nod of acknowledgement. 'I doubt there would be many who would tangle with you in your other guise. All right, how much space will you need?'

'You!' Femke gasped as she suddenly noticed Calvyn's real appearance. She staggered away from him and fell to the floor as she abandoned his support. She stared up at him as if she had seen a ghost and continued to scrabble away, as if consumed by fear. 'Shanier! What are you doing here?'

'Helping you, it seems,' Calvyn replied calmly. 'Yes, I remember you from Mantor. *Ambassador* Femke, wasn't it? At least that was how you were announced. I thought at the time there was more to you than met the eye, but I could see you had no ill intent towards the King of Thrandor, so I left you to your devices.'

'Why are you helping me? You led thousands of Shandese Legionnaires to their deaths. It was on your account I was sent to Thrandor to foster peace between our countries. What is your purpose here?'

'Is this true? Are you Lord Shanier?' Commander Lutalo asked sharply, his hand automatically going to his sword hilt. Reynik, too, looked at him with suspicion.

Calvyn sighed. 'Yes and no. Yes, in body I was Shanier, the cold-blooded sorcerer. However, I was a soulless puppet of Vallaine when I was given that name. I think it's fair to say that I was not my true self for much of the time I held it.'

'Why should we believe you?' Femke snapped. 'You betrayed the Legions.'

'True, but you have to see it from my perspective, Femke. I'm Thrandorian, not Shandese. They believed I had betrayed them because I was leading the Shandese Legions. By deliberately leading the Legions away from Mantor and into battle with our enemies, the Terachites, I saved my home country from conquest by your troops. Does this make me a traitor? You're a spy, or at least you were. I don't know what your status is now, but given the same opportunity to save Shandar, what would you have done?'

'I . . . I don't know.'

'I think you do,' Calvyn continued. 'However, let's put that aside for now. I bear you no ill will. I'm presently studying here in Shandar. Whilst my allegiance will always be to Thrandor, I can see your Empire needs a stable, rational leader if Thrandor is to remain unthreatened. I'll do everything in my power to help you and your friends achieve this.'

Femke nodded, wincing as pain spiked again with the slight movement.

'Your shoulder needs treatment. Let me heal it and you'll be able to think more clearly.' Calvyn turned back to Commander Lutalo, noting that his hand was still resting on his sword hilt. I won't need much space, sir. Enough to lay Femke down and treat her. I'll do the rest.'

Lutalo paused for a moment, unsure of what to do. Calvyn's steady gaze remained unthreatening. Finally the Commander nodded. With brief, precise directions, he issued orders to the soldiers who had escorted them in. The men reacted swiftly, dispersing into defensive positions and preparing for a possible assault. Two of the men were sent out to fetch reinforcements. The final soldier paused before leaving. It was the Legionnaire who had taken custody of Calvyn's sword.

'Before I go, you'll be wanting this back, sir.' He handed over the sheathed blade. 'It's strange. I've been desperate to give you this back ever since I first touched it. Did you place a spell on me?'

Calvyn smiled. 'I said it was a special sword. One of its qualities is that it knows its owner. I didn't work any magic on you. What you were feeling was the desire of the blade to return to me.'

The Legionnaire did not look convinced, but he nodded and left.

'Come. Bring your injured friend through here. This room will have to suffice. It's not big, but we'll try to keep any from entering.' Lutalo took a torch from a nearby bracket and led them through one of three doors leading out of the guardroom.

Calvyn and Reynik supported Femke as they moved through the doorway into a square box of a room. There was only one small window on the wall to the left of the door. The walls were whitewashed stone and the flooring was of uneven wooden boards, untreated and bare. The only furniture was a single trellis table and two stools. There was no fireplace and the air in the room felt cold and damp.

'We use it as a cell for those caught out after curfew,' Lutalo explained. 'It's neither big, nor comfortable, but it's the best I can offer.'

'This will be fine, Commander,' Calvyn replied. 'We won't stay long. As soon as I can, I shall cloak the three of us within another illusion and we'll move on to safer lodgings.'

Calvyn and Reynik helped Femke through the doorway and over to the side of the room furthest from the window. Reynik took off his cloak and spread it on the floor for Femke to sit on. The front of her tunic was dark with blood and a steady flow still ran down her arm, dripping from her fingers. Her face was a deathly pale white in the dim light of the single torch. That she had said little since the soldiers had captured them was an indication to Reynik of how badly she was hurt. He knew she had a high pain threshold. He had seen her cope with injuries before.

Once Femke was seated, Reynik took the torch from his father and thanked him again.

'It's no trouble, son. I hope your magician friend will be able to help her. She looks to have lost a lot of blood. Are you sure you don't want me to send for a medic?'

'If Calvyn says he can heal her, then I believe him. He's proved a most capable ally so far.'

'Fair enough. How long will it take?'

'Just a few minutes, sir,' Calvyn said, kneeling to examine the wound. 'I don't mean to be rude, but if you would leave us now, I would appreciate quiet in order to concentrate. Reynik, come here, would you? I'd like you to brace Femke while I remove the knife. If you kneel behind her – that's right. Femke, lean back against Reynik . . .'

Lutalo left, closing the door behind him. Calvyn took a quick look around the room and muttered a spell under his breath. A slight shimmer in the air gave Reynik the clue that Calvyn was creating another illusion, but what form it took was unclear, for when Calvyn was finished, the room looked no different. Reynik wanted to ask about it, but Calvyn was already concentrating on the wound again.

'I'm afraid this is going to hurt, Femke,' Calvyn said with a frown. 'I'm going to draw the blade. Are you ready?'

She nodded, teeth gritted against the anticipated increase

in pain. Calvyn placed forefinger and thumb of his left hand on the flesh either side of the blade, and grasped the handle with his right hand. Femke gasped as he wrenched the blade free. A fresh flood of bright red blood flowed over Calvyn's left hand as he initially pinched the flesh together. He checked the blood and blade for any obvious signs of poison, but there was no discolouration. He then checked the wound, probing it first with fingers, then with magic. It appeared clean.

Aside from the initial gasp, Femke remained silent throughout the examination. The only sign she gave of her discomfort was a wince as Calvyn opened the wound in order to look inside. To Reynik's eyes what followed was little short of a miracle.

Calvyn's lips began to move again as he silently mouthed his spell in the strange language of magic. His eyes shut as his concentration became absolute, and Reynik found his own gaze alternating between Calvyn's face and Femke's wound.

At first nothing appeared to be happening, but then the flow of blood from the wound slowed from a steady flow to a trickle, before stopping altogether. Reynik could hardly believe his eyes as the deep, ugly hole in Femke's shoulder slowly closed, knitting itself back together as he watched. As Calvyn finished his spell, Femke gave a sigh and slipped into a deep sleep. Reynik felt her relax against him and he looked in wonder at her totally healed shoulder. There was not so much as the faintest scar to show where the knife had struck.

Reynik opened his mouth to speak when the door to the

little room burst open. His father stumbled in through the doorway, having been pushed hard from behind. A figure dressed in the black garb of the Guild followed him inside and scanned the room from under his dark hood. His eyes passed over the three of them without pause.

'Where are they?' demanded the assassin, his voice hard as granite.

'Gone.'

'That much is evident, Commander. Now tell me something useful. Where have they gone to?'

'I sent them under escort to find a medic,' Lutalo replied, a defiant edge in his voice. 'The girl was hurt. Her wound needed urgent attention.'

'Why did my men not see them leave? Is there another way out of here?'

'No. Look for yourself. Your watchers must have missed them. They left by the way you came in.'

'Unlikely. Are you seeking death, Commander?' The assassin raised his blade towards Lutalo's chest.

Reynik tensed, reaching automatically for a knife, but Calvyn put a hand out in a calming gesture and shook his head. Reluctantly, Reynik lowered his hand and continued to watch in silence. He wondered what sort of illusion Calvyn had spun that had fooled the assassin so completely. The figure in black was only standing a couple of paces away, yet he was totally unaware of them. It was not Shalidar; his build, his stance and his voice were not those of his sworn adversary. This was not one of the Brothers with whom Reynik was familiar.

'Not at all. I do not fear death, yet neither do I invite it.

227

I don't believe you'd kill me without a contract. You see I know something of your Guild. For you to kill me would violate your creed and thus invite death upon yourself. I find it unlikely you would want to do that.'

Lutalo kept his voice calm and reasonable, yet his words were almost taunting. His stance mirrored his conviction. Where the assassin was taut and menacing, the Commander stood tall and relaxed. Confidence oozed from him like an aura. The atmosphere between them was thick with tension.

'Don't overdo it, father. If you push him too hard he might snap,' Reynik thought, his stomach tight with anxiety.

'I could always claim self-defence,' the assassin suggested. 'You're a soldier. People would expect you to pick a fight with me.'

'Are you looking for an excuse to kill me then? Is that the true nature of the Guild? Do you itch to kill any who irritate?' He paused for a moment, his eyes flashing with righteous fire. Then with an apparent change of heart, he continued with a more conciliatory tone. 'To answer your question, I don't know why your men did not see them leave. I'm also not sure which medic post my men will have taken the three curfew-breakers to. I didn't give them specific orders on that detail. The two most likely ones are the main guard post on the Western Avenue, or the one on the south side of the central Civic Square. If you catch up with them, please try not to injure my men. I don't take kindly to folk who do that. If I find that you've hurt anyone under my command, then you can be sure that I'll make it my personal mission to find those responsible and bring them to justice.'

The assassin laughed then, his barking chuckle sharp, like the regular rapping sound of a nail driven home by a carpenter wielding a metal hammer.

'You think to threaten me, soldier! You know that was almost worth coming for tonight. Your kind has never been able to trouble the Guild. Bring your legions into Shandrim if you wish. You will not break us. We're like the wind that slips through your fingers. You'll neither trace us, nor catch us. Go send your troops to catch a moonbeam. Your chances of success will be far higher.'

With a swirl of black material, the assassin was gone. Commander Lutalo remained where he was. Once he was sure the assassin had definitely left, he glanced directly at the three fugitives and raised a quizzical eyebrow before going out through the door.

'What did you do, Calvyn?' Reynik asked in a hoarse whisper. 'What did the assassin see when he entered?'

'I moved the wall so that it was between the assassin and us. It was a simple illusion, but effective. He was expecting a small cell. He saw what he expected to see.'

'You know I'm surprised that the Emperor does not employ magicians within his spy network. With such skills the work of a spy would be easy. Do you not find such power seductive?'

'In what way?'

'Well, you could have anything you wanted,' Reynik replied. 'If you wanted to steal something, you could simply use your powers to open the locks, walk in and take it.'

Calvyn looked thoughtful for a moment.

'Yes, I suppose I could, if I wanted to. There's a sort of unwritten code of conduct amongst the magicians that I've associated with. For the most part they seem to have very high moral standards. Stealing, or using our powers for vast material gain, would be to corrupt the gift we've been given. There are those who would use their powers in this way, but mercifully they're very few.'

'I suppose Lord Vallaine was a good example of one,' Reynik suggested. 'He used his powers to take the Emperor's place.'

'He did?' Calvyn asked, though there was little surprise in his tone. 'I hadn't heard that. Of course, Vallaine wasn't a magician. He was a sorceror – there is a big difference, though it would be difficult for someone untrained in the arcane arts to distinguish. My experience of sorcerors has not been good. Lord Vallaine was possibly the most twisted and corrupt person I've ever known.'

'It's said he wore the Mantle for several months before Femke discovered his secret and exposed him,' Reynik explained.

'Vallaine always was hungry for power,' Calvyn noted. 'What happened to him?'

'Femke poisoned him. She felt it was the only safe way to remove him from the throne.'

Calvyn's face betrayed his surprise as he considered Femke's methods. 'Hmm! I'll bear that in mind if I ever think to cross her. I knew she had a sharp mind, but she's clearly more dangerous than I thought.'

A short while later they woke Femke. Utilising Calvyn's

powers of illusion once more, they took on the guise of Legionnaires, said goodbye to Lutalo, and set out across the city. Reynik found it hard to contain his emotions as they left.

'Please be careful, father. I don't want to lose you again,' he said, more tears threatening as he drew Lutalo into another close embrace.

'You too, son. Keep in touch. If I can be of help, you know you only have to ask.'

Once out from under the watching eyes of the Guild, moving through Shandrim became easy. Femke took the lead, weaving them through the backstreets to one of her less-used safe houses. She had not visited it in over a year, but her agents had seen to its upkeep. There was only one narrow bed, which the two men instantly declined. Femke accepted gracefully. After her recent treatment by the Guild, she was happy to capitalise on their gentlemanly gesture.

The following day Femke was eager to put the location of the Guild beyond all doubt. After a good sleep, she felt fully recovered from her injury. On speaking with Calvyn she was delighted to find he was also able to speed up the healing of the ribs that had troubled her ever since Shalidar had broken them in Mantor some months before. By the time they arrived at the meeting place, Femke felt better than she had in a very long time.

'How much do you two know of accounts?' she asked as they ate a hasty breakfast.

'Don't look at me,' Calvyn replied. 'I know nothing. I grew up on a small farm-holding where most transactions were bartered. After that I was in Baron Keevan's army. I had no reason to learn.'

'My father had me learn the basics,' Reynik admitted. 'He said it may come in useful some day. I hated every second of it.'

'Well, Shand bless Lutalo! I'll be sure to kiss him next time I see him. Before we meet with Kempten I'd like to pay a visit to the Palace to check out a few things. Calvyn, would you mind giving us an illusory makeover? I don't want either of us recognised.'

'Not at all, Femke. What sort of disguise did you have in mind?'

'Could you give us both the appearance of officious auditors? I'd like to give the Head Steward at the Imperial Palace a hard time today and I think an inspection of the Imperial Household accounts, together with a stock check of the cellars in the Palace should give us enough evidence to confirm our suspicions about the location of the Guild headquarters.'

'Are you sure this is necessary, Femke?' Reynik asked. 'Surely the reaction of my visit to the library has all but confirmed it already.'

'You're right, Reynik, but if my suspicions are correct, there will be a physical entrance to the Guild through the Palace cellars somewhere. I'd like to find it before we begin to devise any further plans. Also, through the Steward's accounts we can see if the Guild is vulnerable in other ways. Maybe we could starve them out. There are a lot of people in that underground lair. They must have a regular supply route. It's most likely running through the Palace.

If we could disrupt it sufficiently, the Guild might have no choice but to take direct action. Whatever they do to re-establish a supply route will make them more visible, and therefore more vulnerable.'

Calvyn shook his head in amazement. 'No wonder the Emperor sent you to Thrandor, Femke. You're one devious young lady.'

'Why, thank you, Calvyn. That's possibly the nicest thing anyone's said to me for a very long time.'

'Haunted? Come now, surely you don't believe in such children's tales.' Femke's illusory face was disapproving and she kept her tone harsh.

'It's true ma'am. Shand's truth it is. I'll wait at the door if you don't mind. There's been too many tales of that cellar for my likin'. Where there's rats, there's sickness, if you take my meanin'.'

'What sort of tales are we talking about here? Moaning in the night? Moving shadows?'

'Oh no, ma'am! Much worse than that. It's said that spirits often rearrange the boxes deliberately to trip you up. Also, people 'ave been taken from that chamber, ma'am. You know – taken to the other side.'

'The other side?' Femke asked, curious now about the servant girl's beliefs.

'The spirit world, ma'am. There's been several wot's worked 'ere over the centuries wot've disappeared from this cellar never to be seen in the flesh again. Sometimes, afterwards, their ghosts have been seen 'ere amongst the boxes – searchin'.'

'Searching? Searching for what?'

'No one knows, ma'am. Some say they left their souls 'ere and they come back lookin' for 'em. I'm not so sure about that, ma'am. All I know is there've been far too many sightin's over the years for my likin'.'

Femke smiled at the serving girl, her prim illusory face patronising as she patted the girl's shoulder.

'It's probably one of those practical jokes that's been perpetuated for so long that it's become a part of Palace legend. Don't worry. You don't have to come in if you don't want to. I just need to run a quick inventory check, same as I did in all the other cellars. Wait here. I'll not be long.'

The door creaked in protest as she opened it, the juddering noise changing to a high-pitched squeal of metal on metal as it reached fully open. The eerie sound echoed slightly in the dark cellar and the hairs on the back of Femke's neck prickled. 'Don't be silly,' she chided herself silently. 'It's just a cellar like all the others. The door hinges are probably left untended deliberately in order to add to the atmosphere of the place . . . or to act as a warning for those inside to make themselves scarce in a hurry.' It was not so much the spooky screech that set her nerves jangling, but the thought that a Guild member might be waiting for her inside. What if they had somehow learned of her new disguise?

'Could do with a bit of oil on the hinges,' she said with a sneer, doing her best to dispel her fleeting paranoia.

'Don't make no difference, ma'am. The hinges are oiled ev'ry week, but they squeak just the same.'

234

Femke was certain she had found what she was looking for. She remembered this cellar from her previous experience in the Palace. The stonework was identical to that in the Guild headquarters. It was hard to tell for sure, but it also appeared to be one of the deepest Palace cellars. Moving boxes, ghost legends, and a healthy fear of the place by the Palace staff were all good clues. If there were a way into the Guild from the Palace, then it was likely to be found here.

She entered, holding her torch aloft. The flickering light played, gleefully revealing large, lurking bales and twisted stacks of boxes, whilst simultaneously making shadows duck and lunge. It was a big room, half again as big as the other cellars she had visited. Given its size, however, there appeared to be little held in storage here.

'There's not much in here, is there?' she said, peering over a low wall of boxes.

'We never normally keep much 'ere, ma'am. This bein' the biggest of the cellars, Steward has us bring the deliveries down 'ere and use the space to sort through the goods, before takin' 'em out into the other cellars for storage. The only stuff as gets stored 'ere is overflow from the other cellars really.'

Moving deeper into the cellar, Femke paused to light two of the wall-mounted torches. The extra light helped dispel the last vestiges of her unease. The hairs on her neck settled back down and she set about marking up an inventory on her slate. For the most part, she just noted the markings on the boxes, taking them at face value. As she had in previous cellars, however, she chose three crates at random and opened them to see that the contents matched the notations on the outside. They did.

All the while that she was moving around the cellar scratching notes on her slate, Femke discreetly scanned the walls and floor for any sign of a concealed door. If, as she strongly suspected, there was one, then it was very well hidden. The cellars were all clean and well organised. It had ever been so. The Head Steward always kept a close eye on matters of storage and the organisation of his resources.

With one last look around she walked across to the wall-mounted torches and used the metal snuffer to extinguish them. As she put out the second torch she whirled, holding the torch in her right hand high above her head to maximise the spread of light. Something had moved. She was sure of it.

'What is it, ma'am? Is everything all right?'

Femke peered around the chamber suspiciously. The unease that she had felt when entering the cellar returned in a rush. Her pulse raced. She doubted the Guild would hold her prisoner again if they recognised her. Ferdand would have little choice but to order her execution. However, whilst she was content to let the servant girl think the reputation of the cellar had got to her, she did not want to let her nervous reaction run out of control.

Ten quick steps and she reached the doorway. 'Everything's fine,' she said, injecting confidence into her tone that for the briefest instant she did not feel. Femke swung the door closed behind her. The squealing groan of protest from the hinges was followed by a solid thud as it met the frame, shutting whatever had moved inside. She turned the key in the lock and handed the bunch back to the serving girl. 'All done here. Let's go back upstairs, shall we? I need to talk to Master Jarran and compare notes.'

'Very well, ma'am.' The look that the serving girl gave her as she took the keys spoke volumes. It was obvious what she thought of Femke's bluster. The cellar had got to her as it had to countless others. Whether she liked it or not, she had added to the legend.

They climbed the stairs back to the surface levels of the Palace and the serving girl led Femke through to the Head Steward's office, where she found Reynik. He was perched at the Steward's desk with piles of parchments and slates stacked in obscenely tidy fashion on either side of the work surface. He looked up as she entered and gave her a thin-lipped smile before returning to his scrutiny of the document in front of him.

'So how did it go, Mistress Adele?' Reynik asked. 'Are the cellars in good order?'

'They seem to be, Master Jarran,' Femke responded, walking primly around to peer over his shoulder. 'I shall need some time to total up my slates and compare them with the inventory, but at first glance the organisation appears to be of a satisfactory standard. The main distribution cellar was a most intriguing place. The staff believe it to be haunted.'

'Haunted, you say?' Reynik repeated, not looking up from the parchment. He kept his tone deliberately bland and disinterested, but Femke knew she had his full attention. 'Hmm, well I've not come across a place as big and old as this yet that didn't have a ghost or two hiding in the closets.'

'How about the books? Do the numbers add up?'

'I found a few minor errors, but from what I've seen so far it appears there is little for the new Emperor to be concerned about. I think I've done about enough here for one day. How about you?'

'Yes,' Femke agreed. 'A bite to eat would be welcome. I'm going to take my slates with me so that I can get the numbers straight by tomorrow. The comparison with the inventory shouldn't take long after that. How long will you need to finish auditing the figures?'

'Well, I suppose if I take a bit of work with me this evening, I could finish tomorrow as well,' he said thoughtfully. 'I had hoped to relax tonight, but it makes little sense to stay longer than necessary.'

Femke nodded, strolling around the room casually and looking at some of the familiar items of décor while Reynik gathered those papers he wanted to study more closely. She was careful not to look too intently at anything on the wall opposite the desk, as she knew there would be at least one spy hidden in a secret compartment there. Talking for the benefit of the spy gave them the opportunity to spread disinformation. It was unclear whom the spy was working for, but it was standard procedure within the Palace for strangers to be watched. No doubt any information gathered by the Imperial spy network would be reported to the new Emperor when he took up residence.

It was not until they were well clear of the Palace and

Reynik was certain that no one was in earshot that he began to talk candidly.

'The cellar you mentioned sounds most intriguing. It might be worth returning to the Palace to see if we can find false walls or hidden doors. From what I've learned, I imagine those ghosts have quite an appetite for food and drink.'

'So there are discrepancies in the book-keeping!'

'No, actually there aren't. Or if there are, then I'm not skilled enough to discern them,' he admitted. 'The books are so squeaky clean they practically gleam. That's what makes me think that all is not as it seems. It's most unlikely that an organisation as big as the Palace runs without at least a little corruption. It goes with the territory. The books are clean, but the Head Steward is most certainly not.'

'What do you mean?' Femke asked, her curiosity piqued.

'Just that he lives very well for someone on a Head Steward's wage. I've seen from the books what he earns officially. His lifestyle and his income don't match. He's getting more money from somewhere. It's not clear where. He might have another legitimate source of income, but I find that unlikely. He has a busy job here. I doubt he would have the time or the energy to hold down another. I think we both know where his money comes from. Proving it would be difficult, but I don't think we'll need to. If you've found a physical entrance to the hidden complex, then our job is done.'

Femke did not respond. She knew the Steward, of course. Having worked in the Palace as long as she had, it would have been an incredible coincidence for their paths not to cross at some point. He had not struck her as the extravagant type, but then she had never had cause to study his circumstances before.

They were approaching the tavern where they were to meet up with Calvyn, Jabal and Lord Kempten. The sign sporting a sadly flaking image of a proud griffin was creaking gently as it swung back and forth in the breeze. Overhead the early evening sky was a deep blue, punctuated with small puffs of white cloud that hurried past as if racing to reach some distant destination before the sun dived below the horizon. The late-afternoon sun reflected off the cobbles. They were slick with a wet sheen left by a recent shower. The street was not busy, but those who were about moved with the same urgency as the clouds. Although there was some time remaining until curfew, it was clear that no one wanted to be outside later than necessary.

'Let's hope that we can clean out the cause of all the trouble and get life in Shandrim back to normal,' she responded eventually. 'It's time the city was restored to peace. The Shandese people are proud and strong like that griffin up there, but just as his paint is flaking, so too is the resilience of the city. The military are doing what they can to maintain order, but why should they have to? Shandrim does not deserve this treatment. A period of restoration is overdue.'

The inn was busy. The curfew had compacted available drinking time to a very short window of opportunity. The regulars were there, but so were the more casual drinkers and socialites. All made the most of the short time between the end of the working day and the new enforced closing time. With the general buzz of conversation being much louder than normal, it was easy to use it as a mask for their meeting. Calvyn and Jabal had secured a table in the corner away from the main crowd around the bar. Kempten was with them, though Femke would never have recognised the Lord if Reynik had not pointed him out.

'Femke? Is that really you?' Kempten asked, keeping his voice low.

'Yes, my Lord. Calvyn's illusion is far better than any disguise I could devise. I must say your appearance is equally impressive.'

Quiet introductions were made all around. Jabal had dispensed with his illusory disguise, as had Calvyn. It was deemed unlikely that anyone would be looking for them.

'I'm glad to have you back, Femke. Reynik has proved himself a worthy tactician in your absence, but I think we shall all value your experience in deciding what to do next.'

'Thank you, my Lord,' she replied, giving him a warm smile. 'I should first warn you that if the Guild finds out you're alive, they will look to reinstate your deceased status in double quick time. Let's hope my threat to Toomas held him to silence whilst I was imprisoned, or things could get awkward. From what little I learned, the Guild are backing Lord Tremarle to become the next Emperor.'

'Then they have already succeeded in that much,' Kempten replied. 'The news is everywhere. The Imperial Court has declared him Emperor Designate. The coronation ceremony is only a few days away. He's already moved into the Palace.'

'The ceremony is an irrelevance, my Lord,' Femke stated with conviction. 'You are the true Emperor Designate. As soon as it becomes known that you're alive, the coronation of Tremarle will be declared void.'

Lord Kempten nodded. 'It appears, however, that the Guild may be doing more than just backing Tremarle for the Mantle. Were you aware that Lord Tremarle has adopted a son?'

'No, my Lord, but why should that make any difference? Whether he has an heir, or not, does not change your claim.'

'It might make a difference when the son goes by the name of Shalidar.'

'Shand!' breathed Femke and Reynik as one.

'Are you sure it's the same man? ' Femke asked, incredulous. 'If so, how on earth did Shalidar manipulate him into that? He murdered the man's eldest son, for Shand's sake! The audacity of it is breathtaking. Unless, of course, Tremarle wanted Danar dead . . . No! I can't believe him that callous. There's got to be more to this than meets the eye.'

'Yes,' confirmed Kempten. 'It does appear to be the same Shalidar who gave you all the trouble in Mantor. No one seems to know what prompted the adoption, but there are no signs that it was forced on Tremarle. He seems genuinely taken with the man. If the Guild are behind Tremarle, do you not think it likely that they're ultimately looking to put the Mantle upon the shoulders of one of their own?'

Femke frowned as she thought. If she had not known how the present Guildmaster felt about Shalidar as a person, she might have been tempted to agree. Crafty as Ferdand was, however, she did not believe his intense dislike of Shalidar to be feigned. The idea of Shalidar as Emperor would repulse him as much as it did her. The silence grew as her mind raced, twisting possibilities and trying to view the situation from all angles. In the end she shook her head.

'It's no good,' she said. 'I can't make sense of it. I'm not sure what part the Guild had in getting Shalidar adopted, if any, but something doesn't feel right here. Shalidar has always played his own game. That has been proven time and again. I wouldn't be surprised if he's acting independently. It's easy to see the benefits to the Guild, but I think we're missing a vital piece of the puzzle.'

'What else do we know?' asked Kempten, his brows furrowed as he considered the information they had gathered so far. 'If we pool our knowledge, we might be able to make more sense of it all.'

'Well, Femke and I have established firm links between the Imperial Palace and the Guild,' Reynik offered.

'Links? What sort of links?' Kempten whispered eagerly.

'Well, I believe the Head Steward is in the employ of the Guild. There is certainly a lot of circumstantial evidence to support this theory. Femke believes there is also a physical connection from one of the Palace cellars to the Guild headquarters. Though the presence of such a passage is yet to be physically confirmed, it is logical to assume this is the case. All the evidence points to the existence of such a link. I suspect that the Guild piggybacks their supplies through the Imperial supply chain.'

'A passage from the cellars into the Guild headquarters!' Lord Kempten exclaimed. 'Shand's teeth! That means the Guild have been using the Palace for centuries!'

'Please, my Lord,' Femke hissed, her eyes subtly scanning the nearer tables to see if any had shown any interest in his words. 'Not so loud! This place is not known to be frequented by spies, but one can never be too careful.'

'Of course,' he said apologetically in a low voice. 'Sorry about that. It's just that I was shocked.'

'Understandably, my Lord. I thought I was beyond being surprised, but if this last couple of months have taught me anything, it's that there's always something bubbling below the surface of Shandese politics, lurking in wait to shock and amaze those who thought they'd seen everything.'

'So where does this passage start and end?' Kempten asked. 'I thought Reynik's previous experience of the Guild had led us to believe there was no conventional entrance.'

'That's a good question, my Lord,' Femke answered, dropping her volume still lower. 'There's a particular cellar in the Palace where if I were to gamble, I would lay every sennut I had on there being an opening to the Guild. However, during my explorations of the Guild complex I saw no corresponding evidence of any passage leading upwards. To be fair, I may not have seen half of it. What about you, Reynik? You spent more time than me in there. Did you see anything in the Guild complex that made you suspect such a way existed?'

Reynik looked thoughtful for a moment, but was quick to shake his head. 'Changing the subject a moment, did you find anything at the library, Master Jabal?' he asked.

The magician shook his head. 'The books you spoke of were conspicuous by their absence,' he said. 'My trip to the library was fruitless, I'm afraid.'

Reynik nodded. 'I expected as much,' he said. 'We could follow up the lead of the bakery on Western Avenue, but I don't think it would get us far. It would be more likely to lead them to us than the other way around. I remember openly asking the Guildmaster about a physical link to the surface once,' Reynik continued thoughtfully, 'but he flat-out denied it. He said that the only way in and out was by use of the icons. He could have been lying, of course. If I had been in his position, I would have lied to protect the secrecy of such a passage. As Guildmaster I wouldn't want the other assassins to think they had tied their bodies to magical icons for nothing. I'd actively seek to conceal such information.'

Femke nodded. 'That makes sense,' she agreed. 'But where does all this leave us? I'm fairly convinced we have a potential avenue of attack, but even if it does exist, to utilise it will not be easy. For a successful strike we'll need to get a considerable force into the depths of the Imperial Palace, find the entrance to the passageway, and launch an attack, all without raising the suspicion of the Guild.'

'None of those things will be easy, Femke,' Lord

Kempten observed. 'Have you any idea how we could do any of them?'

Femke looked Lord Kempten squarely in the eyes. 'Are you willing to see this through, my Lord?' she asked. 'There's no half-measure here. It's all or nothing.'

Kempten sighed as he met her gaze. 'It depends,' he temporised. 'If I'm to gamble with my life and the lives of my family, then you'll have to convince me that you have a plan that will work. I agree that we've come a long way in the last few weeks. We're closer to breaking the Guild than any have come in centuries, but "close" is not good enough. I need to be convinced. Can you convince me?'

A slow smile spread across Femke's face. 'I think I can, my Lord. This might sound a little bizarre, but I've just had a moment of clarity. Everything suddenly fits together. It might take some refining, but what do you think of this for a plan of action . . .'

Five minutes later and Lord Kempten's face mirrored the incredulity in his voice.

'Are you telling me you just thought all this up on the spur of the moment?' he asked.

Femke's plan was both daring and audacious. It also relied on the cooperation of people who might be difficult to coerce into such a venture. On the positive side, however, Kempten could see that there were plenty of points during the preparation phase at which they could back out if all were not going the way they intended. Looking around the table he could see from the expressions of the others that they were taken with Femke's ideas.

'Well I had a lot of thinking time whilst I was being held

prisoner. This is a variation on something I'd dreamed up for a different reason, but I believe the principles are sound.'

'Some of the people you want to bring in on this will no doubt require remuneration for their efforts,' Kempten observed.

'Yes, my Lord, and I suspect that some of them will not come cheaply.'

'I saw the bills from some of your other escapades, Femke. Are you set on depleting the Imperial Treasury and making the Emperor a pauper in his Palace?'

Femke grinned. 'I can see how I might give that impression sometimes. Let's just say that the bill will represent good value for money, shall we? You will have rid Shandrim of the Guild, whilst securing your rightful place as Emperor. Surely that's worth spending a little gold on? I also have ideas on how to attract some of the people we need at the public's expense. Let me explain . . .'

CHAPTER THIRTEEN

'Do you plan to use *any* real actors in this endeavour?'

Femke gave Devarusso her most winning smile. It had always been a source of amusement to her that she had never yet revealed her true name to the troupe leader and the irony of the response she had to his question tickled her all the more. To Devarusso, she had always been Dana, the actress. If he had deduced her true occupation, he had never said anything.

'Of course,' she replied. 'There'll be you and me. We'll also need at least one or two of your regular troupe. I only want your most trustworthy people to be involved, though. We can't afford to have the true nature of this play leaked to the tattle touts.'

Devarusso pursed his lips. 'And have any of the others you propose to involve ever acted on stage before?' he asked.

'That's unlikely, which is why they will only have minimal roles. Theirs will be visual, rather than speaking

248

parts. By necessity some of them may have to speak one or two lines, but not many. The beauty of using *The True King's Gambit*, aside from the irony, is that we'll only need four main speaking actors, and it will take minimal adaptation to include the rest of my team as a supporting cast.'

'And what am I supposed to do with the rest of the troupe? I don't want to lose them. They're good people.'

'Tell them they can have a paid holiday, Devarusso,' Femke replied. 'I'm sure they'll work all the better for a short break. The Treasury will pay. Won't it, my Lord?'

Kempten nodded, never taking his eyes off Devarusso.

'You're assuming, of course, that you're going to be successful,' the troupe leader pointed out. 'What if you're not? Who will pay then?'

'I will give you the money in advance from my own pocket,' Lord Kempten said, watching the actor intently. 'That way you'll lose nothing by going along with this venture.'

Devarusso drummed his fingers on the tiny table, his brows knitted together in a deep frown. Femke got the distinct impression that if there had been space within the wagon, he would have been pacing. It was as well that the actor was a tidy person. Living in such a small space required constant discipline to avoid clutter building up. The inside of Devarusso's wagon was immaculate. It was clear that he was not one to be tempted into acquiring possessions that were excess to requirement. For such a flamboyant person, his quarters displayed remarkable restraint.

'Tell me again about your plans for a theatre, my Lord. I can see so many things to go wrong that I need something positive to focus on.'

Kempten looked across at Femke, his eyebrows raised in an unspoken question. She gave him a solemn wink in return.

'Are you saying you'll help us?' Kempten asked.

'Can I trust you to keep your promise of building a public theatre?'

'You can. It will be one of my first acts on becoming Emperor.'

'Then, Shand help me, I'll do my best. To be honest, I think it'll be a disaster, but I'll try. When can I see the adapted script, Dana?'

Femke's eyes twinkled as she responded. 'Right after we finish writing it down, Devarusso.'

'The adaptation is not written yet! When did you say we're going to go public with this?'

'Like I said, it won't need much adaptation,' Femke said casually. 'Besides, the few changes that will be required are right here,' she added, tapping her head with her finger. 'All we need to do is put it down onto parchment.'

'All we have to do, she says! *All* we have to do! All we have to do is rewrite a play to feature more characters than have ever been seen in a production in Shandrim before, train a bunch of novices to play the parts and make it so good that we get invited to stage it at the Imperial Palace. Oh, and we have a whole ten days until the first performance! No problem.' Devarusso looked up at the ceiling as if seeking divine intervention. 'Shand's teeth,

Dana! You've been in plays before. You know such a task is impossible.'

'Nothing is impossible, Devarusso. Difficult, but not impossible. Oh, and I think you should know that Dana is not my real name.'

'I suppose I should have guessed,' he replied with a rueful smile. 'Every time you turn up here I discover something new and unexpected about you. Why not a different name? Come tell me, what is your true name?'

'Femke.'

'A strong name. It suits you. Well, *Femke*, I shall see you tonight. I'll tell the troupe that the performance at the sixth call will be the last. Be here by the eighth call. I just hope you know what you're doing. Bring parchment, pen and ink with you. I have an old copy of *The True King's Gambit* you can mutilate, but I don't have writing materials here.'

They all rose to their feet. Devarusso had to stoop slightly to avoid hitting his head on the roof of the wagon. It seemed amazing to Femke that he had not developed a permanent hunch living like this.

Kempten gave Devarusso a firm handshake. 'Thank you for doing this,' he said fervently.

'My Lord, the promise of a proper theatre is thanks enough. Acting has always been my life. The idea that I could be instrumental in making plays more popular and accessible to the population of Shandrim is something I have often dreamed of. Let's pray that you're successful.'

'I think even the least pious of us could say a quick prayer for that,' Femke agreed.

*

251

The look Serrius gave Femke was one of total outrage.

'You go too far, Femke! Play-fighting on stage – you had better be jesting. I've never feigned a fight in my life. When I fight, I fight for real. If there's no danger, then there's no fight. Such a staged dance with blades would be a fiasco – and it would look as such.'

'Call it sparring then if you must. You must have practised with other fighters to become as good as you are. I promise you this is no jest, Serrius. I'd like you to approach some of the other top gladiators and bring them in on this. If you want to make the fight scenes serious, then that's fine. Make the on-stage clashes as real as you like – the more spectacular, the better in fact. My only condition is that you're careful not to kill or maim one another. It is the fighting off-stage that's important. That will be deadly enough, I assure you. It's this fighting you'll get your money for, so there must be no scope for you to forget yourselves and allow old rivalries to get in the way.'

'So the blades will be real?' Serrius asked

'Yes.'

'And whom exactly is it that we'll be fighting off-stage?'

'The Guild of Assassins,' Femke answered, watching his response carefully. 'Are they dangerous enough to add the risk you crave?'

'What, *all* of them?'

'Well there aren't that many of them,' Femke pointed out. 'And you would have some help. If all goes well, we'll hit them with the element of surprise firmly on our side. The idea is to kill them, not give a swordplay demonstration. None are to be left alive. This is probably the most

252

severe test of your abilities as a swordsman that you could find outside of the arena. Members of the Guild of Assassins have a certain reputation for having masterful skills with all weapons. What do you think? Is it enough of a challenge for you?'

Serrius stared at her through narrowed eyes. She had not expected convincing the ex-gladiator to be easy. Ever since he had started fighting in the arena, the challenge of being the best fighter in the land had dominated his thinking. Making him appreciate that there was anything else in life worth doing was always difficult. Without the help of Serrius, they were unlikely to find fighters capable of facing Guild assassins in single combat. He was the vital last element to the plan. If she could not convince him, then they would have to scrap the plan and start again.

'Who would be the help?' Serrius asked cautiously.

'We have a Legion Commander willing—'

'No soldiers,' Serrius interrupted.

Femke took a deep breath. 'Very well, no Legionnaires. There are also two magicians.'

'No . . .'

'Whom you cannot veto,' Femke continued quickly, 'as we have discovered the assassins use magic. We'll need to counter that magic somehow. One of the magicians is also a strong swordsman. I'm sure he wouldn't mind some sparring if it would set your mind at rest.'

The ex-gladiator's brow furrowed deeper. 'Anyone else?' Serrius growled after a short pause, his eyes sparking.

'A couple of street entertainers.'

'And what are they going to do? Keep the assassins laughing whilst the rest of us chop them into little pieces, I suppose,' he said with a twisted smile that matched his sarcasm.

'As it happens, the two men I've hired are the two best knife-throwers in Shandrim. I think you might find them useful to have along.'

'Derryn and Bartok?'

'The same,' Femke confirmed.

The expression on his face softened a little. 'I've seen their acts. They're both very skilled,' he said. He picked up his glass of water from the table and took a sip. The silence in the room grew as he contemplated Femke's proposal.

As the silence grew louder, Femke found that her need to say more grew with it. The overwhelming urge to give an impassioned plea for help blossomed until she felt ready to explode, but instinctively she held her peace. If there was one discipline she had learned over her years as a spy, it was to trust her instincts.

She was right.

'Very well, Femke,' Serrius conceded, his voice killing the ringing silence with the same sharp precision he displayed in his swordplay. 'I'll speak to Nadrek and the other top fighters. I can't promise anything, but if I keep the details of what they'll have to do for their money to a minimum, the fee should be enough to entice most of them.'

'Thank you. Secrecy is everything at this stage. If word were to reach the street of what we're doing, then I'm sure

I don't have to tell you how vulnerable we'd become. As long as we maintain the element of surprise, then we have a good chance of success.'

'Surprise is a useful ally, but don't rely on it to the exclusion of all else, Femke. A good plan should see us triumph whether we maintain that ally to the very end, or not. When this is over you will likely see that it's the speed and accuracy of the strike that has won the day. I'm trusting you to be the person directing the strike, rather than being on the receiving end.'

'Rikala, I need your help,' Femke began.

'Yes, dear, I can see that. Those clothes are positively dreadful! Where in Shand's name did you get them? The seamstress deserves to be shot for such shoddy work.'

Femke smiled. Rikala always spoke her mind when it came to clothing, but her tone on this occasion made her sound every bit as pompous as Femke did when in disguise as Lady Alyssa. Rikala had only ever known Femke as Alyssa, so it was not surprising that she sought to imitate in order to please.

'No, Rikala, it's not clothing for me ... Well, yes it is ... and it isn't.'

'Well, my Lady, which is it?' the seamstress asked. 'Is it for that young man again? He's quite a good-looking young fellow. You could do a lot worse for yourself. He has nice legs.' Rikala gave her a saucy wink, which seemed strange coming from the stout little woman.

'Rikala! No, I'm not here for Reynik. I'm here because I would like to utilise your skills in preparing the costumes for a play. Have you been to the open-air stage and seen Devarusso's company perform?'

'I have,' she said. 'They're very good. He has nice legs too!'

Femke ignored her teasing.

'Well, they're going to perform a special play, which they're trying to prepare in very quick time. I'm the patron, so naturally I wish to see the players get what they need for the production. I'm also very excited, as Devarusso has agreed to let me play a small part as well. I've seen many plays over the years. To take part in one has been a dream for a very long time. How quickly could you turn out costumes, do you think?'

Rikala thought for a moment, the fingers of her right hand stroking absently across her chin. The woman was no fool. Femke knew the seamstress suspected there was more to Lady Alyssa than met the public eye. However, the woman had held her tongue up until now and there was little reason to suspect she would suddenly lose her sense of discretion.

'What sort of costumes are we talking about and when will I get to measure up the actors and actresses taking part?'

'The play is to be a variation on the classic, *The True King's Gambit*, so it's all set around a Royal Court. Most of the costumes will be for courtiers, but there'll also be the King's costumes, an assassin's garb, a couple of magicians and some soldiers' uniforms. A lot of the military stuff should be obtainable ready-made, though I'd like to give them a different look from anything normally seen in

Shandar. I'll make some enquiries to see what I can give you to start with. The troupe has courtiers' clothing, but it's all rather tired. I've promised to pay for the costumes, so Devarusso intends to make the most of the opportunity and get something that will last. I can't say I blame him. As for measuring, well some of the actors could come straight away, but the others may be a couple of days. If you show me the measurements you want, I could collect them myself more quickly.'

Rikala nodded.

'Measuring's not difficult. A Lady of your intelligence should have no problem with it,' she agreed. 'Here, take my knotted string. This is how I like the notations.'

The seamstress pulled out a piece of parchment from a dresser drawer and spread it onto the central table. It took just a few minutes to explain what all the notations meant. Femke agreed that it was straightforward and that she would have no problem remembering which measurement was which.

'The King's costumes might take a little while to produce, as they will need to be fancy, but colourful clothing for the courtiers will be simple enough. I could turn several of those out each day. If you're not worried about them being stitch-perfect, then I could possibly turn them out even faster.'

'Whatever you produce is likely to be of a far higher quality finish than the players are used to,' Femke said with a grin. 'I think the majority of the clothing that they work with is barely tacked together.'

'Then I'll give them something that will last through

many repeat performances,' she replied. 'Come back and see me as soon as you can with the measurements. In the meantime, what costume will you need for yourself?'

Devarusso rubbed his eyes for the third time in as many minutes. Dawn was breaking and the early-morning bird-song was nearing the peak of its daily crescendo. Dark rings encircled his eyes. Femke was still hunched over the stack of parchments working like a woman possessed.

'For Shand's sake, Femke!' he swore. 'Take a rest. You've earned it. Your spin on the play is great. You've utilised all the extra characters in a way that will see them needing minimal acting practice. As long as their weapons play is good, then they'll look spectacular on stage. Your instinct for drama, irony and use of language is excellent. I'm beginning to share this vision of yours in spite of myself.'

'But we're so close to finishing . . .'

'Which means it will not take long to do so when we resume. Go. Get a couple of hours of rest and come back when you're ready. I need sleep, even if you don't. If anyone had ever told me they could adapt a play to give it such a different feel in a single night, I'd have declared them mad. Had I not witnessed you do it, I'd never have believed it possible. I can see where you're going with it. Some of the amended lines will need work, but you've held to the traditional storyline, which has always worked well. We'll sort out the casting and start rehearsing this afternoon. However, we won't be able to do that if you're dead on your feet.'

Femke sat up and looked at the page of text on the table.

It blurred in and out of focus as she struggled to read the notes she had written. For a moment she felt dizzy, as the world seemed to spin out of control. She placed her hands flat on the table in front of her and pressed down hard in an effort to restore her sense of balance.

'Are you all right?' Devarusso asked, his voice suddenly full of concern.

'I just sat up too quickly, that's all. You're right. I'm tired.' She got to her feet slowly to avoid any further dizziness. 'I'll see you in a few hours. Thanks for all your help, Devarusso. I'd never have got that much done without you.'

He shook his head self-deprecatingly. 'The work was yours. All I did was nudge you every now and then. If you ever get tired of getting into trouble, I'd be happy to have you back here as one of my actors – you know that. After seeing this, I'd be happy to have you rewrite plays for me too.'

Femke gave a weary smile as she reached for the door handle. 'Thanks, I appreciate the sentiment but, inspired or not, this will most definitely be my first and last. I'll see you in a couple of hours. It would be good to get the amended script finished before we begin rehearsing.'

'Good, yes – essential, no. Rest. I'll see you when you're feeling recovered. I've plenty to work with for today.'

Lady Kempten could not sleep. Her imagination would not stop creating dire images of what might be happening in Shandrim. Bad dreams had troubled her every night since her husband had left and she was becoming paranoid that buried somewhere in the nightmares there might dwell a grain of truth.

There were many who believed in the power of dreams. Some claimed they could interpret them. Isobel did not normally believe in such things, but the dreams were beginning to wear at her sense of reality. The more she worried, the more she convinced herself that something bad was happening, or going to happen.

She rolled over again, plumping the pillow before trying to settle her cheek into it. No position felt comfortable this evening. Despite the heavy blankets she felt cold and alone without her husband.

A flicker of light against her closed eyelids had her sitting upright in an instant. 'I didn't imagine it,' she thought, her heart racing. 'That was a real light, I know it was.' With shaking hands she reached out to the bedside table and felt around to the back leg nearest to the bed where she had tied a small dagger. It was well that she had tied it in place with a bow, or she would have struggled to make her trembling fingers untie the knot.

Cautiously, with the dagger clutched tightly in her right hand, she swung her feet out of bed and took her first step across the floor towards the door. A distant grumble of thunder brought her to a stop. The flicker had been lightning! Relief spread through her stomach, bringing a flush of warmth and making her feel foolish. There had been an unusually large number of storms this spring. Why should another be any surprise?

She lowered her dagger and chuckled quietly at her melodramatic reaction as she turned back to the bed. The room was dark, but not completely so, and her eyes had long since adapted to the low light. She could see that the covers on the large four-poster were rucked and twisted from her tossing and turning. It would be as well to straighten them before getting back in, she thought. Getting comfortable was proving impossible enough without starting out tangled in a mess of blankets and sheets.

Placing the dagger on the bedside table, Isobel methodically stripped back the blankets and sheets, re-making the bed layer by layer until all the bedding was flat and tightly tucked under the mattress. She sighed and pulled back the corner in preparation to climb in. Again lightning flickered at the window, the blue-white light dancing through the curtains with the seductive allure of fairy-like magic. As a little girl, Isobel had always found the sight of distant lightning against the night sky enchanting. It was a beautiful phenomenon. Despite the late hour she felt little inclination towards sleep, and the chance to recapture something of her childhood innocence was appealing.

Moving to the curtains, she drew them apart. By chance, as the curtains moved, so the thunder rolled. However, the distant rumble was augmented by a sudden flurry of sound that caused Isobel such a fright she leaped back in shock. A pair of pigeons roosting on the deep windowsill had startled into flight, disturbed by the sudden movement of the curtains behind them. Once again she found her heart pounding and her face flushing, as she experienced feelings of foolishness for being so on edge.

'For Shand's sake!' she muttered. 'What is wrong with you tonight, Izzie?'

It took a few moments for her nerves to settle, but when they did she moved forwards and looked out from the window at the dark, silhouetted countryside. The treetops were unmoving in the breathless stillness. Lady Isobel opened the window to better appreciate the beauty of the crisp, calm night air. The distant flash drew her eyes instantly as lightning once again forked down from the heavens. The jagged fingers of incandescent energy were beautiful. At this distance it was hard to imagine that something so pretty could wreak damage and destruction. It seemed almost like a momentary glowing spider web, connecting heaven and earth.

A movement down on the lawn by the pond drew her eye. It was hard to see much after the brightness of the lightning. Her night vision had gone, but there was definitely something out there moving stealthily through the cover of darkness. She narrowed her eyes, trying her utmost to see through the after-image of the forked web of light. Then she caught a glimpse of it again – a dark shape, creeping silently towards the house. What was it? It was hard to get any sort of perspective of size in this light.

The roll of thunder this time lasted a little longer than the previous ones, though it was no louder. As it died away a barn owl flew from the roof of the manor house down across the lawn towards the willow tree by the pond. Isobel watched its ghostly passage, and was most pleased that she did not start when it let out its high-pitched hunting screech. Another flash of lightning lit the sky, casting shadows and momentarily exposing the nightly hunters to their prey. The shape on the lawn was recognisable in an instant. It was a fox, doubtless looking to see if it could break into the chicken coop. It was unlikely to succeed. The coop and shed were sturdy structures and the servants maintained them well.

Isobel drew in a deep breath, enjoying the evening air. As she did so, a hand suddenly clamped across her mouth and nose from behind, pulling her away from the window. She felt the prick of a dagger at her throat and instinctively tried to scream. It was useless. Her assailant's hand was clamped too firmly for anything but a muffled squeak to escape.

'Silence!' whispered a voice in her ear. 'If you cry out, or try to attract attention in any way, I'll cut your throat. Understand?'

For a moment she thought about trying to get free. The dagger on the bedside table gave her brief hope. If she could just break his grip and get her weapon, she might stand a chance. After a few seconds, she realised the futility of her thinking. The man holding her was strong. His body felt hard against her back. He had made no sound as he approached her. Given the circumstances it was quite likely that he was a trained assassin, or at the least a professional spy. The point of the dagger under her chin pressed slightly harder.

'Understand?' he repeated.

She gave the slightest of nods, careful not to press any harder against the dagger for fear of it breaking her skin.

'Good. Now I'm going to take my hand from your mouth and you're going to answer my questions. Just look straight ahead at the window. So long as you do as I say, you won't be hurt.' He gradually loosened his hand from her mouth and nose, replacing it over her forehead to better tilt back her head and expose her throat. 'Where is Lord Kempten?' he asked. The man's voice was hard as granite, with a rough texture to match.

'He knows,' she thought frantically. 'What can I tell him that will satisfy him?'

'He's dead and buried. What more do you want from him?' she answered with a sniff.

'Don't try to be clever, my Lady. I know the assassination was a fake. Kempten's alive. Where is he?'

Isobel paused for a moment. There was nothing she could do. Given that the man already knew her husband was alive, any information she gave about his whereabouts would do little damage.

'He's gone to Shandrim, to claim what is rightfully his.'

'So he's going to take the Mantle then?'

'Of course! What else could he do? Surabar made him his heir. The Mantle of an Emperor is not something to be thrown aside lightly.'

The man fell silent. She could feel him breathing as the seconds dragged from one to the next, but the pressure of the knifepoint at her throat did not waver.

'Whereabouts in Shandrim is he staying?' he asked.

'I don't know. He didn't tell me that.'

'And do you know what he intends for the Guild?'

'The Guild? Which Guild?'

'Don't play the fool, my Lady. It doesn't become you. You know exactly what I'm talking about.'

Isobel's thoughts raced. 'Whatever I say now will land

me in trouble. What do I say? What do I say?' When in doubt, a lie was more likely to be obvious. She decided that the safest course was still the truth.

'That very much depends,' she answered carefully.

'Don't tease me, my Lady. I don't take well to that. Come on – spit it out. It depends on what?'

Isobel paused for effect.

'It depends on whether he can find a sure-fire way of destroying the Guild once and for all.'

The man grunted. To her relief, he appeared to accept her answer. The pressure of the knifepoint eased a fraction. Once again the silence grew and her mind played through the possibilities of what would happen next. 'If he's a Guild member, the man's unlikely to kill me. Without a contract it's against the man's creed to kill . . . unless someone has taken out a contract. But who? Who would want me dead? What if he isn't a member of the Guild, but one of their hired hands? Would he still be bound by the creed?'

'Very well, my Lady. Thank you for your cooperation. Now, much as I'd like to leave you here and pursue your husband, I'm afraid I have specific orders that I'm bound to comply with.'

'He's going to kill me. I'm going to die,' she thought frantically.

'Please, don't make this any more difficult than it needs to be. I'm going to lead you out of the house. Make a noise, or try to attract attention in any way, and I'll kill you without hesitation. If you do draw the attention of others, you'll be killing them as surely as if you ran them through with a sword. There's no one in this house capable of stopping me, so unless you'd like me to stain your lovely carpets with copious amounts of blood, I suggest you concentrate on doing exactly as I say. Now, I'm going to guide you forwards. Walk as silently as you can. Let's go.'

'Well, I'd never have believed it unless I'd seen it with my own two eyes! Shand, but that's the dog's danglies! And you can provide a backdrop like this to every scene?'

Devarusso was sitting on the audience steps about a third of the way up the tiered seating and looking on as Jabal created the illusion that converted the stage into a forest. The troupe leader's jaw had dropped in amazement as the transformation occurred. He got to his feet, his eyes still wide. Huge trees had sprung from nowhere, and anyone not knowing that it was a stage would swear blind that the forest went on for as far as the eye could see between the enormous tree trunks.

Was that birdsong he could hear? And the other background woodland noises . . . this was beyond anything he had imagined possible.

'To be honest, I'd rather not have to unless it's totally necessary,' Jabal answered. 'It takes a lot of energy and I'll need to have considerable reserves if I'm to face the Guild's master stone after the show.'

'I could do it, Master,' Calvyn offered, his quiet voice sounding confident. 'I know you don't approve of sorcery as an alternative to magic, but in this instance it makes sense to play to the strengths of the available disciplines. I was trained by some of the most powerful sorcerers in

Shandar. To create something like this would be simple. May I demonstrate?'

Jabal frowned, and his acolyte wondered for a moment if he had misread his master. Calvyn would not have suggested such a demonstration to any other Grand Magician. To do so would have been to invite a string of unpleasant penances. No magician liked to admit there were things that the other arcane disciplines made easier, but Jabal was more of a liberal than most. After a considerable pause, Jabal nodded his permission.

'Please, take a seat, Master. This will only take a moment,' Calvyn said. 'Before I begin, I feel I should explain what I'm doing, Devarusso. What you've just seen was a magically-created illusion. A magician draws energy from the elements around him and harnesses that energy through the binding power of the runic language. In this way he can disrupt the natural order of things. What you'll see next is not quite the same, though I'd be surprised if you could see the difference. Sorcery works very differently from magic. It relies on the strength of the sorcerer's mind. The clarity with which he can picture images and the strength with which he can project them into the minds of others is the critical factor to being a powerful practitioner.'

True to his word, within moments he had recreated the forest scene in every detail. He walked across the stage amongst the huge trees and turned to face his master and Devarusso.

'There is another advantage to my producing the illusions,' he said without so much as a hint of superiority

267

in his tone. 'I can add texture and substance to them. Look.' Devarusso and Jabal both found their eyes widening with amazement as Calvyn leaned up against one of the trees. 'I discovered during my time with Vallaine that my magical training gave my illusions something that none of the other sorcerers appeared able to create – a sense of reality that was a step on from the visual. To do this takes a little more concentration, but is not really any more draining than producing a ghost image. I didn't let on to the other sorcerers that I could do this, as it would likely have been viewed with as much horror by them, as my use of sorcery was by the masters in the Magicians' Academy.'

Jabal was speechless, but Devarusso was quick to jump in with a question.

'So you can take any backdrop I describe to you and convert the stage into something approaching the reality?' he asked excitedly.

'Actually it's better than that, Calvyn replied. 'You only have to picture the scene you require and I can take that scene from your mind and recreate it exactly as you picture it. Go ahead. Think of a setting.'

Calvyn reached into Devarusso's mind with his own and smiled as he saw the scene the actor was picturing. The actor was clearly attempting to picture something impossible to recreate on stage. The image was the deck of a ship in the midst of a storm. Men were staggering across the heaving deck as waves crashed over the railing, sending plumes of water into the air and washing knee-deep across the decking.

An instant later and the stage was the deck. Beyond the deck all the two viewers could see was the raging sea. Sailors ran, slid and climbed, fighting with the rigging as they struggled to control the ship amid the monstrous waves. Shouted orders could barely be heard above the howl of the wind. Two barrels broke loose from their stowage point and were swept on a wave towards the rail. One of the barrels crashed through the railing, taking a sailor over the side with it.

Through the drama, Calvyn stood in the centre of the heaving deck, unmoving amidst the chaos and seemingly unaffected by the pitching movement of the ship around him.

'Wait a minute!' Devarusso exclaimed. 'You can create characters as well?'

'Of course,' Calvyn replied.

Devarusso began to laugh. To begin with it was a chuckle, but the chuckle developed quickly into a full-blown belly laugh. Calvyn dissolved the illusion and exchanged puzzled glances with Jabal. His master shrugged.

'You ... can ... create ... characters ... ha, ha, ha!' Devarusso was beyond communication for some time. He sat holding his sides, doubled up to the point that his head was almost on his lap and his dark curtain of wavy hair prevented any sight of his face. When he sat up and brushed his hair back with his fingers there were tears still rolling down his cheeks. He shook his head, lost in mirth and repeated the same words over and over again whilst waggling a finger in Calvyn's direction. When he finally recovered enough composure to speak, the two magicians were keen to share in what was so funny about the revelation.

'Don't you see?' Devarusso asked. 'If you can create characters, then there's no need for lengthy rehearsals. All I have to do is to sit and read the manuscript. Calvyn can take the images from my mind as I picture them from the script and produce them on stage. One or two practices will probably do it. All our "actors" will have to do is practise their curtain call bow, and Calvyn could probably recreate that, too, if he wanted to. No one will ever realise that they were never on stage at all. Shand's teeth, Calvyn! You could put me out of business overnight if you had a mind to, or make me rich in very quick time if you joined me. Why would anyone ever want to watch live actors again when they could view something as spectacular as this?'

'Oh, I don't know,' Jabal replied. 'There's a certain charm about watching live theatre. I shouldn't worry too much. I don't think you'll find many sorcerers wanting to take away your trade.'

'I'm glad to hear it!' Devarusso said with feeling. 'Now, come on. We might as well go and give Femke and Kempten the good news. Femke's plan to spill the final fight scene off the stage and out into the corridors of the Palace was a good one, but fraught with many dangers. If the Imperial guards were quick and well organised, they might cut off the attack party before they ever reached the cellars. Also, because by its very nature, the plan would have scattered the party out through multiple doors, there was always the chance that individuals might not have managed to rejoin the main strike force.'

Jabal and Calvyn still looked on, bemused by Devarusso's extravagant enthusiasm.

'Don't you see?' the troupe leader continued. 'Femke's original plan has just become obsolete. If we utilise Calvyn's ability to the full, then Femke can lead her team on a secret strike from the dressing rooms, whilst the vast majority of the Palace is distracted by the play.'

CHAPTER FOURTEEN

'There are others who think as I do, Brother Dragon,' Fox purred. 'The Guildmaster is no longer fit to lead us. We must act now if the Guild is to survive. Kempten lives. If we're to keep our identity in Shandar, then he cannot be allowed to gain the Mantle. The Guildmaster would have us blackmail him into renouncing his position. Since when has the Guild resorted to such base tactics? Kempten should be removed from the picture cleanly and permanently. That's what we're here for. That's what we do.'

Shalidar's satisfied smile beneath the shadow of his deep hood was almost a reflection of the toothy grin of the dragon image woven into the tapestry on the opposite wall. Fox was doing his dirty work for him, without so much as the subtlest of prompting. It was almost too good to be true.

He shifted his weight in his chair and extended his right leg fully before crossing it over his left. The wound in his thigh bothered him more if he did not stretch the muscles regularly. Fox lounged suggestively in the only other chair in his living chamber. A split in the lower part of her robes fell open, revealing the flesh of her leg to just above the knee. Shalidar pointedly turned his focus away. He knew Fox's reputation. No matter how attractive she might be under those robes, Shalidar knew better than to be tempted. Fox had the heart of a cold-blooded killer. Despite his instinct for survival and talent at dealing death to others, he was under no illusion. To share more than a platonic relationship with such a woman would be to invite trouble.

'So what do you suggest, Brother Fox? Are we to kill the Guildmaster as well? That's a drastic measure. We're already down on numbers. He's a most accomplished assassin. Don't make the mistake of underestimating him because of his age. His reactions might not be what they were, but he's no fool.'

'I never said he was a fool, Brother. I know his mind is sharp, but despite his abilities he's led the Guild into this crisis. There are several of us who don't believe he can lead us out again. The Guildmaster cannot retire, so we'll have to retire him.'

'Two kills with one arrow,' he thought, his grin broadening even further. 'What's more, it was not I who loosed it.'

'So who do you hope will be the next Guildmaster? Are you looking to take the position? Or is there someone else you think might make a strong leader for the present circumstances?'

Fox's change in posture answered his question before she opened her mouth. Shalidar read her pose as easily as he would read words from a slate. She got to her feet, moved across to one of Shalidar's two bookcases and started running her elegant fingers gently back and forth across the spines.

'I would stand if it went to a ballot,' she admitted, 'but in that event it will be up to the members to decide who can best lead us during these dark times.'

It was clear that she felt she had a good chance. He had to admit she possessed many attributes of a strong leader. She was confident, clever and subtle. She manipulated others with ease, and used her feminine wiles to full advantage. It was not hard to see her winning a considerable number of votes if it were to come to a ballot. The problem facing her, though, was that Guildmasters were rarely selected in such a fashion.

Under normal circumstances a Guildmaster would pre-select his successor. No one, including the Guildmaster's choice, would know whom he had chosen. His decision would be brought to the members by one of the Guildmaster's personal servants in a sealed scroll. The servant would bring the scroll to the central chamber, break the seal, and present it to the assassin whose icon was named inside. Only if the chosen assassin refused the position would the leadership go to a vote.

The leadership of the Guild meant nothing to Shalidar. There had been a time not long ago when he would have challenged if the opportunity had arisen, but now he had ultimate power in Shandar teetering tantalisingly towards his grasp. Guild politics seemed almost petty by comparison.

'Well, I hope you get your opportunity to challenge for the leadership, Brother. I'll not stand in your way if you seek to brush the old man aside. He and I have never seen eye to eye.'

'Thank you, Brother Dragon. I appreciate your support.' Shantella stepped towards the door, allowing her fingertips to run gently down the back of one of the larger silver dragon ornaments on the top of the bookcase as she moved away. Her strutting gait emphasised the irony of her title as a 'Brother'. There were few women who used the power of their femininity with such confidence. 'There's one more Brother whom I trust enough to approach. With his support added, I'll be ready to move. I'll speak with you again in a couple of days.'

She disappeared out through the door, leaving just the faintest hint of exotic perfume in her wake. Shalidar massaged his thigh gently around the area of crossbow bolt wound. The surface damage was healing nicely now. Tremarle's ointment had worked wonders in a very short time, but he was still finding it impossible to walk without a limp.

'A couple of days – perfect,' he thought. 'Long enough to finalise my plans to snatch power, but not long enough to allow the Guildmaster time to interfere. It will take time for a new Guildmaster to find his, or her, feet, and by the time the new leader realises what I'm doing, it'll be too late.'

Shalidar had seen well-laid plans fall apart before. As such he knew instinctively where the weak points in his latest scheme were. 'Tremarle may waver when he discovers that Kempten is not dead,' he mused. 'I must make sure he doesn't do anything foolish. The Guildmaster should be distracted – whatever Fox does will not be half-hearted. I'd better get up to the Palace and see that Tremarle keeps his mind set on being Emperor. Perhaps I can convince him that the coronation should be a private affair – just Tremarle, a few senior Lords and the High Cleric. There would be no reason to delay. We could have it done almost immediately. With those formalities complete I can get back to my unfinished business with Femke and Wolf Spider. . .'

'I thought I'd better drop by and apologise, Rikala. The number of costumes required has substantially reduced. With these complete, we only need –' Femke paused as she mentally ran through the cast and what clothing she had ready for whom. '– three more: the dark cloak for the King and two sets of courtier's clothes. One in Jabal's size and another for Devarusso should cover it. What's the earliest you could have them ready for?'

A small rack of completed garments dominated the tiny living area. The living room clearly doubled as her workroom, as there was an open cabinet with all manner of cloth, boxes of pins, needles, thimbles, buttons and no end of other dressmaking paraphernalia neatly stacked inside. The stout little woman was standing in the doorway between the living room and the kitchen of her tiny town house. Her hands were on her hips and her face was characteristically stern.

'That depends on whether you'd like them thrown

together, or properly sewn,' Rikala replied, her brusque tone leaving Femke in no doubts as to her displeasure. 'By late this afternoon if you're really desperate, I suppose. So what brought on the sudden change? Am I not working fast enough? Have you taken on someone else?'

'No, nothing like that, Rikala. You've worked miracles. We're just going to cheat a little, to speed up the launch of the play, that's all. One of the magicians has agreed to use his skills to take away the need for quite so many costumes.'

'A magician! Pah! As if they know anything of clothing. Ah, well, that's your business, I suppose. I'll be sure to come along and watch the play when you start performing. When's it due to launch?'

'Now that we have the last of the costumes guaranteed, then tomorrow looks likely. Would you like me to reserve you a place?'

'That would be kind, dear. Thank you. I look forward to it. Come in this afternoon at the fifth call and I should have those last items ready for you.'

Femke unhooked the completed costumes from the rack and draped them over her arm. She left through the narrow front door, thanking the stout little seamstress again as she departed. To look at the tiny frontage of her home, it was amazing that Rikala got much trade at all. There was nothing prominent to advertise her presence, but Femke knew that the seamstress had gained her trade through personal referral and reputation. Having built her little business to capacity on that basis, she did not need fancy window displays.

The narrow street was bustling with people about their morning business. Seeing one of the streetwise tattle touts leaned up against a wall and chatting with a particularly shady character was a timely reminder that she needed to catch up on the street gossip. Since her release from the Guild complex, she had been totally focused on the plan. There had been no time for anything else, so it had been a considerable while since she had last done the rounds of the city.

A last glance at the tattle tout settled her mind on the matter. Up-to-date news and gossip would be useful before entering the next phase, to say nothing of starting a few strands of gossip about the production. An effective rumour spread today would pack out the open-air stage seating for the first showing – even if it were staged tomorrow.

Femke hurried through the busy city streets to where Devarusso's wagon was parked near the open-air stage. When she knocked on his door there was no response. The door was not locked, so she cracked it open and cautiously peered inside. There was no sign of Devarusso. 'He's probably at the stage with Calvyn,' she thought. 'There's no point in disturbing their rehearsal.' Leaving the costumes on the bed, she closed the door behind her and headed back into the city, excited at the thought of getting back to doing what she knew she did best.

'Ah, Shalidar! It's good to see you, son.' Tremarle savoured the word 'son'. Although most would consider the deal he had struck before adopting Shalidar unsavoury, it brought him great pleasure to know that the man he now called 'son' had avenged his firstborn. It seemed ever more poetically fitting that the avenger should take the place of the avenged.

Shalidar had a strong presence, and a sense of calm about him that few possessed. He was not Danar, of course, but that was not necessarily all bad. Whilst he had loved Danar, Tremarle had always felt his eldest son to be shallow, and at times had despaired that the boy would ever mature. All he and his idle friends had thought about was their trivial hobbies, and which young lady he planned to seduce next. Shalidar's focus was on more serious issues.

'Father,' Shalidar acknowledged, bowing respectfully. He walked fully into the drawing room, working hard to minimise his limp. 'Are you having a good day?'

'I've had better . . . but I've also had a lot worse. Come. Sit by me. There are some things I wanted to talk with you about.'

Tremarle was sitting in one of four large armchairs arranged in a semi-circle, facing the windows of the drawing room. This was an area of the Palace that Shalidar doubted the previous Emperor had ever even visited. Surabar had stayed closeted in his bleak study on the first floor of the Palace for the majority of the time. It was said that he left it only to sleep and to attend sessions of the Imperial Court.

In contrast to the dark study of Surabar, with its minimal furnishing and feeling of military functionality, this drawing room was opulent in décor, rich with bright gold and glowing purples. It was bright and airy, with tall windows facing south across the manicured gardens of the Palace grounds. The high ceilings displayed ornate coving and a beautiful ceiling rose, from which depended a crystal chandelier laden with candles. Great pictures by master artists graced the walls, whilst ornaments of the highest quality were tastefully placed on the marble mantelpiece, on dahl tables and in purpose-built display cabinets.

A wood fire was burning in the grate. It had burned down to a flicker, but the occasional pop and crackle still punctuated the air as the logs were slowly consumed. The scent of wood smoke hung heavy, though there was no haze to suggest that the flue was restricted in any way.

Shalidar sat down in the chair next to the thickset old Lord. Tremarle shifted in his chair, angling his body more towards his adopted son.

'There are some interesting rumours circulating the streets at the moment,' Tremarle began.

'Rumours? What sort of rumours?' Shalidar asked, keeping his tone calm and politely interested.

'Well to start with there's a rumour that Lord Kempten is not dead, but living out at his country estate with his wife.'

'I shouldn't pay credence to such nonsense, my Lord. Lord Kempten was assassinated. Everyone knows that.'

'Indeed,' Tremarle agreed, noting Shalidar's casual dismissal of the story with interest. 'But the truth and "what everyone knows" are not always the same thing at all. Still, if Kempten were alive, and he did want the Mantle, all he would have to do is come forward and claim it. As Surabar's chosen successor, that is his right.'

'But he has not done so,' Shalidar pointed out.

'Which means either he is dead, or he does not want the Mantle,' Tremarle finished.

'A logical conclusion.' Shalidar did not like the way this conversation was going. He had thought to tackle the Kempten issue in a slightly different fashion. To his surprise, however, Tremarle suddenly dropped the issue and changed the subject to something completely trivial.

'Out of interest, have you heard anything about the new play starting on the city stage tonight?' the old Lord asked, taking him by surprise.

Shalidar paused to consider the question for a moment, trying to see if there was more to this sudden change of direction than met the eye. There was no obvious danger in the subject, so he replied.

'No, I don't believe I have. What's it about?'

'Apparently the current city troupe have produced a new adaptation of *The True King's Gambit*. If the rumours are true, they're utilising magic to create some of the backdrops. It opens tonight. I was thinking of going along. Would you like to come?'

Shalidar's mind raced. Having Tremarle go out into such a large mass of public before he had formally accepted the Mantle would be very risky. Any decent assassin could make a successful hit under those conditions, no matter what security precautions were taken. With Wolf Spider and Femke out in the city somewhere, he did not want to lose sight of Tremarle for any more time than was absolutely necessary.

'I'm not sure that would be a good idea before the coronation, my Lord. There's a rogue assassin loose in the city at the moment. It would be just his style to utilise such an opportunity in order to increase his profile. The Guild is currently trying to track him down, but he's clever. So far he's eluded the extensive network of snares set for him. To make matters worse, he's joined forces with one of Surabar's top Imperial spies, which has given him certain advantages. It's with this in mind that I was going to make a suggestion about your coronation . . .'

'Yes?' Tremarle prompted. 'What sort of suggestion?'

'You might want to make it a private affair, my Lord – a minimum number of witnesses, the High Cleric and you. That would rob the rogue assassin of his chance to make a strike at a time guaranteed to give him maximum publicity.'

Tremarle looked thoughtful for a moment, and not a little worried. 'So you believe this man is definitely out to kill me then?'

'That is my understanding, my Lord, which is why I'll be spending a lot more time with you until he is apprehended. I believe I know his methods well enough to protect you. Once you're Emperor, however, I expect he'll desist. Rogues often continue to play by the Assassins' Creed even after they've broken from the Guild. Adhering to the creed lends a veneer of legitimacy to their business.'

Tremarle' eyebrows raised. 'A veneer of legitimacy? That could also be said of the Guild, you know, but I take the point. You know my feelings on the Guild. I believe they're a necessary part of our society. They've played an important role in Shandese culture for centuries. What do you suggest? Is there any other way I can protect myself further?'

'That's simple, my Lord – bring forward the coronation

ceremony. Have it tomorrow in private. Once you are the Emperor, he's a lot less likely to touch you.'

Tremarle nodded. 'That makes sense. And the play? I'd really like to see it. I've always enjoyed attending the plays at the open-air stage. Could I not go in disguise or something?'

'You'll be Emperor, my Lord. Why not have them come to you? They could give a private performance in the Palace ballroom, or the Great Hall. There's plenty of space in there.'

'What an excellent idea, Shalidar! I love it. I'll send someone to invite the players immediately.' Tremarle got to his feet, his face beaming with enthusiasm, and walked towards the bell pull.

'You might want to schedule your coronation before the play, my Lord. Just in case the assassin managed to infiltrate the group,' Shalidar offered casually, keeping his eyes focused out through the window at the Imperial gardens.

'A wise precaution – yes, that makes a lot of sense,' the Lord replied, pausing mid-way across the room. 'Very well, I'll send for the High Cleric and some of the senior Lords. We can have a private ceremony in the morning and I'll ask the company of players to stage their new play here in the evening. I could then invite a select audience to celebrate my change of status without all the normal pomp. I never much enjoyed the big state ceremonies anyway. This will be far more pleasant. Thank you.'

'My pleasure, my Lord. I look forward to being able to address you as "your Imperial Majesty" tomorrow.'

*

The rapturous applause was unlike anything Devarusso had ever witnessed before. There was not a single person sitting. The entire crowd was cheering, clapping and whooping with delight at the spectacle they had just witnessed.

'OK, everyone, this is it. Don't trip over your feet. Big smiles. On we go.'

The line of supposed actors was longer than any Devarusso had put on stage before. They filed out to even greater applause. The crowd was literally going wild with delight. When the actors had all reached their positions, they turned and bowed to the audience. They stepped back two paces and prepared to file off the stage, but the applause did not lessen. Devarusso gave the signal and they all stepped forwards again to take a second bow. It took a third bow before the noise began to abate.

Devarusso was beaming as he led the line of his 'cast' off to the left of the stage and out of sight.

'Well, I'd say that went off without a hitch. Do you think anyone at the front noticed that the people on stage at the end were not the people in the play?'

'Not a chance,' Calvyn replied without hesitation. 'They were so caught up in the illusion they'd have believed anything by the end. What I want to know is how did Femke manage to arrange our invitation to the Palace *before* we'd even had a chance to dazzle our first audience? That's a sort of magic I don't understand.'

Femke gave him a quirky grin. 'Knowledge is power,' she observed, tapping her temple with her forefinger. 'It always pays to know the weaknesses of your opponent. Tremarle has been an avid follower of theatre for many years. I saw him at performances many times with my . . . with a group of other Lords.' Her face darkened for a moment as she mentally cursed the source of her memory. 'My main worry was that he might be drawn to the performance here, rather than inviting us into the Palace. That would have made a show at the Palace more difficult to arrange, but not impossible. I had a back-up plan for that eventuality.'

'Why does that not surprise me?' Calvyn replied, shaking his head. 'I feel I severely underestimated you when we first met back in Thrandor. I realised you were devious, of course, but if I'd known just how darned clever you were, I'd never have left King Malo to cope with your wiles.'

Femke's grin widened. 'The important thing is that we're going to get in. The buzz from tonight's show should ensure that there's little danger of a cancellation tomorrow. I watched from the side. It looked *very* impressive. Traditional plays will never be the same again.'

Devarusso's elation visibly deflated. 'That's something that really worries me,' he admitted with a grimace. 'The sort of effects that Calvyn can produce are so spectacular, one has to wonder how I'll ever be able to hold an audience with my regular cast again. Everything will pale into insignificance when compared with this. Are you sure I can't tempt you to join my company, Calvyn? Together we could become very rich, you and I.'

Calvyn smiled. 'No, Devarusso, I'm afraid not. My duty is to my King. I've enjoyed working with you these past few days, but my destiny is not here. I must gain my robes as a magician and return to Thrandor. I'm sorry.'

'Ah, well, it was to be expected, I suppose. You don't

happen to know anyone else with your skills who might like some work, do you?' he asked hopefully.

'The only other sorcerers I've met would not be the sort of people you would want to do business with. I shouldn't worry about any rival companies being able to recreate what we're doing here. I find it highly unlikely that there are any other sorcerers around who would do something like this.'

Out of the corner of her eye, Femke noticed Lord Kempten lurking in a corner nearby. He had not gone out on stage with the others, as it was deemed an unnecessary risk. One of the regular troupe had taken his place for the final bows. Sliding away from the group, she stepped discreetly across to speak with him.

'I gather from the applause that all went well,' he said in a low voice.

'Yes, my Lord – very well. We have our invitation to the Palace for tomorrow and everyone knows the plan. Serrius wasn't happy to see Commander Lutalo and his men, but when I explained that they were to be your bodyguard whilst he and the other gladiators led the assault, he calmed down.'

'Good. So everything is set. Tell me honestly, Femke, do you think the plan will work?'

Femke looked him in the eye and took a deep breath. 'It will have to, my Lord.'

'Have to? You don't sound very sure of something. What's wrong?'

'There's been an unexpected development. I got some bad news from one of my agents this morning. I've been

286

wondering how to tell you this all day. There's no easy way to say it.'

Kempten's face drained of colour. 'What is it, Femke? Tell me. Does the Guild know what we plan? Have we got a traitor in our midst?'

'No, it's not that. I'm afraid it's worse. The Guild has taken Lady Kempten hostage, my Lord. I can only assume that she's being held, as I was, somewhere in the Guild complex.'

'Oh Shand, no!' he breathed. 'I should have listened to you and had her move from the country house. This is exactly the sort of thing I was worried about from the beginning. Have they issued any demands in return for her release?'

Femke nodded.

'Well? What are they?'

Femke pulled out a small piece of folded parchment from an inside pocket. Without a word she handed it to him. He snatched it and opened it with trembling fingers. His eyes raced back and forth across the page, his lips tightening with each line read. When he reached the end, he closed his eyes, drawing the parchment close to his chest.

'I realise this places you in a difficult position, my Lord,' Femke said softly. 'I did think about concealing this until after we had carried out the raid, but I realised that I could not in all conscience bring myself to do it. We're your servants in this, my Lord. I've spoken with Reynik. He feels, as I do, that we pushed you down the road this far. We're ready to face the consequences of our actions if you

287

so desire. We couldn't ask you to choose in our favour.'

Kempten looked down at the parchment again and read it a second time:

> Lord Kempten,
> We have your wife. If you want to see her alive again, you must:
>
> 1 – Renounce your claim to the Imperial Mantle.
> 2 – Hand over the Imperial spy, Femke.
> 3 – Hand over the man who faked your assassination.
>
> To trade, first go to the Imperial Palace and renounce your claim to the Mantle. Then take a room at the Silver Chalice. You will be contacted there by one of our people. You have until the third day of Channis.

'The third day of Channis – that's tomorrow, but it doesn't give a time. Does it mean I have until midnight tomorrow? Or sundown? Or until the end of today? The sun has already set. Am I too late? When did you get this, Femke? How long have you known and not told me?'

Although he kept his voice low, there was no mistaking the anger in Lord Kempten's tone. Femke was not surprised. On the contrary – but she was impressed at how calm he was staying, given the circumstances.

'The interpretation of the letter is debatable, my Lord. I would read it as until midnight tomorrow, but that may be wishful thinking. I got the message this morning, but there's no indication of how old it is. My agent got it from one of the better-known tattle touts in town. He claimed he had not had the message for more than a day. They cannot have been holding Lady Kempten long. I took a trip to see Toomas as soon as I got this. Higher priorities had prevented my doing so until now.'

'What did he say?'

'He was most talkative once I had a blade to his throat. Assuming he told the truth, he didn't sell information about you to the Guild until five days ago, so even if Ferdand moved the instant he heard you were still alive, there's no way he could have got someone to your estate and back more than three days ago. Two is more likely.'

Kempten pursed his lips into a tight line and screwed the parchment into a tight ball. 'That's still two days too many,' he said bitterly. 'Shand, but I should never have agreed to all this! My one concern from the beginning was my family. Now look what I've done.'

'My Lord Kempten, you've done nothing wrong.'

'My actions have placed Izzie in danger. If she's been hurt . . . I . . . I don't know what I'll do.'

'What would you have us do, my Lord?' Femke asked.

'I don't know. Give me some time to think. Damn it, Femke! You should have brought this to me as soon as you received it. If Izzie is already dead, I doubt I'll ever forgive you.'

Femke bowed and turned away. She felt terrible. They were so close to making her plan a reality, yet one word from Lord Kempten and everything she and Reynik had gone through over the past weeks would be rendered a wasted effort. Femke had always known the possibility that her service to the Empire might require her to give up her life. Reynik, as a member of the Legions, was similarly braced for the possibility. It was the manner of that ultimate sacrifice that promised to be galling. To give up her life knowing that they had lost – that the Empire was to fall under the control of the Guild of Assassins – was what hurt most. All she could hope was that Lord Kempten would be brave and bold. In her gut, though, she knew this was unlikely. She knew his heart. He would do anything to save his wife.

CHAPTER FIFTEEN

The decision had been agonising. As Kempten stepped up to the Palace gates with Femke on one side and Reynik on the other, his sense of guilt peaked once more. Had he made the right choice? Would this be a day that he would forever look back on with remorse and guilt?

Femke sensed his growing tension and glanced across at him. The glamour image that Calvyn had given Kempten this time was almost too good. It was reacting to his emotions. The Lord's skin looked almost as grey as his hair. There was little Femke could do to help him with his conscience. Everything she could say to help him had been said.

The Palace gates opened wide to admit them and the guards waved them through without question. A small contingent of guards was waiting inside the wall. The soldiers formed up in loose files on either side of them to escort them into the main building. Given all the recent troubles in Shandrim, it seemed strange to gain such easy access to the Palace, even if the guard force was watching them closely.

They followed the road through the gardens and up to the main Palace entrance, the guards shadowing them silently on either side. The last time Femke had entered through these doors was for Surabar's coronation. It was amazing to think that only a few short months had passed since that day, yet so much had happened since. Was this to be the end? Femke had never been one for morbid thoughts, but she could not shake the air of impending doom that had settled on her heart. Reynik looked as calm and intent as ever. Was that because he had no fear, or because he was better at hiding it?

They climbed the grand steps up to the main entrance to the Palace and entered through the huge double doors. Inside the doors a steward awaited them.

'Are you Devarusso?'

'I am,' Devarusso responded from the front of the line.

Femke turned to Lord Kempten and whispered softly in his ear, 'You've done the right thing, my Lord. Don't worry, we won't let you down.'

Lord Kempten nodded, but he did not try to answer aloud. Femke wished with all her heart that her feelings would match the confidence of her words, but right now she was sick to the core with nerves.

'Come this way and I'll show you where His Imperial Majesty would like you to set up your show.'

'His Imperial Majesty? Has the coronation already taken place, then?' Devarusso's question mirrored the thoughts of many in the party.

'The coronation was a small private ceremony this morning. News of it will be released to the public tomorrow. Your show is to be the highlight of the Emperor's private celebrations. It was commissioned at the request of his son, Lord Shalidar.'

Devarusso gave an elaborate bow. 'We're honoured,' he said.

Femke looked first at Reynik, and then at Kempten. They met her eyes with the same silent questions evident in their features. Does he know it's us? Are we walking into the jaws of another of the Dragon's traps? If he knew, then the game was up. If he didn't . . . the irony of that thought caused Femke's lips to twitch in amusement.

'One way or the other, it'll be the highlight – no doubt about that,' Femke heard Kempten mutter softly.

That much was certainly true, Femke reflected. Morose thoughts surfaced. People were going to die today. The only questions remaining were: who, and how many?

Lord Kempten had made a very brave choice by electing to continue with the plan. It had surprised her, but also had filled her with an added sense of accountability. It was her plan. If it went wrong, all fingers would point at her. What if Lady Kempten were to die? What if the assassins proved better fighters than Serrius and his fellow gladiators? The weight of responsibility pressed down hard on her shoulders. There were nineteen in the party, leaving herself aside. In the past she had only ever had to worry about her own skin, and occasionally that of one or two agents. Today was very different.

She looked back and forth along the line. All were

heavily laden with 'costumes' and props, most of which were totally unnecessary for the play, but served to conceal the very real nature of the weapons and armoured clothing they would use for the assault on the Guild. In all, there were six gladiators, six soldiers and two knife-throwers, plus Reynik, Kempten, Jabal, Calvyn and Devarusso. Feeling responsible for so many people made her wonder for a moment what it must be like to be a military commander, or worse still, Emperor. She did not envy Lord Kempten his future, no matter what the outcome.

Not least of her worries was Reynik's role. She stepped behind Kempten and up alongside the young soldier.

'Are you *sure* you're going to be able to handle Shalidar?' she asked discreetly.

'Yes, Femke. For the last time, I'm sure,' he whispered back. 'I don't want anyone else interfering. He's mine. I have more than one score to settle with him. Don't worry, I won't let him get away this time.'

'Don't forget that I know how good he is, Reynik. No offence, but he is a master swordsman. Your desire for vengeance won't neutralise his abilities. I don't want you doing anything stupid, like letting him kill you.'

He flashed her an amused grin. 'What's the matter? Worried I won't be around to rescue you next time you get into trouble?'

'Something like that,' she said, deliberately looking away so as not to meet his eye. 'Is this just an extreme case of nerves?' she wondered. 'Or am I experiencing forewarnings? Oh, Shand! I hope it's nerves.'

'Don't worry, Femke. I'll have Calvyn, my father and six

highly-trained Legionnaires to help me if I need them. I've crossed blades with him before. I'll be careful. What are you going to do if Jabal can't find the entrance?' he said, turning the tables.

'He appears confident that it won't be a problem,' Femke replied. 'I'll give him his chance. But don't worry, if it's there, then we'll find it one way or another – and I'm sure it's there. I take your point, though. Sorry, but old habits are hard to kill. I'll concentrate on my problems and leave you to handle yours.'

They filed through to the Great Hall. Femke fell silent. She knew better than to whisper in here. The acoustics were such that the echo of a whisper in some parts of the hall would magnify their volume by several factors. It was not a good place for loose talk.

For the majority of the party, this was their first time in the Palace. They looked around in wonder at the immense scale of the architecture. The Great Hall had been designed and built to inspire awe. Its great vaulted ceiling and towering pillars evoked a sense of reverence and majesty not unlike the great temples many cultures built in honour of the gods. The architect had been briefed to build suitably intimidating surroundings in which to host visiting royalty. The hall had achieved that aim for nearly six centuries.

The only people in the party seemingly unaffected by the hall were the six gladiators. If anything they seemed more at home in the hall than they had in the corridors. Femke put that down to their experience in the arena. Standing in that huge, sandy bowl, surrounded on all sides by a high wall and tier after tier of shouting, screaming people would likely be more intimidating than a silent hall, no matter how big. Both structures had been designed to make the person in the centre self-conscious. It was only the context that differed.

'The Emperor thought you might like to use the dais at the far end of the Great Hall as your stage. I assume it is large enough for your needs,' the steward said, sounding pleased with his effort at sly humour.

'I should think it will do. What do you think, chaps?' Devarusso asked, turning to the rest of them with a twinkle of excited amusement in his eyes.

'We can slum it for one night, I suppose,' Reynik quipped. A smattering of chuckles echoed with a disconcerting hollow ring.

'Is there somewhere that we can use as a dressing room? There are quite a lot of us, so we might need more than one. Ideally we'd also like access to the stage from the side. At our open-air stage we have screens to allow the players to get on and off without the audience seeing their approach. Have you anything we might be able to set up for this purpose?'

The steward scratched at the back of his head as he thought for a moment. 'I'm sure we'll have something to suit your purposes,' he said. 'This way.'

The party was led forwards to the dais and then over to a side door to the left of the raised platform. Through the door was a corridor running parallel to the side of the Great Hall. An Imperial guard was positioned on the other side of the door. Lover of the theatre or not, Tremarle was clearly not prepared to let the troupe of players have the run of the Palace. Once through the door, the steward turned right along the corridor. He did not take them far. There were two doors on the left. Both were open.

'Here you are,' he said. 'I'll go and see what we can do about setting up screens. Do you need them on both sides of the dais, or will just the one side do?'

'Ideally, both,' Devarusso said without hesitation, 'but we can manage with one if that's not possible to arrange in time.'

'Very well. I'll see what I can do. These two rooms should suffice for your dressing area. If you need anything further, ask one of the guards. The Imperial party will begin to assemble at the seventh call. You should be ready to begin shortly after that time. Good luck.'

'Thank you.' Devarusso turned to the rest of the party. 'All right, everyone. Bring all the gear in here,' he said loudly, indicating the left door of the two. 'Group one should then gather all their things and go next door to prepare. We have about an hour, maybe a little more, so we need to be slick, people.'

The steward, seeing that the company was now in the right place and being chivvied into motion by Devarusso, set off at a brisk walk to find suitable screens with which to form the wings of the stage. Femke took her bundle of costumes into the room and then returned to Devarusso, who was clearly pleased to find his orders followed so swiftly and precisely.

'You know, it makes a change to see a group react to commands so swiftly,' he said with a bemused smile. 'I normally have to talk myself hoarse trying to get the troupe organised in time for a performance. I think perhaps I ought to look out for a few ex-military people who fancy a spell on the stage. They might whip the others into some sense of order. Look, the gladiators are just as efficient. Tell them to do something and they get on with it. I could get used to this.'

Femke patted him affectionately on the shoulder. He was to stay with Lord Kempten, Reynik, Calvyn and the six Legionnaires whilst Femke led Serrius, his fellow gladiators, the knife-men and Jabal in the assault on the Guild.

'Are you content with your part of the plan?' she asked the troupe leader.

'Absolutely. If Calvyn can recreate the atmosphere he did last night, then I guarantee the audience will be spellbound. You'll not have any problems on that score. What about those guards in the corridor? Are they going to prove a problem?'

'With the resources I have to draw on, they could have put a Legion out there and we'd get past them,' Femke said with a wicked grin. 'Don't worry about the guards. We'll deal with them when the time comes.'

'Good luck then, Femke. Be careful, won't you?'

'You can count on it.'

She crossed the room to where Reynik was chatting with his father. On seeing her approach, Lutalo nudged his son and turned away to concentrate on changing into his uniform. They faced each other awkwardly for a moment and then Reynik stepped forward and drew her into a tight hug. Neither of them spoke. There was nothing left to be said. After a long moment, Reynik took a half step backwards, still gripping her upper arms loosely with his hands.

'You know, I quite like you as a redhead,' he said, his eyes sparkling with cheeky humour as his illusory face twisted into a recognisable parody of his boyish grin. 'And the green eyes are fantastic. I think I'll tell Calvyn he's not to change them back. They suit you.'

'What's this?' she asked with a spark in her tone that most would take as a gentle warning. 'Am I your doll then, to dress as you see fit?'

'No, but when this is all over I'd like you to be more than just a friend,' he said softly, his cheeks colouring at the admission.

Femke put her arms around his waist and pulled him back close again. 'You're already more than just a friend,' she whispered in his ear. 'Make sure you're still alive when I get back and I'll prove it to you.'

She kissed him. The kiss was not long, but both felt the significance of it. It was a pivotal gesture. When she stepped away this time, she turned quickly and left the room without looking back. Reynik did not feel slighted. He understood perfectly. Femke needed to focus, and so did he.

The hour passed quickly. Everything was in position. The steward had managed to find screens. Ordinarily they would not have been adequate, but Devarusso was quick to assure the steward that the actors would make do with them. In truth they were not required at all, but the entire plan hinged on perception.

As Calvyn began to create the opening sequence of imagery, Femke gathered her assault party together.

'Master Jabal, I intend to have our team of gladiators take out the guards. I must admit a certain amount of ignorance as to the scope of your abilities. I've not worked with magicians before. If the gladiators kill the guards, there's likely to be some noise. Is there any way you can contain the noise they make?'

The magician nodded. 'I can,' he said thoughtfully. 'But it might be better if I deal with the guards. They've done nothing wrong other than to draw an unfortunate duty. There's no need to harm them. Let me put them to sleep. Trust me – if I put them to sleep, they'll not wake up for anything other than the counter-spell,' he said.

Serrius frowned, looking at Femke with clear disapproval. His 'I told you so' went unspoken, but Femke could read it in his expression as easily as if he had shouted it.

Femke thought for a moment. 'How long will it take?' she asked.

The gladiator's eyebrows shot up, his questioning expression reflecting his disgust.

'Give me about two minutes,' Jabal replied.

'Let the magician use his skills, Serrius,' Femke ordered, her voice low, but firm. 'Your turn will come soon enough.'

Serrius muttered something inaudible under his breath and turned away. Femke ignored his reaction. She knew him well enough to see that his response was born out of a desire for action. The waiting was all but done. He would get over it as soon as they were on the move.

The old magician closed his bright blue eyes and fiddled for a moment with his ponytail of steel-grey hair. His lips began to move as he formed the runes in his mind. With the sequence fully formed, he pictured the runes spinning out through the door and along the corridor in both directions to the unsuspecting guards, who then unwittingly inhaled them like smoke. When Jabal opened his eyes again, there was an air of mischief about his expression. 'You can send your men out to get them if you like,' he said. 'They're sleeping like babies.'

The look that Serrius gave the old magician before opening the door was sceptical, but when he and the other gladiators re-entered the room less than a minute later carrying the two sleeping guards, his eyes held considerably more respect.

'Serrius – you're with me. We'll lead. Derryn will follow. Bartok – take backward point. Is everyone ready? OK, let's go.'

They swept through the Palace at a fast pace to the main stairwell down to the cellars. They met no one along the way. The Palace servants were too busy to be abroad in the corridors. Those who were not preparing the food and rooms for the celebrations to follow the play were hanging around the Great Hall trying to get a glimpse of the show.

In silence they descended to the lower levels. When they reached the cellar door, three of the men lit spare torches at Femke's direction. These were spread through the party and held aloft to give a reasonable level of light with which to aid their silent movement.

The assault team moved into the cellar. Femke immediately had two men bar the door from the inside and listen out for anyone approaching. The rest she bade be silent whilst Jabal searched for the opening. The magician moved to the centre of the room and began muttering in the strange runic language of magic. As he muttered, he turned slowly full circle. The sound of his low, whispered syllables seemed to reverberate unnaturally in the large cellar space, the echoes growing until it sounded as if there were a chorus of magicians muttering spells. He kept turning round and around. Everyone else watched, mesmerised by the strange sight and ghostly whispering.

Suddenly Jabal stopped moving, but his whispering voice did not falter. He was facing diagonally across the room at the wall to the right of the door. He stepped forwards, at first tentatively taking a single pace. Then he took another step and another. Within three strides he was walking forwards with conviction.

The point on the wall that he walked to looked no different from any other. As he reached the wall, Jabal spread his hands and placed them against the surface in front of him as if he intended to push against it. The pattern of his muttered sequence of syllables changed, and his voice grew from a whisper until he was speaking in an everyday volume. His tone became at once more commanding yet lost the echoing quality of just a few seconds earlier.

Femke walked quietly across until she was standing just a few paces behind the magician. If she had not been so close, she would have been unlikely to hear the tiny *snick* of the lock opening within the wall. A large section of the wall, about double the width of a normal doorway, suddenly began to retreat silently from Jabal's hands. There was barely the tiniest of scraping sounds as it slid first back, and then to the side to reveal a dark, descending stairwell on the other side.

A gesture to the rest of the group and they were all in motion. Femke let Serrius and Derryn lead the way. If there was to be a physical confrontation, it made sense to have those best suited to dealing with it at the front. Femke and Jabal slotted into the middle of the group. After a dozen steps down, the stairwell turned through ninety degrees to the left. Another dozen steps followed and a further right-angled turn. Down and down they ran, flight after flight, turn after turn, until finally they reached the bottom. Ahead was a long, straight passageway wide enough for two people to pass with ease. They raced along it until they reached a closed door at the end. Serrius took a quick look back to see that everyone was in position and then he turned the handle. The door was locked. Femke signalled to him from her position in the middle of the group and silently moved through to the front, drawing out her lock picks as she went. The men pulled back a few paces to give her more space, while Serrius held a torch to give her light to work with.

It was not a complex lock. Femke made no noise as she opened it. Having done so, she moved back to allow Serrius and Derryn to resume their positions in the lead. Derryn had a knife in each hand and Serrius had drawn the shorter of his two swords. The tension was palpable as she weaved between the fighters and back into her position next to Jabal. The gladiators looked poised, almost eager, while Derryn and Bartok looked decidedly nervous. Jabal was positively white in the flickering orange light of the torches.

'Are you all right?' she whispered.

'I'm beginning to experience the effects that Calvyn told me about. I can counter them, but it will take a lot of concentration and I don't want to use more magic until I have to,' he replied. 'It seems Darkweaver was very protective of his projects. What he has done here must have taken a huge amount of magical energy.'

Femke nodded, but did not respond further because as Jabal finished his explanation, Serrius threw open the door and they were carried forward in the surge out into the corridor. As soon as she entered the corridor, Femke knew instantly where she was. The straight passageway must run underneath the main chamber, she realised, for they were on the level of the Guildmaster's quarters and this was the corridor that led straight to his door.

A servant emerged from the left-hand side of the corridor about twenty paces ahead of Serrius and Derryn. The man in his brown robes had barely turned into the corridor before Derryn's knife struck him squarely in the throat. He sank to the ground, clutching at the handle but completely unable to cry out.

Serrius ran forward and plunged his blade through the man's heart. The unfortunate servant's legs kicked once, then he was still. The entire encounter had taken just a few seconds and had been blessedly silent. Femke hissed at Serrius to stop for a moment.

'Serrius, have your men set up a defensive position here and wait. I won't be long, but I need to pay a quick visit to the Guildmaster's quarters before we go any further.'

'Do you want to take some of the men with you?' Serrius responded in a forced whisper.

'That won't be necessary. I'm confident I can handle one old man. Besides, I have a score to settle with the leader of the Guild. Only move if you're forced to. I should be no more than a couple of minutes.'

Serrius nodded. His eyes were bright with anticipation of the coming conflict. Now that they were underground his earlier reticence had disappeared and he looked more alive than Femke had seen him since he was at the height of his gladiatorial career. He did not waste any time. Even as Femke drew one of her knives and ran lightly down the corridor to the Guildmaster's door, he was already directing the men into a defensive formation with silent gestures.

She paused at the door, a knife in one hand, her other hand on the handle and her right ear pressed against the wood, listening intently for any sounds inside. She could hear no movement or noise of any kind emanating from within, so she threw the door open and performed a diving roll into the room to minimise her vulnerability to an instant attack.

As she rolled to her feet, she spotted the Guildmaster sitting in an armchair on the far side of the room. He was wearing his black cloak, but the hood was back and his face exposed. He did not flinch at her sudden entrance. Indeed, he was completely motionless. Was he pretending to be asleep? Was this one of his ploys to lull her into a false sense of security? He had fooled her several times before, so she was exceptionally wary as she stalked across the room towards him.

Had his hands not been in plain sight on the arms of the chair, Femke would not have approached him so directly, but she trusted her own reflexes to be faster than her old mentor's. As it was, she was careful not to tread on the oval-shaped rug in the centre of the room for fear of what might be hidden underneath. Instead she stepped around the outside of it, testing each footstep before putting her full weight down. After his refusal to give in to the other Guild members who wanted her killed, she did not think he would look to kill her now, but she was not about to take unnecessary risks.

'Lord Ferdand?' she said softly. No response. 'Lord Ferdand?' she said again, a little louder this time. Still no response. She moved closer. His eyelids were fluttering and his lips trembling. This had all the makings of a trap. Femke stopped and looked around the room again. There was nothing obvious that could pose a threat, but the hairs on the back of her neck were prickling. Something did not feel right here.

Keeping her knife back where Ferdand would not be able to snatch it from her easily, she stretched forwards slowly with her fingertips and touched the back of his left hand. With startling abruptness his eyes opened wide and he took a sharp, deep intake of breath, as if in extreme fright. Femke gasped and stumbled backwards with shock at the ghastly, unfocused stare of her former mentor.

'Femke?' he mumbled. 'Femke? Is that you?'

'Yes, it's Femke,' she replied. 'What's wrong with you, Ferdand? What are you doing?'

'Poisoned . . . Brother Fox.'

'One of your own assassins poisoned you!' Her mind leaped on the irony of it, and revelled in the thought that his treachery had led ultimately to his downfall. Justice had sought him out after all, she thought with grim satisfaction. For all his manipulating and devious schemes, he had been laid low by one of his own – a poetic end for a traitor. However, as fast as the triumphant thoughts entered her mind, accompanying feelings of guilt and compassion welled within her. 'What sort of poison? Do you have the antidote?' she asked tentatively, irritated that she cared.

'Seritriss . . . taken antidote . . . too late . . . too old.'

Femke could see he was right. The poison had gained too great a hold on his system. There were some antidotes that could be as fatal to the elderly as the poisons they had been devised to combat. Seritriss was a particularly nasty poison that affected the nervous system. The antidote, whilst effective at blocking the nerve agent, had side effects that would strain the systems of a young person's body. Ferdand had long since left youth and strength behind. It was obvious to her that he was dying. Even had she wanted to help, there was nothing she could do.

With a quick look around to ensure that she was still alone with Ferdand, she sheathed her knife and dropped to one knee in front of his chair. Looking into his tortured eyes, the final edges of her anger and resentment melted away. It was hard to see any person suffering in this way, but particularly someone whom she had once thought of as a father figure.

'Is there anything I can do?' she asked.

'Listen . . .' he croaked. 'Mission . . . for the Emperor . . . old Emperor . . . before Surabar . . . infiltrate the Guild . . .'

'Infiltrate the Guild? What are you talking about? Reynik infiltrated the Guild.'

'Me.' He tapped his chest feebly. 'Trapped by icon . . . forced . . . stay undercover . . . lived double life.' He coughed, a wheezing cough, too weak to clear his throat. 'Over at last,' he sighed.

Femke's heart pounded in her chest. Could it be true? Had Ferdand really infiltrated the Guild on a mission only to find himself trapped by the same sort of bond that now threatened Reynik? It was possible. She had always known Ferdand to be an exceptional spy. Had he preceded Reynik in infiltrating the Guild? If so, why was he now their leader?

'So the Guild trapped you with the icon. How did you remain under cover so long without being discovered?'

'Long-term mission . . . discovered that without refreshing bond . . . I would die . . . icon would kill me.'

'So you stayed undercover. But why didn't you tell me? How long have you been a member of the Guild?'

The revelation brought unbidden tears to her eyes. Part of her did not want to believe him. Inside, she repeated over and over again that he had betrayed her. He was a traitor to the Empire. The problem was that she could hear the truth in his voice. In her heart she knew it was just the sort of impossible mission at which he would have succeeded where everyone else had failed. He had always been the perfect spy. To penetrate the Guild and maintain his cover to the point of becoming Guildmaster was just like him.

'I might have been able to help,' she added lamely.

Ferdand shook his head. He swallowed hard several times and forced more words up. 'Many years . . . no time left . . . go . . . finish mission . . . done well . . . proud of you.'

'Oh, Ferdand! Why did it have to be this way? I misjudged you so many times. I still don't know what to think. I don't think I've ever really known you, but I so wanted to. I loved you as a father. You know that, don't you?'

The corners of the Guildmaster's lips twitched upwards slightly and he gave the faintest of nods. Femke got up, leaned forward and kissed him on the forehead.

Jerking and twitching against the combined effects of the poison and antidote in his system, Ferdand raised his right hand to the button at the front of his cloak.

'You want to open it?'

Again, he gave the slightest of nods. Femke reached to the button and undid it. She pulled the two corners of the cloak back and over his shoulders. Underneath, the old Lord was wearing one of the wide cravats that she remembered him wearing often when they had lived together at his residence. With extreme effort and violently trembling fingers, he raised the top layer of the cravat. Femke's breath caught in her throat. There was a silver clasp underneath: a clasp in the shape of a panther reaching down from a branch. It was his icon. It had to be.

'Take it,' he gasped.

'But . . .'

'Take it!' he growled, his body rigid with the effort of enunciating the order. He relaxed again, looking totally spent. Almost as an afterthought he whispered, 'Please.'

Femke was torn. She had entered Ferdand's sanctuary with her heart hardened and fully prepared to kill him if she was given the chance. Now he was begging her to take his life and she felt that if she did so, her heart would break. Staring deep into his eyes, she reached out with her right hand and gently unclipped the silver panther. Ferdand nodded and sighed, closing his eyes.

With eye contact broken, Femke looked down at the tie clip. It was a beautifully-crafted piece of silverwork. A closer inspection revealed the same clever touch and styling as the wolf spider pendant that Reynik wore. She wrapped her fingers over the icon, squeezing it in the palm of her hand until the sharper edges began to generate spikes of pain. Leaning forward, she gave him another kiss on the forehead.

'Goodbye, my Lord. I'm sorry I doubted you,' she whispered softly. Then she stood up straight, turned and walked towards the door with as much resolution as she could muster. The icon began to tingle in her hand before she had gone more than a handful of paces and she heard the gasp behind her. She desperately wanted to turn and run back, but she pursed her lips and kept walking. Suddenly there was nothing in her hand and she knew that any thoughts of turning back were irrelevant. Without another backward glance, she slipped out of the door and back into the corridor.

As she closed the door silently behind her, she drew a blade again. A deep *BONG* suddenly reverberated through the corridor and her eyes met those of Serrius, whose alert expression turned questioning at the sound. It was as if someone had struck an enormous gong somewhere in the complex, though if it had been a gong that had created the sound, it would have to be a bigger instrument by far than any she had ever seen. She had heard the noise once before, when Reynik and Calvyn had come to her rescue. It was a detail she had forgotten to ask Reynik about in the aftermath of their escape.

The noise had to be an alarm of some sort. 'The assassins are being called to arms,' she thought. 'If the assassins join forces, we could quickly become outnumbered.'

Femke raced to rejoin the others. This time she took point, with Serrius and Derryn directly behind her. Together they raced up the nearby spiral staircase, taking two steps at a time. As they reached the top of the dark spiral steps she slowed, paused, and peered cautiously around the large central chamber. The Guildmaster's raised podium was nearby and she could see the alcoves in all directions were empty. Torches were burning at regular intervals around the main walls, but there was no sign of life. All was silent.

It had only been a matter of seconds since the alarm had rung, but Femke was surprised not to find assassins appearing from every alcove. If the signal had been a call to arms, then they would have reacted more quickly than this. It must have meant something else. Then it dawned on her – the gong noise had sounded very shortly after the

311

moment of Ferdand's death. If the noise were related to that, then there was no reason for the assassins to come running, but it was likely they would eventually come out of curiosity or duty.

One thing was certain – the female assassin known as Brother Fox would be in no hurry. She would know exactly what had caused the alarm. Femke remembered that the woman had been one of those calling for her death when she had been held prisoner here. It was easy to remember her voice with its rich and sultry tones. 'Let's see how sultry Brother Fox sounds with a knife in her chest,' she thought.

CHAPTER SIXTEEN

Femke leaped up the last few steps and marshalled the rest of the group. As Derryn emerged, she pulled him to one side.

'You stay with Serrius,' she whispered to the knife-thrower. She kept her voice soft enough to ensure no one else would hear her orders. 'Try not to let him get carried away. Make sure you get Lady Kempten out safely. Don't get sidetracked.'

Derryn nodded.

With a rapid sequence of hand signals, she paired off four of the other gladiators and directed them into the alcoves of the bear and the griffin respectively. According to Reynik's information, the secret cavern containing the master stone of the icons was accessed through the wall between these two alcoves. Clearing these two entry points to the central cavern would therefore be the first step to preventing Jabal and his guards from being surprised at short range.

Nadrek and Bartok she assigned to protect Jabal. The master magician looked very pale, as if he were on the verge of vomiting. Serrius gave Jabal a look bordering on contempt as he led Derryn off towards the alcove with the sea snake symbol on the gate. Femke suffered a flash of annoyance, but it quickly became apparent that Jabal was oblivious to the gladiator's slight.

Jabal looked sick, but his focus was already on the wall where they knew the secret opening to the chamber of the bonding stone to be. Magic was his business. She knew better than to interfere. The gladiators were also about their work. With a final 'thumbs up' signal to Nadrek and Bartok, she quickly scanned the chamber until she found the particular symbol she was looking for. The fox's head had a sinister grin. She ignored its malevolent stare and ran lightly across the chamber to the fox alcove.

Vaulting the gate, she landed with catlike silence in an attack crouch. The inner door was shut. With painstaking care not to make even the slightest of sounds, she turned the handle, cracked open the door and slipped shadow-like into the corridor beyond.

Serrius gave a mental 'tut' as he gestured to Derryn to follow him. 'Bloody magic users!' he thought as he ran lightly across the chamber to the alcove displaying the sea snake symbol. 'One look at him and I knew he wasn't cut out for this. Femke should have left the Guild to the fighters. Now we have to waste good people protecting him. What was she thinking of?'

It seemed likely that the Guild would have secured Lady

Kempten in the same holding room in which they had held Femke. Serrius blocked out his negative thoughts and focused his concentration on the task at hand. They needed to get Lady Kempten out of the fray before it turned really ugly. The trick would be to get her out quickly and cleanly. It was the most delicate part of the operation and, despite his respect for the abilities of his fellow gladiators, he fully understood Femke's assignment of this element to him. With unspoken coordination, Derryn and Serrius entered the alcove, each covering for the other as they negotiated first the gate and then the door. The corridor beyond was empty, but there were voices in conversation not far ahead.

Whilst he thought little of the old magician, he had to concede respect to Derryn. The entertainer was far from young, but he appeared in good physical shape. He moved easily, and his breathing remained quiet despite the speed at which they raced down the passageway. 'If I move half as well at his age, I'll consider myself very fortunate,' he thought as he approached the entrance to the assassin's chambers. The door was wide open, so they did not quite achieve the element of surprise they had hoped for. The guards in the room saw them coming in time to scramble for weapons.

Serrius leaped through the doorway with the grace of a dancer, his second sword appearing from its scabbard with a chilling ring. There were three men in brown robes in the centre of the room and a fourth figure robed in black beyond them. A single ring of steel on steel and Serrius had run the first man through with the blade in his right hand. He twisted to meet the blade of the man in black with his left, as both the other brown robes fell with knives protruding from their chests. The figure in black flowed forward, his movements fluid and fast. Serrius parried and blocked three times with the blade in his left hand before managing to draw his other blade free. This was no novice, he realised. The man in black was a dangerous opponent, possessing both poise and speed.

Balance restored, and both weapons available, Serrius whipped into the offensive, only to see the man stagger back with a knife buried to the hilt in the middle of his chest.

'He was mine!' Serrius growled, whirling to face his partner with an angry scowl.

Derryn raised an eyebrow in surprise. 'Sorry,' he said with a hint of sarcasm. 'I didn't realise you were possessive of your enemies. Don't worry. I'm sure there are plenty more to play with. I'll try to let you have more fun next time.'

Serrius let go of his momentary irritation and gave the knife-thrower a lopsided grin as he realised how foolish he must seem. 'Good!' he said gruffly. 'See that you do.'

A resounding BONG echoed along the corridor and filled the room with its after tones. Seconds later another followed. 'Quick! The keys.' They searched the four guards for keys to the inner room, but there was no sign of them. Whatever that noise signalled, the rest of the Guild would be unlikely to ignore it sounding with this frequency. Time was running out.

'The table,' suggested Derryn. Serrius nodded. They picked it up and turned it on its side. 'If you can hear me,

Lady Kempten, get away from the door,' Derryn warned, projecting his voice without shouting. The table was heavy enough to make an efficient battering ram. Serrius took the weight at the mid point with Derryn lending momentum at the back. Together they charged the door. The first impact had little effect. They tried again. On the second strike they were rewarded with the sound of splintering wood. 'Once more should do it.' They charged a third time. The door gave way, unable to resist another blow of such force. It split squarely down the middle and the doorframe ripped off the leading two legs of the table.

Serrius and Derryn threw the broken table aside and forced their way through the remains of the door. Lady Kempten was huddled in the far corner of the room. She looked dishevelled and frightened.

'Don't worry, my Lady. We're not going to hurt you,' Serrius said gently. 'Derryn here is going to take you to safety as fast as he can. Lord Kempten will be most glad to see you alive and well. He's been most worried about you. Come.'

Derryn stepped forwards and offered Lady Kempten his arm. With as much dignity as she could muster, she took his arm, got to her feet and brushed down her filthy clothing.

Frightened she might be, but Serrius could see the un-broken spirit in her eyes. This was a strong woman, he thought.

'I'll cover you back to the staircase,' Serrius said to Derryn. 'From there, you'll be on your own. Be careful.'

Derryn nodded. He had recovered his knives when

searching for the keys. He drew one of them again. Lady Kempten noticed the fresh blood on the blade and pointedly switched her focus elsewhere. It was not that she was squeamish, but she did not want to reinforce in her mind that she was arm in arm with a killer, no matter how noble his intentions.

They moved quickly past the dead bodies in the outer room and into the corridor beyond. Serrius stalked ahead with both blades drawn again. They moved swiftly with no fuss and little noise. When they reached the central chamber, a quick glance around revealed three figures in black emerging from different alcoves. Nadrek and Bartok still held their positions, but the assassins had clearly become aware of them. There was no sign of Jabal, or Femke.

'Go! Go!' Serrius urged. 'I'll cover you. Just run.'

There was one assassin to their right emerging two gates along from where Nadrek and Bartok held guard. The other two were to their left. Serrius moved swiftly to place himself between the two assassins on his left and the fleeing figures of Derryn and Lady Kempten. Holding his relative position, he angled out to meet them. Out of the corner of his eye, he saw Nadrek and Bartok move to engage the third.

'Rats in a sewer – it's funny, but that's always been how I've thought of the Guild of Assassins. Didn't expect it to be quite this true, though,' Serrius taunted in a loud voice. The two figures in black moved towards him. Both drew blades. Neither man spoke, nor looked at one another. Both moved forwards with caution, showing no signs of anger at his insult.

Another figure emerged from an alcove in front of Serrius. Derryn and Lady Kempten reached the staircase. The assassins did not appear concerned. Serrius was the centre of their focus. From Reynik's briefing, the gladiator knew that the assassins thought the only way out of the Guild complex was by using a magical icon. They had no knowledge of the conventional exit into the Palace, so they would view any efforts to run and hide as futile. Derryn disappeared down the dark stairwell behind Lady Kempten. Serrius relaxed.

He hoped some of his fellow gladiators would reappear soon. He had once triumphed over five opponents simultaneously in the arena, but they had been novices and he had been at the peak of his fitness and ability. He was under no illusions that to engage multiple Guild members alone would invite a swift death. 'But what a glorious death,' he thought, allowing a cold smile to grow. 'No rheumatism and old age, but a swirling dance of blood and steel. I can think of no better end.'

This was no time for fancy footwork or dramatic gestures. He needed to kill the men in black swiftly and with the minimum of effort. As the two men closed on him, the man to Serrius's left drew a knife and threw. Instinct born of numerous fights in the arena gave Serrius speed he did not realise he still possessed. With a flashing twist of his sword he deflected the thrown dagger, in a move that brought the thrower to a disbelieving halt. Once his blade was in motion, Serrius followed through with the momentum and took the fight to his opponent.

The assassin's shock at his target's apparent superhuman

319

reactions caused him to freeze for just an instant too long. Although he managed to parry a couple of strokes, he was off balance and simply unprepared for the icy fury of his opponent. Serrius all but beheaded him with a vicious cross cut and then spun out of reach of the other assassin, who had moved rapidly into position to attack the gladiator from behind.

The second assassin also paused his forward motion as he found Serrius suddenly facing him with perfect balance, poised with one blade in a classic defensive position and the other held ready for another attack. Another reverberating gonglike sound echoed around the chamber, followed shortly afterwards by another and then a third. Serrius could sense the third assassin was moving closer.

He turned slowly, concentration at a maximum as he strove to keep both assassins within his field of vision. He heard the clash on the far side of the chamber, but ignored it. His dance was with these two for the time being. Everything else was irrelevant. A feint to his left drew the response he desired. With a stunning turn of speed he spun and leaped, closing down the distance on the second man. He was still mid-leap when it happened. One second he was engaged in a full on attack, the next he was sent flying through the air and darkness swallowed him with an angry, deafening roar.

The moment Jabal stepped up into the chamber, his head began to spin with the chaotic magical energy that tugged and twisted at his senses. The first thing that struck him was that Calvyn had somehow managed to enter this place and get out again. For anyone open to magical influence, the cavern offered a huge danger. It would be easy to lose oneself here – to lose control and never be able to find reality again. Whatever Darkweaver had done to this chamber was specifically designed to keep magicians from interfering with his work. However, despite the apparent stagnation in the mindset of magicians over the last few centuries, some progress in magical arts had been made.

It took a few moments to create a shield that would protect his mind from the effects of the chaos. The vaulted chamber was impressive and imposing by design. It was hard to imagine that even folk blind to the forces at work here would not feel something of the magic in the air, but one look at the faces of his two companions and he could see they were oblivious. With his mind shield in place he was able to regain his focus.

He looked around. Aside from his two guards, the others had all disappeared to complete their various missions.

'Are you all right, master Jabal?' Bartok asked, his body tense and his dark eyes scanning the chamber for signs of danger.

'Yes, thank you, Bartok. I'm fine now. Come. Let's see if I can open the hidden entrance.'

The magician strode across to the wall where Reynik had reported the secret passage to begin. His two guardians loitered in his wake – alert and poised for action. He studied the stone carefully for a moment. The fact that Darkweaver had placed one trap for magicians here made him wary that there could be more. His caution served him well. It took a few moments, but he cast a complex spell of revelation that unveiled a particularly nasty trap. Any magician who blindly tried an opening spell would trigger a chain reaction. The reaction was designed to concentrate a large amount of the chaotic power of the chamber and unleash it in a single magical blast at the person casting the spell.

A bead of sweat began to trickle down his forehead as Jabal sought the key to opening the inner sanctum of the Guild. There was more magical energy flowing around the chamber than he cared to think about. One wrong move and no shield he could create would be strong enough to protect him from the consequences. The more he thought about it, the more he realised that the solution could not be a magical one. This entire complex had been set up to repel magic users. The Guildmaster would therefore not use magic to unlock the barrier. It had to be something basic – a password or a particular sequence of gestures. The problem was there was no magical way of discerning such a key.

'Damn you, Derrigan Darkweaver!' he muttered, irritated at being made to look the fool. The realisation that he was no better placed to force an entry than his two bodyguards made a mockery of his presence.

To Jabal's complete amazement, as soon as he uttered the long dead magician's name, a doorway appeared in the wall directly in front of him. For a moment all he could do was stare in disbelief. Was it another trap? Was there a metaphorical spider waiting to pounce on him the moment he entered? Why had the door opened? It took a moment for it to sink in that it was Darkweaver's name that had opened the way.

'Of all the egotistical . . .' He stopped, lost for words. He had read once that Darkweaver had been a man intent on making his mark in history. Discovering he would make his own name an unchangeable password for such a place made Jabal realise just how desperate the magician must have been to ensure that memory of his name did not die.

'What is it? Can we go in?' Nadrek and Bartok were both fascinated by the appearance of the passageway through what had appeared to be solid rock. They peered in from either side, but Jabal stopped them from going any further.

'No! Do not step across the threshold. There were traps set on the door for the unwary. I imagine there'll be more inside. If you inadvertently triggered one of them, you would die without knowing what had hit you. I must proceed alone. Please, wait here until I return. I'll try to be as quick as I can.'

The two men nodded. Nadrek looked more than content to wait at the doorway, but Bartok's nod was more reluctant. The faint green glow emanating from somewhere along the dark passageway had clearly piqued his curiosity, but he did as he was told and remained with the gladiator as Jabal unhooked a burning torch from the wall nearby and stepped cautiously inside.

He would not have thought it possible, but the buzz of magic in the air ahead was even stronger than in the chamber he had just left. So much so that the power was manifesting to the naked eye. The rocks ahead were glowing with a vast store of magical energy, the like of which Jabal had never encountered before. Even the flickering orange light of his torch did not mask the eerie green glow.

'What in Shand's name has Derrigan done?' he whispered, totally awestruck as he moved forwards step by tentative step. About ten paces along the passage, Jabal felt the magical barrier reform behind him, but he was not concerned by it. The verbal key was unlikely to be different on exit, so he could open it again when needed. His immediate concern was what awaited him ahead.

He emerged into the cave with eyes so wide they bulged from their sockets. The walls were alive with magic! Power surged and flowed, pulsating around the chamber in waves of ghostly green, yet the large altarlike stone in the centre of the chamber appeared cold and untouched by any magical influence. With tentative caution, he stepped into the chamber, his eyes darting about constantly with wonder and nervous apprehension at the phenomenon. About four paces from the central stone he stopped stock-still. There was no mistaking the sensation. The stone began to draw energy from him like a leech sucking blood. The flow was not dangerous; in fact it was barely more than a tiny trickle, but it gave him cause to pause and consider why the stone would react to his presence in such a way.

A simple adaptation of his mind shield expanded the barrier around his entire body and transformed it such that the stone's energy-draining effects were unable to touch him. With his barrier in place, he stepped forward to the altar. Even as he approached, a sparkle of magical energy began to form in one of the shaped recesses on the surface of the stone. As the fizzing motes of light subsided, Jabal saw a silver griffin icon nestled in the recess. With no warning a loud BONG reverberated through the chamber. He clamped his hands over his ears, but he was a moment too slow. The resounding noise was so loud that the shock of it hitting his eardrums felt as if someone were spiking them with giant needles. The ringing aftershock vibrated through his body such that his teeth ached and his eyes watered.

No sooner had the first noise died away than another sparkle of energy announced the arrival of a second icon. Jabal was ready this time. He kept his hands clamped over his ears like limpets, gritted his teeth and screwed his eyes shut. This made the second BONG far more tolerable. When the aftershocks had receded, he was slow to remove his hands from his ears, but quick to begin studying the central stone. The pain thrumming through his head from the intense overload of sound served as a focus for achieving his goal: destroying the stone before it rang again.

Given the arrival of the two icons in quick succession, it appeared that the rest of the team were being at least partially successful. The thought that his companions were engaged in mortal combat gave impetus to his study of the master stone. Although it did not appear to be bursting with energy like the rest of the cavern, he did not want to destroy the stone without taking some precautions against any possible magical backlash.

With infinite care, Jabal began to cast a spell to reveal all the magical bonds he knew to exist between the master stone and the remaining icons. As he completed the spell, a spider web of glowing blue energy mixed with the green light emanating from the walls. Strands of pulsating magic reached out from the master stone like fingers of lightning stroking the walls in a variety of directions and angles. It was clear that the energy was emanating from the central stone, rather than reaching in from each individual icon. However, what fascinated Jabal more than the strands was a faint blue nimbus that coloured the air throughout the chamber. The subtle glowing indicated another, weaker link, but one that was omni-directional. The only space that was not filled with the faint haze was the small space inside the bubble of his shield.

'Shand's teeth, Derrigan!' The shock of revelation, as Jabal realised what Darkweaver had done, was mind-blowing. 'A magical accumulator! You built a magical accumulator! Gods, you were a genius!'

The magician came alive as he realised exactly what he was dealing with. The centre stone had been quietly drawing energy from its surroundings for centuries. Doubt-less, Darkweaver's original intention had been to make the system self-sustaining. This was the powerhouse that fed the icons the energy they needed in order to transfer the assassins between their associated satellite stones.

If Jabal were to make an educated guess, he would say Derrigan had set the master stone to attract a tiny surplus of energy based on an average usage of the system. Over the centuries that surplus had built and built until now so much magical energy was amassed in the rock walls that it was a miracle the chamber did not implode. A closer look at the wall revealed a containment barrier at the surface of rock face that acted like a dam, only allowing a trickle of energy through, whilst holding back a vast flood of magic that unchecked could wreak a disaster of calamitous proportion on far more than just this chamber.

One look at the pattern of power and the solution was obvious. In theory, all Jabal had to do was to smash the stone. The magical magnet effect would then be disrupted and cease to attract more energy, the bonds with the icons should sever, and the energy in the walls would gradually disperse again, though that process might take decades. Despite this assessment, he felt a sudden reluctance to smash the stone.

His purpose in coming here had been to destroy the Guild's ability to use this magic, but on seeing what had been done, he found he wanted to share his discovery with other magicians. The system created by Darkweaver was sheer genius. It displayed simplicity, yet was also complex. Somehow he had harnessed vast amounts of magical energy and contained it in such a way as to present a marvel for any that understood even the most rudimentary precepts of magic. If kept intact, magicians from all over the continent would flock to see what had been done here.

A sparkling on the surface of the bonding stone gave the warning that another icon was appearing. Then another fizzing apparition appeared, and another. Jabal put his fingers in his ears and braced for the alarm. Three ringing tones resonated through the chamber in quick succession. The assassins were being eliminated, but at what cost? It was no use. He knew he could not delay any further.

Strengthening his personal magical barrier with as much power as he dared in his current surroundings, Jabal prepared a spell that would deliver a crushing blow to the top of the bonding stone. He drew every last ounce of energy he felt he could safely control from the walls around him and hurled it into the spell. He had not wielded this amount of energy for many years and the burning sensation inside his head gave him warning that he was reaching his limits. Any more and he risked burning his mind. With gritted teeth, he released the spell and staggered backwards with the effort. There was a thunderous crack as the invisible force smashed into the stone from above like an enormous pile driver. The bonding stone split and with agonising sluggishness it fell into five main pieces, with many smaller pieces crumbling from the edges as it went.

The weblike tendrils of energy winked out instantly and the echoing aftershock of the stone's destruction faded to silence. Jabal sat down, exhausted. Tears hung in his eyes as he surveyed his handiwork. The eerie green glow of the walls gave a ghoulish edge to the quiet. It was done. The bonds between stone and icons, and between icons and assassins, would no longer function.

Unable to look at the broken stone any longer, he bowed his head and allowed his tears to run. He had always sought to create, rather than to destroy. Intense weariness from channelling vast amounts of magical energy mixed with a heavy sense of responsibility for his actions, to leave him feeling empty and sad. He doubted he would ever truly forgive himself, but he had done it out of friendship and loyalty to his friend, Kempten. Sometimes maintaining friendships required personal sacrifice. He wondered for a moment what repercussions this particular sacrifice might have over the coming years. It was impossible to tell.

It was the subtle change in the colour of the light in the chamber that alerted him first. The hairs on the back of Jabal's neck began to rise as he realised something catastrophic was happening. He looked up and his jaw dropped in horror. In the centre of the pile of rubble a brilliant point of light was growing in size and intensity. Vortices of energy were forming all around the cavern, swirling and growing in speed and size even as he watched, feeding vast amounts of energy into that central point in a flow that no magician in Shandar could hope to stop. Somehow, Darkweaver must have set a final trap that he had not detected. The point of light in the centre of the chamber was becoming brighter by the second, its core burning with the intensity of a tiny sun.

'Bloody . . .' Jabal didn't bother to finish his oath. He forced himself to his feet and scrambled away down the passageway towards the exit. He had to get out of the chamber as fast as he could. When that ball of energy reached a critical mass it would explode. With the amount of energy in that chamber, no thickness of rock could be enough to make Jabal feel safe from the resulting forces.

As he staggered along the corridor towards the exit, he instinctively drew further energy into his personal shield, pushing his already depleted reserves to the limits once more. His breath was ragged and his heart thumping wildly as he bounced from one side wall of the corridor to the other like a drunkard. The intense flash of light gave him an instant of warning.

'Sh—'

His voice was cut off mid-syllable. The primary wave of

magical energy as the coruscating ball exploded, brushed through his personal shield as if it were not there. Jabal was vaporised where he stood. Any tiny remnants of his person were swept along with the unstoppable wave of force. The magical door at the end of the corridor was held in place by the separate energy source in the central Guild chamber. The magic of the illusory door proved stronger than the rock walls to either side of it. However, the split second of resistance offered by the walls of the chamber was sufficient to reduce the power of the shock wave, thus preventing the full destructive force of the blast from ripping through the Guild complex.

Bartok was unfortunate to be standing to the left of the magical barrier as the wave blew out the rock wall. He was killed instantly as a huge chunk of rock smashed into his body with hideous force. By chance, Nadrek had moved behind the magical door relative to the blast, having just despatched the assassin with whom he had been battling. He felt rock and debris sweep past on either side of him as all the torches in the cavern extinguished simultaneously, but was fortunate enough not to suffer any injury. The last thing he saw before the inky-black darkness clamped in on the chamber was Serrius and his two opponents being flung across the chamber like leaves on the wind.

'Come in, darling. Don't skulk about out there in the corridor. If you have something to say to me, then come in and say it.'

Femke paused just out of sight. How had the Fox known she was there? Her movement along the corridor had been totally silent. How the assassin had detected her was irrelevant. The crucial element of surprise was lost. Femke was now faced with tackling the confrontation on even terms – not ideal, she realised, but she felt confident of her abilities.

Knife held in front of her, she stepped into the open and through the doorway.

'Ah, the Emperor's pet spy!' Shantella exclaimed. 'I suppose I should have expected to see you turn up again about now. The Guildmaster was a fool to keep you alive. Had it been my choice I would have killed you at the first opportunity. What do you want?'

Femke took in the layout of the personal chamber. It was similar in shape and size to the others she had seen. As was the case with Reynik's quarters, images of the assassin's designated predator dominated the room. Her eyes completed their sweep of the chamber and settled on her adversary. The Fox was wearing her cloak with her hood drawn forward such that Femke could see nothing significant of her facial features. She had a glass of red wine in her left hand and was clearly concealing something in her right.

'If the Guildmaster was a fool, it was for trusting you to be a member of the Guild,' Femke said, her voice cold and emotionless. 'That error cost him his life. *Your* mistake was to kill him. Now I feel obliged to take your life in recompense. What did you think I would want?'

'You're honest. I like that,' Fox replied, clearly amused by the notion. 'But you're in way out of your depth, Femke. I would never allow you to stick me with that little knife of yours, no matter how good you are with it. I confess, though, I'm intrigued to know what Ferdand was to you . . . Yes, I know his real name. The Guild rule about not knowing the real identity of the other members was always one I felt to be tiresome, so I made a conscious effort to break it at every opportunity. Ferdand had a much higher public profile than most here, so it was not hard to figure him out.'

Femke watched her intently as she spoke. Her body language was relaxed. There was no sign of tension in the way she held the glass of wine – probably the celebration glass for having disposed of Ferdand, she thought, an acid taste burning at the back of her mouth. The move, when it came, was so fast that Femke barely saw it. In one motion the Fox dropped her glass, drew and threw a blade at a speed that beggared belief.

Instinct saved her. She ducked under the thrown knife and dived forwards, simultaneously making an underarm throw of her own. Her throw was true, but at a height that allowed the Fox to dodge it with fluid ease. Femke rolled to her feet, deflecting her opponent's vicious front kick with her left wrist, and instantly driving a fingertip thrust towards the woman's throat with her right. Her thrust was met by a solid block.

The hand-to-hand fight that ensued was ferocious. If either had possessed lesser skill they would have been overwhelmed in seconds. Punches, kicks and knife hand strikes were matched with blocks and counterstrikes of equal skill and speed. Seconds ticked and the two blurred in a whirling dervish of flashing arms and legs, but neither could gain a clear advantage over the other.

Femke fought with a single-minded intensity she had not felt since she had battled Shalidar on the roof of the Royal Palace in Thrandor. Had the Fox not been encumbered with her cloak, she might have possessed an edge. It was impossible to tell and irrelevant to the situation. Despite wanting to know who was concealed beneath the dark hood, Femke was not about to encourage the Fox to gain more freedom of movement.

It was a back kick that turned the fight. Femke spun and kicked out backward with her right heel. The power of the strike was such that it drove through the Fox's defensive block and caught her squarely in the solar plexus. The kick was so hard that it lifted the assassin from her feet and threw her across the chamber. She landed with a *whoof* on her back, not far from the transfer stone.

Femke saw the woman's eyes shift to the stone, but her kick had left her awkwardly placed to prevent the Fox from reaching her goal. Femke spun and dived, both fists outstretched. It was an all-or-nothing strike that would leave her horribly vulnerable if she missed her target, but fast as she was, Fox had far less ground to cover.

Something silver flashed in her hand as the Fox slapped it down on the transfer stone.

Femke literally flew across the intervening gap, but even with her lightning-fast reactions, she was not fast enough. Sparkling motes of energy swirled in place of the assassin and Femke felt a chill race down her spine as she passed through the space that the Fox had occupied a split second before. She landed hard, but felt no pain as she scrambled to her feet.

'Damn!' she cursed, smashing her fist down on the transfer stone in frustration. There was nothing she could do. She did not even know where Fox would emerge, so there was no chance of catching up with her. There was nothing to be gained by remaining here in her chamber. It was unlikely that Fox would come back for a while – if ever, assuming Jabal could destroy the bonding stone.

It was as she bent to pick up her knife from where it had come to rest on the floor that the chamber lurched in the most alarming fashion. There was the shortest of pauses before the blast wave hit. The force of the impact picked her from her feet and smashed her body into the nearby bookcase. Femke's last fleeting thought was that the entire underground complex was collapsing, and then there was nothing.

The shock wave rocked Rikala's front room as if it were a ship running aground at speed. The little seamstress placed her arms over her head and closed her eyes tight as the sound of falling pots and pans mixed with that of breaking glass and shattering pottery. When the shaking stopped, she cautiously lifted her head. The first thing to catch her eye was the alarmingly wide crack in the wall in front of her. Without a second thought for her possessions, she staggered up out of her chair and ran out through her front door into the street, terrified that the house might fall down around her at any moment.

No sooner had she stepped out through the door than a piece of falling masonry twice the size of a large man fell from the sky, crashing through the front wall of the house opposite. Rikala screamed in terror. Turning towards the Palace, she saw a huge mushroom cloud billowing upwards, black and forboding.

'What in Shand's holy name could have created that?' she mouthed in astonishment. Even as she completed the thought, a deadly rain of smaller pieces of stone began to shower down, clattering and crashing into the rooftops and across the cobbled streets. Dangerous though it may be to remain inside with a huge crack in your wall, to stand out in this would be to invite death with open arms.

Cowering as she ducked back inside, Rikala dashed into her tiny kitchen and dived under the table, where she remained, quaking and weeping uncontrollably. The noise of the falling debris was terrifying as death and destruction rained down across the city. To Rikala it seemed as though the Creator himself had decided to shatter the mundane life of Shandrim with a thunderbolt from heaven. Whatever had caused this, one thing was sure – life would never be the same again. Anyone who survived would recall the day of the great cloud of devastation.

CHAPTER SEVENTEEN

One second Reynik was on his feet, talking tactics in hushed tones with his father in the corridor outside the Great Hall, the next he was flat on his face, convinced the end of the world had come. A series of rumblings, smashing and crashing noises followed, along with hysterical screams and panicked shouting emanating from the Great Hall.

'What in hell . . .'

A quick glance around revealed that no one had managed to stay on his feet through the explosive quake. His father and the other Legionnaires were all scattered across the floor like so many twigs shaken from a tree by high winds. Even Calvyn, whom Reynik expected to still be upright through some magical means, was sprawled flat on his back. No one appeared badly injured, though Calvyn's face had suddenly lost all its usual colour and vitality.

'Master?' he mouthed, his voice not audible above the noise from the Great Hall, but the word clearly formed on his lips.

Reynik leaped to his feet and ran to Calvyn's side. 'What has Jabal done?' he asked urgently, grabbing the young acolyte by the hand and helping him sit up. 'What's happened, Calvyn? What has Jabal done?'

'Master . . .' Calvyn whispered again, his voice thick with sorrow and tears forming in his eyes. He gave no outward sign of having registered Reynik's presence. His body was limp with grief and his eyes distant. Reynik realised the futility of his questions. He would get no quick answers from the magician. Calvyn was in a deep state of shock. Reynik tried shaking him, but without success. Calvyn could not help.

He turned to Lord Kempten. The Emperor Designate did not appear hurt. His glamour disguise was gone. Instinctively, Reynik glanced down at his own appearance. All the glamours had dissipated. The explosion must have had magical repercussions, he realised. Calvyn was in no state to reform them, but it no longer mattered. The time for disguise was past.

'Are you ready, my Lord?' Reynik asked urgently. 'It sounds like pandemonium in the Great Hall. Shand only knows what's happening in there. If you're going to take control, then you need to do it now.'

Kempten nodded. Lutalo and the other Legionnaires were all scrambling to their feet. They gathered in a defensive group around Lord Kempten and were ready within a matter of a few seconds.

Reynik gave his father a brief nod and stepped through the doorway into the chaos beyond.

At first it was hard to make sense of the mess. There

seemed altogether too much debris for the relatively small hole in the roof and the larger hole in the end wall above the altar. It was only when Reynik focused on the huge chunk of masonry that had crashed down in the centre of the dais that he realised it had not fallen, but had been hurled through the end wall of the hall from elsewhere.

'Good grief!' he uttered as he scanned the vast hall. One of the great pillars had crumbled and fallen right across the middle of the audience. By some miracle, the section of the roof that it had supported had not caved in, but was sagging precariously. Reynik's instinctive assessment was that it was poised to come down at any moment. Noblemen were scrambling to pull friends and loved ones from under the debris, but for the most part the pieces of stone were simply too heavy to move. Others were dithering, or running for exits, or simply sitting, held in mesmerised thrall by the shock of the moment. The pained screams of the injured joined with the wailing of those cast into instant mourning at the sudden, crushing death of those nearby. The sounds echoed and rang around the hall in a way that accentuated the panic and pain of the moment.

Tremarle was clearly visible in the middle of the chaos. He was one of the few actively trying to coordinate efforts to free a nobleman trapped underneath one of the smaller sections of fallen stone. It took a moment or two for Reynik's searching eyes to find Shalidar, but then his eyes came to rest on his sworn enemy.

'Shalidar mustn't get away,' he said quickly, already in motion before making the conscious decision to attack.

'You must protect Lord Kempten, father, but if I fall, do what you can to see Shalidar stopped.'

The assassin was halfway across the Great Hall, clearly looking to escape through one of the side doors. The first thing that Reynik noted was that he was limping, but either the injury he had sustained was a minor one or it was not a fresh wound, for he looked to be moving with relative ease in spite of his uneven gait.

'Stand and face me, Shalidar!' The shout was loud enough to cut through the chaos and confusion. Shalidar froze in his tracks. The assassin's face instinctively twisted into a sneer of contempt. Reynik closed the distance between them quickly, bounding and vaulting over fallen masonry with determined purpose.

The assassin's eyes narrowed as he recognised his adversary. His sneer twisted further to become a snarl of anger. It looked for the briefest of moments as if he might make a run for the side door. The indecision was clear in his eyes, a flicker of uncertainty before accepting the challenge.

Reynik noted the fleeting inner conflict with a sense of satisfaction. Shalidar was not so sure of himself now, he realised. It was one thing to attack someone on a dark street with the advantage of surprise, but to face a determined, talented fighter, who knew exactly what to expect from the encounter was a different prospect.

Across the Great Hall, another had frozen at Reynik's shouted challenge.

'Leave my son be,' Tremarle called out, alarmed by the sight of Reynik bounding through the debris with a murderous expression on his face. If Reynik heard the call, he gave no indication of it.

'Your son, Tremarle? You have no sons.'

The response came from the dais, and Tremarle was quick to identify the speaker's voice.

'Kempten! I heard whispers that you were still alive, but I gave them little credence. What is it to you if I have adopted Shalidar as my son? And what is the meaning of all this? If you wanted the Mantle, you could have taken it. You were the named heir,' he said, gesturing around at the devastation of the Great Hall with a look that spoke of personal injury.

'You're making a fool of yourself, Tremarle, though I suspect you've done so unwittingly. Shalidar has used you. Don't you see it? You're too wily to have let his profession escape you. You know who he is – what he is. But did you know that it was he who killed Danar?'

A clash of blades rang loud through the silence that followed Kempten's last statement.

'Shalidar killed Danar?' Disbelief was heavy in his tone and evident in his expression, though it quickly wavered in the face of Lord Kempten's steady gaze. His misgivings about Shalidar's hidden agenda had troubled his heart for some time, but this? Bile rose to the back of his throat as he recognised the truth in Kempten's eyes. The realisation that he had fallen victim to the very worst kind of deception hit him with cruel force.

Shalidar timed his attack with precision. He waited until the critical instant when Reynik committed to hurdling the final piece of fallen masonry between them. As Reynik leaped, Shalidar palmed and flung one of his knives. The blade flashed through the air, the finely-honed steel streaking with deadly accuracy towards the centre of Reynik's torso. The young Legionnaire saw the blade leave Shalidar's hand and in that second his mind and body accelerated, the world appearing to slow as the adrenalin spike in his system provoked an entirely new turn of speed.

With a spectacular twist mid-leap, Reynik somehow arched his body such that the blade passed by, missing him by the finest of margins. In that moment, his entire consciousness seemed to reach a new level. He assimilated details that under normal circumstances would never have been possible: the fine ebony handle of the blade as it zipped past, the brushing sensation of its passage and the flashing expression of disappointment on Shalidar's face. Every detail etched itself into his mind.

With a catlike sensitivity to the force of gravity, Reynik managed to complete his twist and land on his feet, though he was not at all in balance as he hit the floor. He fell forwards and tucked into an acrobatic, twisting roll that he had learned from Femke. In a flash he was back on his feet, his momentum intact and his desire to engage with Shalidar burning more fiercely than ever. His mind and body lurched back into its normal speed of thought and reaction. With his blade in the guard position, he rushed forwards.

Shalidar did not allow his flash of disappointment at failing to stop his adversary affect him. With his customary grace, he whipped out his sword and adopted a strong, defensive stance to meet the oncoming Legionnaire.

The first exchange was both vicious and blindingly fast.

Reynik launched a flashing attack in a deadly combination of hard, accurate strokes. To his surprise, Shalidar's previously evident limp disappeared and he defended with apparent ease. Displaying the neat efficiency of a master swordsman he deflected each of Reynik's blows, remaining in perfect balance throughout. If Reynik had not seen the assassin's limping gait before shouting his challenge, then he would have thought he was facing Shalidar in top physical condition.

Sparks showered from the clashing blades and the ring of steel on steel suddenly became the only sound in Reynik's ears. All else faded out of existence as his world shrank to a bubble containing just the two of them. Their deadly dance was everything. In his mind it became an entire cosmos of whirling order and chaos: good against evil, light battling the darkness, right striving to overcome wrong.

Lessons with the gladiator, Serrius, had improved his swordsmanship out of all recognition from the raw skills he had possessed as a freshly-graduated Legionnaire, but he was no blademaster – not yet at least. His opponent, however, had honed his skills with a sword over years. Shalidar fought with confidence and a fire in his eyes that would have made even the best of swordsmen blanch. Reynik did not allow the assassin's gaze to distract him. He did not notice it. Instead he did exactly what Serrius had taught him to do – focused on the centre of his opponent's torso, watching for the tell-tale shifts in balance that would allow him to anticipate his opponent's moves. At the same time he kept his own balance and poise as perfect as he could make it.

After the first exchange, the two protagonists began to circle. Reynik could see that the assassin was favouring his right leg, but his limp had definitely lessened since engaging in the fight. No doubt the pumping adrenalin would be dimming the pain, he thought as he watched for another opening.

From beginning the fight on the defensive, Shalidar switched to the offensive during the second exchange. His sudden lunge was well disguised. Reynik barely had time to react, but his sharp reflexes and his newfound balance served him well. He deflected the blade and whipped a cross cut in response, which was quickly parried. Another rapid string of ringing blows ended with a momentary stalemate, as they finished with swords locked hilt to hilt in a muscle-twitching struggle of strength, each looking to gain the advantage of position.

Face to face, Reynik could no longer totally ignore Shalidar's fiery gaze.

'Prepare to die, Wolf Spider. You're no match for me.'

'I'll see you rot in hell first,' Reynik growled in response. He shoved away hard and swung at Shalidar's neck. He was blocked. He struck again and again, testing Shalidar's speed of reflex with every swing, but he could get nothing past the assassin's defences. Worse, the counter-attacks were becoming harder to fend off. Twice in quick succession he barely deflected counter-strokes that unchecked would have landed mortal blows. Femke's misgivings suddenly appeared well founded. It was clear that he was outmatched. Unless he could find a chink in Shalidar's defence quickly, then he was unlikely to survive the encounter.

An idea formed. He attacked again, concentrating on upper body, neck and head, eventually drawing Shalidar into committing to a vicious cross cut at neck height. With his weight on his back foot, Reynik spun through ninety degrees, swaying his upper body away and underneath the blade, whilst his front foot lashed out in an explosive kick. He was aiming for Shalidar's front knee in the hope of damaging the joint, but in his enthusiasm the kick landed high, glancing off Shalidar's right thigh. In a flash he was back in a defensive stance from which he deflected Shalidar's return stroke.

The glancing kick had not landed well, but the gasp of pain from Shalidar told Reynik all he needed to know. He had found the man's weak spot. The assassin's reaction had been out of all proportion to the strength of the contact. The pain in his face was genuine.

Reynik gave a nasty grin at Shalidar's discomfort, but he was not given the luxury of enjoying the moment long. The assassin attacked again, this time with a dazzling pattern of strokes that Reynik found even his reflexes and instincts could not totally counter. The fury displayed on Shalidar's features was no longer contained, but Reynik was unaware of it as he was reduced to purely defending with no thoughts of counter-attack. The blinding barrage of lightning-fast strokes began to take their toll. In quick succession, he felt stings on his sword arm, his chest and his right thigh. None felt serious, but each would be sure to sap his strength.

The assassin did not let up the pace, but continued to press forwards, determined to make his kill. Their blades clashed again and again in what seemed like an endless ringing of metal on metal. A sudden change in tone and a feeling of imbalance in his blade gave Reynik no more than a half second warning before his sword broke two hand spans from the hilt. He tried to leap backwards to gain space from Shalidar, but in doing so he tripped over a piece of fallen masonry and fell crashing to the floor.

Shalidar was over him in an instant. Reynik saw the eyes of his nemesis flash with triumph as he raised his sword for the killing blow. He lunged, but somehow Reynik twisted and, using the remains of the broken blade, turned Shalidar's sword sufficiently aside for it to miss him and strike the stone floor.

'Die, damn you!'

Shalidar shifted to strike again, but suddenly straightened and started to turn, his eyes widening with the shock of unexpected pain. Reynik did not hesitate, but launched upwards with all his strength and rammed the remnant of his blade into the assassin's belly. Shalidar gasped again. His sword fell from his fingers as he staggered back. He turned. To Reynik's amazement there was a dagger stuck deep in the middle of the assassin's back. He shifted his focus beyond Shalidar, fully expecting to see his father. Instead his eyes met those of an unexpected ally – Lord Tremarle. Lutalo and two other Legionnaires were approaching fast, but it was the would-be Emperor who was standing behind Shalidar.

'Why, you old fool?' Shalidar gasped as he sank to his knees.

'I just learned that you killed Danar, you merciless son of

a bitch. How you had the gall to sit at my side as my adopted son, I shall never know.'

Lord Tremarle drew his sword and stepped forwards. Reynik looked away as the old Lord gave a snarl and swung his blade in a lethal arc at Shalidar's unprotected neck. The sound of the impact was horrible. Reynik doubted he would ever forget it. He wanted to vomit, but his pride would not let him. The one thought in his mind was that it was over – finally. With Shalidar dead, he could go back to his life with a sense of peace.

An ominous creaking far above him snapped his mind back to the present. Even as he looked up to the roof, high above, there was a loud cracking noise and it began to collapse. Great beams detached, followed by huge areas of slated roofing, all accelerating with deadly momentum. It was an awe-inspiring sight, the implications of which took but a fraction of a second to sink in.

'RUN! Lord Tremarle! Father – run!'

Reynik was on his feet and sprinting as he had never done before. Another surge of adrenalin fired his body into action, drawing deep on reserves he did not realise he possessed. Behind him, the Legionnaires scattered whilst Lord Tremarle looked up and froze in fascinated horror as a great section of the roof detached and fell towards him in what seemed like slow motion. Those who saw it happen said afterwards that at the last second before impact he threw his arms wide as if to embrace his fate. The huge weight of falling debris crushed him instantly.

A final running dive carried Reynik clear. He landed hard and rolled some distance before coming to rest against the side wall of the Great Hall. A wave of dust and splintered slate scattered in all directions. He huddled in a ball with his arms protecting his head, as splinters rained against his back and legs.

The rumbling crash settled to the occasional clatter of odd pieces of slate falling or settling. There was still some echoing noise in the hall. The survivors were still whimpering, and the injured still crying out for help, but the sounds of them seemed subdued in the aftermath of the collapse. Cautiously, he unravelled his body and rolled over. Tears formed in his eyes as he peered back through the settling dust cloud. He knew instantly that Lord Tremarle had not made it clear. The old Lord had saved his life, only to lose his own just a few seconds later. It did not seem right that he should suffer such a cruel twist of fate.

After a moment, Reynik looked around the Great Hall again. His father gave him a shaky wave from where he was regaining his feet and dusting himself down. All the visible evidence suggested that Lord Tremarle was just one casualty amongst many today. For the first time since the quake had thrown him from his feet, Reynik started to think outside of his immediate circumstances. A slow, creeping sensation of horror coiled around him as his mind finally made the connection between the explosion and Femke.

'Oh please, no!' he breathed. 'Not Femke . . .'

Even as he uttered his plea, Derryn and Lady Kempten stumbled into the Great Hall through one of the nearby doorways. The Lady looked dishevelled, but composed. A trickle of blood ran down the left side of her face, originating somewhere under her hair. Despite her physical appearance, however, there was no mistaking her for anything but nobility.

'Are you all right, my Lady?'

'I'm fine, thank you, Reynik. I shall feel even better if you give me news of my husband.'

'He's well, my Lady. Look, he's over there coordinating the rescue efforts. Part of the roof collapsed and one of the stone pillars fell. There are people trapped under the rubble.'

'Then I shall go and help him. Thank you.'

'Have you seen anything of the others, Derryn?' Reynik asked the aging knife-thrower.

Derryn shook his head. 'We were on our way out of the Guild passages when we were thrown from our feet by the shock wave. I've no idea what caused it, but you'll have to be careful if you're intending to go down there, Reynik. A blast of that magnitude will have done a lot of damage. The entrance to the Guild is open, but even if the passage-ways are not blocked, I'm not confident that the caves will be stable any more. It would be easy to get trapped.'

'Thanks, Derryn. I'll do my best to be careful. Can you show me the way?'

Lutalo grabbed his son by the arm, having approached in the middle of the conversation.

'Are you sure this is a good idea, son?' he said, stopping Reynik as he made to leave. 'You're bleeding. There are others who can lead the search. Get your wounds seen to.'

'Femke's down there somewhere, father. I'm not going to rest until I know she's safe.'

'She's that special then?' Lutalo asked pointedly, giving his son a knowing look.

'That special and more,' he replied, returning his father's look with an uncompromising one of his own. 'What would you do in my position?'

Lutalo paused for a moment. 'Exactly what you're doing, son. Let me bring a few men. We'll go together.'

'Wait! I'm coming too.'

Reynik looked around in surprise. It was Calvyn. Reynik had thought him too deep in shock to take any further part in the action. To see him here, pale, but with a determined look on his face, was completely unexpected.

'You might want to be aware that the West Wing of the Palace has totally gone,' Calvyn added. 'I took a quick look. There's nothing to mark where it stood other than a huge crater. Master Jabal is dead – at least I can detect nothing of his life force from here – but I must make sure. I would not abandon him in an hour of need. That explosion involved a magnitude of magical energy the like of which I doubt has ever been seen in Shandar before. I must come with you.'

'Calvyn? Are you sure?' Reynik asked. 'You don't look well. Remember how you felt last time you entered the Guild complex? I don't want to have to carry you out.'

'I doubt it will affect me this time. Whatever Jabal did down there will have changed the magical properties of the Guild complex forever. You might require my specialist help. If there's need, then I can use magic to clear the way, or to shore up the roof. Both, if necessary.'

Reynik nodded. 'I'd be a fool to turn down the

company of one with such abilities. If you're sure, then let's go.'

Femke felt sure she must have died. The darkness was complete and her body numb. The combination of the total lack of light, together with the lack of tactile feeling, gave her the sensation of floating in an eternal void of darkness. She felt dizzy and sick. Was she spinning in the void? Once the idea had entered her mind, it was difficult to banish. Also, there was pain. 'Is this the sort of echo of pain one suffers on losing a limb, still feeling sensations where the limb used to be?' she wondered. 'Am I a spirit now feeling pain where once I enjoyed a body?

It was the noise that gave her the first flash of hope – the distant sound of someone talking. At first she thought it might be her imagination, but after a moment or two, she realised that there was more than one voice. What was more, they were coming closer.

She tried to move; tried to do anything that might take away the sensation of floating in the darkness. It was hopeless. She tried to call out, but that also proved impossible. Her efforts, whilst not spectacular, did result in a noise. It was faint, but she was sure it had been real. If the noise was real, then the people she could hear talking were real, and if they were real . . .

She tried again. The sound she made was muffled, but louder. A faint haze of light filtered through to her eyes. It was not enough for her to see anything, but the voices were still coming closer. There was a sudden sound of running feet. A weight suddenly lifted from her and she flinched

350

from the burning light of the torches that suddenly flooded her sight.

'Over here! Under the fallen bookcase. Femke? Are you all right? Can you hear me?'

It was Reynik. More pain flooded her body as blood flowed back into limbs. Her chest, constricted for so long, began to expand and contract normally again. He was touching her face gently, stroking her hair and her back. Shand, but it felt good!

'Fine,' she mumbled. 'Fine now. Others?'

There was a pause. Some of them had not made it. Reynik would not have paused if everyone else had survived. A sudden tingling across her body caused her to shudder. Something was happening. Something unnatural. The pain was receding. Life and energy were returning to her.

'What's wrong with her, Calvyn? Is she badly hurt? That bookcase was heavy.'

Another pause.

'No. She should be fully recovered in no time. There's nothing broken. I've just healed the worst of the bruising and abrasions.'

'Can you move now, Femke?' Reynik asked.

She opened her eyes again, squinting in the light of the torches. The first thing Femke saw as she pushed herself up into a sitting position was the anxious look on Reynik's face. She reached for him and he wrapped his arms around her and drew her into a tight embrace. Over his shoulder she saw Calvyn. He looked terrible. She patted Reynik on the back and, though she was reluctant to break the intimacy of the moment, she pushed him gently away.

'Jabal?' she asked Calvyn.

He shook his head sadly.

'I'm so sorry. What did he do? Was it he who caused the blast wave?'

Calvyn gave an apologetic shrug. 'My guess is that Darkweaver left a trap for any who tried to destroy his work. Master Jabal was an excellent magician, but he didn't have the devious mind of Darkweaver. The force generated by the destruction of the bonding stone blasted half of the Palace out of existence. It appears that the weakest point in the cavern was directly above the stone, which was fortunate for you, as the majority of the explosion released straight upwards. The cavern was directly underneath the West Wing of the Palace. Before we came down, I heard witnesses say that they saw chunks of masonry hurled halfway across Shandrim by the blast.'

Femke tried to picture it, but found such an image beyond her? 'What will you do without him?'

'My duty remains. I'll return to the Academy and continue my studies. The other masters there will be sad to hear of his passing, but I'm sure they will not attribute blame. Darkweaver's legacy of magic has caused them more than one hurt in recent times. Jabal was a popular man and an excellent teacher. He will be sorely missed.'

'I certainly liked him. I've not had many dealings with magicians in the past, but Jabal was a good man. My deepest condolences, Calvyn. This mission was always fraught with danger. I'm sorry that you've been burdened with this loss. I appreciate this might seem insensitive, but

I must also ask about the others . . .' Femke looked at Reynik for information.

'Only Nadrek, Derryn and one other gladiator from your party survived the blast. Derryn got Lady Kempten to safety.'

'Serrius didn't make it?' she asked. Inside she felt a measure of surprise that anything could have killed Shandrim's most deadly gladiator.

'No. His neck was broken when he was thrown on the blast wave across the central chamber. Nadrek says he saw him in those last seconds. He was fighting three of the Guild members at the time of the explosion – fighting and winning, as only Serrius could. Nadrek says he'll ensure that the tale of his final fight adds to his legend.'

Femke nodded. 'He would have appreciated that. And Shalidar?'

'Also dead,' Reynik said grimly.

'You're sure?'

'Positive.'

'Then it's over,' she whispered with a satisfied sigh.

'You could say that,' Reynik replied. 'Except that there are four of the assassins still unaccounted for, unless you know the whereabouts of the Fox.'

'No. She's gone,' Femke said, her tone bitter. 'She transported shortly before the blast wave, but I shouldn't worry unduly. I'll catch up with her eventually. In the meantime, what will the remaining assassins do? The Guild no longer has a headquarters. The majority of the organisation is dead or scattered, and they no longer have a magical getaway system to rely on. They're a broken force.'

'Don't underestimate the Fox, Femke. She's as cunning as her namesake. I wouldn't put anything past her. She reminds me somewhat of you . . . but with longer legs.'

Femke cocked one eyebrow and gave him a dangerous look that set him laughing. Even Calvyn managed a watery smile at the expression. Femke could not hold the look long, for Reynik's laughter was infectious and she found herself joining in. He reached out, grabbed her hands and helped her up to her feet.

'Do you plan to return to the Legion now, Reynik?' she asked him softly, as they picked their way through the wreckage of the room and out into the passageway beyond.

'Actually, I was thinking of asking for a long-term secondment,' he replied. 'I've found the last couple of months working with the Imperial spy network most informative. I thought I might suggest to my Legion Commander that I build on my recent experience by working directly for the Emperor with a view to a permanent transfer.'

'Really? Is that the case?' Femke said brightly. 'You'd need a lot more training, of course.'

'Of course.' He slipped his arm around her waist.

'I wonder who the Emperor will assign to train you?'

'Oh, I'm sure he'll find someone with the relevant experience,' Reynik said sagely. 'If I ask nicely he might even assign me a female operative. Of course she'd have to have very long legs . . .'

Calvyn shook his head, wincing. 'And I thought I was the naïve one when it came to women!' he said as Femke gave

Reynik a punch to the stomach that was only half playful. 'You might be a good soldier, Reynik, but I'm beginning to think you have a death wish.'

EPILOGUE

It felt strange to be back in the Emperor's study, Femke realised, particularly now that Emperor Kempten had placed his personal touch upon it. Gone was the sparse, military Court room feel. The room felt warm and friendly, with soft rugs on the floor and bright, cheerful wall hangings. There were comfortable chairs and dahl tables, plants on stands and bookshelves filled with books and ornaments.

It only seemed like yesterday she had poisoned Vallaine's wine here, and browbeaten Surabar into becoming Emperor. Did that make her responsible for Surabar's death as well? It was a question that had nagged her ever since hearing the Imperial Bell the night she and Reynik had first escaped the Guild complex. Femke did not think she would ever truly be able to resolve that question. If she had not twisted General Surabar's arm to become Emperor, it was most likely that he would be alive today. However, it had been Surabar's idea to take on the Guild.

Femke had not had any part in that decision. Looking around the room she felt echoes of the previous three occupants, as if their ghosts were watching on with interest to see what she would do next.

The spy shuddered inwardly at the thought.

'Sit down, Femke. Please, make yourself comfortable. It's good to see you again. Did you enjoy your break? Are you feeling rested?'

'Yes, thank you, your Majesty. It's been good to relax for a while, but I'm ready to come back to work.'

'So you wish to remain in the Imperial spy network, then. I'm glad.' Kempten's voice held the warmth of genuine feeling. 'I was worried that after all your trials during Surabar's brief reign, you might decide to try your hand at something different.'

Femke laughed. 'I briefly considered an apprenticeship as a stonemason, your Majesty. Members of that particular guild are all walking around with fixed grins at the moment. The work created by the destruction of the West Wing, combined with your commission of the new theatre has them all very excited. You've given them enough work to last generations.'

Emperor Kempten smiled. 'Well at least I can be sure of the unreserved support of one of the guilds.'

'The truth is, your Majesty, I don't think I'm suited to much else. I thrive where the action is. Also, Reynik has decided that he would like to transfer from the Legions to join the network, which has brought an added attraction to the work.'

'Ah, I see. He's a fine young man, full of fire and

enthusiasm. You'll make a good match, I feel.' Kempten paused for a moment and tapped his forehead as if trying to remember something. Suddenly he raised his finger as his mind located the elusive scrap of memory. 'Femke, do you happen to know someone named Kalheen?'

'Yes, your Majesty. He's a servant here in the Imperial Palace.'

'Ah, then his claims are not totally without foundation.'

'What has he been saying, your Majesty? I trust he's not compromised my status.' Femke looked concerned as she remembered Kalheen's incessant storytelling during their trip to Thrandor.

'No, I don't think so. He's currently locked in a cell. He's been there ever since the night of Surabar's death. It was he who rang the Imperial Bell.'

'He did?' Femke was genuinely surprised.

'He says he received a letter from one of the Emperor's advisors telling him to do it. He gave your name as the author of the letter, but would say no more. I'm told he has been driving the guards mad by constantly begging for them to confirm his story from the moment they confined him. He's due to be tried for treason later this week.'

'I didn't write the letter, your Majesty,' Femke said thoughtfully, 'but Shalidar knew that Kalheen and I were acquainted. He also knew that Kalheen was aware of my status here in the Palace. I would not be surprised to find Shalidar used my name in order to enlist Kalheen's co-operation. Kalheen is many things, but he's no traitor, your Majesty. I'll vouch for him in this.'

'Good enough. I trust your judgement, Femke. I shall have him released.'

'Thank you, your Majesty. On a different note, has there been any word of the four missing assassins?'

'None.'

'Then we still have a clear-up operation to manage. The Fox in particular should be eliminated. She could prove dangerous if ignored.'

Emperor Kempten shook his head. 'I won't deny that I'd like to see the last of the Guild members apprehended, but I've decided not to expend vital resources chasing them. The power of the Guild is broken. The few remaining members are scattered and weak. I doubt we'll experience any lasting trouble from them. Without their ability to disappear into the night they are vulnerable. Actually, I've another task for you, if you're interested – one threatening more imminent danger. I've been hearing some ugly rumours about a group of Lords who live in the Western quarter. Now I think about it, this is a rather delicate matter that might require more than a single spy to sort out . . .'

Femke grinned as the Emperor allowed his sentence to tail off teasingly. 'You know, ever since I conducted Reynik's initial training, I've been meaning to show him around the Western quarter. His knowledge of that part of the city is sadly lacking. I think it's time I filled that gap in his education. As we'll be in the neighbourhood, we should be able to do a bit of checking for you.'

Lord Kempten nodded. Despite the coronation ceremony, being Emperor did not feel real yet. It was good to know that while he was finding his feet, he had some reliable people to help him re-establish order in Shandrim. As for the rest of the Empire – well, one thing at a time.

'Excellent!' he said aloud. 'In that case let me fill you in on the gory details . . .'

In a world of magic and murder, Femke is entrusted with a vital foreign mission by the Emperor. The task appears straightforward, but the young spy quickly finds herself ensnared in an elaborate trap.

Isolated in a hostile country, hunted by the authorities and with her arch-enemy closing in for his revenge, Femke needs all her wit and skills to survive.Only Reynik, a soldier barely out of training, appears willing to help. But with no knowledge of her true mission, Reynik soon discovers loyalty is a dangerous business.

ISBN: 978-1-41690-185-3

A deadly war has been triggered in the city
of Shandrim. Declared outlaws by the Emperor,
the Guild of Assassins strikes back hard.
Emperor Surabar needs someone to infiltrate
the Guild, but Femke is already known to them.

Reynik steps up to the challenge, but first he
must hone his spy skills with Femke – then
locate the assassins' headquarters.

Penetrating the Guild's inner circle will be
dangerous enough – after all, secrets kept
hidden for over five centuries command a high
price. But there are some perils for which even
the best training cannot prepare him . . .

ISBN: 978-1-4169-0186-0